"The incomparable Linda Howard brings high-voltage power and hard-edged sensuality to this emotional roller coaster of a novel, which is sure to keep readers riveted until the final nail-biting conclusion. They don't get much better than this."

—Jill M. Smith, *Romantic Times*

"Ms. Howard has wonderful pacing, a good ear for dialogue and knows how to turn on the steam. *Dream Man*'s mix of drama, violence, paranormal ability and sex makes it a perfect candidate for a USA Original Picture."

—Suzanne Kennemer Dent,
Birmingham (AL) *Post-Herald*

". . . Steamy romance. . . . Hollister makes the perfect romantic hero. . . . Howard's writing is compelling, especially the murder scenes."

—*Publishers Weekly*

"Linda Howard always writes wonderful contemporary romances. . . . Keep the romantic tension high by picking up Linda Howard's stunning romantic suspense novel *Dream Man*."

—*Heart to Heart* (B. Dalton Booksellers)

Books by Linda Howard

Kill and Tell
A Lady of the West
Angel Creek
The Touch of Fire
Heart of Fire
Dream Man
After the Night
Shades of Twilight
Son of the Morning

Published by POCKET BOOKS

For orders other than by individual consumers, Pocket Books grants a discount on the purchase of **10 or more** copies of single titles for special markets or premium use. For further details, please write to the Vice-President of Special Markets, Pocket Books, 1633 Broadway, New York, NY 10019-6785, 8th Floor.

For information on how individual consumers can place orders, please write to Mail Order Department, Simon & Schuster Inc., 200 Old Tappan Road, Old Tappan, NJ 07675.

LINDA HOWARD
Shades of Twilight

POCKET BOOKS

New York London Toronto Sydney Tokyo Singapore

This book is a work of fiction. Names, characters, places and incidents are products of the author's imagination or are used fictitiously. Any resemblance to actual events or locales or persons living or dead is entirely coincidental.

An *Original* Publication of POCKET BOOKS

POCKET BOOKS, a division of Simon & Schuster Inc.
1230 Avenue of the Americas, New York, NY 10020

Copyright © 1996 by Linda Howington

All rights reserved, including the right to reproduce this book or portions thereof in any form whatsoever. For information address Pocket Books, 1230 Avenue of the Americas, New York, NY 10020

ISBN: 0-671-01971-6

First Pocket Books printing July 1996

10 9 8 7 6

POCKET and colophon are registered trademarks of Simon & Schuster Inc.

Front cover illustration by Ben Perini

Printed in the U.S.A.

To

Beverly Beaver, a wonderful woman and dearly loved friend, for all the years of camaraderie and support, as well as taking the time to escort me around Tuscumbia and Florence, tell me who is sleeping with whom, and show me where all the bodies are buried. (Just joking, folks . . . you hope.)

And to Joyce B. R. Farley, sister extraordinaire. Here's to dolls, both blond and redheaded; tricycles with no brakes; attack roosters; graveyards for socks; hair rollers and bonfires; makeup and Molotov cocktails. You're the only other person I know who understands the reason behind wearing a Groucho mask and a tiara in public—and the only other person I know who's done it.

(For the curious: if you wear a Groucho mask and a tiara, people will figure you're either important, or crazy. Either way, they'll leave you alone. Try it some day when you're feeling grouchy and don't want to be bothered.)

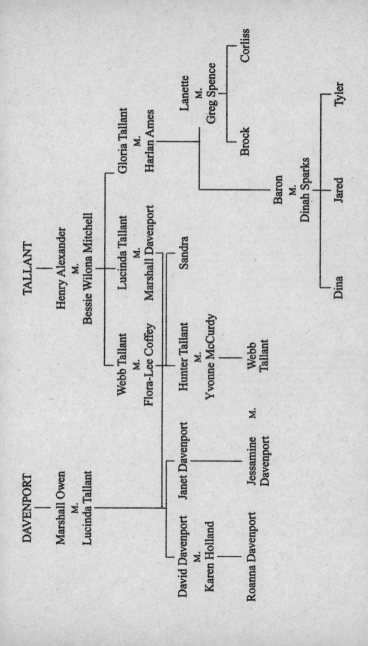

TALLANT

Henry Alexander
M.
Bessie Wilona Mitchell

Webb Tallant
M.
Flora-Lee Coffey

Lucinda Tallant
M.
Marshall Davenport

Gloria Tallant
M.
Harlan Ames

Hunter Tallant
M.
Yvonne McCurdy

Sandra

Brock

Lanette
M.
Greg Spence

Corliss

Webb
Tallant

Baron
M.
Dinah Sparks

Dina

Jared

Tyler

DAVENPORT

Marshall Owen
M.
Lucinda Tallant

David Davenport
M.
Karen Holland

Janet Davenport

M.

Jessamine
Davenport

Roanna Davenport

Prologue

She heard her own soft cries, but the pleasure exploding in her body made everything else seem unreal, distanced somehow from the hot magic of what he was doing to her. The noon sunlight wormed its way through the rustling leaves overhead, blinding her, dazzling her as she arched upward against him.

He wasn't gentle with her. He didn't treat her like a hothouse flower, the way the other boys did. Until she'd met him, she hadn't known how boring it was to always be treated like a princess. To the others, the Davenport name had made her a prize to be sought but never sullied; to him, she was just a woman.

With him, she *was* a woman. Though she was nineteen, her family treated her as if she were still a child. The protectiveness had never chafed her, until two weeks ago when she'd met him for the first time.

Naive and innocent she might be; stupid she wasn't. She knew when he'd introduced himself that his family was little better than white trash, and that *her* family would be horrified that she had even spoken to him. But the way his muscled torso had strained the fabric of his too-tight T-shirt had made her mouth go dry, and the swaggering masculini-

1

ty of his walk had started a strange tighening deep in her abdomen. His voice had lowered seductively when he spoke to her, and his blue eyes had been hot with promise. She'd known then that he wouldn't limit himself to hand-holding or necking. She knew what he'd wanted of her. But the wild response of her body was out of her experience, beyond her control, and when he asked her to meet him, she had agreed.

She couldn't get away at night without everyone knowing where she went, but it was easy to go out alone for a ride during the day and easy to arrange a meeting place. He had seduced her that very first time, stripping her naked beneath this very same oak tree—no, she couldn't pretend that it was a seduction. She had come here knowing what would happen, and she had been willing. Despite the pain of the first time, he had also shown her a wild pleasure she hadn't known existed. And every day, she came back for more.

He was crude sometimes, but even that excited her. He had been proud that he was the one to "bust her cherry," as he'd put it. Sometimes he said something, with a sneer in his voice, about a Neeley screwing a Davenport. Her family would be horrified if they knew. But still she dreamed, dreamed of how he would look in a nice suit and with his hair freshly cut and neatly combed as they stood together and informed the family that they were going to get married. She dreamed of him going to work at one of the family businesses and showing everyone how smart he was, that he could rise above the rest of his family. He would be a gentleman in public, but in private he would roll her on the bed and do these nasty, delicious things to her. She didn't want that part to change at all.

He finished, groaning with his climax, and almost immediately rolled off of her. She wished he would hold her for a moment before withdrawing, but he didn't like to cuddle when the weather was so hot. He stretched out on his back, the sunlight dappling his naked body, and almost immediately began dozing. She didn't mind. With two weeks' experience, she knew that he would awaken ready to make

2

love again. In the meantime, she was content to simply watch him.

He was so exciting that he made her breath catch. She lifted herself onto her elbow beside him and reached out with one lightly exploring finger to trace the cleft in his chin. The corners of his mouth twitched, but he didn't awaken.

The family would have a collective conniption fit if they knew about him. The family! She sighed. Being a Davenport had ruled her life from the day she was born. It hadn't all been onerous. She loved the clothes and jewelry, the luxury of Davencourt, the prestigious schools, the sheer snobbery of it all. But the rules of behavior had chafed; sometimes she wanted to do something wild, just for the hell of it. She wanted to drive fast, she wanted to jump fences that were too high, she wanted . . . this. The rough, the dangerous, the forbidden. She loved the way he would tear her delicate, expensive silk underwear in his hurry to get to her. That perfectly symbolized all she wanted in this life, both the luxury and the danger.

That wasn't what the family wanted for her, however. It was assumed that she would marry the Heir, as she thought of him, and take her place in Colbert County society, with lunches at the yacht club, endless dinner parties for business and political associates, the dutiful production of two little heirs.

She didn't want to marry the Heir. She wanted this instead, this hot, reckless excitement, the thrill of knowing that she flirted with the forbidden.

She ran her hand down his body, sliding her fingers into the thatch of pubic hair that surrounded his sex. As she had expected, he stirred, wakening, and his sex did, too. He gave a low, rough laugh as he lunged upward, rolling her down to the blanket and settling on top of her.

"You're the greediest little bitch I've ever screwed," he said and shoved roughly into her.

She flinched, more from the deliberate crudity of his words than the force of his entry. She was still wet from the last time, so her body accepted him easily enough. But he

3

seemed to like saying things that he knew would sting her, his eyes narrowed as he watched her reaction. She knew what it was, she thought, and forgave him. She knew he wasn't entirely comfortable being her lover, he was too aware of the social distance between them, and this was his way of trying to bring her nearer to his own level. But he didn't have to bring her down, she thought; she was going to bring him up.

She tightened her thighs around him, slowing his strokes so she could tell him before the growing heat in her loins made her forget what she wanted to say. "Let's get married next week. I don't care about a big wedding, we can elope if—"

He paused, his blue eyes flashing down at her. "Married?" he asked and laughed. "Where'd you get a stupid idea like that? I'm already married."

He resumed thrusting. She lay beneath him, numb with shock. A light breeze stirred the leaves overhead, and the sunlight pierced through, blinding her. *Married?* Granted, she didn't know much about him or his family, only that they weren't respectable, but a wife?

Fury and pain roared through her, and she struck out at him, her palm lashing across his cheek. He slapped her in return and caught her wrists, pinning them to the ground on each side of her head. "Goddamn, what's wrong with you?" he snapped, temper flaring hotly in his eyes.

She heaved beneath him, trying to throw him off, but he was far too heavy. Tears stung her eyes and ran down her temples into her hair. His presence inside her was suddenly unbearable, and each stroke seemed to rasp her like a rusty file. In her paroxysm of pain, she thought she would die if he continued. "You liar!" she shrieked, trying to jerk her hands free. "Cheat! Get *off* me! Go—go screw your *wife!*"

"She won't let me," he panted, hammering at her with cruel enjoyment of her struggles plain in his expression. "She just had a kid."

She screamed with rage and managed to jerk one hand

free, clawing him across the face before he could grab her. Cursing, he slapped her again, then drew back and swiftly flipped her onto her stomach. He was on her before she could scramble away, and she screamed again as she felt him plunge deep into her. She was helpless, flattened by his weight, unable to reach him to either hit or kick. He used her, hurting her with his roughness. Not five minutes before, the rough handling had excited her, but now she wanted to vomit, and she had to clench her teeth hard against the hot, rising nausea.

She pressed her face into the blanket, wishing she could smother herself, that she could do anything other than simply endure. But worse than the pain of betrayal, of realizing that she was nothing more than a convenience to him, was the bitter knowledge that it was her fault. She had brought this on herself, eagerly sought him out and not only let him treat her like a piece of trash, but enjoyed it! What a fool she was, spinning fairy tales of love and marriage to justify what was nothing more than a walk on the wild side.

He finished, grunting with his climax, and pulled out of her to fall heavily beside her. She lay where she was, trying desperately to pull the shattered pieces of herself back into some semblance of humanity. Wildly, she thought of revenge. With her torn clothes and the marks of his hand on her face, she could hurry home in very real hysterics, charge him with rape. She could make it stick, too; after all, she was a Davenport.

But it would be a lie. The fault, the weakness, was hers. She had welcomed him into her body. These last few minutes after she had changed her mind were little enough punishment for her monumental stupidity. It was a lesson she would never forget, the humiliation and sense of worthlessness a mental hair shirt she would wear for the rest of her life.

The burden of guilt pressed down on her. She had willingly traveled down this path, but now she had had enough. She would marry the Heir, the way everyone expected her to do, and spend the rest of her life being a dutiful Davenport.

Silently she sat up and began dressing. He watched her with drowsy malice in his blue, blue eyes. "What's the matter?" he sneered. "Did you think you were something special to me? Let me tell you something, baby: snatch is snatch, and your fancy name don't make yours anything special. What I got from you, I can get from any other bitch."

She put on her shoes and stood up. The pain of his words lashed at her, but she didn't let herself react to them. Instead she merely replied, "I won't be back."

"Sure you will," he said lazily, stretching and rubbing his chest. "Because what you got from me, you *can't* get anywhere else."

She didn't look back at him as she walked to where her horse was tied and painfully hauled herself into the saddle, the motion accomplished without her usual grace. The thought of returning to be used like a whore made the nausea rise hot and bitter in her throat again, and she wanted to kick him for his malicious, supreme confidence. She would forget the heated, soul-destroying pleasure he had given her and content herself with the life that had been planned for her. She could think of nothing worse than to come crawling to him and see the triumph in his eyes as he took her.

No, she thought as she rode away, *I won't come back. I'd rather die than be Harper Neeley's whore again.*

BOOK ONE

An End and a Beginning

CHAPTER

1

What are we going to do with her?"

"God knows. *We* certainly can't take her."

The voices were hushed, but Roanna heard them anyway and knew they were talking about her. She curled her skinny little body into a tighter knot, hugging her knees to her chest as she stared stolidly out the window at the manicured lawn of Davencourt, her grandmother's home. Other people had yards, but Grandmother had a lawn. The lawn was a deep, rich green, and she had always loved the feel of her bare feet sinking into the thick grass, like walking on a live carpet. Now, however, she had no desire to go outside and play. She just wanted to sit here in the bay window, the one she had always thought of as her "dreaming window," and pretend that nothing had changed, that Mama and Daddy hadn't died and she'd never see them again.

"It's different with Jessamine," the first voice continued. "She's a young lady, not still a child like Roanna. We're simply too old to take on someone that young."

They wanted her cousin Jessie, but they didn't want *her*. Roanna stubbornly blinked to hold back the tears as she listened to her aunts and uncles discuss the problem of what to "do" with her and list the reasons why they'd each be

9

glad to take Jessie into their homes, but Roanna would simply be too much trouble.

"I'll be good!" she wanted to cry but held the words inside just as she held the tears. What had she done that was so terrible they didn't want her? She tried to be a good girl, she said "ma'am" and "sir" when she talked to them. Was it because she had sneaked a ride on Thunderbolt? No one ever would have known if she hadn't fallen off and torn her new dress and gotten it dirty, and on Easter Sunday, at that. Mama had had to take her home to change clothes, and she'd had to wear an old dress to church. Well, it hadn't exactly been old, it had been one of her regular church dresses, but it hadn't been her gorgeous new Easter dress. One of the other girls at church had asked her why she hadn't worn an Easter dress, and Jessie had laughed and said because she'd fallen in a pile of horse doo-doo. Only Jessie hadn't said doo-doo, she'd used the bad word, and some boys had heard, and soon it was all over church that Roanna Davenport had said she'd fallen in a pile of horseshit.

Grandmother had gotten that disapproving look on her face, and Aunt Gloria's mouth had pursed up like she'd bitten into a green persimmon. Aunt Janet had looked down at her and just shook her head. But Daddy had laughed and hugged her shoulder and said that a little horseshit never hurt anybody. Besides, his Little Bit needed some fertilizer to grow.

Daddy. The lump in her chest swelled until she could barely breathe around it. Daddy and Mama were gone forever, and so was Aunt Janet. Roanna had always liked Aunt Janet, even though she'd always seemed so sad and hadn't liked to cuddle much. Still, she'd been a lot nicer than Aunt Gloria.

Aunt Janet was Jessie's mama. Roanna wondered if Jessie's chest hurt the way hers did, if she'd cried so much that the insides of her eyelids felt like sand. Maybe. It was hard to tell what Jessie thought. She didn't think a grubby kid like Roanna was worth paying any attention to; Roanna had heard her say so.

As Roanna stared unblinkingly out the window, she saw Jessie and their cousin Webb come into view, as if she had dreamed them into being. They walked slowly across the yard toward the huge old oak tree with the bench swing hanging from one of the massive lower limbs. Jessie looked beautiful, Roanna thought, with all the unabashed admiration of a seven-year-old. She was as slim and graceful as Cinderella at the ball, with her dark hair twisted into a knot at the back of her head and her neck rising swanlike above the dark blue of her dress. The gap between seven and thirteen was huge; to Roanna, Jessie was *grown,* a member of that mysterious, authoritative group who could give orders. That had happened only within the last year or so, because though Jessie had always before been classified as a "big girl" to Roanna's "little girl," Jessie had still played dolls and indulged in the occasional game of hide-and-seek. No longer, though. Jessie now disdained all games except Monopoly and spent a lot of time playing with her hair and begging Aunt Janet for cosmetics.

Webb had changed, too. He had always been Roanna's favorite cousin, always willing to get down on the floor and wrestle with her, or help her hold the bat so she could hit the softball. Webb loved horses the way she did, too, and could occasionally be begged into riding with her. He got impatient with that, though, because she was only allowed to ride her old slowpoke pony. Lately, Webb hadn't wanted to spend any time with her at all; he was too busy with other things, he'd say, but he sure seemed to have a lot of time to spend with Jessie. That was why she'd tried to ride Thunderbolt on Easter morning, so she could show Daddy that she was old enough for a real horse.

Roanna watched as Webb and Jessie sat down in the swing, their fingers laced together. Webb had gotten a lot bigger in the past year; Jessie looked little sitting beside him. He was playing football, and his shoulders were twice as wide as Jessie's. Grandmother, she'd heard one of the aunts say, doted on the boy. Webb and his mama, Aunt Yvonne, lived here at Davencourt with Grandmother, because Webb's daddy was dead, too.

Webb was a Tallant, from Grandmother's side of the family; she was his great-aunt. Roanna was only seven, but she knew the intricacies of kinship, having practically absorbed it through her skin during the hours she'd spent listening to the grown-ups talk about family. Grandmother had been a Tallant until she'd married Grandpa and turned into a Davenport. Webb's grandfather, who had also been named Webb, was Grandmother's favorite brother. She had loved him a whole lot, just as she had loved his son, who had been Webb's father. Now there was only Webb, and she loved him a whole lot, too.

Webb was only Roanna's second cousin, while Jessie was her first cousin, which was a lot closer. Roanna wished it were the other way around, because she would rather be close kin to Webb than to Jessie. Second cousins weren't much more than kissing cousins, was what Aunt Gloria had said once. The concept had so intrigued Roanna that at the last family reunion she had stared hard at all her relatives, trying to see who kissed who, so she would know who wasn't really kin. She had figured out that the people they saw only once a year, at the reunion, were the ones who did the most kissing. That made her feel better. She saw Webb all the time, and he didn't kiss her, so they were closer than kissing cousins.

"Don't be ridiculous," Grandmother said now, her voice cutting sharply through the muted arguments over who would be stuck with Roanna, and jerking Roanna's attention back to her eavesdropping. "Jessie and Roanna are both Davenports. They'll live here, of course."

Live at Davencourt! Equal parts of terror and relief displaced the misery in Roanna's chest. Relief that someone wanted her after all, and she wouldn't have to go to the Orphans' Home like Jessie had said she would. The terror came from the prospect of being under Grandmother's thumb all day, every day. Roanna loved her grandmother, but she was a little afraid of her, too, and she knew she'd never be able to be as perfect as Grandmother expected. She was always getting dirty, or tearing her clothes, or dropping something and breaking it. Food somehow always managed to fall off her fork and into her lap, and sometimes she forgot to pay attention when reaching for her milk, and knocked the glass over. Jessie said she was a clumsy clod.

Roanna sighed. She always *felt* clumsy, fumbling around under Grandmother's eagle eye. The only time she wasn't clumsy was when she was on a horse. Well, she had fallen off Thunderbolt, but she was used to her pony and Thunderbolt was so fat she hadn't been able to get a good grip with her legs. But usually she stuck to the saddle like a cocklebur, that's what Loyal always said, and he took care of all Grandmother's horses so he should know. Roanna loved riding almost as much as she had loved Mama and Daddy. The upper part of her felt like she was flying, but with her legs she could feel the horse's strength and muscles, as if *she* was that strong. That was one good part about living with Grandmother; she would be able to ride every day, and Loyal could teach her how to stay on the bigger horses.

But the best part was that Webb and his mama lived here, too, and she'd see him every day.

Suddenly she jumped down from the window seat and raced through the house, forgetting that she was wearing her slick-soled Sunday shoes instead of her sneakers until she skidded on the hardwood floor and almost slid into a table. Aunt Gloria's sharp admonition rang in the air behind her, but Roanna ignored it as she wrestled with the heavy front door, using all of her slight weight to tug it open enough that she could slip through. Then she was running across the lawn toward Webb and Jessie, her knees kicking up the skirt of her dress with every step.

Halfway there the knot of misery in her chest suddenly unwound, and she began sobbing. Webb watched her com-

13

ing, and his expression changed. He let go of Jessie's hand and held his arms out to Roanna. She hurled herself into his lap, setting the swing to bumping. Jessie said sharply, "You're making a mess, Roanna. Go blow your nose."

But Webb said, "Here's my handkerchief," and wiped Roanna's face himself. Then he simply held her, her face buried against his shoulder, while she sobbed so violently that her entire little body heaved.

"Oh, God," Jessie said in disgust.

"Shut up," Webb replied, holding Roanna closer. "She's lost her parents."

"Well, I lost my mama, too," Jessie pointed out. "You don't see me squalling all over everybody."

"She's just seven," Webb said while he smoothed Roanna's tousled mop of hair. She was a pest most of the time, tagging along after her older cousins, but she was just a little kid, and he thought Jessie should be more sympathetic. The late afternoon sun slanted across the lawn and through the trees, catching in Roanna's hair and highlighting the glossy chestnut, making the strands glitter with gold and red. Earlier in the afternoon they had buried three members of their family, Roanna's parents and Jessie's mother. Aunt Lucinda had suffered the most, he thought, because she had lost both of her children at once: David, Roanna's daddy, and Janet, Jessie's mama. The huge weight of grief had bowed her down under the past three days, but it hadn't broken her. She was still the backbone of the family, lending her strength to others.

Roanna was quieting down, her sobs dwindling into occasional hiccups. Her round little head bounced against his collarbone as, without looking up, she scrubbed her face with his handkerchief. She felt frail in his strong young arms, her bones not much bigger than matchsticks, her back only about nine inches wide. Roanna was skinny, all pipe-stem arms and legs, and small for her age. He kept patting her while Jessie wore a long-suffering expression, and eventually one slanted, tear-wet eye peeped out from the security of his shoulder.

"Grandmother said that Jessie and I are going to live here, too," she said.

"Well, of course," Jessie replied, as if any other place would be unacceptable. "Where else would I live? But if I were them, I'd send you to the Orphans' Home."

Tears welled in that eye again and Roanna promptly reburied her face in Webb's shoulder. He glared at Jessie, and she flushed and looked away. Jessie was spoiled. Lately, at least half the time he thought she needed a good spanking. The other half of the time he was enthralled by those new curves to her body. She knew it, too. Once this summer, when they were swimming, she had let the strap of her bathing suit top fall down her arm, baring the upper part of one breast almost to the nipple. Webb's body had reacted with all the painful intensity of recent adolescence, but he hadn't been able to look away. He had just stood there, thanking God that the water was higher than his waist, but the part of him that had been above water had been dark red with mingled embarrassment, arousal, and frustration.

But she was beautiful. God, Jessie was beautiful. She looked like a princess, with her sleek dark hair and dark blue eyes. Her features were perfect, her skin flawless. And now she would be living here at Davencourt with Aunt Lucinda . . . and with him.

He returned his attention to Roanna, jostling her. "Don't listen to Jessie," he said. "She's just spouting off without knowing what she's talking about. You won't ever have to go anywhere. I don't think there *are* any orphanages anymore."

She peeked out again. Her eyes were brown, almost chestnut colored like her hair, just without the red. She was the only person on either the Davenport or Tallant sides of the family who had brown eyes; everyone else had either blue or green eyes or a mixture of the two. Jessie had teased her once, telling her that she wasn't really a Davenport because her eyes were the wrong color, that she'd been adopted. Roanna had been in tears until Webb had put a stop to that, too, telling her that she had her mother's eyes, and he knew she was a Davenport because he remembered going to see her in the hospital nursery when she'd just been born.

"Was Jessie just teasing?" she asked now.

"That's all it was," he replied soothingly. "Just teasing."

Roanna didn't turn her head to look at Jessie, but one small fist darted out and hammered Jessie on the shoulder, then was quickly retracted back into the safety of his embrace.

Webb had to swallow a laugh, but Jessie erupted into fury. "She hit me!" she shrieked, lifting her hand to slap Roanna.

Webb shot his hand out, catching Jessie's wrist. "No, you don't," he said. "You deserved it for telling her that."

She tried to jerk away but Webb held her, his grip tightening and his darkened eyes telling Jessie that he meant business. She went still, glaring at him, but he ruthlessly exerted his will and superior strength, and after a few seconds she sullenly subsided. He released her wrist, and she rubbed it as if he had really hurt her. He knew better, though, and didn't feel guilty as she intended. Jessie was good at manipulating people, but Webb had seen through her a long time ago. Knowing her for the little witch she was, though, only made it more satisfying that he had forced her to back down.

His face flushed as he felt himself getting hard, and he shifted Roanna slightly away from him. His heart was beating faster, with excitement and triumph. It was just a little thing, but suddenly he knew that he could handle Jessie. In those few seconds their entire relationship had changed, the casually close ties of kinship and childhood becoming the past, while the more intricate, volatile passions of male and female took their place. The process had been happening all summer long, but now it was completed. He looked at Jessie's sulky face, her lower lip pouting, and he wanted to kiss her until she forgot why she was pouting. Maybe she didn't quite understand yet, but he did.

Jessie was going to be his. She was spoiled and sulky, her emotions volcanic in intensity. It would take a lot of skill and energy to stay on top of her, but someday he would be there physically as well as mentally. He had two trump cards that Jessie didn't yet know about: the power of sex, and the lure of Davencourt. Aunt Lucinda had talked to him a lot the night of the car wreck. They had been sitting up alone, Aunt Lucinda rocking and quietly weeping as she dealt with the death of her children, and finally Webb had worked up the courage to approach and put his arms around her. She had broken down then, sobbing as if her heart would break—the only time she had so completely given in to her grief.

But when she had composed herself, they had sat alone far into the early hours of the morning, talking in hushed tones. Aunt Lucinda had a great reservoir of strength, and she had brought it to bear on the task of securing Davencourt's safety. Her beloved David, heir to Davencourt, was dead. Janet, her only daughter, was equally beloved but had not been suited in either nature or desire to handle the massive responsibilities involved. Janet had been quiet and withdrawn, her eyes dark with an inner pain that never quite went away. Webb suspected it was because of Jessie's father—whoever he was. Jessie was illegitimate, and Janet had never said who had fathered her. Mama said it had been a huge scandal, but the Davenports had closed ranks and the upper echelon of Tuscumbia society had been forced to accept both mother and child or face Davenport retaliation. Since the Davenports were the wealthiest family in the northwest quarter of Alabama, they had been able to carry it off.

But now, with both her children dead, Aunt Lucinda had to safeguard the family properties. It wasn't just Davencourt, the center jewel; it was stocks and bonds, real estate, factories, timber and mineral rights, banks, even restaurants. The sum total of Davenport holdings required an agile brain to understand it and a certain quality of ruthlessness to oversee it.

Webb was fourteen, but the morning after that long midnight talk with Aunt Lucinda, she had taken the family lawyer into the study, closed the door, and designated Webb as the heir apparent. He was a Tallant, not a Davenport, but he was her adored brother's grandson, and she herself had been a Tallant, so that wasn't a great hindrance in her eyes. Perhaps because Jessie had started life with such a huge strike against her, Aunt Lucinda had always shown a marked preference for Jessie over Roanna, but Aunt Lucinda's love was never blind. As much as she might wish otherwise, she knew Jessie was too volatile to take up the reins of such a huge enterprise; given a free hand, Jessie would have the family bankrupt within five years of attaining her majority.

Roanna, the only other direct descendant, wasn't even considered. She was only seven, for one thing, and completely unruly. It wasn't that the child was disobedient, exactly, but she had a definite talent for finding disaster. If there was a mud puddle within a quarter mile, Roanna would somehow manage to fall in it—but only if she was wearing her best dress. If she was wearing expensive new slippers, she would accidentally step into a horse pile. She constantly turned over, dropped, or spilled whatever was in her hands or merely nearby. The only talent she had, apparently, was an affinity for horses. That was a big plus in Aunt Lucinda's eyes, as she, too, loved the animals, but unfortunately didn't make Roanna any more acceptable in the role of main heiress.

Davencourt was going to be his, Davencourt and all the vast holdings. Webb looked up at the huge white house sitting like a crown in the middle of the lush green velvet of the lawn. Deep, wide verandas completely encircled the house on both stories, the railings laced with delicate ironwork. Six enormous white columns framed the front portico, where the veranda widened at the entrance. The house had an air of graciousness and comfort, imparted by the cool shade promised by the verandas, and the airy spaciousness, indicated by the vast expanse of windows. Double French doors graced each bedroom on the upper story, and a Palladian window arched majestically over the center entrance.

Davencourt was a hundred and twenty years old, built in the decade before the war. That was why there was a gently curving staircase on the left side, to provide a discreet entrance to the house for carousing young men, back when the bachelors of the family had slept in a separate wing. At Davencourt, that wing had been the left one. Various remodelings over the past century had done away with the separate sleeping quarters, but the outside entrance to the second floor remained. Lately, Webb had used the staircase a time or two himself.

And it was all going to be his.

He didn't feel guilty over being chosen to inherit. Even at fourteen, Webb was aware of the force of driving ambition within him. He *wanted* the pressure, the power of all that Davencourt entailed. It would be like riding the wildest stallion alive but mastering it with his own force of will.

It wasn't as if Jessie and Roanna had been disinherited, far from it. They would still both be wealthy women in their own right when they came of age. But the majority of the stocks, the majority of the power—and all the responsibility—would be his. Rather than being intimidated by the years of hard work that lay before him, Webb felt a fierce joy at the prospect. Not only would he own Davencourt, but Jessie came with the deal. Aunt Lucinda had hinted as much, but it wasn't until a few moments ago that he'd realized fully what she meant.

She wanted him to marry Jessie.

He almost laughed aloud in exultation. Oh, he knew his Jessie, and so did Aunt Lucinda. When it became known that he was going to inherit Davencourt, Jessie would instantly decide that she, and no one else, would marry him. He didn't mind; he knew how to handle her, and he had no illusions about her. Most of Jessie's unpleasantness was due to that massive chip on her shoulder, the burden of her illegitimacy. She deeply resented Roanna's legitimate status and was hateful to the kid because of it. That would change, though, when they married. He would see to it, because now he had Jessie's number.

Lucinda Davenport ignored the ongoing chatter behind her as she stood at the window and watched the three young people sitting in the swing. They belonged to her; her blood ran in all three of them. They were the future, the hope of Davencourt, all that was left.

When she had first been told of the car accident, for a few dark hours the burden of grief had been so massive that she had felt crushed beneath it, unable to function, to care. She still felt as if the best part of herself had been torn away, with huge gaping wounds left behind. Their names echoed in her mother's heart. *David. Janet.* Memories swam through her mind, so that she saw them as tiny infants at her breast, rambunctious toddlers, romping children, awkward adolescents, wonderful adults. She was sixty-three and had lost many people whom she had loved, but this latest blow was almost a killing one. A mother should never outlive her children.

But in the darkest hour, Webb had been there, offering her silent comfort. He was only fourteen, but already the man was taking shape in the boy's body. He reminded her a lot of her brother, the first Webb; there was the same core of hard, almost reckless strength, and an inner maturity that made him seem far older than his years. He hadn't flinched from her grief but had shared it with her, letting her know that despite this massive loss, she wasn't alone. It was in that dark hour that she had seen the glimmer of light and known what she would do. When she had first broached to him the idea of training to take over the Davenport enterprises, of eventually owning Davencourt itself, he hadn't been intimidated. Instead his green eyes had gleamed at the prospect, at the very challenge of it.

She had made a good choice. Some of the others would howl; Gloria and her bunch would be outraged that Webb had been chosen over any of the Ameses, when after all they were the same degree of kin to Lucinda. Jessie would have good cause to be angry, for she was a Davenport and direct kin, but as much as she loved the girl, Lucinda knew Davencourt wouldn't be in good hands with her. Webb was the best choice, and he would take care of Jessie.

She watched the small tableau in the swing play itself out in silence and knew that Webb had won that battle. The boy already had the instincts of a man, and a dominant man at that. Jessie was sulking, but he didn't give in to her. He continued comforting Roanna, who as usual had managed to cause some sort of trouble.

Roanna. Lucinda sighed. She didn't feel up to assuming the care of a seven-year-old, but the child was David's daughter, and she simply couldn't allow her to go anywhere else. She had tried, out of fairness, but she couldn't love Roanna as much as she loved Jessie, or Webb, who wasn't even her grandchild, but a great-nephew.

Despite her fierce support for her daughter when Janet was pregnant without benefit of a husband, Lucinda had expected to, at best, tolerate the baby when it came. She had been very much afraid that she would actively dislike it, because of the disgrace it represented. Instead she had taken one look at the tiny, flowerlike face of her granddaughter and fallen in love. Oh, Jessie was a high-spirited handful with her share of faults, but Lucinda's love had never wavered. Jessie *needed* love, so much love, soaking up every snippet of affection and praise that came her way. It hadn't been a starvation diet; from her birth, she had been cuddled and kissed and made over, but for some reason it had never been quite enough. Children sensed early when something about their lives was out of kilter, and Jessie was particularly bright; she had been about two when she had started asking why *she* didn't have a daddy.

And then there was Roanna. Lucinda sighed again. It had been as difficult to love Roanna as it was easy to love Jessie. The two cousins were total opposites. Roanna had never been still long enough for anyone to cuddle her. Pick her up for a hug, and she was squirming to get down. Nor was she pretty the way Jessie was. Roanna's odd mix of features didn't fit her small face. Her nose was too long, her mouth too wide, her eyes narrow and slanted. Her hair, with its un-Davenport-like tinge of red, was always untidy. No matter what she wore, give her five minutes and the garment would be dirty and likely torn. She favored her mother's people, of course, but she was definitely a weed in the Davenport garden. Lucinda had looked hard, but she couldn't see anything of David in the child, and now any resemblance would have been doubly precious had it existed.

But she would do her duty by Roanna, and try to mold her into some sort of civilized being, one who would be a credit to the Davenports.

Her hope, though, and the future, lay with Jessie and Webb.

CHAPTER
2

Lucinda wiped away the tears as she sat in Janet's bedroom and slowly folded and packed away her daughter's clothing. Both Yvonne and Sandra had offered to do this for her, but she had insisted on doing it alone. She didn't want anyone to witness her tears, her grief; and only she would know which items were precious, because of the memories, and which could be discarded. She had already performed this last task at David's house, tenderly folding away shirts that still faintly carried the scent of his cologne. She had wept, too, for her daughter-in-law; Karen had been well liked, a cheerful, loving young woman who had made David very happy. Their things had been stored in trunks at Davencourt for Roanna to have when she was older.

It had been a month since the accident. The legal formalities had promptly been taken care of, with Jessie and Roanna permanently installed at Davencourt and Lucinda as their legal guardian. Jessie, of course, had settled right in, commandeering the prettiest bedroom as her own and cajoling Lucinda into redecorating it to her specifications. Lucinda admitted that she hadn't needed much cajoling, because she understood Jessie's fierce need to regain control of her life, impose order on her surroundings again. The

23

bedroom was only a symbol. She had spoiled Jessie shamelessly, letting her know that even though her mother had died, she still had a family who supported and loved her, that security hadn't vanished from her world.

Roanna, however, hadn't settled in at all. Lucinda sighed, holding one of Janet's blouses to her cheek as she pondered David's daughter. She simply didn't know how to get close to the child. Roanna had resisted all efforts to get her to choose a bedroom, and finally Lucinda had given up and chosen for her. A sense of fairness had insisted that Roanna's bedroom be at least as big as Jessie's, and it was, but the little girl had merely looked lost and overwhelmed in it. She had slept there the first night. The second night, she had slept in one of the other bedrooms, dragging her blanket with her and curling up on the bare mattress. The third night, it had been yet another empty bedroom, another bare mattress. She had slept in a chair in the den, on the rug in the library, even huddled on the floor of a bathroom. She was a restless, forlorn little spirit, drifting around in search of a place of her own. Lucinda estimated that the child had now slept in every room of the house except for the bedrooms occupied by others.

When Webb got up every morning, the first thing he did was go on a Roanna hunt, tracking her down in whichever nook or cranny she had chosen for the night, coaxing her out of her blanket cocoon. She was sullen and withdrawn, except with Webb, and had no interest in anything but the horses. Frustrated, not knowing what else to do, Lucinda had given her unlimited access to the horses, at least for the summer. Loyal would look out for the child, and Roanna had an uncommonly good touch with the animals anyway.

Lucinda folded the blouse, the last one, and put it away. Only the contents of the nightstand remained, and she hesitated before opening the drawers. When that was finished, it would all be finished; the townhouse would be emptied, closed, and sold. All traces of Janet would be gone.

Except for Jessie, Janet had left precious little of herself.

After she'd gotten pregnant, most of her laughter had died, and there had always been sadness in her eyes. Though she'd never said who fathered Jessie, Lucinda suspected it was the oldest Leath boy, Dwight. He and Janet had dated, but then he'd gotten in an argument with his father and enlisted and somehow ended up in Vietnam in the early days of the war. Within two weeks of setting foot in that miserable little country, he'd been killed. Over the years Lucinda had often looked at Jessie's face, searching for some resemblance to the Leaths but instead saw only pure Davenport beauty. If Dwight was Janet's lover, then he had been mourned until the day of her death, because she had never dated anyone else after Jessie's birth. It wasn't that she hadn't had the opportunity either; despite the awkwardness of Jessie's illegitimacy, Janet was still a Davenport, and there were plenty of men who would have wanted her. The lack of interest had all been on Janet's part.

Lucinda had hoped for more for her daughter. She herself had known deep love with Marshall Davenport and had wished the same for her children. David had found it with Karen; Janet had known only pain and disappointment. Lucinda didn't like to admit it, but she had always sensed a certain restraint in Janet's manner toward Jessie, as if she were ashamed. It was the way Lucinda had expected to feel but hadn't. She wished Janet could have gotten past the pain, but she never had.

Well, putting off an unpleasant chore wouldn't make it any less unpleasant, Lucinda thought, unconsciously straightening her spine. She could sit here all day musing over the intricacies of life, or she could get on with it. Lucinda Tallant Davenport wasn't one to sit around whining; right or wrong, she got things done.

She pulled open the top drawer of the nightstand, and tears filled her eyes again at the neatness of the contents. That was Janet, tidy to the bone. There was the book she'd been reading, a small flashlight, a box of tissues, a decorative tin of her favorite peppermint candy, and a leather-bound journal with the pen still stuck between the pages. Curious, Lucinda wiped away her tears and pulled out the journal. She hadn't known that Janet kept one.

She smoothed her hand over the journal, knowing full well what information might be on the pages. It could be only private comments on day-to-day life, but there was the possibility that here Janet had divulged the secret she'd carried to her grave. At this late date, did it really matter who Jessie's father was?

Not really, Lucinda thought. She would love Jessie no matter whose blood ran in her veins.

But still, after so many years of wondering and not knowing, the temptation was impossible to resist. She opened the journal to the first page and began reading.

Half an hour later, she blotted her eyes with a tissue and slowly closed the journal, then placed it on top of the pile of clothes in the last box. There hadn't been all that much to read: several anguished pages, written fourteen years ago, then very little after that. Janet had made a few notations, marking Jessie's first tooth, first step, first day in school, but for the most part the pages were blank. It was as if Janet had stopped living fourteen years ago, rather than just a month. Poor Janet, to have hoped for much and settled for so little.

Lucinda smoothed her hand over the journal's leather cover. Well, now she knew. And she had been right: it didn't make any difference at all.

She picked up the roll of masking tape and briskly sealed the box.

BOOK TWO

Torn Asunder

CHAPTER
3

*R*oanna bounced out of bed with the dawn, hurrying to brush her teeth and drag her hands through her hair, then scrambling into jeans and a T-shirt. She grabbed her boots and socks on the way out the door and ran barefoot down the stairs. Webb was driving up to Nashville, and she wanted to see him before he left. She didn't have any particular reason other than that she seized every opportunity to have a few private minutes with him, precious seconds when his attention, his smiles, were only for her.

Even at five o'clock in the morning, Grandmother would have had her breakfast in the morning room, but Roanna didn't even pause there on her way to the kitchen. Webb, while thoroughly comfortable with the wealth that was at his disposal, didn't give a snap of his finger for appearances. He would be scrounging around in the kitchen, preparing his own breakfast since Tansy didn't come to work until six, then eating it at the kitchen table.

She burst through the door, and as she had expected, Webb was there. He hadn't bothered with the table and was instead leaning against the cabinet while he munched on a jelly-spread slice of toast. A cup of coffee steamed gently beside his hand. As soon as he saw her, he turned and dropped another slice of bread into the toaster.

"I'm not hungry," she said, poking her head into the huge double-doored refrigerator to find the orange juice.

"You never are," he returned equably. "Eat anyway." Her lack of appetite was why, at seventeen, she was still skinny and barely developed. That and the fact that Roanna never simply *walked* anywhere. She was a perpetual motion machine: she skipped, she bounded, occasionally she even turned cartwheels. At least, over the years, she had finally settled down enough to sleep in the same bed every night, and he no longer had to search for her every morning.

Because it was Webb who'd made the toast, she ate it, though she rejected the jelly. He poured a cup of coffee for her, and she stood beside him, munching dry toast and alternately sipping orange juice and coffee, and felt contentment glowing warmly deep in her middle. This was all she asked out of life: to be alone with Webb. And to work with the horses, of course.

She gently inhaled, drawing in the delicious scents of his understated cologne and the clean, slight muskiness of his skin, all mingled with the aroma of the coffee. Her awareness of him was so intense it was almost painful, but she lived for these moments.

She eyed him over the rim of her cup, her whiskey brown eyes glinting with mischief. "The timing of this trip to Nashville is pretty suspicious," she teased. "I think you just want to get away from the house."

He grinned, and her heart flip-flopped. She seldom saw that cheerful grin any more; he was so busy that he didn't have time for anything but work, as Jessie consistently, relentlessly complained. His cool green eyes warmed when he smiled, and the lazy charm of his grin could stop traffic. The laziness was deceptive, though; Webb worked hours that would have exhausted most men.

"I didn't plan it," he protested, then admitted, "but I jumped at the chance. I guess you're going to stay in the stables all day."

She nodded. Grandmother's sister and her husband, Aunt Gloria and Uncle Harlan, were moving in today, and Roanna wanted to be as far from the house as possible. Aunt Gloria was her least favorite of aunts, and she didn't care much for Uncle Harlan either.

"He's a know-it-all," she grumbled. "And she's a pain in the—"

"Ro," he said warningly, drawing out the single syllable. Only he ever called her by the abbreviation of her name. It was one more tiny connection between them for her to savor, for she thought of herself as Ro. Roanna was the girl who was skinny and unattractive, clumsy and gauche. Ro was the part of herself who could ride like the wind, her thin body blending with the horse's and becoming part of its rhythm; the girl who, while in the stables, never put a foot wrong. If she had her way, she'd have *lived* in the stables.

"Neck," she finished, with a look of innocence that made him chuckle. "When Davencourt is yours, are you going to throw them out?"

"Of course not, you little heathen. They're family."

"Well, it isn't as if they don't have a place to live. Why don't they stay in their own house?"

"Since Uncle Harlan retired, they've been having trouble making ends meet. There's plenty of space here, so their moving in is the logical solution, even if you don't like it." He ruffled her untidy hair.

She sighed. It was true that there were ten bedrooms in Davencourt, and since Jessie and Webb had gotten married and now used only one room, and since Aunt Yvonne had decided to move out last year and get a place of her own, that meant seven of those bedrooms were empty. Still, she didn't like it. "Well, what about when you and Jessie have kids? You'll need the other rooms then."

"I don't think we'll need seven of them," he said drily, and a grim look entered his eyes. "We may not have any kids anyway."

Her heart jumped at that. She had been down in the dumps since he and Jessie had married two years ago, but

31

she had really dreaded the idea of Jessie having his babies. Somehow that would have been the final blow to a heart that hadn't had much hope to begin with; she knew she'd never had a chance with Webb, but still a tiny glimmer lingered. As long as he and Jessie didn't have any children, it was as if he wasn't totally, finally hers. For Webb, she thought, children would be an unbreakable bond. As long as there were no babies, she could still hope, however futilely.

It was no secret in the house that their marriage wasn't all roses. Jessie never kept it a secret when she was unhappy, because she made a concerted effort to make certain everyone else was just as miserable as she was.

Knowing Jessie, and Roanna knew Jessie very well, she had probably planned to use sex, after they were married, to control Webb. Roanna would have been surprised if Jessie had let Webb make love to her before they were married. Well, maybe once, to keep his interest keen. Roanna never underestimated the depths of Jessie's calculation. The thing was, neither did Webb, and Jessie's little plan hadn't worked. No matter what tricks she tried, Webb seldom changed his mind, and when he did it was for reasons of his own. No, Jessie was *not* happy.

Roanna loved it. She couldn't begin to understand their relationship, but Jessie didn't appear to have a clue about the type of man Webb was. You could appeal to him with logic, but manipulation left him unswayed. It had given Roanna many secretly gleeful moments over the years to watch Jessie try her feminine wiles on Webb and then throwing fits when they didn't work. Jessie just couldn't understand it; after all, it worked on everyone else.

Webb checked his watch. "I have to go." He swiftly gulped the rest of his coffee, then bent to kiss her forehead. "Stay out of trouble today."

"I'll try," she promised, then added glumly, "I *always* try." And somehow seldom succeeded. Despite her best efforts, she was always doing something that displeased Grandmother.

Webb gave her a rueful grin on his way out the door, and

their eyes met for a moment in a way that made her feel as if they were co-conspirators. Then he was gone, closing the door behind him, and with a sigh she sat down in one of the chairs to pull on her socks and boots. The dawn had dimmed with his leaving.

In a way, she thought, they really were co-conspirators. She was relaxed and unguarded with Webb in a way she never was with the rest of the family, and she never saw disapproval in his eyes when he looked at her. Webb accepted her as she was and didn't try to make her into something she wasn't.

But there was one other place where she found approval, and her heart lightened as she ran to the stables.

When the moving van drove up at eight-thirty, Roanna barely noticed it. She and Loyal were working with a frisky yearling colt, patiently getting him accustomed to human handling. He was fearless, but he wanted to play rather than learn anything new, and the gentle lesson required a lot of patience.

"You're wearing me out," she panted and fondly stroked the animal's glossy neck. The colt responded by shoving her with his head, sending her staggering several paces backward. "There has to be an easier way," she said to Loyal, who was sitting on the fence, giving her directions, and grinning as the colt romped like an oversized dog.

"Like what?" he asked. He was always willing to listen to Roanna's ideas.

"Why don't we start handling them as soon as they're born? Then they'd be too little to shove me all over the corral," she grumbled. "And they'd grow up used to humans and the things we do to them."

"Well, now." Loyal stroked his jaw as he thought about it. He was a lean, hard fifty and had already spent almost thirty of those years working at Davencourt, the long hours outside turning his brown face into a network of fine wrinkles. He ate, lived, and breathed horses and couldn't imagine any job more suited to him than the one he had. Just because it was customary to wait until the foals were yearlings before beginning their training didn't mean it had to be that way. Roanna might have something there. Horses had to get used to people fooling around with their mouths and feet, and it might be easier on both horses and humans if the process started when they were foaled rather than after a year of running wild. It should cut down on a lot of skittishness as well as making it easier on the farriers and the vets.

"Tell you what," he said. "We won't have another foal until Lightness drops hers in March. We'll start with that one and see how it works."

Roanna's face lit up, her brown eyes turning almost golden with delight, and for a moment Loyal was struck by how pretty she was. He was startled, because Roanna was really a plain little thing, her features too big and masculine for her thin face, but for a fleeting moment he'd gotten a glimpse of how she would look when maturity had worked its full magic on her. She'd never be the beauty Miss Jessie was, he thought realistically, but when she got older, she'd surprise a few people. The idea made him happy, because Roanna was his favorite. Miss Jessie was a competent rider, but she didn't love his babies the way Roanna did and therefore wasn't as careful of her mount's welfare as she could have been. In Loyal's eyes, that was an unforgivable sin.

At eleven-thirty, Roanna reluctantly returned to the house for lunch. She would much rather have skipped the meal entirely, but Grandmother would send someone after her if she didn't show up, so she figured she might as well save everyone the trouble. But she had cut it too close, as usual, and didn't have time for more than a quick shower and change of clothes. She dragged a comb through her wet hair, then raced down the stairs, sliding to a halt just before she opened the door to the dining room and entered at a more decorous pace.

Everyone else was already seated. Aunt Gloria looked up at Roanna's entrance, and her mouth drew into the familiar disapproving line. Grandmother took in Roanna's wet hair and sighed but didn't comment. Uncle Harlan gave her one of his insincere used-car-salesman smiles, but at least he never scolded her, so Roanna forgave him for having all the depth of a pie pan. Jessie, however, went straight on the attack.

"At least you could have taken the time to dry your hair," she drawled. "Though I suppose we should all be grateful you showered and didn't come to the table smelling like a horse."

Roanna slid into her seat and fastened her gaze on her plate. She didn't bother responding to Jessie's malice. To do so would only provoke even more nastiness, and Aunt Gloria would seize the chance to put in her two cents' worth. Roanna was used to Jessie's zingers, but she wasn't happy at all that Aunt Gloria and Uncle Harlan had moved into Davencourt, and she felt she would doubly resent anything Aunt Gloria said.

Tansy served the first course, a cold cucumber soup. Roanna hated cucumber soup and merely dabbled her spoon around in it, trying to sink the tiny green pieces of herb that floated on top. She did nibble on one of Tansy's homemade poppy seed rolls and gladly relinquished her soup bowl when the next course, tuna-stuffed tomato, was served. She liked tuna-stuffed tomato. She devoted the first few minutes to painstakingly removing the bits of celery and onion from the tuna mixture, pushing the rejects into a small pile at the edge of her plate.

"Your manners are deplorable," Aunt Gloria announced as she delicately forked up a bite of tuna. "For heaven's sake, Roanna, you're seventeen, plenty old enough to stop playing with your food like a two-year-old."

Roanna's scant appetite died, the familiar tension and nausea tightening her stomach, and she cast a resentful glance at Aunt Gloria.

"Oh, she always does that," Jessie said airily. "She's like a hog rooting around for the best pieces of slop."

Just to show them she didn't care, Roanna forced herself to swallow two bites of the tuna, washing them down with most of her glass of tea to make certain they didn't lodge halfway.

She doubted it was tact on his part, but she was grateful anyway when Uncle Harlan began talking about the repairs needed on their car and weighing the advantages of buying a new one. If they could afford a new car, Roanna thought, they could certainly have afforded staying in their own house, then she wouldn't have to put up with Aunt Gloria every day. Jessie mentioned that she would like a new car, too; she was bored with that boxy four-door Mercedes Webb had insisted on buying for her, when she'd told him at least a thousand times she wanted a sports car, something with style.

Roanna didn't have a car. Jessie had gotten her first car when she was sixteen, but Roanna was a rotten driver, forever drifting off into daydreams, and Grandmother had stated that, in the interest of the safety of the citizens of Colbert County, it was best not to let Roanna out on the roads by herself. She hadn't resented it all that much, because she would much rather ride than drive, but now one of her demon imps raised its head.

"I'd like to have a sports car, too," she said, the first words she'd spoken since entering the dining room. Her eyes were round with innocence. "I've got my heart set on one of those Pontiac Grand Pricks."

Aunt Gloria's eyes rounded with horror, and her fork dropped into her plate with a clatter. Uncle Harlan choked on his tuna, then began laughing helplessly.

"Young lady!" Grandmother's hand slammed against the table, making Roanna jump guiltily. Some people might think her mispronunciation of Grand Prix had been the result of ignorance, but Grandmother knew better. "Your behavior is inexcusable," Grandmother said icily, her blue eyes snapping. "Leave this table. I'll speak to you later."

Roanna slipped from her chair, her cheeks red with embarrassment. "I'm sorry," she whispered and ran from the dining room but not fast enough to keep from hearing Jessie's amused, malicious question:

"Do you think she'll *ever* be civilized enough to eat with *people?*"

"I'd *rather* be with the horses," Roanna muttered as she slammed out the front door. She knew she should go back upstairs and change into boots again, but she desperately needed to get back to the stables, where she never felt inadequate.

Loyal was eating his own lunch in his office, while he read one of the thirty horse care publications that he received each month. He caught sight of her through the window as she slipped inside the stable and shook his head in resignation. Either she hadn't eaten anything, which wouldn't surprise him, or she was in trouble again, which wouldn't surprise him either. It was probably both. Poor Roanna was a square peg who stubbornly resisted all efforts to whittle down her corners so she would fit into the round hole, and never mind that most people happily whittled on their own corners. Burdened with almost constant disapproval, she merely hunkered down and resisted until the frustration grew too strong to be repressed, then struck out, usually in a way that only brought more disapproval. If she'd had even one-half of Miss Jessie's meanness, she could have really fought back and forced everyone to accept her on her own terms. But Roanna didn't have a mean bone in her body, which was probably why animals loved her so much. She was chock-full of mischief, though, and that only caused more trouble.

He watched as she drifted from stall to stall, trailing her fingers over the smooth wood. There was only one horse in the stable, Mrs. Davenport's favorite mount, a gray gelding who had injured his right foreleg. Loyal was keeping him quiet today, with cold packs on the leg to ease the swelling. He heard Roanna's crooning voice as she stroked the gelding's face, and he smiled as the horse's eyes almost closed with ecstasy. If her family gave her half the acceptance the horses did, he thought, she would stop fighting them at every turn and settle into the life into which she had been born.

Jessie drifted down to the stables after lunch and ordered one of the hands to saddle a horse for her. Roanna rolled her eyes at Jessie's lady-of-the-manor airs; she always caught and saddled her own horse, and it wouldn't hurt Jessie to do the same. To be honest, she never had any trouble catching a horse, but Jessie didn't have that knack. It only showed how smart horses were, Roanna thought.

Jessie caught her expression out of the corner of her eye and turned a cool, malicious look on her cousin. "Grandmother's furious with you. It was important to her that Aunt Gloria be made to feel welcome, and instead you went into your hick act." She paused ever so slightly and let her gaze drift over Roanna. "If it *is* an act." Having delivered that zinger, so subtly sharp that it slid between Roanna's ribs with barely a twinge, she smiled faintly and walked away, leaving only the miasma of her expensive perfume behind.

"Hateful witch," Roanna muttered, waving her hand to disperse the too-heavy scent while she stared resentfully at her cousin's slim, elegant back. It wasn't fair that Jessie should be so beautiful, know how to get along in public so perfectly, be Grandmother's favorite, and have Webb, too. It just wasn't *fair*.

Roanna wasn't the only one feeling resentful. Jessie seethed with it as she rode away from Davencourt. *Damn* Webb! She wished she'd never married him, even though it was what she'd set her sights on from girlhood, what everyone had taken for granted would happen. And Webb had taken it more for granted than anyone else, but then he'd always been so damn cocksure of himself that sometimes she nearly died with the urge to slap him. That she never had was due to two things: one, she hadn't wanted to do anything that would hurt her chances of ruling supreme at Davencourt when Grandmother finally died; and two, she had the uneasy suspicion that Webb wouldn't be a gentleman about it. No, it was more than a suspicion. He might pull the wool over everyone else's eyes, but she knew what a ruthless bastard he was.

She had been a fool to marry him. Surely she could have gotten Grandmother to change her will and leave Davencourt to her instead of to Webb. After all, *she* was a Davenport, not Webb. It should have been hers by right. Instead she'd had to marry that damn tyrant, and she'd made a big mistake in doing so. Chagrined, she had to admit that she'd overestimated her own charms and her ability to influence him. She thought she'd been so smart, refusing to sleep with him before marriage; she'd liked the idea of keeping him frustrated, liked the image of him panting after her like a dog after a bitch in heat. It had never been quite that way, but she'd cherished the image anyway. Instead, she'd been infuriated to learn that, rather than suffering because he couldn't have her, the bastard had simply been sleeping with other women—while he insisted she be faithful to him!

Well, she'd shown him. He was an even bigger fool than she was if he really believed she'd kept herself "pure" for him all those years while he was out screwing those bitches he met in college and at work. She knew better than to mess up her own playground, but whenever she could get away for a day or a weekend, she quickly found some lucky guy to take the edge off, so to speak. Attracting men was disgustingly easy—just give them a whiff and they came running. She'd done it the first time at the age of sixteen and had immediately discovered a delicious source of power over men. Oh, she'd had to do some pretending when she and Webb had finally married, whimpering and actually squeezing out a tear or two so he'd think his big bad pecker was actually hurting her poor little *virginal* pussy, but inside she'd been gloating that he'd been so easy to fool.

She'd also been gloating because now she was finally going to have the power in their relationship. After years of having to sweetly kowtow to him, she'd thought she had him where she wanted him. It was humiliating to remember how she'd thought he'd be more easily handled once they were married and she had him in bed with her every night. God knows, most men thought with their peckers. All of her discreet liaisons over the years had told her that she wore them out, that they couldn't keep up with her, but they'd all said it with big smiles. Jessie took pride in her ability to screw a man into limp exhaustion. She'd had it all planned: screw Webb's brains out every night, and he'd be putty in her hands during the day.

But it hadn't worked out that way at all. Her cheeks burned with humiliation as she guided her horse across a shallow creek, taking care that the water didn't splash on her shiny boots. For one thing, more often than not she was the one who was left exhausted. Webb could go at it for hours, his eyes remaining cool and watchful no matter how she panted and jerked her hips and worked him over, as if he knew she regarded it as a competition and was damned if he'd let her win. It hadn't taken her long to learn that he could outlast her, and she would be the one left lying exhausted on the twisted sheets, her loins throbbing painfully from such hard use. And no matter how hot the sex, no matter how she sucked or stroked or did anything else, once it was finished and Webb was out of bed, he went about his business as if nothing had happened, and she could just make the best of it. Well, damned if she would!

Her biggest weapon, sex, had proven to be ineffective against him, and she wanted to scream at the injustice of it. He treated her as if she were a disobedient child rather than an adult, and his wife. He was nicer to that brat, Roanna, than he was to her. She was sick and tired of being left at home every day while he roamed all over the nation, for God's sake. He said it was business, but she was certain that at least half of his "urgent" trips were conceived at the last moment just to prevent her from doing something fun. Just last month he'd had to fly to Chicago the morning before they were supposed to go on vacation in the Bahamas. And then there was the trip to New York last week. He'd been gone for three days. She'd begged to go with him, dying with excitement at the thought of the shops and theaters and restaurants, but he'd said he wouldn't have time for her and left without her. Just like that. The arrogant bastard; he was probably screwing some silly little secretary and didn't want his wife around to mess up his plans.

But she had her revenge. A smile broke across her face as she reined in the horse and spotted the man who was already lying stretched out on the blanket beneath the big tree, almost hidden in the secluded little cove. It was the most delicious revenge she could have imagined, made all the sweeter by her own uncontrolled response. It frightened her sometimes that she desired him so savagely. He was an animal, totally amoral, as ruthless in his way as Webb was, though without the cool, precise intellect.

She remembered the first time she'd met him. It hadn't been long after Mama's funeral, after she had moved into Davencourt and wheedled Grandmother into letting her redecorate the bedroom she'd chosen. She and Grandmother had been in town to choose fabrics, but Grandmother had run into one of her cronies in the fabric shop and Jessie had quickly gotten bored. She had already chosen the fabric she liked, so there was no reason to hang around listening to two old biddies gossip. She had told Grandmother she was going to the restaurant next door to get a Coke and made her escape.

She *had* gone there; she had learned early that she could get away with a lot more if she simply did what she really wanted to do after she'd done what she'd said she was going to do. That way she couldn't be accused of *lying,* for heaven's sake. And people knew how impulsive teenagers were. So, icy Coke in hand, Jessie had then whisked herself down to the newsstand where dirty magazines were sold.

It wasn't really a newsstand, but a grimy little store that sold hobby kits, a smattering of makeup and toiletries, some "hygienic" items such as rubbers, as well as newspapers, paperbacks, and a wide selection of magazines. The *Newsweek*s and *Good Housekeeping*s were prominently displayed up front with all the other acceptable magazines, but the forbidden ones were kept on a rack behind a counter in back, and kids weren't supposed to go back there. But old man McElroy had arthritis real bad, and he spent most of his time sitting on a stool behind the checkout counter. He couldn't really see who was in the back area unless he stood up, and he didn't stand up very often.

Jessie gave old man McElroy a sweet smile and wandered over to the cosmetic section, where she leisurely inspected a few lipsticks and selected a sheer pink lip gloss, her reason for being there should she get caught. When a customer claimed his attention, she whisked herself out of sight and slipped into the back area.

Naked women cavorted on various covers, but Jessie spared them only a brief disdainful glance. If she wanted to see a naked woman, all she had to do was strip off her clothes. What she liked were the nudist magazines, where she could see naked men. Most of the time their peckers were small and limp, which didn't interest her at all, but sometimes there would be a picture of a man with a nice, long, fat one sticking out. The nudists said there was nothing sexy about running around naked, but Jessie figured they lied. Otherwise, why would those men be getting hard like Grandmother's stallion did when he was about to mount a mare? She had sneaked into the stables to watch whenever she could, though everyone would have been horrified, just *horrified,* if they'd known.

Jessie smirked. They didn't know, and they wouldn't. She was too smart for them. She was two different people, and they didn't even suspect. There was the public Jessie, the princess of the Davenports, the most popular girl in school who charmed everyone with her high spirits and who refused to experiment with alcohol and cigarettes the way all the other kids did. Then there was the real Jessie, the one she kept hidden, the one who slipped the paperback porn books under her clothes and smiled sweetly at Mr. McElroy as she left his store. The real Jessie stole money from her grandmother's purse, not because there was something she couldn't have just for the asking, but because she liked the thrill of it.

The real Jessie loved tormenting that little brat, Roanna, loved pinching her when no one could see, loved making her cry. Roanna was a safe target, because no one really liked her anyway and they would always believe Jessie rather than her if she carried tales. Lately, Jessie had begun to really hate the brat, rather than just disliking her. Webb was always taking up for her, for some reason, and that made Jessie furious. How dare he take Roanna's side instead of hers?

A secret little smile curved her mouth. She'd show him who was boss. Lately she had discovered a new weapon, as her body had grown and changed. She had been fascinated by sex for years, but now physically she was beginning to match her mental maturity. All she had to do was arch her back and take a deep breath, thrusting out her breasts, and Webb would stare so fixedly at them that it was all she could do to keep from laughing. He'd kissed her, too, and when she rubbed her front against him, he had started breathing real deep, and his pecker had gotten hard. She had thought about letting him do it to her, but an innate cunning had stopped her. She and Webb lived in the same house; she would be taking too much of a chance that others would find out, and that might change the image they had of her.

She had just reached out for one of the nudist magazines when a man spoke behind her, his voice low and raspy. "What's a pretty little gal like you doin' back here?"

Alarmed, Jessie snatched her hand back and whirled to face him. She was always so careful not to let anyone see her in this section, but she hadn't heard him approach. She stared up at him, blinking wide, startled eyes at him as she prepared to go into her act of the innocent young girl who had wandered back here by accident. What she saw in the hot, impossibly blue eyes looking down at her made her hesitate. This man didn't look as if he would believe any explanation she could make.

"You're Janet Davenport's kid, ain't you?" he asked, still keeping his voice low.

Slowly, Jessie nodded. Now that she'd had a good look at him, a strange thrill ran through her. He was probably in his thirties, way too old, but he was really muscular and the expression in those hot blue eyes made her think he must know some really nasty things.

He grunted. "Thought so. Sorry about your mama." But even as he said the conventional words, Jessie had the feeling that he didn't really care one way or the other. He was looking her up and down in a way that made her feel peculiar, as if she belonged to him.

"Who are you?" she whispered, casting a weather eye toward the front of the store.

A feral grin bared his white teeth. "The name's Harper Neeley, little darlin'. Mean anything to you?"

She caught her breath, because she knew the name. She had snooped through Mama's things on a regular basis. "Yes," she said, so excited she could barely stand still. "You're my daddy."

He'd been surprised that she'd known who he was, she thought now, watching him as he lazed beneath the tree while he waited for her. But as excited as she'd been at meeting him, he really hadn't given a damn that she was his daughter. Harper Neeley had a bunch of kids, at least half of them bastards. One more, even if that one was a Davenport, didn't mean anything to him. He'd approached her just for the hell of it, not because he really cared.

Somehow, that had excited her. It was like meeting the secret Jessie, walking around in her father's body.

He fascinated her. She had made a point of meeting with him occasionally over the years. He was rough and totally selfish, and she often felt as if he were laughing at her. It infuriated her, but whenever she saw him, she still felt that same electric excitement. He was so nasty, so totally unacceptable to her social circle . . . and he was hers.

Jessie couldn't remember exactly when the excitement had turned sexual. Maybe it had always been like that, but she just hadn't been ready to recognize it. She had been so focused on bringing Webb to heel, so careful to indulge herself only when she was safely away from her home area, that it simply hadn't occurred to her.

But one day, about a year ago, when she had seen him, the usual excitement had suddenly sharpened, turned almost feral in its intensity. She had been furious with Webb— what was new about that?—and Harper had been right there, his thickly muscled body enticing her, his hot blue eyes drifting down her body in a way no father should ever look at his daughter.

She had hugged him, cuddled against him, sweetly called him "Daddy," and all the while she had been rubbing her breasts against him, rolling her hips against his pecker. That was all it had taken. He'd laughed down at her, then crudely grabbed her crotch and shoved her to the ground, where they had gone at each other like animals.

She couldn't stay away from him. She had tried, knowing how dangerous he was, knowing that she had no power to control him, but he drew her like a lodestone. There were no games she could play with him, because he knew her exactly for what she was. There was nothing he could give her and nothing that she wanted from him, except for the mindless, heated sex. No one had ever screwed her the way her daddy did. She didn't have to gauge her every reaction or try to manipulate his response; all she could do was simply lose herself in the hot nastiness of the sex. Whatever he wanted to do to her, she was willing. He was trash, and she loved it, because he was the best revenge she could ever have chosen. When Webb got into bed beside her at night, it served him right that he was sleeping with a woman who, only hours before, had been sticky with Harper Neeley's leavings.

CHAPTER

4

*R*oanna stared after Jessie as she rode away from Davencourt, up toward the hilly part of the Davenport lands. Jessie usually preferred a less demanding ride, over fields or level pastures. Why would she deviate from custom? Come to think of it, she had ridden that way a couple of times before, and Roanna had noticed it but not paid attention to it. For some reason, this time she was puzzled.

Maybe it was because she still felt resentful at Jessie's last zinger, though God knows it hadn't been any worse than the usual cut at her fragile self-esteem. Maybe it was because she, unlike everyone else, *expected* Jessie to be up to no good. Maybe it was that damn perfume. She hadn't been wearing it at lunch, Roanna thought. A scent that strong would have been noticed. So why had she doused herself with perfume before going for a ride by herself?

The answer dawned on her with blinding clarity. "She's got a boyfriend!" she whispered to herself, almost overcome with shock. Jessie was slipping around behind Webb's back and seeing someone! Roanna almost suffocated on her indignation on Webb's behalf. How could *any* woman, even Jessie, be fool enough to jeopardize her marriage to him?

Quickly she saddled Buckley, her current favorite, and set

46

out in the same direction she'd seen Jessie take. The big gelding had a long, slightly uneven gait that would have been jarring to a less experienced rider but covered distance at a fast clip. Roanna was used to his stride and settled herself into his rhythm, moving fluidly with the motion as she kept her eyes on the ground, following the fresh imprints of Jessie's horse.

Part of her didn't believe Jessie really had a boyfriend—it was just too good to be true, and besides, Jessie was too smart to drop her bread butter-side down—but she couldn't resist the tantalizing possibility that she might be right. Gleefully she began plotting some vague revenge against Jessie for the years of hurts and slights, though she didn't know exactly what she could do. Real revenge wasn't part of Roanna's makeup. She was far more likely to punch Jessie in the nose than she was to plot and carry through some long-term plan, and she would get a lot more enjoyment out of it. But she simply couldn't pass up the opportunity to catch Jessie doing something she shouldn't; it was usually she who was goofing up and Jessie who was pointing it out.

She didn't want to overtake Jessie too quickly, so she reined Buckley to a walk. The July sun broiled down so white and merciless that it should have washed out the colors of the trees, but it didn't. The top of her head burned from the heat. Usually she crammed a baseball cap on her head, but she was still dressed in the silk blend slacks and shirt she had worn to lunch, and the baseball cap, like her boots, was in her bedroom.

Dawdling was easy in that heat. She stopped and let Buckley drink from a small stream, then resumed her leisurely tracking. There was a slight breeze blowing into her face, which was why Buckley caught the scent of Jessie's mount and gave a soft whicker, alerting her. She immediately backtracked, not wanting the other horse to alert Jessie to her presence.

After tethering Buckley to a small pine, she quietly made

her way through the trees and up a small hill. Her thin-soled sandals slipped on the pine needles, and she impatiently kicked them off, then clambered barefooted the rest of the way to the top.

Jessie's mount was about forty yards below and to the left, calmly cropping a small patch of grass. A large, moss-covered rock jutted up just over the crest of the hill, and Roanna crept over to crouch behind its bulk. Carefully she peeked around it, trying to locate Jessie. She could hear voices, she thought, but the sounds were odd, not really words.

Then she saw them, almost directly below her, and sank weakly against the hot surface of the rock, shock clanging through her body. She had thought to catch Jessie meeting with one of her friends from the country club, maybe necking a little, but not *this*. Her own sexual experience was so severely limited that she couldn't have formed the images in her mind.

A bush partially concealed them, but still she could see the blanket, Jessie's pale, slim body, and the darker, more muscled form of the man on top of her. They were both stark naked, he was moving, and she was clinging to him, and they were both making sounds that made Roanna cringe. She couldn't tell who he was, could only see the top and back of his dark head. But then he moved off Jessie, rising up on his knees, and Roanna swallowed hard as she stared at him, her eyes huge. She had never seen a naked man before, and the shock was jarring. He pulled Jessie up on her hands and knees and slapped her rear, laughing harshly at the hot, guttural sound she made, then he was driving into her again the way Roanna had once glimpsed two horses doing it, and dainty, fastidious Jessie was clawing at the blanket and arching her back and rotating her butt against him.

Bile rose hotly in Roanna's throat, and she ducked down behind the rock, pressing her cheek against the rough stone. She closed her eyes tight, trying to control the urge to vomit.

48

She felt numb and sick with despair. My God, what would Webb do?

She had followed Jessie out of a perverse, mischievous desire to cause trouble for her hateful cousin, but she had expected something minor: teasing kisses, if another man was involved at all, maybe meeting some of her friends and slipping away to a bar or something. Years ago, after she and Jessie had first come to live at Davencourt, Webb had sternly neutralized Jessie's spitefulness by threatening to spank her if she didn't stop tormenting Roanna, a threat Roanna had found so delicious that she had spent days trying to provoke Jessie, just so she could watch her hateful cousin get her rear end warmed. Amused, Webb had finally taken her aside and warned her that the punishment could come her way, too, if she didn't behave herself. That same impish impulse had prompted her today, but what she had found was far more serious than she had anticipated.

Roanna's chest burned with impotent rage, and she swallowed convulsively. As much as she disliked and resented her cousin, she had never thought Jessie was stupid enough to actually be unfaithful to Webb.

Nausea rose again, and she quickly turned around to drape her arms across her drawn-up knees and rest her head on them. Her movements scraped against some small gravel, but she was too far away for them to hear the slight noises she was making, and at the moment she was too sick to care. They weren't paying much attention to anything around them anyway. They were too busy pumping and humping. God, how silly it looked . . . and how gross, all at the same time. Roanna was glad she wasn't any closer, glad that the bush had hid at least part of them.

She could just *kill* Jessie for doing this to Webb.

If Webb knew, he might kill Jessie himself, Roanna thought, and a chill ran through her. Though he normally controlled it, everyone who knew Webb well was aware of his temper and took care not to arouse it. Jessie was a fool, a stupid, malicious fool.

But she probably thought she was safe from discovery, since Webb wouldn't be back from Nashville until tonight. By then, Roanna thought sickly, Jessie would be all freshly bathed and perfumed, waiting for him and wearing both a pretty dress and a smile, and silently making fun of him because only a few hours earlier she'd been screwing in the woods with someone else.

Webb deserved better than that. But she couldn't tell him, Roanna thought. She could never tell anyone. If she did, the most likely outcome would be that Jessie would lie her way out of it, saying that Roanna was just jealous and trying to make trouble, and everyone would believe her because Roanna *was* jealous, and everyone knew it. Then both Webb and Grandmother would be angry with her rather than with Jessie. Grandmother stayed exasperated at her most of the time anyway for one reason or the other, but she couldn't bear for Webb to be mad at her.

The other possibility would be that Webb *did* believe her. He might really kill Jessie, and then he would be in trouble. She couldn't bear for anything to happen to him. He might find out some other way, but she couldn't do anything to prevent that. All she could do was not say anything herself and pray that if he did find out, he wouldn't do anything to get himself arrested.

Roanna slipped from her place of concealment behind the rock and quickly made her way back over the hill and through the stand of pine trees to where she had tethered Buckley. He blew a soft greeting and shoved his nose at her. Obediently she stroked the big head, scratching behind his ears, but her mind wasn't on what she was doing. She mounted him and quietly walked him away from the scene of Jessie's adultery, heading back to the stables. Misery weighed heavily on her thin shoulders.

She couldn't understand what she'd seen. How could any woman, even Jessie, not be satisfied with Webb? Roanna's childhood hero worship had only intensified in the ten years she had been living at Davencourt. At seventeen, she was painfully aware of other women's response to him, so she knew it wasn't just her opinion. Women stared at Webb with unconscious, or maybe not so unconscious, yearning in their eyes. Roanna tried not to look at him that way, but she knew she wasn't always successful, because Jessie sometimes said something sharp to her about mooning around Webb and making a pest of herself. She couldn't help it. Every time she saw him, it was as if her heart gave a great big leap before starting to beat so fast that sometimes she couldn't breathe, and she would get warm and tingly all over. Lack of oxygen, most likely. She didn't think love caused tingles.

Because she did love him, so much, in a way Jessie never would or could.

Webb. His dark hair and cool green eyes, the slow grin that made her dizzy with delight. The tall, muscled body that made her go both hot and cold, as if she had a fever; that particular reaction had been bothering her for a couple of years now, and it got worse whenever she watched him swimming and he was wearing only those tight brief trunks. His deep, lazy voice, and the way he scowled at everyone until he'd had his morning coffee. He was only twenty-four, but he ran Davencourt, and even Grandmother listened to him. When he was displeased, his green eyes would get so cold that they looked like glacier ice, and the laziness of his tone would abruptly vanish, leaving his words clipped and cutting.

She knew his moods, how he looked when he was tired, how he liked his laundry done. She knew his favorite foods, his favorite colors, which professional sports teams he liked, what made him laugh, what made him frown. She knew what he read, how he voted. For ten years she had absorbed every little detail about him, turning toward him like a shy little violet reaching for the light. Since her parents had died, Webb had been both her defender and her confidant. It was to him that she had poured out all her childish fears and fantasies, he who had comforted her after nightmares or when she felt so alone and frightened.

But for all her love, she had never had a chance with him

and she knew it. It had always been Jessie. That was what hurt most of all, that she could offer herself to him body and soul, and he would still have married Jessie. Jessie, who sometimes seemed to hate him. Jessie, who was unfaithful.

Tears burned Roanna's eyes, and she dashed them away. There was no point in crying about it, though she couldn't help resenting it.

From the time she and Jessie had come to live at Davencourt, Webb had watched Jessie with a cool, possessive look in his eyes. Jessie had dated other boys, and he had dated other girls, but it was as if he allowed her only so much rope, and when she reached the end of it, he would haul her back in. He had been in control of their relationship from the start. Webb was the one man Jessie had never been able to wrap around her finger or intimidate with her temper. A single word from him could make her back down, a feat even Grandmother couldn't match.

Roanna's only hope had been that Jessie would refuse to marry him, but that hope had been so slim as to be almost nonexistent. Once Grandmother had announced that Webb would inherit Davencourt itself plus her own share of the Davenport business concerns, which was fifty percent, it had been a foregone conclusion that Jessie would have married him even if he'd been the meanest, ugliest man on the earth, which he wasn't. Jessie had inherited Janet's twenty-five percent, and Roanna had her father's twenty-five percent. Jessie saw herself as the princess of Davencourt, with the promise of becoming its queen by marrying Webb. There was no way she would have accepted a lesser role by marrying someone else.

But Jessie had been fascinated by Webb, too. The fact that she couldn't control him as she did other boys had both irritated and entranced her, keeping her dancing around his flame and to his tune. Probably, with her overweening conceit, she had thought that once they were married she'd be able to control him with sex by bestowing or withholding her favors according to how he pleased her.

If so, she had been disappointed in that, too. Roanna

knew that their marriage wasn't happy and had been secretly pleased. Suddenly she was ashamed of herself for that, because Webb deserved to be happy even if Jessie didn't.

But how she had gloated every time Jessie hadn't gotten her way! She always knew, because although Webb might control his temper, Jessie never made any attempt to do so. When she was angry, she raged, she pouted, she sulked. In the two years they had been married, the fights had come more and more frequently, with Jessie's yelling heard all over the house, to Grandmother's distress.

Nothing Jessie did, however, could sway Webb from whatever decision happened to displease her. They were locked in almost constant battle, with Webb determined to oversee Davencourt and do his best by their investments, a job that was grinding and often kept him working eighteen hours a day. To Roanna, Webb was obviously adult and responsible, but he was still only twenty-four and had told her once that his age worked against him, that he had to work twice as hard as others to prove himself to older, more established businessmen. That was his primary concern, and she loved him for it.

A workaholic husband, however, wasn't what Jessie wanted in life. She wanted to vacation in Europe, but he had business meetings scheduled. She wanted to go to Aspen at the height of the ski season; he thought it was a waste of time and money because she didn't ski and wasn't interested in learning. All she wanted was to see and be seen. When she lost her driver's license due to four speeding tickets within six months, she would have blithely continued driving and counted on the Davenport influence to keep her out of trouble, but Webb had confiscated all of her car keys, sternly ordered everyone not to let her borrow theirs, and made her sit at home for a month before hiring a driver for her. What had enraged her even more was that she had tried to hire a driver herself, but Webb had anticipated her and stymied that. It hadn't been difficult; there weren't that many limousine services in the Shoals area, and none who would cross him. Only Grandmother hadn't received the rough end of Jessie's tongue during that hellish month when she'd been grounded like a rebellious teenager.

Maybe sleeping with other men was Jessie's revenge against Webb for not letting her have her way, Roanna thought. She was willful enough and spiteful enough to do it.

Bitterly, Roanna knew that she would have made Webb a much better wife than Jessie had, but no one had ever considered it, least of all Webb. Roanna was abnormally observant, a trait developed from a lifetime of being shoved to the side. She loved Webb, but she didn't underestimate his ambition. If Grandmother had made it plain that she would be very pleased if he married Roanna, the way she had with Jessie, then very probably they would now be engaged. Granted, Webb had never looked at her the way he'd looked at Jessie, but she'd always been too young. With Davencourt in the balance, he would have chosen her, she knew he would. She wouldn't have cared that he'd wanted Davencourt more than he wanted her. She would have married Webb on any terms at all, grateful just to get any part of his attention. Why couldn't it have been her? Why Jessie?

Because Jessie was beautiful, and had always been Grandmother's favorite. Roanna had tried hard at first, but she had never been as graceful or as socially adept, or had Jessie's good taste in clothing and decorating. She would certainly never be as pretty. Roanna's mirror wasn't rose tinted; she could plainly see her straight, heavy, untidy hair, more brown than red, and her bony, angular face with her weird, slanted brown eyes, the bump on the bridge of her long nose, and her too-big mouth. She was rail thin and clumsy, and her breasts were just barely there. Despairing, she knew that no one, especially no man, would ever willingly choose her over Jessie. At seventeen, Jessie had been the most popular girl in school, while Roanna, at the same age, had never had a real date. Grandmother had arranged for her to have "escorts" to various functions she'd been forced to attend, but the boys had obviously been shanghaied by their mothers for the duty, and Roanna had always been embarrassed and tongue-tied. None of the draftees had ever volunteered for another opportunity for her company.

But since Webb's marriage, Roanna had tried less and less to fit herself into the mold Grandmother had chosen for her, the appropriate social mold of a Davenport. What was the point? Webb was lost to her. She had begun withdrawing, spending as much time as she could with the horses. She was relaxed with them in a way she never was with people, because the horses didn't care how she looked or if she'd knocked over yet another glass at dinner. The horses responded to her light, gentle touch, to the special crooning note in her voice when she talked to them, to the love and care she lavished on them. She was never clumsy on a horse. Somehow her thin body would move into the rhythm of the powerful animal beneath her, and she would become one with it, part of the strength and grace. Loyal said he'd never seen anyone ride as good as she did, not even Mr. Webb, and he rode as if he'd been born in a saddle. Her riding ability was the only thing about her that Grandmother ever praised.

But she would give up her horses if she could only have Webb. Here was her chance to break up his marriage, and she couldn't take it, didn't dare take it. She couldn't hurt him that way, couldn't take the chance that he would lose his temper and do something irrevocable.

Buckley sensed her agitation, the way horses do, and began to prance nervously. Roanna jerked her attention back to what she was doing and tried to soothe him, patting his neck and talking to him, but she couldn't give him her full attention. Despite the heat, cold chills roughened her skin, and again she felt as if she might vomit.

Loyal was far more attuned to horses than he was to people, but he frowned when he saw her face and came over to take Buckley's reins as she swung down from the saddle. "What's wrong?" he asked bluntly.

"Nothing," she said, then rubbed a shaky hand over her face. "I think maybe I got too hot, that's all. I forgot my cap."

"You know better'n that," he scolded. "Go on up to the house and drink some cold lemonade, then rest up for a while. I'll take care of Buck."

"You told me to always take care of my own horse," she said, protesting, but he cut her off with a wave of his hand.

"And now I'm tellin' you to go on. Scat. If you don't have enough sense to take care of yourself, I don't know that you can take care of Buck."

"All right. Thanks." She managed a weak smile, because she knew she must really look sick for Loyal to bend his rule about the horses, and she wanted to reassure him. She was sick, all right, sick at heart, and so full of impotent rage that she thought she might explode. She *hated* this, hated what she'd seen, hated Jessie for doing it, hated Webb for letting her love him and putting her in this situation.

No, she thought as she hurried up to the house, stricken by the idea. She didn't hate Webb, could never hate him. It would be better for her if she didn't love him, but she could no more stop that than she could stop the sun from rising the next morning.

No one saw her when she slipped in the front door. The huge hall was empty, though she could hear Tansy singing in the kitchen, and a television played in the den. Probably Uncle Harlan was watching one of the game shows he liked so much. Roanna moved silently up the stairs, not wanting to talk to anyone right now.

Grandmother's suite was at the front of the house, the first door on the right. Jessie and Webb's suite was the front one on the left side. Over the years, Roanna had finally settled on one of the back bedrooms, away from everyone else, but to her dismay she saw that Aunt Gloria and Uncle Harlan had chosen the middle suite on the right side of the house, and the door was standing open, Grandmother's and Aunt Gloria's voices coming from within. Listening, Roanna could also make out the voice of the housekeeper,

Bessie, as she worked to unpack their clothes. She didn't want to see any of them, especially didn't want to give Aunt Gloria the opportunity to start in on her, so she reversed her steps and went out the double French doors onto the upper-story gallery that completely encircled the house. Using the gallery, she went around the house in the opposite direction until she came to the French doors that opened into her own bedroom and gained sanctuary.

She didn't know how she could ever look at Jessie again without screaming at her and slapping her stupid, hateful face. Tears dripped down her cheeks, and angrily she dashed them away. Crying never had done any good; it hadn't brought back Mama and Daddy, it hadn't made anyone like her any better, it hadn't kept Webb from marrying Jessie. For a long time now she had fought back her tears and pretended that things didn't hurt her even when she felt as if she would choke on her hidden pain and humiliation.

But it had been such a shock, seeing Jessie and that man actually doing it. She wasn't stupid, she'd been to an R-rated movie a couple of times, but that really never showed anything except the woman's boobs and everything was all prettied up, with dreamy music playing in the background. And once she'd glimpsed the horses doing it, but she hadn't really been able to see anything because she'd sneaked out to the stables for that very purpose and hadn't been able to find a good vantage point. The noises had scared her, though, and she'd never tried that again.

Reality was nothing like the movies. It hadn't been romantic at all. What she'd seen had been raw and brutal, and she wanted to blot it out of her memory.

She took another shower, then collapsed across the bed, exhausted from her emotional upheaval. Perhaps she dozed; she wasn't certain, but all of a sudden the room was darker as twilight gathered, and she realized she had missed supper. Another black mark against her, she thought, and sighed.

She felt calmer now, almost numb. To her surprise she was even hungry. She pulled on some clean clothes and trudged down the back stairs to the kitchen. Tansy had already cleaned up the dishes and gone home, but the industrial-size stainless-steel refrigerator would be full of leftovers.

She was nibbling at a cold chicken leg and a roll, with a glass of tea at her elbow, when the kitchen door opened and Webb strolled in. He looked tired, and he'd removed both coat and tie, the coat slung over his shoulder and hanging from one crooked finger. The top two buttons on his shirt were open. Roanna's heart gave its customary jump when she saw him. Even when he was tired and disheveled, he looked like heaven. The sickness roiled in her stomach again at the thought of what Jessie was doing to him.

"Are you still eating?" he teased with mock amazement, green eyes twinkling.

"Got to keep my strength up," she said, striving for her usual flippancy, but she couldn't quite achieve it. There was a somberness in her tone that she couldn't hide, and Webb gave her a sharp glance.

"What've you done now?" he asked, taking a glass down from the cabinet and opening the refrigerator door to pour himself some iced tea.

"Nothing unusual," she assured him, and even managed a wry, crooked smile. "I opened my big mouth at lunch, and both Grandmother and Aunt Gloria are mad at me."

"So what did you say this time?"

"We were talking about cars, and I said that I wanted one of the Pontiac Grand Pricks."

His broad shoulders heaved as he controlled a spasm of laughter, turning it into a cough. He dropped into the chair beside her. "My God, Ro."

"I know." She sighed. "It just popped out. Aunt Gloria made one of her snide remarks about the way I eat, and I wanted to get her goat." She paused. "It worked."

"What did Aunt Lucinda do?"

"She sent me from the table. I haven't seen her since." She picked at the roll, reducing it to a pile of crumbs, until

58

Webb's strong hand suddenly covered hers and stilled the movements.

"Had you eaten anything before you left the table?" he asked, and there was a stern tone in his voice now.

She made a face, knowing what was coming. "Sure. I had a roll and some tuna."

"A whole roll? How much tuna?"

"Well, probably not an entire roll."

"More than you've eaten of this one?"

She eyed the demolished bread on her plate, as if judiciously weighing each crumb, and was relieved to be able to say, "More than that."

It wasn't much more, but more was more. His expression told her he wasn't fooled, but he let that slide for now. "All right. How much tuna? How many bites?"

"I didn't *count* them!"

"More than two?"

She tried to remember. She knew she'd taken a couple of bites just to show Aunt Gloria that her verbal swipe had fallen short of the mark. She might try to evade the truth, but she wouldn't lie outright to Webb, and he knew it, so he would continue to pin her down with explicitness. With a little sigh she said, "About two, I guess."

"Did you eat anything afterward? Until now, that is?"

She shook her head.

"Ro." He turned his chair toward hers and put his arm around her thin shoulders, hugging her to him. His heat and strength enveloped her the way it always had. Roanna burrowed her untidy head against that broad shoulder, bliss overtaking her. When she'd been young, Webb's hugs had been a haven for a terrified, unwanted little girl. She was older now, and the quality of her delight had changed. There was a heady, faintly musky scent to his skin that made her heart beat faster, and made her want to cling to him.

"You have to eat, baby," he said cajolingly, but with a firm undertone. "I know you get upset and lose your appetite, but I can tell that you've lost even more weight. You're going to damage your health if you don't start eating more."

"I know what you're thinking," she charged, lifting her head from his shoulder to scowl at him. "But I don't make myself throw up or anything like that."

"My God, how could you? There's never anything in your stomach to be thrown up. If you don't eat, soon you won't have the strength to work with the horses. Is that what you want?"

"No!"

"Then eat."

She looked at the chicken leg, her expression miserable. "I try, but I don't like the taste of most food, and p-people are always criticizing how I eat and the food turns into this big wad that I can't swallow."

"You ate toast this morning with me and swallowed just fine."

"You don't yell at me or make fun of me," she muttered.

He stroked her hair, pushing the dark chestnut strands away from her face. Poor little Ro. She had always hungered for Aunt Lucinda's approval, but was too rebellious to modify her behavior to get it. Maybe she was right; it wasn't as if she was a juvenile delinquent or anything like that. She was just different, a quirky wildflower growing in the middle of a sedate, well-ordered southern rose garden, and no one knew quite what to make of her. She shouldn't have to beg for her family's love or approval; Aunt Lucinda should just love her for what she was. But for Aunt Lucinda, perfection was her other granddaughter, Jessie, and she had always made it plain that Roanna fell short in every category. Webb's mouth tightened. In his opinion, Jessie was far from perfect, and he was sick and tired of waiting for her to grow out of some of that selfishness.

Jessie's attitude, too, had a lot to do with Roanna's inability to eat. He had let this rock on for years while he devoted himself to the herculean task of learning how to run Davencourt and all the Davenport business concerns, packing four years of college into three and then going after his master's degree in business, but it was obvious now that the situation *wasn't* going to resolve itself. For Roanna's sake, he was going to have to put his foot down, with Aunt Lucinda as well as Jessie.

Roanna needed calm, peaceful surroundings where her nerves could settle down and her stomach relax. If Aunt Lucinda and Jessie—and now Aunt Gloria, too—wouldn't or couldn't let up on the criticism that they constantly leveled at Roanna, then he wouldn't let Roanna eat with them. Aunt Lucinda had always insisted that they be at the table together, that Roanna conform to social standards, but he was going to override her on this. If she would eat better with her meals served on a tray in the peacefulness of her bedroom, or even out in the stables if she preferred, then that was where she'd have them. If being separated from the family made her feel exiled, rather than the relief he thought it would be, then he'd eat out in the stable with her. This simply couldn't go on, because Roanna was starving herself to death.

Impulsively he scooped her onto his lap, the way he'd done when she was a youngster. She was about five-seven now, but not a lot heavier, and fear clutched at him as he encircled her alarmingly frail wrist with his long fingers. This little cousin had always appealed to his protective side, and what he had always loved best about her was her pluckiness, her willingness to fight back without regard for the consequences. She was full of wit and mischief, if only Aunt Lucinda would stop trying to obliterate those very traits.

She had always snuggled up to him like a kitten and did so now automatically, rubbing her cheek against his shirt. A faint twinge of physical awareness surprised him, making his dark eyebrows draw together in a puzzled frown.

He looked down at her. Roanna was woefully immature for her age, without the normal social skills and defenses teenagers developed in the course of interacting with each other. Faced with disapproval and rejection at home as well as at school, Roanna had responded by withdrawing, so she had never learned how to interact with the kids in her age group. Because of that, subconsciously he had always thought of her as still being a child in need of his protection, and maybe she did still need it. But even if she wasn't quite an adult, physically she was no longer a child either.

He could see the curve of her cheek, her long, dark lashes, the translucence of her temple where the fragile blue veins lay just beneath the surface. The texture of her skin was smooth, silky, and carried the sweet warm scent of womanhood. Her breasts were very small but very firm, and he could feel the nipple, as small and hard as a pencil eraser, of the breast that was nestled against him in her half-turned position. The twinge of awareness intensified into a sudden, definite throb in his loins, and he was abruptly conscious of how round her buttocks were and how they nestled so sweetly on his thighs.

He barely bit back a growl as he shifted her a little, just enough that the side of her hip wasn't rubbing against his hardening penis. Roanna was remarkably innocent for her age, having never dated; he doubted she had ever even been kissed. She had no idea what she was doing to him, and he didn't want to embarrass her. It was his fault for taking her on his lap as if she were still a kid. He'd just have to be more careful from now on, though this was probably a fluke. It had been over four months since he'd had sex with Jessie, because he'd gotten so damn sick and tired of her trying to manipulate him with her body. Their encounters weren't about making love; they were a contest of domination. Hell, he doubted Jessie even understood the concept of making love, of the mutual giving of pleasure. But he was young and healthy, and four months of denial had left him extremely edgy, so much so that even Roanna's skinny body could arouse him.

He jerked his mind back to the issue at hand. "Let's make a deal," he said. "I promise that no one else will say anything to you about how you eat, and if anyone does, you

62

tell me and I'll take care of it. And you, sugar, will start eating regular meals. Just for me. Promise."

She looked up at him, and her whiskey brown eyes held that soft, adoring glow she reserved for him. "All right," she whispered. "For you." Before he had any inkling what she was going to do, she curved her arm around his neck and pressed her sweet, soft, innocent mouth against his.

From the moment he'd scooped her onto his lap, Roanna had been almost breathless with longing and intense excitement. Her love for him flooded her, making her want to moan with pleasure at his touch, at the way he was holding her so close. She rubbed her cheek against his shirt, and felt the heat and resilience of his flesh beneath the fabric. Her nipples throbbed, and blindly she pressed hard against his chest. The resulting sensation was so acute that it shot straight down between her legs, and she had to clench her thighs against the heat.

Then she felt it, that sudden hardness against her hip, and with a thrill she realized what it was. She had seen a naked man for the first time that afternoon, and the shock of the act she'd witnessed had left her weak and nauseated, but this was different. This was Webb. And this meant he wanted her.

The realization shattered her with delight. She stopped thinking. He moved her so that she couldn't feel him against her hip anymore, and he was talking. She watched him, her gaze fastened on his beautiful mouth, barely absorbing his words. He wanted her to eat, just for him.

"All right," she whispered. "For you." She would do anything for him. Then the longing grew so intense she couldn't hold it back any longer, and she did what she had wanted to do for so long that it seemed like her entire life had been spent craving this. She put her arm around his neck and kissed him.

His lips were firm and warm, and hinted of a tantalizing taste that made her quiver with need. She felt him jerk, as if

63

startled, felt his hands move to her waist and tighten as if he would lift her away from him. "No," she sobbed, suddenly terrified that he would push her away. "Webb, please. Hold me." And she tightened her hold on him and kissed him even harder, shyly daring to lick his lips the way she'd seen it done in a movie.

He quivered, a long shudder running through his muscled body, and his hands clenched on her. "Ro—" he began, and her tongue slipped in between his opened lips.

He groaned, his entire body tensing. Then suddenly his mouth opened and moved, and control of the kiss was no longer hers. His arms closed around her, hard, and his tongue moved deep into her mouth. Roanna's neck bent back under the pressure, and her senses dimmed under the onslaught. She had thought about kissing, even practiced it on her pillow at night, but she hadn't realized a kiss could make her feel so hot and weak, or that his taste would be so delicious, or that the feel of him against her would unleash such terrible longing. She twisted on his lap, seeking to get closer, and fiercely he turned her so that her breasts were against his chest.

"You two-timing bastard!"

The shriek battered Roanna's ears. She leaped from Webb's lap, her face white as she pivoted to face her cousin. Jessie's features were twisted with rage as she stood just inside the door, glaring at them, her hands clenched into white-knuckled fists.

Webb got to his feet. Dull red stained his cheeks, but his gaze was steady as he too faced his wife. "Calm down," he said in an even tone. "I can explain."

"I just bet you can," she sneered. "This should be good. Damn you, no wonder you haven't been interested in touching me! All this time you've been fucking this stupid little whore!"

A red mist edged Roanna's vision. After what Jessie had been doing this afternoon, how dare she talk to Webb like this over a kiss! Without realizing she even moved, suddenly she found herself in front of Jessie, and she shoved her against the wall so hard that her head slammed against it.

"Roanna, stop it!" Webb said sharply, catching her and roughly setting her aside.

Jessie straightened and shoved her hair out of her eyes. Quick as a cat, she lunged past Webb and slapped Roanna across the face with all the strength in her arm. Webb grabbed her and swung her to one side, holding her with a firm grip on the collar of her blouse while he caught Roanna by the nape of her neck.

"That's enough, God damn it," he said with clenched teeth. Webb didn't normally swear in front of women, and the fact that he did now was a measure of his anger. "Jessie, there's no sense in letting the whole house in on this. We'll talk about it upstairs."

"We'll talk about it upstairs," she mimicked. "We'll talk about it right here, damn you! You want to keep it quiet? Tough shit! By tomorrow night, everyone in Tuscumbia is going to know you've got a taste for young ass, because I'm going to yell it on every corner!"

"Shut up," Roanna growled, ignoring her burning cheek and glaring her hate at Jessie. She tried to wriggle free of Webb's punishing hold on her neck, but he merely tightened his grip.

Jessie spat at her. "You've always been after him, you slut," she hissed. "You set it up for me to find you two together like this, didn't you? You knew I was coming down to the kitchen. You weren't content to fuck him behind my back, you wanted to lord it over me for once."

The scope of the lie stunned Roanna. She darted a glance at Webb and saw the sudden suspicious, condemning glare in his eyes. "Both of you shut up," he growled, his voice so low and icy that chills ran down her back. "Jessie. Upstairs. Now." He released Roanna and all but frog-marched Jessie to the door. He paused there to flick Roanna with a glacier gaze that cut like a whip. "I'll take care of you later."

The door swung shut behind them. Roanna sank weakly against the cabinets and covered her face with her hands.

Oh, God, she'd never meant for anything like this to happen. Now Webb hated her, and she didn't think she could bear it. Pain welled in her, tightening her throat, choking her. She had never been a match for Jessie in slyness and cunning, and Jessie had proved it once again, effortlessly spewing out the lie that would turn Webb against her. Now he thought she'd caused all this deliberately, and he would never, never love her.

Grandmother wouldn't forgive her for this ruckus. She rocked back and forth, overwhelmed with misery, wondering if she'd be sent away. Jessie had been telling Grandmother that Roanna should go away to some girl's college up north, but Roanna hadn't wanted to go and Webb had supported her, but now she doubted Webb would lift a finger if they wanted to send her to the Gobi Desert. She had caused him so much trouble he'd never forgive her, even if she could convince him that Jessie lied, which she doubted. In her experience, they always believed Jessie.

In the space of a few minutes, her entire world had crumbled around her. She had been so happy, those few, sweet moments in his arms, and then it had turned to hell. She would likely have to go away, and she'd lost Webb forever.

It wasn't fair. Jessie was the one who was the whore. But Roanna didn't dare tell, couldn't tell, no matter what happened. She couldn't defend herself against the vicious lies Jessie was even now telling about her.

"I hate you," she whispered thinly to her absent cousin. She cowered against the cabinets like a frightened little animal, her heart pounding against her ribs with a force that almost made her faint. "I wish you would die."

CHAPTER

5

*R*oanna lay huddled tensely in her bed. She was cold with misery despite the heat of the summer night, and sleep was as distant now as it had been when she had first escaped upstairs to her room.

The hours since Jessie had caught her kissing Webb had been a nightmare. The uproar had, of course, brought the rest of the household running. There was no need for questions, because Jessie had screamed curses at both Webb and Roanna the entire time he was dragging her upstairs, but both Grandmother and Aunt Gloria had hammered Roanna with endless queries and accusations anyway.

"How *dare* you do such a thing?" Grandmother had asked, glaring at Roanna with eyes as cold as Webb's had been, but Roanna remained mute. What could she say? She shouldn't have kissed him; she knew it. Loving him was no excuse, at least not one that would matter to the unanimous condemnation she faced.

She couldn't defend herself by pointing to Jessie's behavior. Webb might hate her now, but still she couldn't tell something that would so hurt him and might cause him to do something rash. She would rather take all the blame

67

herself than risk anything bad happening to him. And in the final analysis, Jessie's actions didn't excuse her own. Webb was a married man; she shouldn't have kissed him. She writhed inside with shame at what her heedless, impulsive act had caused.

The battle raging upstairs had been clearly audible to everyone else. Jessie had always been unreasonable when thwarted and doubly so when her vanity was involved. Her screams had sliced over the deep rumble of Webb's voice. She'd called him every filthy name imaginable, using words that Roanna had never heard spoken aloud before. Grandmother was usually able to overlook anything Jessie did, but even she winced at the language being used. Roanna heard herself called a whore, a horse-faced little slut, and a stupid animal good only for barnyard screwing. Jessie had threatened to have Grandmother cut Webb out of her will—hearing this, Roanna had darted a terrified look at Grandmother, because she would die if she'd cost Webb his inheritance, but Grandmother had lifted her elegant brows in surprise at hearing this threat—and to have Webb arrested for statutory rape.

Of course, Grandmother and Aunt Gloria had instantly believed that Roanna had been sleeping with Webb, and this brought their hard glares and recriminations down on her again, though Uncle Harlan had merely lifted his thick gray brows and looked amused. Embarrassed, miserable, Roanna had shaken her head dumbly, not knowing any way to defend herself that they would believe.

Webb wasn't a man to take threats lying down. Until then, he'd been furious but kept his temper under control. Now there was a crash, and the sound of glass breaking, and he roared: "Get a goddamn divorce! I'll do whatever it takes to get rid of you!"

He'd come down the stairs then, his face hard and set, his eyes burning cold and green. His furious gaze touched on Roanna, and his eyes narrowed, making her shudder with dread, but he didn't stop. "Webb, wait," Grandmother said, reaching out a staying hand. He ignored her, slamming out of the house. A moment later they saw the headlights of his car slice across the lawn.

Roanna didn't know if he'd returned yet, because only loud vehicles could be heard from inside the house. Her eyes burned as she stared up at the ceiling, darkness weighing down on her like a blanket, suffocating her.

What hurt most of all was that Webb hadn't trusted in her; even knowing Jessie, he'd believed her lies. How *could* he think for one moment that she would deliberately do anything that would cause him any trouble? Webb was the center of her existence, her one champion; if he turned away from her, then she had no foundation, no security in this world.

But fury and disgust had been in his eyes when he'd looked at her, as if he couldn't stand the sight of her now. Roanna curled in a ball, whimpering with the pain that seemed so overwhelming she thought she could never recover from it. She loved him; she wouldn't have turned away from him, no matter what he did. But he had turned away from her, and she shrank in on herself as she realized what the difference was: he didn't love her. She hurt all over, as if she'd bruised herself in this headlong crash into the brick wall of reality. He'd liked her, been amused by her, maybe felt some sort of family tie with her, but he hadn't loved her the way she wanted him to love her. With sudden, shattering clarity, she saw that he'd felt sorry for her, and the humiliation of it scoured her raw inside. Pity was never what she'd wanted from Webb or from anyone else.

She'd lost him. Even if he gave her the chance to defend herself and if he then believed her, it would still never be the same again. He thought she had betrayed him, and his lack of trust was a betrayal of her. That knowledge would always be there in her heart, an icy, burning knot to mark her loss.

She had always clung fiercely to Davencourt and to Webb, resisting any effort to pry her loose. Now, for the first time, she thought about going away. There was nothing left here, she might as well go away to college the way everyone wanted her to and start fresh, where people didn't know her and have preconceived ideas about how she should look and act. Before, the very thought of leaving Davencourt had brought panic, but now she felt only relief. Yes, she wanted to get away from everyone and everything.

But first, she would fix things for Webb. One last gesture of love, and then she would put all this behind her and move on.

She glanced at the clock as she got out of bed. It was after two; the house was silent. Jessie was probably asleep, but Roanna frankly didn't give a damn. She could just wake up and listen, for once, to what Roanna had to say.

She didn't know what she would do if Webb were there, but she didn't really expect him to be. He'd been in such a temper when he'd left that he probably hadn't returned yet, and even if he had, he wouldn't crawl into bed with Jessie. He'd either be downstairs in the study or asleep in one of the other bedrooms.

She didn't need a light; she had wandered Davencourt so much at night that she knew all of its shadows. Silently she drifted down the hallway, her long white nightgown making her look like a ghost. She *felt* like a ghost, she thought, as if no one ever really saw her.

She paused in front of the door to Webb and Jessie's suite. A light was still on inside; a thin bright ribbon was visible at the base of the door. Deciding not to knock, Roanna turned the knob. "Jessie, are you awake?" she asked softly. "I want to talk to you."

The shrill scream tore through the soft fabric of the night, a long, raw sound that seemed to go on and on, straining, until it broke on a hoarse note. Lights flared in various bedrooms, even down in the stables where Loyal had his own apartment. There was a gabble of sleepy, confused voices crying out, asking questions, and the thud of running feet.

Uncle Harlan was first to reach the suite. He said,

"Godawmighty," and for once the too-smooth, too-hearty tone was absent from his voice.

Her hands stuffed into her mouth as if to keep another scream from escaping, Roanna slowly backed away from Jessie's body. Her brown eyes were wide and unblinking, the expression in them curiously blind.

Aunt Gloria rushed into the room despite Uncle Harlan's belated attempt to stop her, with Lucinda close behind. Both women stumbled to a halt, horror and disbelief stunning them to immobility as they took in the gory scene. Lucinda stared at the tableau presented by her two granddaughters, and every vestige of color washed out of her face. She began to tremble.

Aunt Gloria put her arms around her sister, all the while staring wildly at Roanna. "My God, you've killed her," she blurted, each word rising with hysteria. "Harlan, call the sheriff!"

The driveway and courtyard were a snarl of vehicles parked at random angles, bar lights flashing eerie blue strobes through the night. Every window in Davencourt blazed with light, and the house was crowded with people, most of them wearing brown uniforms, some of them wearing white.

All of the family, except for Webb, sat in the spacious living room. Grandmother was weeping softly, her hands ceaselessly twisting a delicately embroidered handkerchief as she sat with slumped shoulders. Her face was ravaged with grief. Aunt Gloria sat beside her, patting her, murmuring soothing but meaningless words. Uncle Harlan stood just behind them, rocking back and forth on his toes, importantly answering questions and offering his own opinions on every theory or detail, soaking in the limelight currently shining on him because of his luck in being the first one on the scene—discounting Roanna, of course.

Roanna sat alone on the opposite side of the room from everyone else. A deputy stood nearby. She was dully aware that he was a guard, but she couldn't bring herself to care.

She was motionless, her eyes dark pools in a colorless face, her gaze both unseeing and yet encompassing as she stared unblinkingly across the room at her family.

Sheriff Samuel "Booley" Watts paused just inside the doorway and watched her, wondering uncomfortably what she was thinking, how she felt about this silent but implacable rejection. He assessed the thin frailty of her bare arms, noted how insubstantial she looked in that white nightgown, which wasn't much whiter than her face. The pulse at the base of her throat beat visibly, the rhythm too fast and weak. With the experience of thirty years in law enforcement behind him, he turned to one of his deputies and said quietly, "Get one of the paramedics in here to see about the girl. She looks shocky." He needed her lucid and responsive.

The sheriff had known Lucinda for most of his life. The Davenports had always been hefty contributors to his campaign funds when election time rolled around. Politics being what they were, he'd done a lot of favors for the family over the years, but at the base of their longtime relationship was genuine liking. Marshall Davenport had been a tough, shrewd son of a bitch but a decent one. Booley had nothing but respect for Lucinda, for her inner toughness, her refusal to relax her standards in the face of modern decline, her business acumen. In the long years after David's death, until Webb had become old enough to begin taking over some of the burden, she had run an empire, overseen a huge estate, and raised her two orphaned granddaughters. Granted, she'd had the benefit of immense wealth to smooth the way for her, but the emotional burden had been the same on her as it would have been on anyone else.

Lucinda had lost too many loved ones, he thought. Both the Davenport and Tallant families had suffered untimely deaths, people taken too young. Lucinda's beloved brother, the first Webb, had died in his forties after being kicked in the head by a bull. His son, Hunter, had died at the age of thirty-one when his small plane crashed in a violent thunderstorm in Tennessee. Marshall Davenport had been only sixty when he died from a burst appendix that he ignored, thinking it was just an intestinal upset, until the infection had become so massive his system couldn't fight it off. Then both David and Janet, as well as David's wife, had been killed in that car wreck ten years ago. That had nearly broken Lucinda, but she'd stiffened her spine and soldiered on.

Now this; he didn't know if she could bear up under this latest bereavement. She'd always adored Jessie, and the girl had been mighty popular in the elite society of Colbert County, though Booley himself had had his own reservations about her. Sometimes her expression had seemed cold, emotionless, like that of some of the killers he'd seen through the years. Not that he'd ever had any trouble with her, never been called on to cover up any minor scandals; whatever Jessie was really like, under the flirtatiousness and party manners, she'd kept her nose clean. Jessie and Webb had been the sparks in Lucinda's eyes, and the old girl had been nearly bursting a seam with pride when the two kids had gotten married a couple of years ago. Booley hated what he had to do; it was bad enough that she'd lost Jessie, without involving Webb, but it was his job. Politics or not, this couldn't be swept under the carpet.

A stocky paramedic, Turkey MacInnis, entered the room and crossed to where Roanna was sitting, hunkering down in front of her. Turkey, so called because of his ability to imitate a turkey call without benefit of any gizmos, was both competent and soothing, one of the better paramedics in the county. Booley listened to the casual matter-of-fact voice as he asked the girl a few questions, assessing her responsiveness as he flicked a tiny penlight in her eyes, then took her blood pressure and counted her pulse. Roanna answered the questions in a flat, almost inaudible tone, her voice sounding strained and raw. She regarded the paramedic at her feet with a total lack of interest.

A blanket was fetched and wrapped around her, and the paramedic urged her to lie down on the sofa. Then he brought her a cup of coffee, which Booley guessed to be heavily sweetened, and cajoled her into drinking it.

Booley sighed. Satisfied that Roanna was being taken care of, he couldn't put off his onerous duty any longer. He rubbed the back of his head as he walked over to the small group on the other side of the room. For at least the tenth time, Harlan Ames was recounting the event as he interpreted it, and Booley was getting heartily sick of that greasy, too-loud voice.

He sat down beside Lucinda. "Have you found Webb yet?" she asked in a strangled tone, as more tears slipped down her cheeks. For the first time, he thought, Lucinda looked her age of seventy-three. She had always given the impression of being lean and strong, like the finest stainless steel, but now she looked shrunken in her nightgown and robe.

"Not yet," he said uncomfortably. "We're looking for him." That was an understatement if he'd ever made one.

There was a slight disturbance at the door, and Booley looked around, frowning, but relaxed when Yvonne Tallant, Webb's mother, strode into the living room. Technically no one was supposed to be allowed in, but Yvonne was family, even though she had distanced herself several years back by moving out of Davencourt into her own little house across the river in Florence. Yvonne had always been a woman with an independent streak. Just now, though, Booley wished she hadn't shown up, and he wondered how she'd found out about the trouble here tonight. Ah, hell, no use worrying about it. That was the trouble with small towns. Someone in dispatch, maybe, had called home and said something to a family member, who'd called a friend, who'd called a cousin who knew Yvonne personally and had taken it upon herself to let her know. That was always how it worked.

Yvonne's green eyes swept the room. She was a tall, slim woman with streaks of gray in her dark hair, the type described more as handsome than pretty. Even at this hour, she was impeccably clad in tailored slacks and a crisp white blouse. Her gaze lit on Booley. "Is it true?" she asked, her voice cracking a little. "About Jessie?" Despite Booley's own reservations about Jessie, she had always seemed to get along with her mother-in-law. Besides, the Davenport and Tallant families were so close that Yvonne had known Jessie from the cradle.

Beside him, Lucinda gulped on a sob, her entire body trembling. Booley nodded an answer at Yvonne, who closed her eyes against welling tears.

"Roanna did it," Gloria hissed, glaring across the room at the small, blanket-wrapped figure lying on the sofa.

Yvonne's eyes flew open, and she gave Gloria an incredulous look. "Don't be ridiculous," she snapped, and purposefully strode over to Roanna, crouching down beside her and stroking the tumbled hair back from the colorless face, murmuring softly to her as she did. Booley's opinion of Yvonne jumped up several notches, though he doubted, from the look on her face, that Gloria shared it.

Lucinda bowed her head, as if unable to look across the room at her other granddaughter. "Are you going to arrest her?" she whispered.

Booley took one of her hands in his, feeling like a meaty, clumsy ox as his thick fingers folded around her cold, slender ones. "No, I'm not," he said.

Lucinda shuddered slightly, some of the tension leaving her body. "Thank God," she whispered, her eyes squeezing shut.

"I'd like to know why not!" Gloria shrilled from Lucinda's other side, rearing up like a wet hen. Booley had never liked Gloria nearly as much as he did Lucinda. She'd always been prettier, but Lucinda had been the one who'd caught Marshall Davenport's eye, Lucinda who had married the richest man in northwest Alabama, and envy had nearly eaten Gloria alive.

"Because I don't think she did it," he said flatly.

"We saw her standing right over the body! Why, her feet were in the blood!"

Irritably, Booley wondered why that was supposed to

75

have any significance. He reached for patience. "From what we can tell, Jessie had already been dead for several hours before Roanna found her." He didn't go into the technical details about the progression rate of rigor mortis, figuring Lucinda didn't need to hear it. It wasn't possible to pin down the exact time of a death unless it was witnessed, but it was still a sure thing that Jessie had died at least a couple of hours before midnight. He didn't know why Roanna had paid her cousin a visit at two in the morning—and he'd definitely find out—but Jessie had already been dead.

The little family group was frozen, staring at him as if they couldn't comprehend this latest twist. He took out his little notebook. One of the county detectives normally would have done the interviewing, but this was the Davenport family, and he was going to give the case his personal attention.

"Mr. Ames said that Webb and Jessie had a lulu of a fight tonight," he began, and saw the sharp look that Lucinda gave her brother-in-law.

Then she took a deep breath and squared her shoulders as she mopped at her face with the mangled handkerchief. "They argued, yes."

"What about?"

Lucinda hesitated, and Gloria stepped into the breach. "Jessie caught Webb and Roanna carrying on in the kitchen."

Booley's gray eyebrows rose. Not much surprised him anymore, but he felt mildly astonished at this. Dubiously, he glanced at the frail, huddled little form across the room. Roanna seemed, if not childish, still oddly childlike, and he wouldn't have figured Webb for being a man who was turned on by that. "Carrying on, how?"

"Carrying on, that's how," Gloria said, her voice rising. "My God, Booley, do you want me to draw you a picture?"

The idea of Webb having sex with Roanna in the kitchen struck him as even more unlikely. He was never surprised at the depth of stupidity supposedly smart people could exhibit, but this didn't ring true. Odd, that he could see Webb

76

committing murder, but not fooling around with his little cousin.

Well, he'd get the true story about the kitchen episode from Roanna. He wanted something else from these three. "So they were arguing. Did the argument turn violent?"

"Sure did," Harlan replied, only too eager to take the spotlight again. "They were upstairs, but Jessie was screaming so loud we could hear every word. Then Webb yelled at her to get a divorce, that he'd do anything to get rid of her, and there was the sound of glass breaking. Then Webb came storming downstairs and left."

"Did any of you see Jessie after that, or maybe hear her in the bathroom?"

"Nope, not a sound," Harlan said, and Gloria shook her head. No one had tried to talk to Jessie, knowing from experience that it was better to let her cool down first or her fury would erupt on the erstwhile mediator. Lucinda's expression was one of growing disbelief and horror as she realized where Booley's questioning was headed.

"No," she said violently, shaking her head in denial. "Booley, no! You can't suspect Webb!"

"I have to," he replied, trying to keep his voice gentle. "They were arguing, violently. Now, we all know Webb has quite a temper when he's stirred up. No one saw or heard a peep out of Jessie after he left. It's a sad fact, but any time a woman's killed, it's usually her husband or a boyfriend who does it. This hurts me bad, Lucinda, but the truth is Webb is the most likely suspect."

She was still shaking her head, and tears were dribbling down her wrinkled cheeks again. "He couldn't. Not Webb." Her voice was pleading.

"I hope not, but I have to check it out. Now, what time was it when Webb left, as near as you can remember?"

Lucinda was silent. Harlan and Gloria looked at each other. "Eight?" Gloria finally offered, uncertainty in her voice.

"About that," Harlan said, nodding. "That movie I wanted to watch just had come on."

Eight o'clock. Booley considered that, chewing on his lower lip as he did so. Clyde O'Dell, the coroner, had been doing his job for just about as long as Booley had been doing his, and was damn good at guessing the time of death. He had both the experience and the knack for adding the degree of rigor with the temperature factor and coming up with pretty close to the right answer. Clyde had put the time of Jessie's death at "Oh, ten o'clock or thereabouts," with a rocking motion of his hand to indicate the actual time could slip either way. Eight o'clock was a mite early, and though it was still within the realm of possibility, that did throw a bit of doubt into the mix. He had to make damn sure of his case before he presented it to the county prosecutor, because old Simmons was too slick a politician to take on a case involving the Davenports and Tallants unless he was sure he could make it stick. "Did anyone hear a car or anything later on? Did Webb maybe come back?"

"I didn't hear anything," Harlan said.

"I didn't either," Gloria confirmed. "You'd have to be driving a transfer truck before we could hear it in here, unless maybe we were in bed and the balcony doors were open."

Lucinda rubbed her eyes. Booley had the feeling she wished her sister and brother-in-law would shut the hell up. "We can't normally hear anyone driving up," she said. "The house is very well insulated, and the shrubbery deadens the sound, too."

"So he could have returned and you wouldn't necessarily have known it."

Lucinda opened her mouth, then closed it without replying. The answer was obvious. The upstairs balcony that circled the huge, elegant old house was accessible from the outside stairs on Webb and Jessie's side of the house. Moreover, each bedroom had double French doors that opened onto the balcony; it would have been ridiculously easy for anyone to go up those stairs and enter the bedroom without anyone else in the house seeing them. From a security standpoint, Davencourt was a nightmare.

Well, maybe Loyal had heard something. His apartment in the stables probably wasn't as soundproof as this massive old house.

Yvonne left Roanna's side and came to stand right in front of Booley. "I heard what you've been saying," she said quietly, her tone even despite the way her green eyes were boring a hole in him. "You're barking up the wrong tree, Booley Watts. My son didn't kill Jessie. No matter how mad he was, he wouldn't have hurt her."

"Under normal circumstances, I'd agree with you," Booley replied. "But she was threatening to have Lucinda cut him out of her will, and we all know what Davencourt means to—"

"Bullshit," Yvonne said firmly, ignoring the way Gloria's mouth tightened like a prune. "Webb wouldn't believe that for a second. Jessie always exaggerated when she was mad."

Booley looked at Lucinda. She wiped her eyes and said faintly, "No, I would never have disinherited him."

"Even if they divorced?" he pressed.

Her lips trembled. "No. Davencourt needs him."

Well, that undercut a damn good motive, Booley thought. He wasn't exactly sorry. He would hate like hell to have to arrest Webb Tallant. He'd do it, if he could build a strong enough case, but he'd hate it.

At that moment a flurry of voices came from the front entrance, and they all recognized Webb's deep voice as he said something curt to one of the deputies. Every head in the room, except Roanna's, swiveled to watch as he strode into the room, flanked by two deputies. "I want to see her," he said sharply. "I want to see my wife."

Booley got to his feet. "I'm sorry about this, Webb," he said, his voice as tired as he felt. "But we need to ask you some questions."

79

CHAPTER
6

Jessie was dead.

They hadn't let him see her, and he desperately needed to, because until he saw it for a fact himself, Webb found it impossible to truly believe it. He felt disoriented, unable to sort out his thoughts or feelings because so many of them were contradictory. When Jessie had yelled at him that she wanted a divorce, he'd felt nothing but relief at the prospect of being rid of her, but . . . dead? Jessie? Spoiled, vibrant, passionate Jessie? He couldn't remember a day of his life when Jessie hadn't been there. They had grown up together, cousins and childhood playmates, then the fever of puberty and sexual passion had locked them together in an endless game of domination. Marrying her had been a mistake, but the shock of losing her was numbing. Grief and relief warred, tearing him apart inside.

Guilt was there, too, in spades. Guilt, first and foremost, because he could feel relief at all, never mind that for the past two years she had done her best to make his life hell, systematically destroying everything he'd ever felt for her in her relentless quest for the fawning adoration she'd thought she wanted.

And then there was the guilt over Roanna.

He shouldn't have kissed her. She was only seventeen, damn it, and an immature seventeen at that. He shouldn't have held her on his lap. When she had suddenly thrown her arms around his neck and kissed him, he should have gently pushed her away, but he hadn't. Instead he'd felt the soft, shy bloom of her mouth under his, and her very innocence had aroused him. Hell, he'd already been aroused by the feel of her round bottom on his lap. Instead of breaking the kiss, he had deepened it, taking control, thrusting his tongue into her mouth for an explicitly sexual kiss. He'd turned her in his arms, wanting to feel those slight, delicate breasts against him. If Jessie hadn't walked in at that point, he probably would have had his hand on those breasts and his mouth on the sweetly pebbled nipples. Roanna had been aroused, too. He'd thought she was too innocent to know what she was doing, but now he saw it differently. Inexperienced wasn't the same as innocent.

No matter what he'd done, he doubted Roanna would have lifted a hand or spoken a word to stop him. He could have taken her there on the kitchen table, or sitting astride his lap, and she would have let him.

There was nothing Roanna wouldn't do for him. He knew it. And that was the most horrible thought of all.

Had Roanna killed Jessie?

He'd been furious with both of them, and with himself for allowing the situation to happen. Jessie had been screaming her filthy insults, and abruptly he'd been so fed up with her that he knew it was the end of their marriage for him. As for Roanna—he never would have thought she was devious enough to set up the scene in the kitchen, but when he'd looked at her after Jessie's vicious accusation, he hadn't seen shock on Roanna's too-open, too-expressive face; he'd seen guilt. Maybe it was caused by the same dismay he'd been feeling, because they shouldn't have been kissing, but maybe . . . maybe it was more. For an instant he had seen something else, too: hate.

They all knew that Roanna and Jessie didn't get along, but he'd also known for quite some time that, for Roanna, the animosity had been very bitter. The reason for it had been obvious, too; only a blind fool could have missed seeing how much Roanna adored him. He hadn't done anything to encourage her, romantically speaking, but neither had he discouraged her. He was fond of the little brat, and that unquestioning hero worship of hers had definitely stroked his ego, especially after one of the endless battles with Jess. Hell, he supposed he loved Ro, but not in the way she wanted; he loved her with the amused exasperation of an older brother, he worried about her lack of appetite, and he felt sorry for her when she was humiliated by her own social awkwardness. It hadn't been easy for her, forever being cast as the ugly duckling to Jessie's beautiful swan.

Could she have believed that ridiculous threat Jessie had made, about having him cut out of Aunt Lucinda's will? He'd known it was nonsense, but had Roanna? What would she have done to protect him? Would she have gone to Jessie, tried to reason with her? He knew from experience that reasoning with Jessie was wasted effort. She would have turned on Roanna like a bear on fresh meat, dredging up even more hateful things to say, vicious threats to make. Would Roanna have gone to such extreme lengths to stop Jess? Before that episode in the kitchen, he would have said no way, but then he'd seen the expression on Roanna's face when Jessie burst in on them, and now he wasn't certain.

They said she'd been the one to find Jessie's body. His wife was dead, murdered. Someone had bashed her head in with one of the andirons from the fireplace in their suite. Had Roanna done it? Could she have done it deliberately? Everything he knew about her said no, at least to the second question. Roanna wasn't cold-blooded. But if Jessie had taunted her, made fun of her looks and her feelings for him, made more of those stupid threats, maybe then she could have lost her temper and hit Jessie.

He sat alone in Booley's office, bent over with his head cradled in his hands as he tried to bring some sort of order to the turmoil of his thoughts. Evidently he was the prime suspect. After the fight he and Jess had had, he supposed that was logical. It made him so angry he wanted to punch someone, but it was logical.

He hadn't been arrested, and he wasn't particularly worried, at least not about that. He hadn't killed Jess, so unless some evidence was fabricated against him, there was no way to prove that he had. He was needed at home to take care of things. From the brief glimpse he'd had of her, Aunt Lucinda had been devastated; she wouldn't be up to making the funeral arrangements. And Jess was his wife; he wanted to do this last service for her, mourn her, grieve for the girl she had been, the wife he had hoped for. It hadn't worked out for them, but still she hadn't deserved to die like that.

Tears burned his eyes, dripped through his fingers. Jess. Beautiful, unhappy Jess. He had wanted her to be a partner rather than a parasite that constantly demanded more and more, but it hadn't been in her nature to give. There hadn't been enough love in the world to satisfy her, and eventually he had stopped even trying.

She was gone. He couldn't bring her back, couldn't protect her.

But what about Roanna?

Had she killed his wife?

What should he do now? Tell Booley his suspicions? Throw Roanna to the wolves?

He couldn't do it. He didn't, couldn't, believe that Roanna would deliberately have killed Jessie. Hit her, yes. The blow might even have been struck in self-defense, because Jessie was—had been—perfectly capable of physically attacking Roanna. Ro was only seventeen, a juvenile; if she were arrested and tried and found guilty, her sentence would be light, for the crime. But even a light sentence would be a death sentence for her. Webb knew as sure as he was sitting there that Roanna wouldn't survive so much as a year's sentence to a juvenile detention hall. She was too frail, too vulnerable. She would stop eating altogether. And she would die.

He thought of the scene at the house. He'd been hustled out of the house before he'd been able to speak with anyone, though his mother had tried. But what he'd seen in that brief moment was branded on his mind: Yvonne, fiercely protective, ready to do battle for him, but then he'd expected nothing else from his stalwart mother; Aunt Lucinda, staring at him with numb grief; Aunt Gloria and Uncle Harlan, horrified, fascinated accusation in their eyes. No doubt about it, they thought he was guilty, damn them. And Roanna, in pale and frozen isolation on the other side of the room, not even lifting her head to look at him.

He'd spent the past ten years protecting her. It had become second nature to him. Even now, as angry as he was at her, he couldn't stop the instinct to shield her. If he thought she'd done it deliberately, that would be different, but he didn't. So here he was, protecting with his silence the girl who had probably killed his wife, and the bitterness of the choice filled his gut.

The office door opened behind him and he straightened, brusquely wiping the remaining dampness from his eyes. Booley walked around the desk and sank heavily into the creaky leather chair, his shrewd eyes on Webb's face, taking note of the evidence of tears. "I'm sorry about this, Webb. I know it's a shock."

"Yeah." His voice was rough.

"I got a job to do, though. You were heard telling Jessie you'd do anything to get rid of her."

The best way through this minefield, Webb figured, was to tell the truth—up to a point, when it would be best to say nothing at all. "Yeah, I said it. Right after I told her to get a divorce. I meant I'd agree to any settlement."

"Even giving up Davencourt?"

"Davencourt isn't mine to give, it's Aunt Lucinda's. That decision would be hers."

"Jessie threatened to have Lucinda cut you out of her will."

Webb gave an abrupt shake of his head. "Aunt Lucinda wouldn't do anything like that just because of a divorce."

Booley crossed his arms behind his head, linking his fingers to form a cradle for his skull. He studied the young man before him. Webb was big and strong, a natural athlete; he had the strength to crush Jessie's skull with one blow, but had he done so? He abruptly changed the subject. "Supposedly Jessie caught you and Roanna at some hanky-panky in the kitchen. Want to tell me about it?"

Webb's eyes flashed with a hint of the cold, ferocious fury he was holding bottled up inside. "I was never unfaithful to Jess," he said shortly.

"Never?" Booley let a little doubt slide into his tone. "Then just what did Jessie see that set her off?"

"A kiss." Let Booley have the unvarnished truth, as far as it went.

"You kissed Roanna? For God's sake, Webb, don't you think she's a mite young for you?"

"Damn it, of course she's too young!" Webb snapped. "It wasn't like that."

"Wasn't like what? What do you have going with her?"

"I don't have anything going with her." Unable to contain himself any longer, Webb lunged to his feet, causing Booley to tense and automatically lay his big hand on the butt of his pistol, but he relaxed when Webb began pacing the confines of the small office.

"Then why did you kiss her?"

"I didn't. She kissed me." Initially, that is. Booley didn't need to know the rest of it.

"Why'd she do that?"

Webb rubbed the back of his neck. "Roanna's like a kid sister to me. She was upset—"

"Why?"

"Aunt Gloria and Uncle Harlan moved in today. She doesn't get along with Aunt Gloria."

Booley made a grunting sound, as if he could understand that. "And you were . . . comforting her?"

"That, and trying to get her to eat. If she's upset or

nervous, she can't eat, and I was worried about what this would do to her."

"You think she's—what's the word—aner-something? Starving herself to death?"

"Anorexic. Maybe. I don't know. I told her that I'd talk to Aunt Lucinda and make the others stay off her back, if she would promise to eat. She threw her arms around my neck and kissed me, Jessie walked in, and all hell broke loose."

"Is that the first time Roanna's kissed you?"

"Except for pecks on the cheek, yes."

"So there's nothing at all romantic going on between the two of you?"

"No," Webb said, the word clipped.

"I heard she's got a crush on you. A sweet young girl like that, a lot of men would be tempted."

"She depends on me a lot, has since her folks died. It's no big secret."

"Was Jessie jealous of Roanna?"

"Not to my knowledge. She had no reason to be."

"Even though you get along real good with Roanna? From what I hear, you and Jessie hadn't been getting along at all. Maybe she was jealous about that."

"You hear a lot, Booley," Webb said tiredly. "Jessie wasn't jealous. She threw temper tantrums whenever she didn't get her way. She was mad at me for going to Nashville this morning, and when she saw Roanna kissing me, that was just an excuse to raise hell."

"The argument turned violent, didn't it?"

"I threw a glass and broke it."

"Did you hit Jessie?"

"No."

"Have you ever hit her?"

"No." He paused, and shook his head. "I spanked her ass once when she was sixteen, if that counts."

Booley restrained a grin. Now wasn't the time for amusement, but Jessie getting her rear end tanned was something he'd liked to have seen. A lot of kids nowadays, boys and girls both, would benefit greatly from the same treatment.

Webb would have been just seventeen at the time, but he'd always been older than his years.

"What happened then?"

"Jessie was getting more and more out of control. I left before things could get out of hand."

"What time did you leave?"

"Hell, I don't know. Eight, eight-thirty."

"Did you go back?"

"No."

"Where did you go?"

"I drove around a while, over to Florence."

"Did anybody you know see you, so they can verify it?"

"I don't know."

"What did you do? Just drive around?"

"For a while, like I said. Then I went to the Waffle Hut on Jackson Highway."

"What time did you get there?"

"Ten o'clock, maybe."

"What time did you leave?"

"After two. I didn't want to come home until I'd cooled down."

"So you were there about four hours? I reckon the waitress would remember that, don't you?"

Webb didn't reply. He thought it likely, because she had tried several times to strike up a conversation, but he hadn't been in the mood for chitchat. Booley would check it out, the waitress would verify his presence, and that would be the end of it. But who would Booley look at as a suspect then? Roanna?

"You can go on home," Booley said after a minute. "Don't guess I have to tell you to stick close. No going out of town on business trips or anything like that."

Webb's gaze was cold and hard. "I'd hardly be scheduling a business trip when I have to bury my wife."

"Well, as to that. Considering the nature of her death, there's gotta be an autopsy. Normally that only delays the funeral a day or two, but sometimes it can be longer. I'll have to let you know." Booley leaned forward, his jowly

87

face earnest. "Webb, son, I'll tell you plain, I don't know about this. It's a sorry fact that when a woman gets killed, it's usually her husband or boyfriend who did it. Now, you've never struck me as the type, but then neither have a lot of other folks I've wound up arresting. I gotta suspect you, and I gotta check everything out. On the other hand, if you have any suspicions yourself, I'd appreciate hearing about them. Families always have their little twists and secrets. Why, your folks were sure Roanna had killed Jessie, and they were treating her like she was poison or something, until I told them that I didn't think she'd done it."

Booley was a country-plain, unsophisticated good old boy, but he'd been in law enforcement for a long time, and he knew how to read people. In his way, he used the same tactics Columbo had made famous on television, just kind of easing around and carrying on casual conversations and putting the pieces together. Webb resisted the invitation to confide in the sheriff, instead saying, "May I go now?"

Booley waved a meaty hand. "Sure. But like I said, stick close to home." He heaved his bulk out of the chair. "I might as well drive you home myself. It's already morning, so I'm not going to get any sleep anyway."

Roanna was hiding, not the way she had when she was little by crawling under furniture or burrowing deep in a closet, but nevertheless she had removed herself from the grim, hushed activity in the house. She had retreated to the bay window where once she had watched Webb and Jessie sit in the garden swing, while behind her the rest of the family had discussed what to do with her. She was still wrapped tight in the blanket the paramedic had put around her, holding the edges together with cold, bloodless fingers. She sat watching the slowly arriving dawn, ignoring the hum of voices behind her, shutting it all out.

She tried not to think about Jessie, but no amount of effort could erase that bloody scene from her mind. She didn't have to actively *think* about it, it was just there, like the window. Death had so altered Jessie that at first Roanna had simply stood there, gaping at the body without quite realizing that it was real, or even recognizing her cousin. Her head had been oddly misshapen, flattened around a huge open wound where her skull had literally been cracked open. She had been awkwardly sprawled with her neck bent as her head rested against the raised rock hearth.

Roanna had turned on the light when she'd entered the suite, blinking her eyes as she tried to adjust her vision, and walked around the sofa on her way to the bedroom to wake Jessie and talk to her. She had literally stumbled on Jessie's sprawled legs, and stared down in silent stupefaction for a long moment before she realized what she was seeing and began to scream.

It wasn't until later that she realized she'd been standing on blood-soaked carpet and that her bare feet were stained red. She didn't remember how they had gotten clean, if she had washed them or someone else had.

The window reflected the scene behind her, the swarm of people coming and going. The rest of the family had arrived, singly and in pairs, adding their questions and tears to the confusion.

There was Aunt Sandra, Webb's aunt on his father's side, which made her Grandmother's niece. Aunt Sandra was a tall, dark-haired woman with the Tallant good looks. She had never married, instead pursuing an advanced education in physics, and now worked for NASA in Huntsville.

Aunt Gloria's daughter and her husband, Lanette and Greg Spence, had arrived with their two teenagers, Brock and Corliss. Corliss was Roanna's age, but they had never gotten along. No sooner had they arrived than Corliss had slipped up to Roanna and whispered, "Were you really standing in her blood? What did she look like? I heard Mama tell Daddy that her head was cracked open like a watermelon."

Roanna had ignored the avid, insistent voice, keeping her face turned toward the window. "Tell me!" Corliss insisted.

A vicious pinch on the back of her arm made Roanna's eyes sting with tears, but she stared straight ahead, refusing to acknowledge her cousin in any way. Eventually Corliss had given up and left to badger someone else for the gory details she craved.

Aunt Gloria's son, Baron, lived in Charlotte; he and his wife and three kids were expected to arrive later in the day. Even without them, that meant ten family members were grouped in the living room or around a comforting pot of coffee in the kitchen, with the makeup of the groups changing as people shifted back and forth.

No one was allowed to go upstairs yet, though Jessie had long since been taken away, because the investigators were still taking pictures and gathering evidence. With the deputies and all the others there in various official capacities, the big house was teeming with people, but still Roanna managed to shut them all out. She felt very cold inside, a strange chill that had spread to every cell of her body and formed a protective shell, keeping her inside and everyone else outside.

The sheriff had taken Webb away, and she had nearly choked on her guilt. This was all her fault. If only she hadn't kissed him! She hadn't done it on purpose, but then none of the messes she caused were on purpose.

He hadn't killed Jessie. She knew it. She'd wanted to scream at them for even thinking something so ugly about him. Now that was all Aunt Gloria and Uncle Harlan were talking about, how shocking it was, as if he'd already been tried and convicted. Only a few hours before, they had been equally convinced that Roanna was the killer.

Webb couldn't do something like that. He could kill; somehow Roanna knew that Webb would do whatever was necessary to protect those he loved, but killing under those circumstances wasn't the same as murder. No matter how nasty Jessie had been, no matter what she'd said or even if she'd attacked him with a poker or something, he wouldn't have harmed her. Roanna had seen him tenderly helping a foal into the world, sitting up all night with a sick animal, taking turns with Loyal walking a colicky horse for hours on end. Webb took care of his own.

It wasn't her fault Jessie was dead, but because Roanna loved Webb and hadn't been able to control her stupid impulses, it had set in motion a chain of circumstances that caused Webb to be blamed for Jessie's death. She had no idea who had killed Jessie, her thoughts hadn't gone that far; she only knew that it wasn't Webb. With every cell in her body, she knew he couldn't have done it, just as she knew this was all her fault and he'd never forgive her.

When Sheriff Watts had taken Webb away for questioning, Roanna had been paralyzed with shame. She hadn't even been able to lift her head and look at him, sure that she would see nothing but hatred and contempt in his eyes if he happened to look at her, and she knew that she couldn't have borne it.

She had never felt so alone, as if there was an invisible bubble around her, preventing anyone from getting close. She could hear Grandmother behind her, softly weeping again, and hear Aunt Gloria's murmured attempts at consolation, but it didn't quite touch her. She didn't know where Uncle Harlan was; she didn't care. She would never forget the way they had accused her of killing Jessie, the way they had pulled back from her as if she had the plague. Even when Sheriff Watts had said he didn't think she'd done it, none of them had approached or apologized. Not even Grandmother, though Roanna had heard the soft "Thank God" she'd uttered when the sheriff had said he thought she was innocent.

All her life she'd tried so hard to earn these people's love, to be good enough, but she had never succeeded. Nothing about her had ever equaled the standards of the Davenports and Tallants. She wasn't pretty, she wasn't even presentable. She was clumsy, untidy, and had the unfortunate habit of saying the most appalling things at the most inappropriate time.

Deep inside her, something had given up. These people had never loved her, never would. Only Webb had cared, and now she had messed that up, too. She was alone in a fundamental way that left a huge, aching void inside. There was something devastating in knowing that if she simply walked out of this house and never came back, no one would care. The despair that she had faced earlier, when she realized that Webb didn't love her or trust her, had settled into mute acceptance.

All right, so they didn't love her; that didn't mean she had no love to give. She loved Webb with every fiber in her body, something that wasn't going to change no matter how he felt about her. There was also love for Grandmother, despite her obvious preference for Jessie, because after all it had been Grandmother who had firmly said, "Roanna will live here, of course," easing the terror of a seven-year-old who had abruptly lost everything. Even though she had more often found disapproval than approval from Grandmother, she still felt enormous respect and affection for the indomitable old woman. She hoped that someday she could be as strong as Grandmother, rather than the bumbling, unwanted fool she was now.

Both of the people Roanna loved had lost someone dear to them. All right, so she herself had despised Jessie; Grandmother and Webb hadn't. It wasn't her fault that Jessie was dead, but if Webb were blamed for it, that definitely would be her fault because of that kiss. Who really had killed Jessie? The only person who readily sprang to mind was the man she had seen with Jess the day before, but she had no idea who he was and wasn't certain she could either describe him now or even identify him if he walked in the door. Her shock had been so great that she hadn't paid a great deal of attention to his face. If she had decided before to keep quiet about what she'd seen, her reasons now were even more crucial. If Sheriff Watts found out that Jessie had been having an affair, he would see that as a motive for Webb to kill her. No, Roanna decided dazedly, she would only hurt Webb by disclosing what Jessie had been doing.

A murderer would go free. Roanna thought about that,

but her reasoning was simple: telling the sheriff about it wouldn't guarantee that the murderer was caught, because she couldn't give him any more information than that, and Webb would be harmed. For Roanna, there was no question of justice or truth, and she was too young and unsophisticated for subtleties of philosophy. The only thing that mattered was protecting Webb. Right or wrong, she would keep her mouth shut.

She watched as a county car silently rolled up the long driveway and stopped. Webb and Sheriff Watts got out and walked toward the house. Roanna watched Webb; her gaze stuck to him like a magnet to steel. He was still dressed in the clothes he'd worn yesterday, and he looked exhausted, his hard face shadowed with both fatigue and a day's growth of beard. At least he was home, she thought, her heart leaping, and he wasn't in handcuffs. That must mean the sheriff wasn't going to arrest him.

As the two men walked up the semicircle of brick-paved sidewalk, Webb glanced up to where she sat in the big bay window, outlined by the lights behind her. Though it still wasn't full daylight, Roanna saw the way his face hardened, then he looked away from her.

She listened to the confused, awkward flurry of family members behind her when Webb entered the house. Most of them didn't speak to him, but instead made an effort to make their own conversations seem casual. Under the circumstances, the effort was ridiculous, and they merely sounded stilted. Only Yvonne and Sandra rushed to him, and were gathered into his strong arms. In her reflective window, Roanna watched him bend his dark head down to them.

He released them and turned to Sheriff Watts. "I need to shower and shave," he said.

"Upstairs is off-limits for now," the sheriff replied.

"There's a bath with a shower next to the kitchen. Would you have a deputy bring me some clean clothes?"

"Sure." The arrangements were made, and Webb left to

clean up. The voices behind her resumed a more normal rhythm. Watching them, Roanna could tell that both Aunt Yvonne and Aunt Sandra were furious with the others.

Then suddenly her view of the room was blotted out as Sheriff Watts appeared directly behind her. "Roanna, do you feel up to answering some questions?" he asked in a tone so gentle it seemed out of place, coming from such a rough, burly man.

She clutched the blanket even tighter and silently turned around.

His huge hand closed over her elbow. "Let's go where it's quieter," he said, helping her to slide from the window seat. He wasn't quite as tall as Webb but was easily twice as wide. He was built like a wrestler, with a barrel chest and thick belly, and without any jiggle to his middle.

He led her into Webb's study, seating her on the sofa rather than in one of the big leather armchairs, and eased down beside her.

"I know it's hard for you to talk about it, but I need to know what happened tonight, and this morning."

She nodded.

"Webb and Jessie were arguing," Sheriff Watts said, watching her carefully. "Do you know—"

"It was my fault," Roanna interrupted, her voice flat and hollow and strangely raspy. Her brown eyes, usually so lively and full of golden lights, were dull and haunted. "I was in the kitchen trying to eat when Webb came home from Nashville. I—I'd missed supper. I was upset . . . Anyway, I k-kissed him, and that's when Jessie came in."

"You kissed him? He didn't kiss you?"

Miserably Roanna nodded. It didn't matter that, after a few seconds, Webb had held her tight and returned her kiss. She had initiated it.

"Has Webb ever kissed you?"

"Some. Mostly he ruffles my hair."

The sheriff's lips twitched. "I mean on the mouth."

"No."

"Do you have a crush on him, Roanna?"

She went still, even the breath halting in her chest. Then she squared her thin shoulders and gave him a look of such naked despair that he swallowed. "No," she said with pitiful dignity. "I love him." She paused. "He doesn't love me, though. Not like that."

"Is that why you kissed him?"

She began to rock back and forth, the movement slight but significant as she fought to control her pain. "I know I shouldn't have done it," she whispered. "I knew it then. I never would have done anything to cause Webb so much trouble. Jessie said I'd done it on purpose, that I knew she was coming down, but I didn't. I swear I didn't. He was being so sweet to me, and all of a sudden I couldn't resist it. I just grabbed him. He never had a chance."

"What did Jessie do?"

"She just started screaming at us. She called me all sorts of ugly names, and Webb, too. She accused us of—you know. Webb tried to tell her it wasn't like that, but Jessie never listened to anybody when she was pitching one of her fits."

The sheriff put his hand over hers, patting it. "Roanna, I have to ask you this, and I want you to tell me the truth. Are you sure there's nothing between you and Webb? Have you ever had sex with him? This is a serious situation, honey, and nothing but the truth will do."

She gave him a blank look, then hot color washed into her white face. "No!" she sputtered, and turned an even darker red. "I've never—with anyone! I mean—"

He patted her hand again, mercifully interrupting her mangled reply. "There's no need to be embarrassed," he said kindly. "You're doing the smart thing, placing such a high value on yourself."

Miserably Roanna thought that she didn't have a high value on herself at all; if at any time Webb had so much as crooked his finger at her, she would have come running and let him do whatever he wanted to her. Her virginity was due to his lack of interest, not her own morals.

"What happened then?" he prompted.

95

"They went upstairs, still arguing. Or rather, Jessie was. She was screaming at him, and Webb was trying to calm her down, but she wouldn't listen."

"Did she threaten to have him cut out of Lucinda's will?"

Roanna nodded. "But Grandmother just looked surprised. I was so relieved, because I couldn't have stood it if I caused Webb to lose Davencourt."

"Did you hear anything violent happening in their room?"

"Some glass breaking, then Webb yelled at her to go ahead and get a divorce, and he left."

"Did he tell her he'd do anything to get rid of her?"

"I think so," Roanna answered readily, knowing that the others had likely confirmed this. "I don't blame him. I'd have added my allowance to her alimony, if that would have helped."

The sheriff's lips twitched again. "You didn't like Jessie?"

She shook her head. "She was always hateful to me."

"Were you jealous of her?"

Roanna's lips trembled. "She had Webb. But even if she hadn't, I know that he wouldn't be interested in m-me. He never has been. He was nice to me because he felt sorry for me. After she caused such a ruckus last night—I mean after *I* caused it—I decided I might as well go away to college the way they'd been wanting me to do. Maybe then I could make some friends."

"Did you hear anything from their room last night after Webb left?"

Roanna shuddered, an image of Jessie as she'd last seen her flashing through her brain. She gulped. "I don't know. Everybody was mad at me, even Webb. I was upset and went to my room. It's at the back of the house."

"All right now, Roanna, I want you to think carefully. When you go up the stairs, their rooms are across the front hall to the left. If there's a light on in the room, you can see it under the door. I checked that myself. When you went to your room, did you look in that direction?"

She remembered that very well. She had cast a fearful

glance at Jessie's door, afraid she would come storming out of it like the Wicked Witch in *The Wizard of Oz,* and she had tried to be very quiet so Jessie wouldn't hear her. She nodded.

"Was there a light on?"

"Yes." She was certain of it, because otherwise she would have thought Jessie had gone on into the connecting bedroom and thus wouldn't hear her.

"Okay, now tell me about later, when you found her. What time was it?"

"After two. I hadn't been asleep. I kept thinking how I'd messed everything up and caused Webb so much trouble."

"You were awake the entire time?" the sheriff asked sharply. "Did you hear anything?"

She shook her head. "I told you, my bedroom's on the back, away from everyone else. It's real quiet back there. That's why I like it."

"Could you tell when the others came up to bed?"

"I heard Aunt Gloria in the hall about nine-thirty, but my door was closed and I couldn't tell what she was saying."

"Harlan said that he started watching a movie about eight. It shouldn't have been off at nine-thirty."

"Maybe he finished watching it in their room. I know they have a television in there, because Grandmother had a connection run for them before they moved in."

He pulled out his notebook and scribbled a few words, then said, "Okay, let's go back to when you went to Jessie's room this morning. Was the light on then?"

"No. I turned it on when I went in. I thought Jessie was in bed, and I was going in there to wake her up so I could talk to her. The light was bright, and I couldn't see good for a few minutes, and I—I stumbled over h-her."

She shuddered again and started shaking. The bright color of a moment before leached out of her face, leaving it chalky again.

"Why were you going to talk to her?"

"I was going to tell her that it wasn't Webb's fault, that he didn't do anything wrong. It was just me—being stupid, as

97

usual," she said dully. "I never meant to cause him any trouble."

"Why not wait until morning?"

"Because I wanted to fix it before then."

"Then why didn't you talk to her before you went to bed?"

"I was a coward." She gave him an ashamed look. "You don't know how nasty Jessie could be."

"I don't think you're a coward at all, honey. It takes guts to say something's your fault. A lot of grown-ups never do learn how to do it."

She began rocking again, and the haunted look came back. "I didn't want anything bad to happen to Jessie, not bad like that. I'd have laughed if her hair fell out or something. But when I saw her head . . . and the blood . . . I didn't even recognize her at first. She was always so beautiful."

Her voice trailed off, and Booley sat in silence beside her, thinking hard. Roanna said she'd turned on the light. All doorknobs and light switches had already been dusted for fingerprints, so it should be her print on that particular switch, something easy enough to check. If the light had been on when she'd gone to her room, and off when she went to talk to Jessie, then that meant either Jessie had turned off the light herself after Webb had gone, or someone else had. Either way, Jessie had been alive when Webb had left the house.

That didn't mean he couldn't have returned later and gone up the outside stairs. If his alibi at the Waffle Hut checked out, though, that meant they likely didn't have enough circumstantial evidence to charge him. Hell, there was no motive anyway. He wasn't having an affair with Roanna, not that Booley had pinned much credence to that theory to begin with. It had been a shot in the dark, nothing more. The hard facts were, Webb and Jessie had argued over something Roanna said was her fault while totally absolving Webb. Jessie had threatened him with the loss of Davencourt, but no one had believed her, so that didn't count. In a temper, Webb had yelled at her to go ahead and get a divorce, and slammed out of the house. Jessie had been alive then, according to both Roanna's testimony and the coroner's estimate of time of death, based on the degree of rigor mortis and the temperature of Jessie's body. No one had seen or heard anything. Webb had been at the Waffle Hut close to the time of Jessie's death. Now, they weren't talking about any great distance here, nothing that couldn't be driven in about fifteen or twenty minutes, so it was still within the realm of possibility that he could have returned, bashed her in the head, and then calmly driven to the Waffle Hut to establish his alibi, but the odds of convincing any jury of that were pretty slim. Hell, the odds of convincing the county prosecutor to press charges on that basis were even slimmer.

Someone had killed Jessie Tallant. Not Roanna. The girl was so painfully open and vulnerable, he doubted she knew how to lie. Besides, he'd have bet money she didn't have the strength to pick up that andiron, which was one of the heaviest he'd ever seen, specially made for the oversize fireplaces here in Davencourt. Someone strong had killed Jessie, pointing to a man. The two other men at Davencourt, Harlan Ames and the stableman, Loyal Wise, had no motive.

So, the killer was either Webb—and unless Webb confessed, Booley knew there was no way of proving it—or a stranger. There was no sign of forced entry, but to his amazement he'd discovered that none of the people here locked their balcony doors, so force wouldn't have been necessary. Nor was there anything stolen, which would have given them robbery as a motive. The plain fact was, Jessie was dead for no good reason that he could tell, and it was damn hard to make a murder charge stick without giving a jury a motive it could believe.

This was one murder that wasn't going to be solved. He could feel it in his bones, and it made him sick. He didn't like for law-breaking slime to get away with so much as stealing a pack of chewing gum, much less murder. It didn't make any difference that Jessie had evidently been a bitch of the first water; she still hadn't deserved to have her head bashed in.

Well, he'd try. He'd check out all the angles, verify Webb's alibi, and present what he had to Simmons, but he knew the prosecutor was going to say they didn't have a case.

He sighed, got to his feet, and looked down at the forlorn little figure still on the sofa, and he was moved to offer her some comfort. "I don't think you give yourself enough credit, honey. You aren't stupid, and you aren't a coward. You're a sweet, smart girl, and I like you fine."

She didn't reply, and he wondered if she'd even heard him. She'd been through so much in the last twelve hours, it was a wonder she hadn't cracked under the strain. He patted her on the shoulder and quietly left the room, leaving her alone with her regrets, and her nightmare images.

CHAPTER

7

*T*he next few days were hell.

The entire Shoals area, which consisted of Tuscumbia, Muscle Shoals, Sheffield, and Florence, the four towns that butted together where Colbert and Lauderdale Counties met at the Tennessee River, were riveted by the spectacle of the bloody murder of a member of Colbert County's premier family and the ensuing investigation of her husband as the killer. Webb was as well known, if not quite as respected yet, as Marshall Davenport had been, and of course everyone who was anyone had known Jessie, the star of the local top society. Gossip ran rampant. Webb hadn't been arrested, and Sheriff Watts would say only that he had been questioned and released, but as far as everyone was concerned that was as good as saying he'd done it.

Why, look at how his only family treated him, the whispers ran. Lucinda cried every time she saw him, and she couldn't bring herself to talk to him yet. Gloria and Harlan Ames were convinced Webb had killed Jessie, and though publicly they didn't say anything, they had made a few comments to their closest friends, the "just between you and me" kind. The more moral souls were disapproving

101

when the confidential gossip was spread, but that didn't stop it from growing like kudzu.

Gloria and Harlan's two children, Baron and Lanette, kept their respective families as far away from Webb as they could.

Only Webb's mother, Yvonne, and his aunt Sandra seemed convinced of his innocence, but of course they would be. He'd always been Sandra's favorite, while she practically ignored Gloria's grandchildren. A definite rift was growing in the family. And as for Roanna, who had discovered the body, she was said to be suffering from shock and had all but sequestered herself. She had always been like a puppy dog at Webb's heels, but not even she had anything to do with him. Word was that they hadn't spoken since Jessie's death.

The insidious vines of gossip spread the rumor that Jessie had been savagely beaten before she'd been killed; someone else said she'd been mutilated. They said that Webb had been caught *in flagrante delicto* with Roanna, the little cousin, but credulity stopped short of actually believing that. Maybe he'd been caught, but with *Roanna?* Why, she was skinny as a rail, unattractive, and had no idea how to make herself appealing to a man.

Anyway, obviously Webb had been caught with *someone*, and gossip ran hot with speculation on the unknown woman's identity.

The autopsy on Jessie's body was completed, but the results weren't released pending the results of the investigation. Funeral arrangements were made, and so many people attended the service that the church couldn't hold everyone. Even people who hadn't known her personally attended out of curiosity. Webb stood alone, an island around which everyone else moved but never quite touched. The minister extended his sympathies. No one else did.

At the cemetery, it was much the same thing. Lucinda was heartbroken, weeping uncontrollably as she stared at Jessie's flower-laden casket, supported on brass rails over the raw, open mouth of the grave. It was a hot summer day, without a cloud to mar the sky, and the white-molten sun soon had everyone dripping with sweat. Handkerchiefs and miscellaneous bits of paper were used to languidly fan perspiring faces.

Webb sat on one end of the first row of folding chairs that had been placed under the canopy for the immediate family. Yvonne sat beside him, firmly holding his hand, and Sandra sat beside her. The rest of the family had taken the other chairs, though no one seemed eager to be the one sitting directly behind Webb. Finally Roanna slipped into that chair, a frail wraith who had grown even thinner in the days since Jessie's murder. For once, she didn't stumble or drop anything. Her face was white and remote. Her dark chestnut hair, usually so untidy, was pulled sternly back from her face and tied with a black bow. She had always jittered around, as if she had too much energy to control, but now she was oddly still. Several people gave her curious glances, as if not quite certain of her identity. Her too-big features, so unsuited for the thinness of her face, somehow looked better suited to the remote severity that now swathed her. She still wasn't pretty, but there was something . . .

The prayers were said, and the mourners tactfully steered away from the gravesite so the casket could be lowered and the grave filled. No one actually left the cemetery, except for a few who had other things to do and couldn't wait around any longer for something to happen. The rest milled around, pressing Lucinda's hand, kissing her cheek. No one approached Webb. He stood alone, just as he had at the funeral home and then the church, his expression hard and closed.

Roanna stood it as long as she could. She had avoided him, knowing how he must hate her, but the way people were treating him made her bleed inside. She moved to his side and slipped her hand into his, her cold, frail fingers clinging to the hard, warm strength of his. He glanced down at her, his green eyes as welcoming as ice.

"I'm sorry," she whispered, her words audible only to

103

him. She was acutely aware of all the avid eyes trained on them, speculating on her gesture. "It's all my fault people are treating you like this." Tears swam in her eyes, blurring his outline as she looked up at him. "I just wanted you to know that I didn't . . . I didn't do it on purpose. I didn't know Jessie was coming downstairs. I hadn't talked to her since lunch that day."

Something flickered in his eyes, and he drew in a long, controlled breath. "It doesn't matter," he said, and gently but firmly removed his hand from her grip.

The rejection was like a blow to the face. Roanna swayed under the impact, her expression stark with despair. Webb muttered a curse under his breath and reluctantly lifted his hand to steady her, but Roanna stepped back. "I understand," she said, still in a whisper. "I won't bother you anymore." Then she slipped away, as insubstantial as a black-clad ghost.

Somehow she kept her control. It was easier now, as if the layer of ice that encased her kept everything from spilling out. Webb's rejection had almost cracked the ice, but after the initial blow, the layer had thickened in self-defense, becoming even stronger. The hot sun beat down on her, but Roanna wondered if she would ever be warm again.

She had scarcely slept since the night she'd found Jessie's body. Every time she closed her eyes, the bloody image seemed to be painted on the inside of her eyelids, where she couldn't escape it. Guilt and misery kept her from eating more than a few bites, and she had lost even more weight. The family was being kinder to her, perhaps because of their own guilt about the way they had treated her immediately after she'd found Jessie's body, when they had thought Roanna had killed her cousin, but it didn't matter. It was too little, too late. Roanna felt so distant from them, from everything, that sometimes it was as if she wasn't even there.

After the grave had been filled and the multitude of flowers positioned to cover the raw earth, all of the family and a good many others drove back to Davencourt. The upstairs had been off-limits for two days, then Sheriff Watts had simply sealed off the murder scene and let the remainder of the floor be used, though everyone had felt strange at first. Only Cousin Baron and his family were staying at the house, though, since all of the other relatives lived close by. Webb hadn't slept at Davencourt since Jessie's murder. He spent his days there, but at night he went to a motel. Aunt Gloria had said that she was relieved, because she wouldn't have felt safe with him in the house at night, and Roanna had wanted to slap her. Only a desire not to cause Grandmother more stress had restrained her.

Tansy had prepared huge amounts of food to feed the expected crowd and had been glad of the opportunity to keep herself busy. People wandered in and out of the dining room where the buffet had been arranged, filling plates and returning to gather in small groups where they discussed the situation in hushed voices.

Webb shut himself in the study. Roanna walked down to the stables and stood at the fence, finding comfort in watching the horses graze. Buckley saw her and trotted over, thrusting his head over the fence to be patted. Roanna hadn't been riding since Jessie's death; in fact, this was her first visit to the stables. She scratched behind Buckley's ears and crooned soothingly to him, but her mind wasn't on what she was saying, it was just automatic noise. He didn't seem to mind, though; his eyes half closed in delight, and he made a grunting noise.

"He's missed you," Loyal said, coming up behind her. He had changed out of the suit he'd worn to the funeral and was now clad in his more familiar khakis and boots.

"I've missed him, too."

Loyal propped his arms on the top railing and surveyed his kingdom, his gaze warming as he watched the sleek, healthy animals he loved. "You don't look too good," he said bluntly. "You need to take better care of yourself. The horses need you."

"It's been a bad time," she replied, her voice lifeless.

"Sure has," he agreed. "It still don't seem real. And it's a shame how folks are treating Mr. Webb. Why, he no more killed Miss Jessie than I did. Anybody who knows anything about him would know that." Loyal had been extensively questioned about the night of the murder. He'd heard Webb leave and agreed with everyone else that the time was between eight and eight-thirty, but hadn't heard any cars after that until the sheriff had been called and the county vehicles arrived on the scene. He'd been awakened from a sound sleep by Roanna's scream, a sound that could still make him wince when he remembered it.

"People only see what they want to see," Roanna said. "Uncle Harlan just likes the sound of his own voice, and Aunt Gloria's a fool."

"What do you reckon will happen now? With them living here, I mean."

"I don't know."

"How's Miss Lucinda holding up?"

Roanna shook her head. "Dr. Graves is keeping her on mild sedatives. She loved Jessie a lot. She still cries all the time." Lucinda had been frighteningly diminished by Jessie's death, as if this had been one blow too many for even her nature. She had pinned all her hopes for the future on Webb and Jessie, and now it looked as if her plans had been destroyed, with Jessie dead and Webb suspected of her murder. Roanna had kept waiting for Grandmother to go to Webb and put her arms around him, tell him that she believed in him. But for whatever reason, whether Grandmother was too paralyzed with grief or maybe because she *did* think Webb could have killed Jessie, it hadn't happened. Couldn't Grandmother see how much Webb needed her? Or was she in so much pain that she couldn't see his?

Roanna felt nothing but dread for the coming days.

"We got the results of the autopsy back," Booley said to Webb the day after the funeral. They were in Booley's office again. Webb felt as if he'd spent more time there since Jessie's death than he had anywhere else.

The initial shock had passed, but the grief and anger were

106

still bottled up inside him, all the more potent for having to be kept under restraint. He didn't dare let his control slip, or his rage would explode over everyone: his so-called friends, who had stayed as far away from him as if he'd been a leper; his business associates, some of whom had seemed secretly pleased at his trouble, the bastards; and most of all his loving family, who all apparently thought him a murderer. Only Roanna had approached him and said she was sorry. Because she'd accidentally killed Jessie herself, and was afraid to say so? He couldn't know for certain, no matter what he suspected. What he did know was that she too had avoided him, Roanna who had always done her best to stay right at his heels, and that she was definitely feeling guilty about something.

He couldn't help worrying about her. He could tell that she wasn't eating, and she was alarmingly pale. She had changed in other, more subtle ways, too, ways he couldn't analyze because he was still so angry he couldn't focus on those tiny differences.

"Did you know Jessie was pregnant?" Booley asked.

If he hadn't already been sitting, Webb's legs would have folded beneath him. He stared at Booley in silent shock.

"I guess not," Booley said. Damn, this case had as many hidden little twists as a maze. Webb was still the best bet for Jessie's killer, which wasn't saying much, but the evidence wasn't there. There wasn't much evidence, period; no witnesses and no known motive. He couldn't convict a gnat on the evidence he had. Webb's alibi had checked out, Roanna's testimony had established that Jessie had been alive when Webb had stormed out, so they had nothing but a corpse. A pregnant corpse, as it turned out.

"She was about seven weeks along, according to the report. Had she been puking or anything?"

Webb shook his head. His lips felt numb. Seven weeks. The baby wasn't his. Jessie had been cheating on him. He swallowed the lump in his throat, trying to consider what this meant. He'd had no indication she'd been unfaithful, and there hadn't been any gossip either; in a small town, there would have been gossip, and Booley's investigation would have turned up something. If he told Booley that the baby wasn't his, that would be considered a believable motive for killing her. But what if her lover had killed her? Without even a guess as to who the man might be, there was no way of finding out, even assuming Booley would listen to him.

He had kept quiet when he thought Roanna might have killed Jessie, and now he found himself forced into the same position again. For whatever reason, because he couldn't bring himself to destroy Ro or because disclosing that Jessie's baby wasn't his and bringing even more suspicion down on his own head, his wife's murderer was going to go unpunished. The impotent rage welled up again, eating him alive like acid; rage at Jessie, at Roanna, at everyone, and most of all at himself.

"If she knew," he finally said, his voice hoarse, "she hadn't told me."

"Well, some women know right off, and some don't. My wife didn't miss a period for four months with our first; we had no idea why she was throwing up all the time. Don't know why they call it morning sickness, because Bethalyn puked all hours of the day and night. We never knew what would set it off. But now, with the others, she knew pretty soon. Guess she learned how to spot it. Anyway, I'm sorry about this, Webb. About the baby and all. And, uh, we'll keep the case open, but frankly we don't have jack shit to go on."

Webb sat for a moment, staring at the whiteness of his knuckles as he gripped the arms of the chair. "Does this mean you're not investigating me anymore?"

"I guess it does."

"I can leave town?"

"Can't stop you."

Webb stood up. He was still pale. He stopped at the door and looked back at Booley. "I didn't kill her," he said.

Booley sighed. "It was a possibility. I had to check it out."

"I know."

"I wish I could find the killer for you, but it don't look good."

"I know," Webb said again and quietly closed the door behind him.

Sometime during the short drive to the motel, he made his decision.

He packed his clothes, checked out of the motel, and drove back to Davencourt. His gaze was bitter as he surveyed the grand old house, crowning a slight rise with its graceful and gracious wings spread wide, like welcoming arms. He had loved it here, a prince in his own kingdom, knowing that one day it would all be his. He had been willing to work himself into the ground for the sake of his kingdom. He had married the chosen princess. Hell, he had been more than willing to marry her. Jessie had been his since that long ago day when they had sat in the swing beneath the huge old oak and fought their first battle for dominance.

Had he married her out of pure ego, determined to show her that she couldn't play her little games with him? If he were honest, then yes, that had been part of the reason. But the other part had been love, a strange love compounded of a shared childhood, a shared role in life, and the sexual fascination that had existed between them since puberty. Not a great foundation for marriage, he knew now. The sex had burned itself out pretty damn fast, and their old bonds hadn't been strong enough to hold them together after the attraction was gone.

Jessie had been sleeping with another man. *Men,* for all he knew. Knowing Jessie as he did, he realized she had probably done it out of revenge, because he hadn't kow-towed to her every whim. She'd been capable of just about anything when thwarted, but somehow he'd never expected her to cheat on him. Her reputation in Tuscumbia and Colbert County had been too important to her, and this wasn't some fast-lane big city where lovers came and went and no one paid much attention to it. This was the South, and in some ways still the Old South, where appearances and genteel manners held sway, at least in the middle and upper echelons of society.

But she'd not only slept with someone else, she had neglected to use birth control. Again, out of revenge? Had she thought it would be a delicious joke on him to present him with a child not his own?

In one short, hellish week, his wife had been murdered, his entire life and reputation had been destroyed, and his family had turned on him. He had gone from prince to pariah.

He was fed up with it all. Booley's bombshell today had just topped it off. He had worked like hell for years to keep the family in the manner to which they'd become accustomed, meaning the lap of luxury, sacrificing his private life and any chance he might have had of making a real marriage with Jessie. But when he'd needed his family in a united front, supporting him, they hadn't been there. Lucinda hadn't accused him but neither had she backed him, and he was tired of dancing to her tune. As for Gloria and Harlan and their bunch, to hell with them. Only Mother and Aunt Sandra had believed in him.

Roanna. What about her? Had she set this entire nightmare in motion, striking out at Jessie without any regard to the damage she would do to him? Somehow, on a different level, Roanna's betrayal was more bitter than the others. He'd gotten so accustomed to her adoration, to the comfortable companionship he'd had with her. Her quirky personality and unruly tongue had amused him, made him laugh even when he was so dead tired he was about to fall on his face. *Grand Pricks,* indeed, the little imp.

At the funeral, she'd said that she hadn't deliberately set up that scene in the kitchen, but guilt and misery had been written all over that thin face. Maybe she had, maybe she hadn't. But she too had avoided him, when he'd have sold his soul for comfort. Booley didn't consider Roanna a suspect in Jessie's murder, but Webb couldn't forget the look of hate he'd seen in Roanna's eyes, or the fact that she'd had the chance. Everyone in the house had had the chance to do it, but Roanna was the only one who'd hated Jessie.

He just didn't know. He'd kept his mouth shut to protect her even though she hadn't supported him. He'd kept his mouth shut about Jessie's baby not being his, letting another possible murderer off scot-free, because he himself would have been the more likely suspect. He was goddamn tired of being caught in the middle.

To hell with them all.

He stopped the car in the driveway and stared at the house. Davencourt. It was the embodiment of his ambition, a symbol of his life, the heart of the Davenport family. It had a personality all its own, an old house that had sheltered generations of Davenports within its graceful wings. Whenever he was away on a business trip and thought of Davencourt, in his mind's eye he always saw it surrounded by flowers. In spring, the azalea bushes rioted with color. In summer, the roses and old maids took their bow. In fall there were the chrysanthemums, and in winter the pink and white camellia bushes. Davencourt was always in bloom. He'd loved it with a passion he'd never felt for Jessie. He couldn't put the blame for this totally on the others, because he too was guilty, in the final analysis marrying for the legacy rather than the woman.

To hell with Davencourt, too.

He parked at the walk and went in the front door. The conversation in the living room stilled abruptly, as it had been doing for the past week. He didn't even glance into the room as he strode into the study and seated himself behind the desk.

He worked for hours, completing paperwork, drawing up forms, returning active control of all the far-flung Davenport enterprises into Lucinda's hands. When it was finished, he got up and walked out of the house, and drove away without looking back.

BOOK THREE

The Return

CHAPTER

8

Bring Webb back for me," Lucinda said to Roanna. "I want you to convince him to come home."

Roanna's face didn't show her shock, though it reverberated through her entire body. With controlled grace she replaced her tea glass on the dainty coaster without even the tiniest betraying rattle. Webb! Just the sound of his name still had the power to slice through her, bringing up the old painful longing and guilt, even though it had been ten years since she'd last seen him, since anyone had seen him.

"Do you know where he is?" she asked composedly.

Unlike Roanna's, Lucinda's hand did shake as she set down her glass. Her eighty-three years sat heavily on Lucinda, and the constant tremor in her hands was just another of the tiny ways her own body was failing her. Lucinda was dying, in fact. She knew it, they all knew it. Not immediately, not even soon, but it was summer now and it wasn't likely she'd see another one. Her iron will had stood up to a lot, but had slowly bowed under the inexorable crush of time.

"Of course. I hired a private investigator to find him. Yvonne and Sandra have known all along, but they wouldn't tell me," Lucinda said with a mixture of anger and

115

exasperation. "He's kept in touch with them, and both of them have visited him occasionally."

Roanna veiled her eyes with her lashes, careful not to let any expression show through. So they had known all this time. Unlike Lucinda, she didn't blame them. Webb had made it perfectly plain he had no use for the rest of the family; he had to despise them, and herself most of all. She didn't blame him, considering. Still, it hurt. Her love for him was the one emotion she hadn't been able to block. His absence had been like a slow-bleeding wound, and in ten years it hadn't healed but still seeped pain and remorse.

But she had survived. Somehow, by locking away all other emotions, she had survived. Gone was the coltish, exuberant girl, brimming over with energy and mischief, that she'd been. In her place was a cool, remote young woman who never hurried, never lost her temper, and seldom even smiled, much less laughed aloud. Emotions were paid for with pain; she had learned a bitter lesson when her impulsiveness, her stupid emotionalism, had ruined Webb's life.

She had been worthless and unlovable the way she'd been, so she had destroyed herself and built a new person from the ashes, a woman who would never know the heights but would no longer sink to the depths either. Somehow she had set in motion the chain of events that had cost Jessie her life and banished Webb from theirs, so she had grimly set herself to the task of atonement. She couldn't replace Jessie in Lucinda's affection, but at least she could stop being such a burden and disappointment.

She had gone to college—at the University of Alabama, as it happened, rather than the exclusive all-girl's college that had previously been considered—and gotten a degree in business management so she could be of some help to Lucinda in running things, since Webb was no longer there to take care of everything. Roanna didn't like anything about her courses but forced herself to study hard and get good grades. So what if she found it boring? It was a small enough price to pay.

She had forced herself to learn how to dress, so Lucinda

wouldn't be embarrassed by her. She had taken a course to improve her poor driving skills, she had learned how to dance, how to apply makeup, to make polite conversation, to be socially acceptable. She had learned how to control the wild exuberance that had so often gotten her into trouble as a child, but that hadn't been difficult. After Webb had disappeared, her problem had been in working up any enthusiasm for life rather than the opposite.

She could think of nothing she dreaded more than having to face Webb again.

"What if he doesn't want to come back?" she murmured.

"Convince him," Lucinda snapped. Then she sighed, and her voice gentled. "He always had a soft spot for you. I need him back here. *We* need him. You and I together have managed to keep things going, but I don't have much time left and your heart and soul isn't in it the way Webb's was. When it came to business, Webb had the brain of a computer and the heart of a shark. He was honorable but ruthless. Those are rare qualities, Roanna, the kind that aren't easily replaced."

"That's why he may not forgive us." Roanna didn't react to Lucinda's dismissal of her competence in managing the family empire. It was nothing less than the truth; that was why the burden of decision-making rested, for the most part, on Lucinda's increasingly frail shoulders, while Roanna implemented them. She had trained herself, disciplined herself, to do what she could, but her best would never be good enough. She accepted that and protected herself by not letting it matter. Nothing had really mattered anyway for the past ten years.

Pain flickered across Lucinda's lined face. "I've missed him every day that he's been gone," she said softly. "I'll never forgive myself for what I let happen to him. I should have let folks know that I believed in him, trusted him, but instead I wallowed in my own grief and didn't see what my neglect was doing to him. I don't mind dying, but I can't go easy until I make things right with Webb. If anyone can bring him back, Roanna, you can."

Roanna didn't tell Lucinda that she had reached out to Webb at Jessie's funeral, and been coldly rebuffed. Privately she thought that she had less chance of convincing Webb to come home than anyone else did, but that was something else she'd taught herself: if she couldn't manage to block out her feelings, then her private pain and fears were just that, private. If she kept them inside, then no one but she knew they were there.

It didn't matter what she felt; if Lucinda wanted Webb home, she would do what she could, no matter the cost to herself. "Where is he?"

"In some godforsaken little town in Arizona. I'll give you the folder of information the investigator gathered for me. He's . . . done well for himself. He owns a ranch, nothing on the scale of Davencourt, but it isn't in Webb to fail."

"When do you want me to leave?"

"As soon as possible. We need him here. *I* need him. I want to make my peace with him before I die."

"I'll try," Roanna said.

Lucinda looked at her granddaughter for a long moment, then a tired smile quirked her mouth. "You're the only one who doesn't put on that fake cheerfulness and tell me I'll live to be a hundred," she said, a hint of acerbic approval in her voice. "Damn fools. Do they think I don't know that I'm dying? I have cancer, and I'm too old to waste my time and money on treatment when old age is going to get me pretty soon anyway. I live in this body, for God's sake. I can tell that it's slowly shutting down."

There was no response that wouldn't sound either falsely cheerful or callous, so Roanna made none. She was often silent, letting conversation flow around her, not thrusting out any verbal oars to deflect the tide her way. It was true that everyone else in the household tried their best to ignore the situation, as if it would go away if they didn't acknowledge it. It wasn't just Gloria and Harlan now; somehow, within a year of Jessie's death and Webb's departure, Gloria had managed to move more of her family into Davencourt. Their son, Baron, had decided to remain in Charlotte, but everyone else was there. Gloria's daughter, Lanette, had moved in her entire family: husband Greg and children Corliss and Brock. Not that they were children; Brock was thirty, and Corliss was Roanna's age. Lucinda had let the house fill, perhaps in an effort to banish the emptiness left by losing both Jessie and Webb. Assuming Roanna could convince Webb to return—a major assumption—she wondered what he would make of all this. True, they were all his cousins, but somehow she thought he might be rather impatient with them for taking advantage of Lucinda's grief.

"You know that I changed my will after Webb left," Lucinda continued after a moment, taking another sip of tea. She gazed out the window at the profusion of peach-colored roses, her favorite, and squared her shoulders as if bracing herself. "I made you the main heir; Davencourt and most of the money would go to you. I think it's only fair to tell you that if you can convince Webb to come back, I'll redo it in his favor."

Roanna nodded. That wouldn't make any difference to her efforts; nothing would. She would do her best to talk Webb into coming back but not let herself feel any personal loss when Lucinda changed her will. Roanna accepted that no matter how hard she tried, she simply didn't have the knack for business that Lucinda and Webb possessed. She wasn't a risk taker, and she couldn't muster any enthusiasm for the game of big business. Davencourt would be better off with him in charge and so would the myriad financial investments and interests.

"That was the deal I made with him when he was fourteen," Lucinda continued, her voice abrupt and her shoulders still held stiffly erect. "If he would work hard, study, and train himself to take care of Davencourt, it would all be his."

"I understand," Roanna murmured.

"Davencourt . . ." Lucinda stared out over the perfectly manicured lawn, the flower gardens, the pastures beyond where her beloved horses bent their sleek, muscular necks to graze. "Davencourt deserves to be in the best hands. It isn't just a house, it's a legacy. There aren't many like it left, and I have to choose who I think will be the best caretaker for it."

"I'll try to bring him back," Roanna promised, her face as still as a pond on a hot summer day, when no breeze existed to ripple the surface. It was the face she lived behind, a face of indifference, unreadable and serene. Nothing could pierce the safe cocoon she had woven for herself, except Webb, her only weakness. Despite herself, her thoughts drifted. To have him back . . . it would be heaven and hell combined. To be able to see him every day, listen to his voice, secretly hug his nearness to her in the long, dark nights when all her nightmares became real . . . that was the heaven. The hell was in knowing that he despised her now, that every look he gave her would be one of condemnation and disgust.

But, no, she had to be realistic. She wouldn't be here. When Lucinda—she never thought of her as Grandmother anymore—died, Davencourt would no longer be her home. It would be Webb's, and he wouldn't want her here. She wouldn't see him every day, perhaps not at all. She would have to move out, get a job, face the real world. Well, at least with her degree and experience, she should be able to get a decent job. Maybe not in the Shoals area; she might have to move, in which case it was certain she'd never see Webb. That, too, didn't matter. His place was here. Her thoughtless actions had cost him his inheritance, so it was only right that she do what she could to return it to him.

"Doesn't it matter to you?" Lucinda asked abruptly. "That you'll lose Davencourt if you do this for me?"

Nothing matters. That had been her mantra, her curse, for ten years. "It's yours to leave to whomever you want. Webb was your chosen heir. And you're right; he'll do a much better job than I ever could."

She could tell that her quiet, even voice disturbed Lucinda in some way, but injecting any passion in her words was beyond her.

120

"But you're a Davenport," Lucinda argued, as if she wanted Roanna to justify her own decision for her. "Some folks would say Davencourt should be yours by right, because Webb is a Tallant. He's my blood relative, but he isn't a Davenport, and he isn't nearly as closely related to me as you are."

"But he's the better choice."

Gloria came into the living room in time to hear Roanna's last comment. "Who's the better choice?" she demanded, sinking into the depths of her favorite chair. Gloria was seventy-three, ten years younger than Lucinda, but while Lucinda's hair was unabashedly white, Gloria still stubbornly resisted nature and kept her fluffy curls tinted a delicate blond.

"Webb," Lucinda answered tersely.

"Webb!" Shocked, Gloria stared at her sister. "For goodness sake, what could *he* possibly be the better choice for, except the electric chair?"

"To run Davencourt, and the business side of things."

"You have to be joking! Why, no one would deal with him—"

"Yes, they would," Lucinda said, steel in her voice. "If he's in charge, *everyone* will deal with him, or wish they hadn't been so stupid."

"I don't see why you even brought up his name anyway, since no one knows where he—"

"I found him," Lucinda interrupted. "And Roanna is going to talk him into coming back."

Gloria rounded on Roanna as if she had suddenly sprouted two heads. "Are you out of your mind?" she breathed. "You can't mean to bring a murderer among us! Why, I'd never be able to close my eyes at night!"

"Webb isn't a murderer," Roanna said, sipping her tea and not even glancing at Gloria. She had stopped thinking of Gloria as *Aunt*, too. Sometime during the awful night after Webb had walked out of their lives, the titles of kinship had faded from the way she thought of people, as if her emotional distance couldn't accommodate them anymore.

The people in her family now were simply Lucinda, Gloria, Harlan.

"Then why did he disappear like that? Only someone with a guilty conscience would run away."

"Stop that!" Lucinda snapped. "He didn't run, he got fed up and left. There's a difference. We let him down, so I can't blame him for turning his back on us. But Roanna's right; Webb didn't kill Jessie. I never thought he did."

"Well, Booley Watts certainly did!"

Lucinda dismissed Booley's thoughts with a wave of her hand. "It doesn't matter. *I* think Webb's innocent, there was no evidence against him, so as far as the law's concerned he's innocent, and I want him back."

"Lucinda, don't be an old fool!"

Lucinda's eyes glittered with a sudden ferocity that belied her age. "I think it's safe to say," she drawled, "that no one has ever considered me a fool, old or otherwise." *And lived to tell it,* was the unspoken message in her tone. Eighty-three or not, dying or not, Lucinda still knew the full range of her power as matriarch of the Davenport fortune, and she wasn't shy about letting other folks know it, too.

Gloria backed down and turned on Roanna, the easier target. "You can't mean to do it. Tell her it's crazy."

"I agree with her."

Fury sparked in Gloria's eyes at the murmured statement. "You *would!*" she snapped. "Don't think I've forgotten that you were crawling into bed with him when—"

"Stop it!" Lucinda said fiercely, half rising from her chair as if she would physically attack her sister. "Booley explained what really happened between them, and I won't let it be blown out of proportion. I won't let you badger Roanna either. She's only doing what I asked her to do."

"But why would you even *think* of bringing him back?" Gloria moaned, dropping her aggressiveness, and Lucinda sank back into her chair.

"Because we need him. It takes both Roanna and me to handle things now, and when I die, she'll be buried in work."

"Oh, pish tosh, Lucinda, you're going to outlive—"

"No," Lucinda said briskly, cutting through the statement she'd heard so many times before. "I am *not* going to outlive all of you. I don't want to even if I could. We need Webb. Roanna's going to get him and bring him home, and that's that."

The next night, Roanna sat in the shadows of a small, dingy cantina, her back to the wall as she silently watched a man lounging on one of the stools around the bar. She had been watching him for so long and so hard that her eyes ached from the strain of peering through the dim, smoky interior. For the most part anything she might have heard him say was drowned out by the ancient jukebox in the corner, the clatter of billiard balls striking together, the hum of curses and conversation, but every so often she could discern a certain tone, a drawl, that she knew beyond doubt was his as he made some casual comment to either the man beside him or to the bartender.

Webb. It had been ten years since she'd seen him, ten years since she had felt alive. She had known, accepted, that she still loved him, was still vulnerable to him, but somehow the dreary procession of ten years' worth of days had dulled her memory of how sharp her response to him had always been. All it had taken was that first glimpse of him to remind her. The flood of sensation was so intense that it bordered on pain, as if the cells of her body had been jolted back to life. Nothing had changed. She still reacted just the way she had before, her heart beating faster and excitement zinging through every nerve ending. Her skin felt tight and hot, the flesh beneath it pulsing, aching. The hunger to touch him, to be close enough that she could smell the unique, never-forgotten male muskiness of his scent, was so strong that she was almost paralyzed with need.

But for all her longing, she couldn't work up the courage to walk to his side and get his attention. Despite Lucinda's determined confidence that she could convince him to come home, Roanna didn't expect to see anything in that green gaze except dislike—and dismissal. The anticipation of pain kept her in her chair. She had lived with the pain of his loss every day for the past ten years, but that ache was familiar, and she *had* learned to live with it. She wasn't certain she had the endurance to bear up under any new pain, however. A new blow would crush her, perhaps beyond recovery.

She wasn't the only woman in the bar, but there were enough curious male glances her way to make her nervous. Webb's wasn't one of them; he was oblivious to her presence. It was only because she deliberately didn't attract attention that she had so far been left alone. She had dressed plainly, conservatively, in dark green slacks and a cream camp shirt, hardly the costume of a woman out on the town and looking for trouble. She didn't look anyone in the eye and didn't gaze around with interest. Over the years she had developed the knack of being as unobtrusive as possible, and it had stood her in good stead tonight. Sooner or later, though, some cowboy was going to work up enough nerve to ignore her "stay away" signals and approach her.

She was tired. It was ten o'clock at night, and her plane had left Huntsville at six o'clock that morning. From Huntsville she had flown to Birmingham, then from Birmingham to Dallas—with a stop at Jackson, Mississippi. In Dallas, she had endured a four-hour layover. She had arrived in Tucson at four twenty-seven, mountain time, rented a car, and driven south on Interstate 19 to Tumacacori, where Lucinda's private detective said Webb now lived. According to the information in the file, he owned a small but prosperous cattle ranch in the area.

She hadn't been able to find him. Directions notwithstanding, she had wandered around looking for the correct road, returning time and again to the interstate to get her bearings. She had almost been in tears when she had finally run across a local who not only knew Webb personally, but had directed Roanna to this seedy little bar just outside Nogales, where Webb was in the habit of stopping whenever he had to go to town, which he'd done this particular day.

The desert night had fallen with color and drama on the drive to Nogales, and when the kaleidoscope of hues had faded, it had left behind a black velvet sky full of the biggest, brightest stars she'd ever seen. The starkly beautiful desolation had calmed her, so that by the time she managed to find the bar, her usual remote expression was firmly in place.

Webb had been there when she'd walked in; he was the first person she'd seen. The shock had almost felled her. His head was turned away from her and he hadn't so much as glanced around, but she knew it was him, because every cell in her body screamed in recognition. She had gone quietly to one of the few empty tables, automatically choosing the one in the darkest corner, and here she still sat. The waitress, a tired-looking Hispanic woman in her late thirties, came by every so often. Roanna had ordered a beer the first time, nursed it until it was warm, then ordered another. She didn't like beer, didn't normally drink at all, but thought she should probably order or she'd be asked to leave the table to make room for customers who did.

She looked down at the scarred surface of the table, where numerous knife blades had carved a multitude of initials and designs as well as random scratches and gouges. Waiting wasn't going to make it any easier. She should just get up and walk over to him and get it over with.

But still she didn't move. Hungrily her gaze moved back to him, drinking in the changes ten years had made.

He'd been twenty-four when he'd left Tuscumbia, a young man, mature for his age and burdened with responsibilities that would have felled a lesser person, but still *young*. At twenty-four he hadn't yet learned the full range of his own strengths, his personality had still been a bit malleable. Jessie's death and the ensuing investigation, and the way he'd been ostracized by both family and friends, had hardened him. The ten years since had hardened him even more. It was evident in the grim line of his mouth and the cool, level way he surveyed the world around him, marking him as a man who was prepared to take on the world and bend it to his will. Whatever challenges he had faced, he had been the victor.

Roanna knew some of those challenges, because the file on him was thorough. When rustlers had been decimating his herd of cattle and the local law enforcement hadn't been able to stop it, Webb had single-handedly tracked the four rustlers and followed them into Mexico. The rustlers had spotted him and started shooting. Webb had shot back. They had kept each other pinned down for two days. At the end of those two days, one rustler had been dead, one severely injured, and another suffered a concussion after falling off a rock. Webb had been slightly wounded, a crease that burned along his thigh, and suffered from dehydration. But the rustlers had decided to cut their losses and get away the best they could, and Webb had grimly herded his stolen cattle back across the border. He hadn't been bothered by rustlers since.

There was an air of danger about him now that hadn't been there before, the look of a man who meant what he said and was willing to back it up with action. His character had been honed down to its steel core. Webb had no weaknesses now, certainly not any leftover ones for the silly, careless cousin who had caused him so much trouble.

He wasn't the man she had known before. He was harder, rougher, perhaps even brutal. She realized that ten years had wrought a lot of changes, in both of them, but one thing had remained constant, and that was her love for him.

Physically, he looked tougher and bigger than he had before. He'd always had the muscular build of a natural athlete, but years of grueling physical work had toughened him to whipcord leanness, coiled steel waiting to spring. His shoulders had broadened and his chest deepened. His forearms, exposed by his turned-back cuffs, were thick with muscle and roped with veins.

He was darkly tanned, with lines bracketing his mouth and radiating out from the corners of his eyes. His hair was longer, shaggier, the hair of a man who didn't get into town for a haircut on a regular basis. That was another difference:

it was no longer "styled," it was simply cut. His face was darkened by a shadow of beard, but it couldn't hide a newly healed cut that ran along the underside of his right jaw, from ear to chin. Roanna swallowed hard, wondering what had happened to him, if the injury had been dangerous.

The investigator's file said that Webb had not only bought the small ranch and quickly turned it into a profit-making enterprise, but that he had been systematically buying other parcels of land, not, as it turned out, to expand his ranch, but for mining. Arizona was rich in minerals, and Webb was investing in those minerals. Leaving Davencourt hadn't impoverished him; he'd had some money of his own, and he'd used it wisely. As Lucinda had pointed out, Webb had a rare talent for business and finance, and he'd been using it.

As prosperous as he was, though, you couldn't tell it from his clothes. His boots were worn and scuffed, his jeans faded, and his thin chambray shirt had been washed so many times it was almost white. He was wearing a hat, a dark brown, dusty one. Nogales had a reputation for toughness, but all in all, he fit right in with the rough crowd here in this dingy bar in the small desert border town that was as different from Tuscumbia as the Amazon was from the Arctic.

He had the power to destroy her. With a few cold, cutting words he could annihilate her. She felt sick at the risk she would be taking in approaching him, but she kept seeing the hope that had been in Lucinda's eyes when she'd kissed Roanna good-bye that morning. Lucinda, shrunken with age, diminished by grief and regrets, indomitable but no longer invincible. The end, perhaps, was closer than she wanted them to know. This might be her last chance to heal the rift with Webb.

Roanna knew exactly what she was risking, financially, if she could talk Webb into coming home. As Lucinda's will stood now, she was the major heir of Davencourt and the family financial empire, with some modest bequests going to Gloria and her offspring, some to Yvonne and Sandra, and pensions as well as lump sum amounts settled on the long-time domestic staff: Loyal, Tansy, and Bessie. But Webb had been groomed to be the heir, and if he returned, it would be his again.

She would lose Davencourt. She had blocked her emotions, hadn't let Lucinda see the pain and panic that had threatened to break through her protective barrier. She was human; she would regret losing the money. But Davencourt was worth more to her than any fortune. Davencourt was home, sanctuary, dearly beloved, and every inch familiar. It would tear her heart out to lose Davencourt, but she had no illusion that she would be welcome there if Webb inherited. He would want all of them out, including her.

But he could better care for it than she could. He had been raised with the understanding that, through his alliance with Jessie, Davencourt would be his. He had spent his youth and his young manhood training himself to be the best custodian possible for it, and it was Roanna's fault that he'd lost it.

What price atonement?

She knew the price, knew exactly what it would cost her.

But there was Lucinda, desperately wanting to see him before she died. And there was Webb himself, the exiled prince. Davencourt was his rightful place, his legacy. She owed him a debt she could never repay. She would give up Davencourt to get him to return. She would give up anything she had.

Somehow, her body moving without conscious will, she found herself on her feet and walking through the swirling smoke. She stopped behind him and to the right, her gaze fevered and hungry as she stared at the hard line of his cheekbone, his jaw. Hesitantly, both yearning for the contact but dreading it, she lifted her hand to touch his shoulder and draw his attention. Before she could, however, he sensed her presence and turned his head toward her.

Green eyes, narrowed and cool, looking her up and down. One dark eyebrow lifted in silent question. It was the look of a man on the prowl assessing a woman for availability, and desirability.

He didn't recognize her.

Her breath was rapid and shallow, but she felt as if she wasn't drawing in enough air. She dropped her hand, and ached because the brief contact she had so dreaded had been denied her. She wanted to touch him. She wanted to go into his arms the way she had when she was little, lay her head on his broad shoulder, and find refuge from the world. Instead she reached for her hard-won composure and said quietly, "Hello, Webb. May I talk to you?"

His eyes widened a little, and he swiveled on the bar stool so that he faced her. There was a brief flare of recognition, then incredulity, in his expression. Then it was gone, and his gaze hardened. He looked her over again, this time with slow deliberation.

He didn't say anything, just kept staring at her. Roanna's heart pounded against her ribs with sickening force. "Please," she said.

He shrugged, the movement straining his powerful shoulders against his shirt. He pulled a few bills from his pocket and tossed them on the bar, then stood, towering over her, forcing her to step back. Without a word he took her arm and steered her toward the entrance, his long fingers wrapped around her elbow like iron laces. Roanna braced herself against the tingle of delight caused by even that impersonal contact, and she wished she had worn a sleeveless blouse so she could feel his hand on her bare skin.

The door of the squat building slammed shut behind them. The lighting inside had been dim, but still she had to blink her eyes to accustom them to the darkness. Haphazardly parked vehicles crouched in the darkness, bumpers and windshields reflecting the blinking red neon of the BAR sign in the window. After the close, smoky atmosphere of the bar, the clear night air felt cold and thin. Roanna shivered with a sudden chill. He didn't release her but pulled her across the grit and sand of the parking lot to a pickup truck. Taking his keys out of his pocket, he unlocked the driver's side door, opened it, and thrust her forward. "Get in."

She obeyed, sliding across the seat until she was on the passenger side. Webb got in beside her, folding his long legs beneath the steering wheel and pulling the door shut.

Every time the sign blinked, she could see the iron set of his jaw. In the enclosed cab she could smell the fresh, hard odor of the tequila he'd been drinking. He sat silently, staring out the windshield. Hugging her arms against the chill, she too was silent.

"Well?" he snapped after a long moment when it became evident she wasn't exactly rushing into speech.

She thought of all the things she could say, all the excuses and apologies, all the reasons why Lucinda had sent her, but everything boiled down into two simple words, and she said, "Come home."

He gave a harsh crack of laughter and turned so that his shoulders were comfortably wedged against the door and the seat. "I *am* home, or near enough."

Roanna was silent again, as she often was. The stronger her feelings, the more silent she became, as if her inner shell tightened against any outbreak that would leave her vulnerable. His nearness, just hearing his voice again, made her feel as if she would shatter inside. She wasn't even able to return his gaze. Instead she looked down at her lap, fighting to control her shivering.

He muttered a curse, then shoved the key into the ignition and turned it. The motor caught immediately and settled into a powerful, well-tuned hum. He pushed the temperature control lever all the way over into the heat zone, then twisted his torso to reach behind the seat. He pulled out a denim jacket and tossed it into her lap. "Put that around you before you turn blue."

The jacket smelled of dust and sweat and horses and ineffably of Webb. Roanna wanted to bury her face in the fabric; instead she pulled it around her shoulders, grateful for the protection.

"How did you find me?" he finally asked. "Did Mother tell you?"

She shook her head.

"Aunt Sandra?"

She shook her head again.

"Damn it, I'm not in the mood for guessing games," he snapped. "Either talk or get out of the truck."

Roanna's hands tightened on the edges of the jacket. "Lucinda hired a private detective to find you. Then she sent me out here." She could feel his hostility radiating from him, a palpable force that seared her skin. She'd known she didn't have much chance of convincing him to return, but she hadn't realized how violently he disliked her now. Her stomach twisted sickeningly, and her chest felt hollow, as if her heart no longer lived there.

"So you didn't come on your own?" he asked sharply.

"No."

Unexpectedly he reached out and caught her jaw, his fingers biting into the softness of her skin as he wrenched her head around. A purr of soft menace entered his voice. "Look at me when you're talking to me."

Helplessly she did so, her eyes eating him, tracing every beloved outline and committing it to memory. This might be the last time she ever saw him, and when he sent her away, another piece of her would die.

"What does she want?" he asked, still holding her face in his grip. His big hand covered her jaw from ear to ear. "If she simply missed my smiling face, she wouldn't have waited ten years to find me. So what is it she wants from me?"

His bitterness was deeper than she'd expected, his anger still as hot as it had been the day he'd walked out of their lives. She should have known, though, and Lucinda should have, too. They'd always been aware of the force of his character; that was why, when he'd been only fourteen, Lucinda had picked him as her heir and the custodian of Davencourt. Their betrayal of him had been like pulling a tiger's tail, and now they had to face his fangs and claws.

"She wants you to come home and take over again."

"Sure she does. The good people of Colbert County

wouldn't dirty themselves by doing business with an accused murderer."

"Yes, they would. With Davencourt and everything else belonging to you, they'd have to, or lose a lot of their own income."

He gave a harsh bark of laughter. "My God, she must really want me back if she's willing to buy me! I know she's changed her will, presumably in your favor. What's gone wrong? Has she made a few bad decisions, and now she needs me to pull the family's financial ass out of the fire?"

Her fingers ached to reach out and smooth away the anger that lined his forehead, but she restrained herself, and the effort it cost her was reflected in her voice. "She wants you to come home because she loves you and regrets what happened. She needs you to come home because she's dying. She has cancer."

He glared at her in the darkness, then abruptly released her jaw and turned his head away. After a moment he said, "God *damn* it," and viciously slammed his fist against the steering wheel. "She's always been good at manipulating people. God knows, Jessie came by it honestly."

"Then you'll come?" Roanna asked hesitantly, unable to believe that was what he meant.

Instead of answering, he turned back to her and caught her face in his hand again. He leaned closer, so close she could see the glitter of his eyes and smell the alcohol on his breath. Dismayed, she abruptly realized he wasn't exactly sober. She should have known, she'd watched him drinking, but she just hadn't thought—

"What about you?" he demanded, his voice low and hard. "All I've heard is what Lucinda wants. What do *you* want? Do you want me to come home, little-Roanna-all-grown-up? How did she get you to do her dirty work for her, knowing that you'll lose a lot of money and property if you succeed?" He paused. "I assume that's what you meant, that if I go back she'll change her will again, leaving it all to me?"

"Yes," she whispered.

132

"Then you're a fool," he whispered derisively in return, and released her face. "Look, why don't you trot on back, like the good little lapdog you're turned into, and tell her you gave it your best shot but I'm not interested."

She absorbed the pain of that blow, too, and shoved it into her inner shell where the damage wouldn't show. The expression she turned to him was as smooth and blank as a doll's. "I want you to come home, too. Please."

She could feel his intensifying focus as it settled on her, like a laser beam finding its target. "Now, why would you want that?" he asked softly. "Unless you really are a fool. Are you a fool, Roanna?"

She opened her mouth to answer but he laid one callused finger across her lips. "Ten years ago you started it all by offering me a taste of that skinny little body. At the time, I thought you were too innocent to know what you were doing, but I've thought about it a lot since then, and now I think you knew exactly how I was reacting, didn't you?"

His finger was still covering her lips, lightly tracing the sensitive outline. This was what she had dreaded most, having to face his bitter accusations. She closed her eyes and nodded.

"Did you know Jessie was coming down?"

"No!" Her denial moved her lips against his finger, making her mouth tingle.

"So you kissed me because you wanted me?"

What did pride matter? she thought. She had loved him, in some form, her entire life. First she had loved him with a child's hero worship, then with an adolescent's violent crush, and finally with a woman's passion. The last change had, perhaps, taken place when she had watched Jessie cheating on him with another man and knew she couldn't tell, because to do so would hurt Webb. When she'd been younger, she would have been gleeful at the prospect of getting Jessie in trouble, and told immediately. That time she had put Webb's welfare above her own impulses, but then she had surrendered to another impulse when she kissed him, and he had ended up paying the price anyway.

His finger pressed harder. "Did you?" he insisted. "Did you want me?"

"Yes," she breathed, abandoning any scrap of pride or self-protection. "I always wanted you."

"What about now?" His voice was hard, inexorable, pushing her toward an end she couldn't see. "Do you want me now?"

What did he want her to say? Maybe he just wanted her complete humiliation. If he blamed her for everything that had happened, perhaps this was the price he wanted *her* to pay.

She nodded.

"How much do you want me?" Abruptly his hand slipped inside the jacket and closed over her breast. "Just enough to give me a feel, tease me? Or enough to give me what you offered ten years ago?"

Roanna's breath wheezed to a stop in her chest, frozen with shock. She stared helplessly at him, her dark eyes so huge that they dominated her pale face.

"Tell you what," he murmured, his big hand still burning her breast, lightly squeezing as if testing the firm resilience of her flesh. "I paid for this ten years ago, but I never got it. I'll go back and take care of business for Lucinda—if you'll give me what everyone thought I'd had then."

Numbly, she realized what he meant, realized that the years had made him even harder than she'd suspected. The old Webb never would have done such a thing—or perhaps he'd always had the capability for such ruthlessness but hadn't needed to use it. The iron was much closer to the surface now.

This, then, was his revenge against her for her juvenile romantic ambush, which had cost him so much. If he went back home he would have Davencourt as his payment, but he wanted Roanna's personal payment, too, and his price was her body.

She looked at him, at this man she had loved forever.

"All right," she whispered.

134

CHAPTER

9

The motel room was small and dingy, with a chill that went all the way to her bones. Roanna was certain there had to be better motels in Nogales, so why had he brought her here? Because it was closest or to show her how little she meant to him?

It would take a great deal of ego to think she meant anything to him at all, and ego was one thing Roanna didn't have. She felt small and shriveled inside, and a new guilt had been added to the burden she already carried: he thought he was punishing her, and in a way he was, but a secret part of her was suddenly, dizzily ecstatic that soon she would be lying in his arms.

The secret part was small, and deeply buried. She felt the shame he meant her to feel, and the humiliation. She didn't know if she'd have the courage to go through with it, and desperately she thought of Lucinda, ill and diminished with age, needing Webb's forgiveness before she could die in peace. Could she do this, lie down and let him coldly use her body, even for Lucinda?

But it wasn't just for Lucinda. Webb needed revenge just as much as Lucinda needed forgiveness. If this would help

135

him even the scales, if he could then return to Davencourt, then Roanna was willing to do it. And deep inside, that secret little part of her was giddy with selfish delight. No matter what his reasoning, for a brief time he would be hers, the experience held to her heart and savored during the empty years ahead.

He tossed his hat onto the chair and sprawled on his back on the bed, bunching the pillow up behind his head for support. His narrowed green eyes raked down her body.

"Take off your clothes."

Stunned again, she stood there with her arms hanging at her sides. He wanted her to strip down naked, just like that, with him lying there watching?

"I guess you've changed your mind," he drawled, sitting up and reaching for his hat.

Roanna pulled herself together and reached for the buttons of her shirt. She had decided to do it, so what did it matter if he wanted to look at her first? Shortly he would be doing much more than looking. The enormity of what *she* was doing was what shook her, and her hands trembled as she struggled with the buttons. Odd how difficult this was, to bare herself for him, when she had dreamed of it for years. Was it because she had always dreamed he came to her in love, and in reality it was the opposite?

But it didn't matter, she told herself over and over, using the litany as protection against thinking too much. It didn't matter, it didn't matter.

The buttons were finally undone, and the shirt hung open. She had to keep moving or she'd lose her nerve entirely. With a quick, nervous movement she pulled the cloth off her shoulders and let it drop down her arms. She couldn't look at him, but she felt his gaze on her, narrowed and intense, waiting.

Her bra had a front clasp. Briefly, trembling with cold and embarrassment, she wished it was a sexy, lacy thing, but instead it was plain white, designed for concealment rather than enticement. She unhooked it and pushed the straps down, so that this garment too dropped to the floor at her feet. The cold air swirled around her breasts, making her nipples pucker into tight buds. She knew her breasts were small. Was he looking at them? She didn't dare glance at him to see, because she was terrified she would see disappointment in his gaze.

She didn't know how to undress to please a man. Mortified at her own awkwardness, she knew that there had to be a way to do it gracefully, to tease and interest a man with the slowly revealed promise of her flesh, but she didn't know what that way was. All she knew how to do was unbutton, unhook, unzip, like a schoolgirl changing clothes for gym class.

The best thing to do then was to get it over with before she lost her nerve. Hurriedly she kicked off her sandals, unzipped her slacks, and bent over to push them down. It was icy in the room now, her skin rough with chills.

Only her panties remained now, and her meager supply of nerve was almost gone. Not giving herself time to think, she hooked her thumbs in the waistband and pushed this last garment down to her feet and stepped out of them.

Still he didn't speak, didn't move. Her hands made a brief, aborted motion, as if she would cover herself, but then she let her arms fall to her side again and she simply stood there, staring blindly at the worn carpet beneath her bare feet, wondering if it was possible to die of embarrassment. She forced herself to eat these days but she was still thin, a meager offering on the altar of revenge. What if her naked body wasn't desirable enough for him to have an erection? What if he laughed?

He was completely silent. She couldn't even hear him breathing. Darkness edged her vision, and she fought to drag oxygen into her constricted lungs. She couldn't look at him, but she had the sudden panicked thought that he might have had more to drink than she'd imagined, and gone to sleep while she'd been undressing. What a comment that would be on her practically nonexistent charms!

Then the whisper came, low and rough, and she realized he hadn't fallen asleep, after all: "C'mere."

She closed her eyes, trembling as relief threatened to buckle her knees, and edged toward the whisper.

"Closer," he said, and she moved until her knees bumped the side of the bed.

He touched her then, his hand sliding up the outside of her left thigh, callused fingertips sliding over the softness of her skin and rasping nerve endings to life, leaving a trail of heat behind. Up, up, he moved his hand over the column of her thigh and around to the roundness of her bottom, his long fingers cupping the cool undercurve of both cheeks and burning them with his heat. She quivered, and tried to control the sudden, fierce need to rub her bottom against his hand. She didn't quite succeed; her hips moved in a barely perceptible shimmy.

He gave a low laugh, his fingers tightening on the flesh beneath him. He stroked her buttocks, shaping his palm to the underside of each one as if he could imprint the soft female shape on his hand, and running his thumb down the crease between them.

Roanna began to tremble violently under the combined lash of pleasure and shock, and no amount of willpower could stop the betraying tremors. No one had ever touched her there. She hadn't known that this slow caress could make an empty ache begin between her legs, or make her breasts feel hard and tight. She squeezed her eyes even more tightly together, wondering if he would touch her breast again and if she could bear it if he did.

But it wasn't her breasts that he touched.

"Spread your legs."

His voice now was so low and raspy that she wasn't certain she'd heard him, and yet part of her knew she had. A dull roaring began in her ears, even as she felt herself shifting her stance so that her thighs were open enough to admit his exploration, and felt his hand slipping between her legs.

He ran his fingers along the closed, tender folds, feeling their softness, gently squeezing. Roanna stopped breathing. Tension stretched in her body, pulling tight in an agony of waiting that threatened to shatter her. Then one long finger boldly slipped into the closed slit, opening her, probing with unerring skill, and pushed deep up into her body.

Roanna couldn't stop the cry that broke from her lips, though she quickly choked it off. Her knees trembled and threatened again to buckle. She felt as if she was held erect only by his hand between her legs, his finger inside her. Oh, God, the sensation was almost unbearable, his finger big and rough, rasping against her tender inner flesh. He withdrew it, then quickly pushed it into her again. Over and over he stabbed the finger inside her, and rubbed his thumb against the little nub at the top of her sex.

Helplessly she felt her hips begin to move against his hand, heard breathy little moans forming in her throat and slipping free. In the quietness of the room she could hear his breathing, heard how hard and fast it was coming. She wasn't cold now; great waves of heat were breaking over her, and the pleasure was so acute it was almost painful. Desperately she reached down and seized his wrist, trying to pull his hand away from her, because it was too much, she couldn't bear it. Something drastic was happening to her, something even more drastic was about to happen, and she cried out in sudden fear.

He ignored her efforts as if she were holding his hand rather than trying to push it away. She could feel him probing at her, trying to work a second finger into her alongside the other, felt her body's sudden panicked resistance. He tried again, and she flinched.

He went still, and his low curse exploded in the silence.

Then everything turned upside down as he grabbed her and pulled her down onto the bed, turning her, dragging her across his body to lie beside him. Roanna's eyes flew open to combat the sudden dizziness, then she wished she'd kept them closed.

He leaned over her so close she could see the black striations in his green eyes, so close she could feel the heat of his breath on her face, smell the tequila. She was sprawled on her back with her right leg draped over his hip. His hand still rested between her open thighs, one fingertip moving restlessly around and around the tender opening that had grown moist for him.

She felt another wave of mortification, that she was naked while he was still fully clothed, that he was touching her in her most private place and watching her face while he did so. She felt her cheeks and breasts heat, turn pink.

He moved his finger back into her again, probing deep, and all the while he held her gaze with his. Roanna couldn't hold back another moan, and she yearned for the dubious comfort of her closed eyes, but she couldn't look away. His dark brows drew together over the fierce green glitter of his eyes. He was angry, she realized in confusion, but it was a hot anger instead of the cold disgust she would have expected.

"You're a virgin," he said flatly.

It sounded like an accusation. Roanna stared up at him, wondering how he'd guessed, wondering why he sounded so angry. "Yes," she admitted, and blushed again.

He watched the flush pinken her breasts, and she saw the way the glitter in his eyes deepened. His gaze focused intently on her breasts, on her hardened nipples. He removed his hand from between her legs, his finger damp from her body. Slowly, still staring fixedly at her breasts, he stroked her nipple with that wet finger, spreading her own juices on the tightly puckered nub. A rough, hungry sound rumbled in his throat. He leaned over her and fastened his lips around the nipple he had just anointed, sucking hard on it, taking her taste into his mouth.

The pleasure almost shattered her. The fierce pressure, the rasp of his tongue and teeth, sent pure fire racing through her. Roanna arched in his arms, crying out, and her hands clenched in his hair to hold his head in place. He moved to her other breast and sucked just as hard on that nipple until it too was dark red and wet, and painfully erect.

Reluctantly he lifted his head, staring at his handiwork with feral concentration and hunger. His lips, like her nipples, were red and wet, and slightly parted as his breath moved hard and fast between them. The heat radiating from his big body dispelled any lingering chill she might have felt.

"You don't have to do this," he said, the words so harsh they sounded as if they'd been ripped from his throat. "It's your first time . . . I'll go back anyway."

Disappointment pierced her, sliding like a dagger straight into her heart. All color faded from her face, and she stared at him with a stricken expression in her eyes. Taking off her clothes had been difficult, but once he'd touched her, she had been gradually losing herself in a rising tide of sensual delight, despite the shock she felt at every new caress. The secret part of her had been delirious with ecstasy, savoring every touch of those hard hands, waiting with barely restrained eagerness for more.

Now he wanted to stop. She didn't entice him enough for him to continue.

Her throat closed. A strained whisper was all that could escape the sudden constriction. "Don't—don't you want me?"

The plea was faint, but he heard it. His eyes dilated until only a thin circle of green shimmered around the fierce pools of black. He caught her hand and dragged it down his body, pressed it hard over his straining penis despite her instinctive effort to pull away, an action that underscored her innocence.

Roanna froze in wonder. She felt the hard ridge under the denim. It was long and thick, the heat of it burning through the heavy fabric, and it pulsed with a life of its own. She turned her hand, grasping him through his jeans. "Please, Webb. I want you to do it," she gasped.

For a terrifying moment she thought he would still refuse, but then with a sudden, violent motion he jackknifed off the bed and began stripping off his clothes. She was only dimly aware that he watched her as she watched him. She couldn't keep the fascination from her face as she stared at his body, the broad shoulders and hairy, muscled chest, the ridged abdomen. Carefully he maneuvered the zipper down, then pushed his shorts and jeans off with one motion. She blinked, startled, at his pulsing erection as it thrust forward when freed from the restraint of his jeans. Another blush warmed her cheeks.

He paused, sucking in deep breaths.

Suddenly terrified of doing anything that would make him stop, Roanna held herself still and quiet, forcing herself to look away from his body. She thought she would die if he turned away from her now. But he wanted to do it; she knew he did. She was inexperienced, but that wasn't the same as ignorant. He was very hard, and he wouldn't be if he wasn't interested.

The glare of the light was right in her eyes. She wished he'd turned it off, but didn't ask. The mattress dipped under his weight, and she spread her hands to balance herself, because the cheap mattress didn't give much support.

He didn't give her any time to think, to perhaps change her mind, not even time to panic. He moved on top of her, his hard thighs pushing between hers and spreading them, and his shoulders blotted out the light. Roanna barely sucked in a deep breath before he set his hands on either side of her skull, holding her head as he leaned down and covered her mouth with his. His tongue probed, and she parted her lips to accept it. Simultaneously she felt his hot, rock-hard penis begin pushing at the soft entrance between her legs.

Her heart jumped violently, banging against her ribs. She made a faint sound of apprehension, but his mouth smothered it as he deepened the kiss, penetrating her with both tongue and penis.

It wasn't easy, despite her arousal, despite the dampness that readied her for him. Somehow she had thought he would simply slip into her, but it didn't work that way. He rocked his hips back and forth, forcing himself a little deeper into her with each motion. Her body resisted the increasing pressure; the pain surprised her, dismayed her. She tried to endure it without reaction, but it grew progressively worse with each inward thrust.

She groaned, her breath catching. If she had expected him to stop, she was mistaken. Webb merely tightened his arms and held her firmly beneath him, controlling her with weight and strength, all of his intent and attention focused on penetrating her. She dug her nails into his back, weeping now from the pain. He pushed harder and her tender flesh gave under the pressure, stretching around his thick length as he surged deep inside. Finally he was in her to the hilt, and she writhed helplessly beneath him as she tried to find some level of ease.

Now that his masculine goal was accomplished, he set about soothing her, not withdrawing, but using touch and voice to reassure and calm her. He continued to hold her head in his hands, and he crooned to her as he kissed the salty tears from her cheeks. "Shh, shh," he murmured. "Just lie still, sweetheart. I know it hurts, but it'll ease off in a minute."

The endearment soothed her as nothing else could have. He couldn't truly hate her, could he, if he called her "sweetheart"? Slowly she calmed, relaxing from her frantic struggle to accommodate him. Some of his own tenseness eased, and until then she hadn't realized how tightly drawn his muscles had been. Panting, she softened around him, beneath him.

Her breathing calmed, became deeper. Now that she wasn't in such distress some of her pleasure returned. With growing wonder she felt him deep inside her, pulsing with arousal. This was Webb who penetrated her so intimately, Webb who cradled her in his arms. Only an hour before she had watched him from across a dimly lit bar, dreading the moment when she had to approach him, and now she was naked under his powerful body. She looked up at him and met his brilliant green gaze, studying her as intently as if he could see through her to the bone.

He kissed her, quick, hard kisses that had her mouth trying to catch his, begging for more, preparing her for more. "Are you ready?" he asked.

She didn't know what he meant. She gave him a bewildered look, and a tight smile twitched his lips.

"For what?"

"To make love."

She looked even more confused. "Isn't that what we're doing?" she whispered.

"Not quite. Almost."

"But you're . . . inside me."

"There's more."

Confusion changed to alarm. *"More?"* She tried to draw back from him, pressing herself into the mattress.

He grinned, though it looked as if the effort cost him. "Not more of me. More to do."

"Oh." The word was drawn out, filled with wonder. She relaxed beneath him again, and her thighs flexed around his hips. The movement caused a reaction inside her; his sex jumped, and her enveloping sheath tightened around the thick intruder, caressing him. Webb's breath hissed between his teeth. Roanna's eyes grew heavy lidded, slumberous, and her cheeks pinkened. "Show me," she breathed.

He did, beginning to move, at first thrusting into her in a slow, delicious rhythm, then gradually quickening his pace. Hesitantly she responded, her body lifting to his as her excitement soared. He shifted his weight to one elbow and reached down between their bodies. She gasped as he stroked her tightly stretched entrance, her flesh so sensitive that the slightest touch jolted through her like lightning. Then he moved his attention to the nodule he'd touched before, rubbing his fingertip back and forth across it, and Roanna felt herself begin to dissolve.

It happened fast under his ruthless, sensual assault. He didn't ease her into climax, he hurled her into it. He gave her no mercy, even when she bucked under his hand in an effort to escape the intensity of it. The fierce, rapidly increasing sensation burned her, melted her. He rode her harder, thrusting deep, and the friction was almost unbearable. But he was touching her deep inside in a way that made her cling to him and cry out in a pleasure so strong she couldn't control it. It spiraled inside her, growing stronger and stronger, and when it finally shattered, she arched wildly beneath him, her slender body shuddering as her hips undulated, working herself on his invading shaft. She heard herself screaming, and didn't care.

His heavy weight crushed her into the mattress. His hands pushed beneath her and gripped her buttocks, hard. His hips pistoned back and forth between her widespread, straining thighs. Then he convulsed, slamming into her again and again while harsh sounds tore from his throat, and she felt the wetness of his release.

In the silence afterward, Roanna lay limply beneath him. She was exhausted, her body so heavy and weak that all she could do was breathe. She lapsed into a doze, barely aware of when he carefully separated their bodies and moved to lie beside her. Sometime later the light blinked off, and she was aware of cool darkness, of him stripping the bedspread down and positioning her between the sheets.

She turned instinctively into his arms, and felt them close around her. Her head settled into the hollow of his shoulder, and her hand rested on his chest, feeling the crisp hair beneath her fingers. For the first time in ten years she felt a small measure of peace, of rightness.

She had no idea how long it was before she became aware of his hands moving on her with increasing purpose. "Can you do it again?" he asked, the words low and intense.

"Yes, please," she said politely, and heard a low chuckle as he rolled atop her.

Roanna.
Webb lay in the darkness, feeling her slight weight nestled against his left side. She was asleep, her head on his shoulder, her breath sighing across his chest. Her breasts, small and perfectly shaped, pressed firmly against his ribs. Gently, unable to resist, he rubbed the back of one finger over the satiny outer curve of the breast he could reach. Oh, God, Roanna.

He hadn't recognized her at first. Though ten years had

passed and logically he knew she had grown up, in his mind's eye she had still been the skinny, underdeveloped, immature teenager with the urchin's grin. He hadn't seen any trace of her in the woman who had approached him in the grubby little bar. Instead he'd seen a woman who looked so buttoned-down he'd been surprised that she'd spoken to him. Women like her might go to a bar if they were looking for revenge against a straying husband, but that was about the only reason he could think of.

But there she'd been, too thin for his taste, but severely stylish in an expensive silk camp shirt and tailored slacks. Her thick hair, dark in the uncertain light, was cut in a stylish bob that swung just below chin length. Her mouth, though . . . he'd liked her mouth, wide and full, and had the thought that it would feel good to kiss her and feel the softness of those lips.

She'd looked totally out of place, a country-club woman lost in a low-rent district. But she'd been reaching out to touch him, and when he'd turned, she had dropped her hand and looked at him, her face still and strangely sad, her wide mouth unsmiling, and her brown eyes so solemn he wondered if she ever smiled.

And then she'd said, "Hello, Webb. May I talk to you?" and the shock had nearly felled him. For a split second he wondered if he'd had more to drink than he'd thought, because not only had she called him by name when he would have sworn he'd never seen her before, but she had used Roanna's voice, and the brown eyes were suddenly Roanna's whiskey-colored eyes.

Reality had shifted and adjusted, and he'd seen the girl in the woman.

Odd. He hadn't spent the past ten years sulking about what had happened. When he'd walked out of Davencourt that day, he'd intended it to be forever, and he'd gotten on with his life. He'd chosen southern Arizona because it was starkly beautiful, not because it was about as far as it could get from lush, green, northwestern Alabama and still be inhabitable. Ranching was hard, but he enjoyed the physical work as much as he'd enjoyed the cutthroat world of business and finance. Always a horseman, he'd made the transition easily. His family had narrowed to include only his mother and Aunt Sandra, but he was content with that.

At first he'd felt dead inside. Despite the imminent breakup, despite the fact that she'd cheated on him, he'd mourned Jessie with surprising depth. She'd been a part of his life for so long that he woke up mornings feeling strangely incomplete. Then, gradually, he had surprised himself by remembering what a bitch she had been and laughing fondly.

He could have let the uncertainty eat him alive, knowing that her killer was still out there and wasn't likely to be discovered, but in the end he'd accepted that there was nothing he could do about it. Her affair had been so secret that there had been no hints, no leads. It was a dead end. He could let it destroy his life or he could go on. Webb was a survivor. He'd gone on.

There had been days, even weeks, when he hadn't thought about his old life at all. He'd put Lucinda and the others behind him . . . all except for Roanna. Sometimes he'd hear something that sounded like her laugh, and instinctively turn to see what mischief she was in before he remembered she was no longer there. Or he'd be doctoring a cut on a horse's leg, and he'd remember the concern that had darkened her thin face whenever she'd tended a hurt mount.

Somehow she had wormed her way deeper into his heart than the others had, and it was harder to forget her. He'd catch himself worrying about her, wondering what latest trouble she had managed to get herself into. And over the years, it was the memory of her that still had the power to make him angry.

He couldn't forget Jessie's accusation that Roanna had deliberately made trouble between them that last night. Had Jessie lied? She certainly hadn't been above it, but Roanna's transparent face had clearly revealed her guilt. Over the years, given Jessie's pregnancy by another man, he'd come to the conclusion that Roanna hadn't had anything to do

147

with Jessie's death and the murderer had instead been Jessie's unknown lover, but he still couldn't shake his anger. Somehow Roanna's behavior, though it paled in importance when compared with the other events of that night, retained the power to make him furious.

Maybe it was because he'd always been so dead certain of her love. Maybe it had stroked his ego to be worshipped so openly, so unconditionally. No one else on earth had loved him that way. Yvonne's mother-love was unyielding, but she was the woman who had spanked him when he misbehaved as a child, so she saw his flaws. In Roanna's eyes, he'd been perfect, or so he had thought until she had deliberately caused trouble just so she could get one up on Jessie. He wondered now if he'd ever been anything other than a symbol to her, a possession that Jessie had and she wanted.

He'd had women since Jessie's death. He'd even had one or two lengthy relationships, though he'd never been inclined to remarry. But no matter how hot the sex he enjoyed in other women's beds, it was dreams of Roanna that woke him in the cool early mornings before dawn, drenched in sweat and his dick standing up like an iron spike.

He was never able to remember the dreams clearly, just bits and pieces, like the way her bottom had rubbed against his erection, the way her nipples had pebbled just from kissing him, the way they'd felt when she pressed them against his chest. His lust for Jessie had been a boy's lust, a young man's hormone-crazed lust, a game of dominance. His lust for Roanna, disgusted as it made him with himself, always had an undertone of tenderness, at least in his dreams.

But she was no dream, standing there in the bar.

His first impulse had been to get her out of there, where she didn't belong. She had gone with him without protest or question, as silent now as she had once been mouthy. He was aware that he'd had too much to drink, known that he wasn't in complete control of himself, but putting her off until tomorrow hadn't seemed like a viable option.

At first he'd barely been able to concentrate on what she

was saying. She hadn't even wanted to look at him. She had sat there, shivering, looking every place but at him, and he hadn't been able to keep his eyes off her. She'd changed. God, how she'd changed. He didn't like it, didn't like her silence where once she'd been a chatterbox, didn't like the stillness of her expression where once every emotion she had felt had been written plainly on her little face. There was no mischief or laughter in her eyes, no vibrant energy in her movements. It was as if someone had stolen Roanna and left a doll in her place.

The ugly little girl had turned into a plain teenager, and the plain teenager into a woman who was, if not exactly pretty, striking in her own way. Her face had filled out so that her too-big features had assumed a more pleasing proportion. Her long, high-bridged, slightly crooked nose now looked aristocratic, and her too-wide mouth could only be described as lush. Complete maturity had refined her face so that high, chiseled cheekbones had been revealed, and her almond-shaped, whiskey-colored eyes were exotic. She had put on a little weight, maybe fifteen pounds, that softened her body and made her look less like a refugee from a World War II prison camp, though she could easily carry another fifteen pounds and still be slim.

Memories of the girl had haunted him. The reality of the woman had stirred his long-simmering lust to a hard boil.

But, on a personal level, she had seemed oblivious to him. She had asked him to return to Alabama because Lucinda needed him. Lucinda loved him, regretted their estrangement. Lucinda would give him back everything he'd lost. Lucinda was ill, dying. Lucinda, Lucinda, Lucinda. Every word out of her mouth had been about Lucinda. Nothing about herself, whether or not *she* wanted him to return, as if that long-ago hero worship had never existed.

That had made him even angrier, that he'd spent years dreaming about her while she seemed to have completely cut him out of her life. His temper had soared out of control, and the tequila had loosened any restraint he might have felt. He'd heard himself demand that she go to bed with him as the price for his return. He'd seen the shock on her face, seen it quickly controlled. He had waited for her rejection. And then she'd said yes.

He was angry enough, drunk enough, to follow through. By God, if she was willing to give herself to him for Lucinda's benefit, then he'd damn sure take her up on it. He cranked the truck and drove quickly to the nearest motel before she could change her mind.

Once inside the cheap little room, he had sprawled on the bed because his head had been spinning a little, and ordered her to strip. Once again he'd expected her to refuse. He'd waited for her to back out, or at least lose her temper and tell him to kiss her ass. He wanted to see fire break through the barrier of that blank doll's face, he wanted to see the old Roanna.

Instead she had silently begun to take off her clothes.

She did it neatly, without fuss, and from the moment the first button had slipped free he hadn't been able to think of anything else but the soft skin being revealed by each movement of her fingers. She hadn't tried to be coy; she hadn't needed to. His dick was pressing so hard against his fly that it probably had the imprint of his zipper running down it.

She had lovely skin, a little golden, with the faintest dusting of freckles across those classic cheekbones. She slipped out of her shirt, and her shoulders had a soft, mellow sheen to them. Then she had unhooked that plain, serviceable white bra and removed it, and her breasts had taken his breath. They didn't stick out a lot but were surprisingly round and upright, exquisitely formed, with her nipples drawn into tight, rosy buds that made his mouth water.

Silently she had removed her slacks and panties, standing naked before him. Her waist and hips were narrow, but the cheeks of her ass were as deliciously round as her breasts. The need to touch her was painful. Hoarsely he had ordered her to come to him, and she had silently obeyed, moving to stand beside the bed.

He'd touched her then, and felt her quiver under his hand. The column of her thigh was sleek and cool, her skin delicate in contrast with his tanned, work-roughened hand. Slowly, savoring the texture of her skin, he stroked upward and around to her buttocks; she had moved a little, rubbing herself against his hand, and mingled excitement and delight had roared through him. He had cupped the firm mounds and felt them flex, and she had begun to shake even harder. He teased her with a daring caress and sensed her shock, and he'd looked up to find that her eyes were tightly closed.

Somehow he couldn't quite believe it was Roanna who stood naked before him, yielding her body to his exploration, and yet everything about her was infinitely familiar, and far more exciting than ten years' worth of frustrating dreams.

He didn't have to imagine the physical details now; they were laid out before him. Her pubic hair was a neat, curly little triangle. It had drawn his gaze, and he'd been entranced by the delicate folds, shyly closed, that he could glimpse under the curls. The mysteries of her body had made him ache with need. Roughly he'd told her to spread her legs so he could touch her, and she had.

He'd put his hand on the most private part of her body, and felt her startled response. He'd petted her, stroked her, opened her, and eased one finger into her startlingly tight sheath. He was so hard he thought he might explode, but he held back, because here was the proof that the lust wasn't all on his part. She was slick and damp, and her soft, low moans of arousal had nearly driven him crazy. She seemed shyly bewildered by what he was doing, what she was feeling. Then he'd tried to slip another finger into her, and couldn't. He'd felt her instinctive withdrawal, and a sudden suspicion flared in his tequila-fogged brain.

She'd never done this before. He was abruptly certain of it.

Swiftly he tumbled her down onto the bed, dragging her body across his. With more deliberation he'd probed her body, watching her reaction, fighting the alcohol as he tried to think clearly. He'd been the first with a couple of girls, back in high school and college, and even once since he'd left Alabama, so he noticed the way she blushed, her slight flinch as he pushed his rough finger even deeper. If it hadn't been for her years of horseback riding, he doubted he would have been able to even get his finger inside her.

He should stop this, now. The knowledge seared him. His body damn near revolted. He hadn't meant to let it go this far anyway, but he'd been undone by the tequila, and by his own arousal. He'd had just the wrong amount to drink, enough to slow his thoughts and make him not give a damn, but not enough to soften his dick. He was disgusted with himself for making her do this, and he'd opened his mouth to tell her to put on her clothes when, for an instant, he saw how terribly vulnerable she was, and how he could destroy her with a careless word even if it was for her own good.

Roanna had grown up in Jessie's shadow. Jessie had been the pretty one, Roanna the plain one. Her physical self-confidence, except where horses were concerned, had always been close to zero. How could it not be, when rejection had been more the norm for her than acceptance? For a split second he saw the raw, desperate courage it had taken for her to do this. She had stripped naked for him, something he was certain she'd never done with any other man, and offered herself to him. He couldn't imagine what it had cost her. If he rejected her now, it would devastate her.

"You're a virgin," he'd said, his voice hard and flat with frustration.

She hadn't denied it. Instead she had blushed, a delicate rose tinting her breasts, and the delectable sight had been irresistible. He'd known he shouldn't do it, but he'd had to touch her nipple, and then he'd had to taste her, and he'd felt the answering need in her slender body as it arched to his touch.

He'd offered to stop. It took every ounce of willpower he

had to rein himself in and make that offer, but he'd done it. And Roanna had looked as if he'd slapped her in the face. She had gone white, and her lips had trembled. "Don't you want me?" she'd whispered, the plea so faint that his heart had squeezed. His own defenses, already weakened by the tequila, went down with a crash. Rather than answering, he had simply caught her hand and dragged it down to his groin, pressed it over his erection. He hadn't said anything even then, staying silent as he watched the sense of wonder creep into her eyes, chase away the pain. It was like watching a flower bloom.

Then she had turned her hand to hold him and had said, "Please," and he was lost.

Still, he had tried grimly for control. Even as he shucked off his clothes, he had been sucking in deep breaths, trying to cool the fire inside him. It hadn't worked. God, he was so ready he'd probably come as soon as he put it in her.

He had damn sure wanted to find out.

Somehow, he managed to hold himself back. His control hadn't extended to prolonged foreplay. He had simply mounted her, tucking her delicate body under his much more powerful one, and kissed her while he forced his erection in her to the hilt.

He'd known he was hurting her, but he couldn't stop. All he could do, once he was inside her, was make it good for her. "Ladies first" had always been his motto, and he had experience in achieving his objective. Roanna was startlingly, overwhelmingly responsive to his every touch, her hips moving, her back arching, hot little cries breaking from her lips. Jessie had always held back, but Roanna gave herself without restraint, without pretension. She had climaxed fast, and then his own orgasm had seized him and he had come violently, more violently than he'd ever experienced before, pounding into her and flooding her with semen.

She hadn't pulled away, hadn't jumped up to run into the bathroom and clean herself. She had simply dozed off with her arms still looped around his neck.

Maybe he had dozed, too. He didn't know. But eventually he had roused himself and slid off her, turned out the light, tucked her under the covers, and joined her there.

It hadn't been long before his cock had stirred insistently, lured by the silken body in his arms. And Roanna had welcomed him without hesitation, as she had every other time during the night that he'd reached for her.

It was almost dawn now.

The effects of the tequila had faded from his system, and he had to face the facts. Like it or not, he had blackmailed Roanna into this. The hell of it was, he hadn't needed to. She would have lain down for him without it being a condition for his return.

Something had happened to her, something that had robbed her of her zest, her spontaneity. It was as if she had finally been defeated by all the efforts to force her into a certain mold, and had surrendered herself.

He didn't like it. It made him furious.

He wanted to kick himself for becoming just one more person in a long line of people who had forced her to do something. It didn't matter that she had responded to him. He had to make it plain that his return didn't depend on her giving him the use of her body. He wanted her—hell, yes, he wanted her—but without any conditions or threats between them, and it was his own damn fault that he was in this situation.

He wanted to make his peace with Lucinda. It was time, and the thought of her dying made him regret the lost years. Davencourt and all the money didn't matter, not now. Mending fences mattered. Finding out what had extinguished the light in Roanna's eyes mattered.

He wondered if they were prepared for the man he'd become.

Yeah, he'd go back.

CHAPTER
10

*R*oanna seldom slept well, but she was so exhausted from the day of hard travel and emotional stress that when Webb finally let her sleep, she dropped immediately into a hard, deep slumber. She was groggy when she woke, unable for a moment to remember where she was, but over the years she had become accustomed to waking in places where she hadn't gone to sleep, so she didn't panic.

Instead she lay quietly while reality reassembled itself in her mind. She became aware of some unusual things: One, this wasn't Davencourt. Two, she was naked. Three, she was *very* sore in all her tender places.

It all clicked into place then, and she bolted upright in bed, looking for Webb. She knew immediately that he wasn't there.

He'd gotten up, dressed, and left her alone in this cheesy motel. During the night his heat had melted some of the ice that had encased her for so many years, but as she sat there naked in a tangle of dingy sheets, she felt the cold layer slowly solidify again.

It was the story of her life, it seemed. She had always felt that she could offer herself to him body and soul, and he still wouldn't love her. Now she knew for certain. Along with her body, she'd given him her heart, while he'd simply been screwing.

Had she really been silly enough to think he *cared* for her? Why should he? She'd done nothing but cause him trouble. He probably hadn't even been particularly attracted to her. Webb had always been able to get any woman he wanted, even the prettiest ones. She couldn't compare with the type he was accustomed to, in either face or body; she had simply been handy, and he'd been horny. He'd seen an opportunity to get his rocks off and taken it. Case closed.

Her face was expressionless as she slowly crawled out of bed, ignoring the discomfort between her legs. She noticed then the note on the other pillow, scribbled on the scratch pad stamped with the motel's name. She picked it up, recognizing the black slash of Webb's handwriting immediately. "Be back at ten," it read. The note wasn't signed, but then that wasn't necessary. Roanna smoothed her fingers over the writing, then tore the note from the pad and carefully folded it and slipped it into her purse.

She looked at her wristwatch: eight-thirty. An hour and a half to kill. An hour and a half of grace before she had to listen to him tell her that last night had been a mistake, one he didn't intend to repeat.

The least she could do was crawl back into her severely stylish shell, so she wouldn't look pitiful when he gave her the old heave-ho. She could bear a lot, but she didn't think she could stand it if he felt sorry for her.

Her clothes were as limp and wrinkled as she felt. First she washed out her underwear and draped it over the noisy climate control unit to dry, then turned the temperature control to heat and set the fan on high. She carried her slacks and blouse into the tiny bathroom with her, and hung them over the door while she took a shower in the minuscule stall that sported a cracked floor and yellowed water stains. The cubicle quickly filled with steam, and by the time she finished, both blouse and slacks looked fresher.

The climate control unit was a lot louder than it was efficient, but still the room quickly became stuffy. She shut it off and checked her panties; they were dry except for a lingering bit of dampness in the waistband. She pulled them on anyway, then quickly dressed in case Webb came back earlier than he'd said. Not that he hadn't already seen everything she had, she thought, and touched it as well, but that was last night. By leaving the way he had, he'd made it plain that last night hadn't meant anything to him beyond physical release.

She combed her straight, heavy hair back and left it to dry. That was the major benefit of a good cut: it didn't require much maintenance. The small amount of luggage she'd brought was locked in the trunk of her rental car, which was presumably still parked outside that grimy little bar just off the highway, but she wasn't certain exactly where she was in relation to it. The only makeup she had in her purse was a powder compact and a neutral-colored lipstick. She made quick use of it, not looking at her reflection in the mirror any longer than was required to get the lipstick on straight.

She opened the door to let in the freshness of the dry desert morning, turned on the small television that was bolted to the wall, and sat down in the lone chair in the room, an uncomfortable number with a torn vinyl seat, which looked as if it had been stolen from a hospital waiting room.

She didn't pay much attention to what was on, some morning talk show. It was noise, and that was all she required. Sometimes when she couldn't sleep, she would turn her own television on so the voices could give her the illusion of not being utterly alone in the night.

She was still sitting there when a vehicle pulled up right outside the door. The motor cut off as a cloud of dust blew in. Then a door opened and was slammed shut, there was the sound of booted feet on the concrete walk, and Webb filled the doorway. He was silhouetted against the bright sunlight, his broad shoulders almost stretching from one side of the door frame to the other.

He didn't come any farther inside. All he said was, "Are

you ready?" and she silently got up, turned off the light and the television, and picked up her purse.

He opened the truck door for her, his southern manners still holding sway despite a decade of self-imposed exile. Roanna climbed inside, concentrating on not giving any flinches that betrayed her physical discomfort, and settled herself. Now that it was daylight, she could tell that the truck was gunmetal gray, with a gray interior, and was fairly new. There was an extra stick shift on the floor, meaning it was four-wheel drive, probably a necessity for taking it across the range.

As Webb slid behind the wheel, he slanted her an unreadable glance. She wondered if he expected her to either start planning a wedding or pitch a fit because he'd left her alone this morning. She did neither. She sat silently.

"Hungry?"

She shook her head, then remembered that he liked verbal answers. "No, thank you."

His lips thinned as he started the motor and reversed out of the parking spot. "You're going to eat. You've gained a little weight, and it looks good on you. I'm not going to let you catch your flight without eating."

She hadn't booked a return flight, because she hadn't known how long she would be staying. She opened her mouth to say so, then caught the flinty expression in his eyes and realized he had booked one for her.

"When am I leaving?"

"One o'clock. I managed to get you on a direct flight from Tucson to Dallas. Your connection in Dallas is a bit tight, forty-five minutes, but it'll get you into Huntsville at a reasonable hour. You should get home around ten, ten-thirty tonight. Do you have to call anyone to pick you up in Huntsville?"

"No." She had driven herself to the airport, because no one else had been willing to get up at three-thirty to perform the service. No, that wasn't fair. She hadn't asked anyone to do it. She never asked anyone to do anything for her.

By the time she ate, as he seemed determined for her to

158

do, she would have to leave almost immediately in order to turn in her rental car at the airport and make it to the gate in time to board. He hadn't left her any breathing space, probably by design. He didn't want to talk to her, didn't want to spend any more time in her company than necessary.

"There's a little place not far from here that serves breakfast until eleven. The food's plain, but good."

"Just drop me off at the bar so I can pick up my car," she said as she looked out the window, anywhere but at him. "I'll stop at a fast-food place."

"I doubt it," he said grimly. "I'm going to watch every bite go into your mouth."

"I eat now and then," she replied in a mild tone. "I learned how."

"Then you won't mind if I watch."

She recognized that tone, the one he used when he'd made up his mind that you were going to do something, so you might as well not argue. When she'd been younger, that tone had been of infinite comfort, symbolizing the rock steadiness and security she had so desperately needed after her parents' death. In an odd way it was still comforting; he might not like her, might not desire her, but at least he didn't want her to starve to death.

The little restaurant he took her to wasn't much bigger than the kitchen at Davencourt, with a couple of booths, a couple of tiny tables, and four stools lined up at the counter. The rich scent of frying bacon and sausage was in the air, underlaid with that of coffee and the spiciness of chili peppers. Two sun-baked old men were in the back booth, and they both looked up with interest as Webb escorted Roanna to the other booth.

A thin woman of indeterminate age, her skin baked as hard and brown as that of the two old men, approached the booth. She pulled a green order pad out of the hip pocket of her jeans and held a stubby pencil at the ready.

Evidently there was no menu. Roanna looked at Webb in question. "I'll have the short stack, ham and eggs on the

159

side, sunny side up," he said, "and she'll have an egg, plain scrambled, with dry toast, bacon, and hash browns. Coffee for both of us."

"We can't do eggs sunny side up no more. Health Department rules," the waitress said.

"Then I want them well done but take them up early."

"Gotcha." The waitress tore the top sheet off the pad as she walked over to an opening cut out in the wall. She laid the ticket on the sill. "Betts! Got an order."

"You must eat here often," Roanna said.

"I usually stop by whenever I'm in town."

"What does plain scrambled mean?"

"No peppers."

It was on the tip of her tongue to ask if they called that fancy scrambled but bit the comment back. How easy it would be to fall into the old habits with him! she thought sadly. But she had learned to curb her quips, because most people didn't appreciate even the milder ones. Webb had once seemed to, but perhaps he'd been kind.

The waitress set two steaming cups of coffee in front of them. "Cream?" she asked, and Webb said, "No," answering for both of them.

"It'll take me at least a week, maybe two, to get things squared away here," he said abruptly. "I'm keeping my ranch, so I'll be flying back and forth. Davencourt won't be my sole concern."

She sipped her coffee to hide her relief. He was still coming home! He'd said he would if she'd sleep with him, but until now she hadn't been certain he'd meant it. It wouldn't have made any difference if she'd known for sure he was lying; no matter what the day had brought, last night had been a dream come true for her, and she had grabbed at it with both hands.

"Lucinda wouldn't expect you to sell the ranch," she said.

"Bullshit. She thinks the universe revolves around Davencourt. There's nothing she wouldn't do to safeguard it." He leaned back and stretched out his long legs, carefully avoiding contact with hers. "Tell me what's been going on there. Mother tells me some of the news, and so does Aunt Sandra, but neither of them know anything about the day-to-day operations. I do know that Gloria has managed to move her entire family into Davencourt."

"Not *all* of them. Baron and his family still live in Charlotte."

"Being under the same roof with Lanette and Corliss is enough to make me think about buying my own place in town."

Roanna didn't voice her agreement, but she knew exactly what he meant.

"What about you?" he continued. "I know you went to college in Tuscaloosa. What changed your mind? I thought you wanted to attend college locally."

She had gone away because for a long time that had been easier than staying home. Her sleeping problems hadn't been as bad while she was away, the memories hadn't been as acute. But it had been over a year after he'd left before she had started college, and it had been a year of hell.

She didn't tell him any of that. Instead she shrugged and said, "You know how it is. A person can get along without it, but to have all the *right* contacts you have to attend the university." She didn't have to elaborate on which university, because Webb had gone to the same one.

"Did you do the sorority bit?"

"It was expected."

A reluctant grin tugged at his mouth. "I can't see you as a Greek. How did you get along with the little society snobs?"

"Fine." They had, in fact, been kind to her. It was they who had taught her how to dress, how to apply makeup, how to make social chitchat. She rather thought they had seen her as a challenge and taken her on as a makeover project.

The waitress approached with three plates of steaming hot food. She slid two plates in front of Webb and the remaining one in front of Roanna. "Yell when you need a refill," she said comfortably, and left them alone.

Webb applied himself to his food, buttering the pancakes

and soaking them in syrup, then liberally salting and peppering his eggs. The slab of ham covered half the plate. Roanna looked at the mountain of food, then at his steely body. She tried to imagine the amount of physical labor that required that many calories, and felt an even deeper sense of respect for him.

"Eat," he growled.

She picked up her fork and obeyed. Once she couldn't have managed it, but keeping her emotions controlled had allowed her stomach to settle down. The trick was to take her time and take tiny bites. Usually, by the time everyone else had finished their meal she had managed to eat half of hers, and that was enough.

That was the case this time, too. When Webb leaned back, replete, Roanna laid her fork aside. He gave her plate a long, hard look as if calculating exactly how much she'd eaten, but to her relief he decided not to push it.

Breakfast taken care of, he drove her to the bar. The rental car sat forlornly in the parking lot, looking abandoned and out of place. A CLOSED sign hung lopsidedly on the front door of the bar. In daylight, the building was even more ramshackle than it had appeared the night before.

Dust flew around the truck as he braked to a stop, and Roanna allowed the gritty cloud to settle while she fished the ignition key out of her purse. "Thanks for breakfast," she said as she opened the door and slid out. "I'll tell Lucinda to expect you."

He got out of the truck and walked over to the rental car with her, standing right beside the door so she couldn't open it. "About last night," he said.

Dread filled her. God, she couldn't listen to this. She put the key in the lock and turned it, hoping he would take the hint and move. He didn't.

"What about it?" she managed to say without any expression in her voice.

"It shouldn't have happened."

She bent her head. It was the best thing that had ever happened to her, and he wished it hadn't.

"God damn it, look at me!" Just as he had the night before, he cupped her chin in his hand and lifted her head so that she faced him. His hat was pulled low on his forehead, shadowing his eyes, but she could still see the grimness in them and in the line of his mouth. Very gently, he touched her lips with his thumb. "I wasn't exactly drunk, but I'd had too much to drink. You were a virgin. I shouldn't have made that a condition to going back, and I regret what I did to you."

Roanna held her spine very straight and still. "It was as much my responsibility as yours."

"Not quite. You didn't know exactly what you were getting into. On the other hand, I did know that you wouldn't turn me down."

She couldn't escape that hard, green gaze. This was very like the night before when she had stripped herself naked in front of him, except now she was emotionally naked. Her lower lip trembled, and she quickly controlled it. There was no point in denying what he'd said, because her actions had already proved him right. When he had given her the opportunity to call a stop to what was happening, she had begged him to continue.

"It's never been a secret how I feel about you," she finally said. "All you had to do at any time was snap your fingers, and I'd have come running and let you do anything you wanted to me." She managed a smile. It wasn't much of one, but it was better than weeping. "That hasn't changed."

He searched her face, trying to pierce the remoteness of her expression. A kind of angry frustration flashed in his eyes. "I just wanted you to know that my return doesn't depend on your sleeping with me. You don't have to turn yourself into a whore to make sure Lucinda gets what she wants."

This time she couldn't control her flinch. She pulled away from him and gave him another smile, this one even more strained than the first one. "I understand," she forced herself to say with fragile calm. "I won't bother you."

"The hell you won't," he snapped. "You've been bothering me for most of your life." He leaned forward, scowling at her. "You bother me by being in the same room. You bother me by breathing." Furiously he pulled her against him and ground his mouth down on hers. Roanna was too startled to react. All she could do was hang there in his hard grasp and open her mouth to the demand of his. The kiss was deep and intimate, his tongue moving against hers, and down below she could feel the iron ridge of his erection pressing into her belly.

He pushed her away as suddenly as he had grabbed her. "Now trot on back to Lucinda and tell her mission accomplished. Whether or not you tell her how you did it is up to you." He opened the car door and ushered her inside, then stood for a moment looking down at her. "And you don't understand a damn thing," he said evenly, before closing the door and striding back to his truck.

164

CHAPTER
11

When Roanna reached the long driveway to Davencourt that night, as exhausted from the second day of hard travel as she had been from the first, she groaned aloud at the lights still shining like a beacon from the big house. She'd hoped everyone would have gone to bed, so she could regroup before having to face the inquisition she knew was coming. She'd even hoped she could manage to get as much sleep as she had the night before, though that was unlikely. If she couldn't sleep, then at least she could relive those tumultuous hours, savor the memory of his naked body against hers, the kisses, the touches, the shattering, unending moments when he'd actually been inside her. And when she felt calmer, she would think about the rest of it, the hurtful things he'd said and the fact that he didn't want her again . . . But then why had he kissed her? She was too tired to think straight, so the analysis could wait.

She used the automatic opener for the garage, then braked when her headlights swept across a car already parked in her space. She sighed. Corliss again, taking advantage of Roanna's absence to park her own car inside. The detached garage had only five bays, and those bays were allotted to Lucinda, though she no longer drove herself, Roanna,

Gloria and Harlan, and Lanette and Greg, who each had a car. Brock and Corliss were supposed to park their cars outside, but Corliss had a habit of ignoring that and parking her car in any empty space.

Roanna parked her car beside Brock's and wearily climbed out, hauling her small overnight case with her. She thought about slipping up the outside stairway and around the balcony to her room on the back, but she had locked the French doors before leaving and couldn't get in that way. Instead she would go in through the kitchen and hope she could make it to the stairs unnoticed.

Luck wasn't with her. When she unlocked the kitchen door and opened it, Harlan and Gloria were both sitting at the kitchen table, demolishing thick slices of Tansy's coconut cake. Neither of them were in their nightclothes yet, which meant they had been watching television on the large set in the den.

Gloria hastily swallowed. "You couldn't find him!" she exclaimed, openly gleeful of the fact that Roanna was alone. Then she gave Roanna a sly, conspiratorial look. "Not that you tried very hard, did you? Well, *I* won't say anything. I thought Lucinda had lost her mind anyway. Why on earth would she want to bring him back here? I know Booley didn't arrest him, but everyone knew he was guilty, there was just no way to prove it—"

"I found him," Roanna interrupted. She felt fuzzy headed with fatigue, and wanted to cut the interrogation short. "He had some business to take care of, but he'll be coming home within the next two weeks."

Gloria's color faded, and she gaped openmouthed at Roanna. The cake crumbs thus revealed were unappetizing. Then she said, "Roanna, how could you be so *stupid?*" Each word rose until she was fairly shrieking. "Don't you know what you stand to lose? All of this could have been yours, but Lucinda will give it back to him, you mark my words! And what about us? Why, we could all be murdered in our beds, the way poor Jessie—"

"Jessie wasn't murdered in her bed," Roanna said tiredly.

"Don't split hairs with me, you know what I mean!"

"Webb didn't kill her."

"Well, the sheriff thought he did, and I'm sure he knows more about it than you do! We all heard him say he'd do anything to get rid of her."

"We all heard him tell her to get a divorce, too."

"Gloria's right," Harlan weighed in, knitting his bushy brows with concern. "There's no telling what he's capable of doing."

Normally Roanna didn't argue, but she was exhausted, and every nerve in her body felt raw from her encounter with Webb. "What you're really worried about," she said in a colorless voice, "is that he'll remember how you turned your backs on him when he needed our support, and tell you to find somewhere else to live."

"Roanna!" Gloria gasped, outraged. "How can you say such a thing to us? What were we supposed to do, shelter a killer from the law?"

There was nothing she could say to alter their position, and she was too tired to try any longer. Let Webb handle it when he got back. She had just enough energy to feel a flicker of interest at the prospect. If they thought he'd been intimidating before, wait until they saw what they had to deal with now. He was much harder and more forceful.

Leaving Gloria and Harlan still sputtering their rage into the coconut cake, Roanna dragged herself up the stairs. Lucinda was already in bed; she tired easily these days, another indication of her failing health, and was often asleep by nine. Morning would be plenty of time to tell her that Webb was coming home.

Roanna hoped that she would be able to get some sleep herself.

If wishes were horses . . . Several hours later, she glanced at the lighted dial of her clock and saw the hour hand creeping toward the two. Her eyes felt grainy from lack of sleep, and her mind was so dulled by fatigue she could barely think, but sleep was as far away as it had ever been.

167

She'd endured a lot of nights like this, waiting through the endless darkness for morning to come. All of the books on insomnia advised the sufferer to get out of bed, not to make the bed the site of their frustration. Roanna had already developed that habit, so the book hadn't helped any. Sometimes she read to pass the hours, sometimes she played endless card games for one, but for the most part she would sit in the darkness and wait.

That was what she was doing now, because she was too tired for anything else. She sat curled in a huge, overstuffed easy chair, large enough for two. The chair had been a Christmas present to herself five years ago, and she didn't know what she would do without it. When she did manage to doze off, as likely or not it was in the chair. In winter she would wrap up in her softest, thickest afghan and watch the night slowly creep past her windows, but this was summer and she wore only a thin, sleeveless nightgown, though the hem was tucked over her bare feet. She'd opened the French doors so she could hear the comforting sounds of the warm night. A thunderstorm was passing by in the distance; she could see the flashes of lightning, revealing dark purple clouds, but the storm was so far away that the thunder, when she heard it, was only a faint rumble.

If she had to be awake, summer nights were the best. And between insomnia and the other, she preferred insomnia.

When she slept, she never knew where she would wake up.

She didn't think she'd ever left the house. She'd always been inside, and her feet were never dirty, but still it frightened her to think of herself roaming around unknowing. She'd read about sleepwalkers, too. People could evidently negotiate stairs, drive, even carry on a conversation while still asleep. That wasn't much comfort, because she didn't want to do any of that. She wanted to wake up exactly where she'd been when she went to sleep.

If anyone had ever seen her on her nocturnal strolls, they hadn't mentioned it. She didn't think she did it every time she slept, but of course she had no way of knowing and she didn't want to alert the family to her problem. They did know she was troubled with insomnia, so perhaps if anyone did see her outside her room in the middle of the night, apparently perfectly awake, they assumed she was having trouble sleeping and forgot about it.

If it became known that she walked in her sleep . . . She didn't like to think ill of people without proof, but she didn't think she would trust several members of the household if they knew she was so vulnerable. The possibility for mischief was too great, especially with Corliss. In some ways Corliss reminded Roanna a lot of Jessie, though the relationship was only that of second cousin, which meant they didn't share a lot of genetic material. Jessie had been cooler of thought but hotter of temper. Corliss didn't plan, she acted on impulse, and she wasn't prone to temper tantrums. For the most part she seemed restless and unhappy, and liked to make other people unhappy. Whatever it was she wanted out of life, she hadn't gotten it.

Roanna didn't think Webb would get along with Corliss at all.

Thinking of Webb brought her back full circle to how she had begun the day, not that her thoughts had been off of him for long at any one time.

She didn't know what to think. She was no good at analyzing a man–woman relationship, because she'd never had one. All she knew was that Webb had been angry, and a little drunk. If he hadn't been drinking he probably wouldn't have put the pressure on her that he had, but the fact remained that she had fallen into bed with him without the slightest resistance. The circumstances had been humiliating, but that secret little part of her had reveled in the opportunity.

She wasn't sorry she'd done it. If nothing good ever happened to her for the rest of her life, at least she'd lain in Webb's arms and known what it was like to make love with him. The pain had been more severe than she'd imagined, but it hadn't been able to overshadow the joy she'd felt, and ultimately the satisfaction.

The tequila might account for the first time, and maybe the second, but what about the other times? Surely he'd sobered by the third time he'd reached for her, in the middle of the night, and the fourth, just before dawn. She still ached from his lovemaking, with a tenderness deep inside her body that she cherished because it reminded her of those moments.

He hadn't been a selfish lover. He might have been angry, but still he had satisfied her, sometimes more than once, before allowing himself release. His hands and mouth had been tender on her body, careful not to add to the pain she'd already experienced just in accepting him.

But then he'd slipped out of bed and left her alone in the cheap little motel, as if she were a coyote woman. Wasn't that what the wild, drinking crowd called a woman who was so ugly that, when a man woke up and looked over at her asleep on his arm, he gnawed off his own arm rather than wake her up? At least Webb had left a note. At least he *had* come back, and she hadn't been forced to get back to her rental car as best she could.

He'd said she acted like a whore for Lucinda. He'd said that she'd been a bother to him all her life, and that hurt more than the other comment. No matter what, she had always managed to hold on to the thought of those years before Jessie's death as the sweet years, because she'd had him as a friend and hero. The awful night Jessie had been killed, she'd realized that he felt sorry for her and that had nearly killed her, but still the sweet memories had been there. Now she was mortified to think she'd been fooling herself from the beginning. Kindness wasn't the same as love, patience wasn't the same as caring.

He'd made it plain that she shouldn't expect any continuance of their lovemaking when he returned to Davencourt. It had been a one-night stand, pure and simple. There was no ongoing relationship between them, except that of distant cousins.

But then he'd kissed her, and told her she didn't understand anything. He'd been unmistakably aroused; after the night she'd just spent, she was very familiar with his erections. If he didn't want her, why had he been hard?

One thing was for certain though: he'd still been angry.

She sat curled in her chair, watching the lightning and thinking of Webb, and sometime close to dawn she finally dropped into a doze.

Gloria marshaled her entire family to the breakfast table at the same time, a rare happening, but evidently she thought she needed reinforcements. After a restless night in which sleep had been as elusive as ever, Roanna had gone to Lucinda's room and given her the good news. Buoyed by that, there was more energy in Lucinda's movements that morning, more color in her face, than there had been in a long time. She lifted her eyebrows in surprise at the crowd seated at the table, then grinned and gave Roanna an I-know-what-they're-up-to wink.

Breakfast was a buffet, an efficient setup since more than two of them eating at the same time was pure chance. Roanna filled plates for Lucinda and herself and took her place at the table.

Gloria waited until they had food in their mouths before launching the beginning salvo. "Lucinda, we've all talked about it, and we wish you would reconsider this hare-brained idea to put Webb in charge of the business concerns again. Roanna has been doing a fine job, and we really don't need him."

"We?" Lucinda queried, staring down the table at her sister. "Gloria, I've been grateful for and enjoyed your company for the past ten years, but I think I need to remind you that this is Davenport business, and Roanna and I are the only Davenports here. We talked it over and agreed that we want Webb to resume his rightful place in the family."

"Webb isn't a Davenport," Gloria pointed out, pouncing on this detail. "He's a Tallant, one of *our* family. Davencourt and the Davenport money should be Roanna's. Why, it's only right that it go to her."

Anything to keep Webb out of the picture, Roanna

thought. Gloria would much prefer that her immediate family have the inheritance, but Roanna was evidently the second-best choice. Gloria figured she could manipulate and dominate Roanna, but Webb was a different story. That was the crux of the matter, she realized, not any exaggerated fear that Webb was a killer. It all came down to money, and comfort.

"As I said," Lucinda repeated, "Roanna and I are in agreement on this."

"Roanna's never been logical where Webb's concerned." Harlan weighed in on his wife's side. "We all know you can't trust her judgment in this."

Corliss leaned forward, her eyes bright as she scented trouble. "Why, that's right. Don't I remember something about Jessie catching them canoodling in the kitchen?"

Brock looked up from his breakfast and frowned at his sister. Roanna liked him best of all Gloria's brood. Brock was generally good-natured and was a steady worker. He didn't intend to stay at Davencourt forever but was using the opportunity to save as much money as he could so he could build his own house. He and his long-time girlfriend were planning to marry within the year. He was more forceful than his father, Greg, who let Lanette set the agenda for the family.

"I think that was blown all out of proportion," Brock said.

"What makes you think so?" Lanette asked, leaning forward to look at her son. Corliss smiled with satisfaction at having stirred up the waters.

"Because Webb wasn't a cheater, and I'm glad he's coming back."

Gloria and Lanette both glared at this traitor in their midst. Brock ignored them and returned to his meal.

Roanna concentrated on her own breakfast and did her best to tune out the conversation. Nothing would please Corliss more than provoking her into a response or to see her visibly upset. Corliss lacked Jessie's genius for cutting remarks, or perhaps it was Roanna's reaction that had changed, but she found Corliss merely annoying.

The verbal battering went on the entire meal, with Gloria and Harlan and Lanette taking turns coming up with what they obviously thought were good arguments against Webb's return. Greg frankly wasn't interested and left the protests to Lanette. Brock finished eating and excused himself to go to work.

Roanna concentrated on the chore of eating, saying little, and Lucinda was as immovable as a mountain. Having Webb home was more important to her than anything her sister could say, so Roanna didn't have any worries that Lucinda would change her mind.

Lucinda had lit up like a Christmas tree that morning when Roanna had given her the good news. She had asked question after question about him, how he looked, if he'd changed, what he'd said.

She had seemed undisturbed when Roanna told her that he still bore a grudge.

"Well, of course he does," Lucinda had said readily. "Webb's never been anyone's lapdog. I imagine he'll have plenty to say to me when he gets here, and it'll stick in my craw, but I guess I'll have to listen. I'm really surprised he gave in so easily, though. I *knew* you were the one who could make him listen."

He hadn't listened as much as he'd made a deal with her, and when she had followed through, he'd felt bound to do the same. For the first time, she wondered if he had expected her to flatly refuse, if he'd offered the deal without any expectation of having to keep it.

"Tell me how he looked," Lucinda said again, and Roanna described him as best she could. Was it accurate, when she saw him through eyes of love? Would others find him less dominant, less powerful? She didn't think so.

Certainly Gloria wasn't sanguine about his return. It was hypocritical of her, Roanna thought, because before Jessie's death Gloria had always made a point of fussing over Webb, declaring him her favorite nephew. But then she'd made the mistake of turning on him instead of defending him, and she knew he hadn't forgotten it.

"Where will he sleep?" Corliss drawled, interrupting her grandmother to throw another firebomb into the already volatile conversation. "I'm not giving up the suite, even if it did used to be his."

It had the opposite effect of what she'd expected. Silence fell around the table. After Jessie's death, Lucinda had eventually roused herself to have the suite completely redone, from the carpets to the ceilings. When Lanette and her family moved in, Corliss had immediately claimed the suite as her own, carelessly remarking that it didn't bother her at all to sleep there. It was typical of her callousness that she could even think of Webb reclaiming his old quarters.

Nevertheless, Lucinda's suite was the only one that equaled it in size. Gloria and Harlan occupied a smaller set of rooms, as did Lanette and Greg. Roanna's room was just one room, a spacious one, but not a suite. Brock's room was the same. There were four remaining single bedrooms. It was a picayune problem, but status was a subtle thing. Roanna knew Webb wasn't fixated on it, but he did realize the implications and how to use the symbols of status in order to dominate.

"Even if he doesn't want it, he may not like anyone else sleeping there," Lanette said, eyeing her daughter with a troubled expression.

Corliss scowled. "I'm not giving up my suite!"

"You will if Webb says you will," Lucinda said firmly. "I doubt he'll care, but I want it understood that what he says goes, without any argument. Is that clear?"

"No!" Corliss said petulantly, flinging her napkin to the table. "He killed his wife! It isn't fair that he can just waltz back in here and take over—"

Lucinda's voice cracked like a whip. "Another thing I want understood is that Webb did *not* kill Jessie. If I hear such a thing mentioned again, I will ask the person who said it to leave this house immediately. We didn't support him when he needed it most, and I'm deeply ashamed of myself. He *will* be welcomed back into his home, or I'll know why."

Silence followed this flat statement. To Roanna's sure knowledge, this was the first time Lucinda had ever said anything about evicting any of the current residents of Davencourt. Family was so important to her that her threat demonstrated how strongly she felt about Webb's return. For guilt or for love, or for both, Webb had her unqualified support.

Satisfied that her point had been taken, Lucinda daintily patted her napkin to her mouth. "The bedroom situation is difficult. What do you think, Roanna?"

"Let Webb decide when he gets here," Roanna replied. "We can't anticipate what he'll want."

"That's true. It's just that I want everything to be perfect for him."

"I don't think that's possible. He would probably prefer that we carry on as normal and not make a fuss."

"We're hardly likely to throw a party," Gloria sniped. "I can't think what everyone in town is going to say."

"Nothing, if they know what side their bread is buttered on," Lucinda said. "I'll begin immediately making it clear to our friends and associates that if they value our continued friendship, they'll make certain Webb is treated politely."

"Webb, Webb, Webb," Corliss said violently. "What makes him so special? What about *us?* Why don't you leave everything to Brock, if you're so certain that Roanna can't handle things? We're just as much kin to you as Webb is!"

She jumped up and ran from the room, leaving silence behind. Even Gloria, who generally had the hide of a rhinoceros, looked uncomfortable at such a blatantly materialistic outburst.

Roanna forced herself to eat one more bite before giving up the effort. It looked as if Webb's "welcome" was going to be even more strained than his departure had been.

175

CHAPTER
12

*T*en days later, Webb walked in the front door as if he owned the place, which to all intents and purposes he did.

It was eight o'clock in the morning, and the sunlight poured brilliantly through the windows, giving the cream-colored tiles in the foyer a mellow golden glow. Roanna was just coming down the stairs. She had a nine o'clock meeting with their broker, who was driving in from Huntsville, and was going to go over the particulars with Lucinda prior to the broker's arrival. She had already dressed for the meeting, in a summer-weight peach silk sheath with a matching tunic jacket, and afterward she was scheduled for a county commissioner's meeting. Beige snakeskin pumps were on her feet, and creamy pearl earrings dangled from her ears. She seldom wore jewelry other than her wristwatch, but her sorority sisters had taught her the value of wearing good, understated pieces for business occasions.

The front door opened, and she paused on the stairs, momentarily blinded by the dazzling sunlight reflected on the polished tiles. She blinked at the dark figure whose wide shoulders and wide-brimmed hat filled most of the doorway. Then he stepped inside and closed the door, letting a

176

leather satchel drop to the floor, and her heart nearly stopped as realization dawned.

It had been ten days since he'd sent her home, and he hadn't sent advance word of his arrival. She had begun to fear that he wouldn't come after all, though Webb had always kept his word before. Maybe he'd decided the Davenports weren't worth the trouble; she wouldn't have blamed him if he had.

But he was here, taking off his hat and looking around with narrowed eyes as if assessing the changes made during the gap of ten years. They were few, but she had the feeling he noted every one. His gaze even lingered momentarily on the carpet that covered the stairs. When he'd left, it had been beige; now it was oatmeal, with a thicker and tighter weave.

The physical impact of his presence nearly staggered her. To see him standing there with the same natural assumption of authority, as if he'd never left, gave her an eerie sense of time having stood still.

But the differences in him were sharp. It wasn't just that he was older or that he was dressed in jeans and boots instead of linen slacks and loafers. Before, he had tempered the force of his personality with southern good-old-boy geniality, the way business was done down here. Now, however, he tempered it with nothing. It was there, sharp and hard, and he didn't give a damn if anyone didn't like it.

Her chest felt oddly restricted, and she struggled to breathe. She had seen him naked, had lain naked in his arms. He'd sucked her nipples, penetrated her. The sense of unreality made her dizzy again. In the week and a half since she had seen him, their lovemaking had begun to seem like a dream, but at the sight of him, her body began throbbing anew as if he had just withdrawn from her and her flesh still tingled from the contact.

She found her voice. "Why didn't you call? Someone would have met you at the airport. You did fly in, didn't you?"

177

"Yesterday. I rented a car at the airport. Mother and I spent the night in Huntsville with Aunt Sandra, then drove back this morning."

The intense green gaze was on her now, taking inventory of the suit and pearls, perhaps comparing the sleek stylishness of her clothes with the fashion failure she'd been as a teenager. Or perhaps he was comparing her now to the naked woman who had writhed beneath him, screaming as he brought her to climax. He'd rejected her fast enough, so the vision couldn't have been an enticing one.

She flushed hotly, then felt the color fade as fast as it had come.

She couldn't continue to stand there like an idiot. Carefully regulating her breathing, Roanna came down the last few steps to pause at his side. "Lucinda's in the study. We were going to go over some papers, but I'm sure she'll want to talk to you instead."

"I came back to take care of business," he said briefly, already striding down the hall to the study. "Bring me up to speed. The homecoming party can wait."

Somehow she kept her unruffled facade in place as she followed him. She didn't throw her arms around him, brokenly crying, "You're home, you're home," though that had been her first impulse. She didn't shriek with joy or cry. She merely said to his back, "I'm glad you came. Welcome home."

Lucinda seldom sat at the huge desk that had been her husband's, finding the overstuffed sofa more comfortable to her old bones. She was there now, leafing through several printouts of recent stock performances. She looked up when Webb entered, and Roanna, right behind him, saw the bewilderment in the faded blue eyes as she stared at this big, rough stranger who had invaded her domain. Then she blinked, and recognition dawned as brilliantly as the sunrise, bringing with it a flush of excitement that chased away the grayness of ill health. She struggled to her feet, printouts scattering across the thick Aubusson rug.

"Webb! Webb!"

This was the enthusiastic, tearfully gleeful welcome Roanna had been longing to give him and couldn't. Lucinda rushed toward him with her hands outheld, either not seeing or ignoring his shuttered expression. He didn't open his arms to her, but that didn't stop her from throwing her own arms around him and hugging him tightly, her eyes swimming with tears.

Roanna turned toward the door, intending to give them some privacy; if she and Webb had had a special relationship when she was younger, at least in her own mind, he had definitely had a strong, special relationship with Lucinda that rivaled his feelings for his mother. Even though Webb had come back for Lucinda's sake, there were hard feelings between them that needed to be settled.

"No, stay," Webb said when he noticed Roanna's movement. He put gentle hands on Lucinda's fragile old arms and eased her away but continued to hold her as he looked down at her. "We'll talk later," he promised. "For now, I have a lot of catching up to do. We can start with those." He nodded to the papers on the carpet.

If there was anything Lucinda understood, it was the concept of taking care of business. She wiped her eyes and nodded briskly. "Of course. Our broker will be here at nine for a meeting. Roanna and I have made it a practice of going over our stock performances beforehand, so we are in agreement on any actions before he arrives."

He nodded and bent down to pick up the papers. "Are we still using Lipscomb?"

"No, dear, he died, about . . . oh, three years ago, wasn't it, Roanna? Heart trouble ran in his family, you know. Our broker now is Sage Whitten, of the Birmingham Whittens. We've been pleased with him, for the most part, but he does tend to be conservative."

Roanna saw the wry expression cross Webb's face as he readjusted to the nuances of southern business, where everything was tinged with personal information and family relationships. Probably he had become accustomed to a much more straightforward method of doing things.

He was already studying the papers in his hand as he strolled over to the desk and started to drop into the massive leather chair. He halted and gave Roanna an inquiring glance, as if checking her reaction to this abrupt takeover of both territory and authority.

She didn't know whether to cry or shout. She had never really enjoyed business but had nevertheless staked out her own territory. Because this was the only thing in her life for which she had ever been needed, by Lucinda or anyone else, she had worked doggedly to understand and master the concepts and applications. With Webb's return she was losing that territory, and her usefulness. On the other hand, it would be a relief not to have to sit through any more interminable meetings or deal with businessmen and politicians who questioned her decisions with barely veiled condescension. She was glad to be rid of the duty but had no idea how she was going to replace it.

She allowed none of her ambivalence to show in her expression, however, maintaining the blank wall of indifference she presented to the world. Lucinda resumed her seat on the sofa and Roanna walked over to one of the file cabinets to extract a thick folder.

The fax machine beeped and began to whir as a document printed. Webb glanced at it, then at the rest of the electronic equipment that had been installed since he'd left. "Looks like we're on the information highway."

"It was either that or spend most of my time traveling," Roanna replied. She indicated the computer on the desk. "We have two discrete systems. This computer and printer are for our private records. The other one"—she pointed to the electronic setup in the corner, arranged on a custom-built oak computer desk—"is for communication." The second computer was hooked up to a modem. "We have the dedicated fax line, e-mail, and two laser printers. I'll show you the programs any time you want. There's also a laptop for traveling."

"Even Loyal is on computer now," Lucinda said, smiling. "The bloodlines are thoroughly cross-referenced, and his files include breeding times, results, medical history, and identification tattoos. He'd as proud of the system as he would be if it had four legs and neighed."

He glanced at Roanna. "Do you still ride as much as before?"

"There isn't time."

"You'll have more time now."

She hadn't thought of this benefit to Webb's return, and her heart gave an excited leap. She missed the horses with painful intensity, but her statement had been the flat truth: there simply hadn't been time. She rode when she could, which was enough to keep her muscles accustomed to the exercise, but not nearly enough to satisfy her. For now she had to devote herself to the intricacies of handing over the reins to Webb, but soon—soon!—she would be able to begin helping Loyal again.

"If I know you," Webb said lazily, "you're already planning to spend your days in the stable. Don't think you're going to dump everything in my lap and play hooky. I'll have my hands full with all this and my Arizona properties too, so you're still going to have to handle some of the work."

Work with Webb? She hadn't considered that he'd want her around, or that she would still be of any use. Her heart gave that little leap again at the prospect of being with him every day.

He concentrated then on studying the diagrams and analysis of stock performances and considering the projections. By the time Sage Whitten arrived, Webb knew exactly where they stood in the stock market.

Mr. Whitten had never met Webb before, but by his startled expression when he was introduced, he'd heard the gossip. If he was dismayed by Lucinda's explanation that Webb would henceforth be handling all the Davenport concerns, he hid it well. But no matter what people suspected, Webb Tallant had never been charged with the murder of his wife, and business was business.

The meeting was concluded faster than usual. Scarcely

had Mr. Whitten left than Lanette breezed into the study. "Aunt Lucinda, there's a bag of some sort in the foyer. Did Mr. Whitten—?" She stopped dead, staring at Webb seated behind the desk.

"The bag belongs to me." He scarcely glanced up from the computer, where he was reviewing the history of a stock's dividends. "I'll take it up later."

Lanette's cheeks were blanched, but she rallied with a forced laugh. "Webb! I didn't know you'd arrived. No one told us you were expected today."

"I wasn't."

"Oh. Well, welcome home." Her tone was as false as her laugh. "I'll tell Mama and Daddy. They've just finished breakfast, and I know they'll want to welcome you themselves."

Webb's eyebrows lifted sardonically. "Is that so?"

"I'll get them," she said, and fled.

"About the bag." Webb leaned back in the chair and swiveled so he was facing Lucinda, who was still on the sofa. "Where do I put it?"

"Wherever you want," Lucinda firmly replied. "Your old suite has been completely redecorated. Corliss has taken it over, but if you want it she can move into another room."

He rejected the offer with a slight shake of his head. "I suppose Gloria and Harlan have one of the other suites, and Lanette and Greg the fourth one." He slanted an unreadable look at Roanna. "You, of course, are still in your old room on the back."

He seemed to disapprove of that, but Roanna couldn't imagine why. Left uncertain of what to say, she said nothing.

"And Brock has one of the regular bedrooms on the left side," Lucinda said, confirming his supposition. "It isn't a problem, though. I've been considering what can be done, and it would be a simple matter to connect two of the remaining bedrooms by opening a door between them, and converting one of the rooms into a sitting room. The remodeling could be done within a week."

182

"That isn't necessary. I'll take one of the bedrooms on the back. The one next to Roanna will do fine. It still has a king-size bed, doesn't it?"

"All of the rooms have king beds now, except Roanna's."

He gave her a hooded look. "Don't you like big beds?"

The motel bed where they'd made love had been a double. It should have been too small for the two of them, but when one person was lying on top of the other it reduced the need for space. Roanna barely controlled a blush. "I don't need anything bigger." She glanced at her watch and gratefully got to her feet when she saw the time. "I have to go to the county commissioner's meeting, then I'm having lunch with the hospital administrator in Florence. I'll be back by three."

She leaned over to kiss the wrinkled cheek Lucinda presented to her. "Drive carefully," Lucinda said, as she always did.

"I will." There was an element of escape in her departure, and from the way Webb was looking at her, she was sure he'd noticed it as well.

After lunch, Webb and Lucinda returned to the study. He had endured Gloria and Harlan's effusive, embarrassingly false welcomes, ignored Corliss's sulky bad manners, and been fussed over by Tansy and Bessie. It was plain as hell that only Roanna and Lucinda had wanted him back; the rest of his family obviously wished he'd stayed in Arizona. The reason for that was pretty plain, too: they'd been mooching off Lucinda for years and were afraid he'd boot them out on their asses. It was a thought. Oh, not Gloria and Harlan. As much as he knew he'd dislike having them around, they were in their seventies, and the reasons he'd given Roanna ten years ago for their moving in were even more valid now. But as for the others . . .

He didn't plan to do anything right away. He didn't know the details of their individual situations, and it was a lot easier to get his facts straight before he acted than it would be to repair the damage done by a wrong decision.

"I suppose you want to have your say," Lucinda said

183

crisply, taking her seat on the sofa. "God knows you deserve it. This is your chance to get it off your chest, so go to it. I'll sit here, listen, and keep my mouth shut."

She was as indomitable as ever in spirit, he thought, but dangerously frail. When she'd hugged him, he'd felt the fragility of her brittle bones, seen the crepey thinness of her skin. Her color wasn't good, and her energy level was low. He'd known, from his letters from Yvonne, that Lucinda's health wasn't good these days, but he hadn't realized the imminence of her death. It was a matter of months; he doubted she would even see spring.

She'd been a cornerstone of his life. She had let him down when he'd needed her, but now she was willing to face his ire. It was a measure of her strength that he had tested his budding manhood against her, measured his growth by how well he held his own with her. Damn her, he wasn't ready to let her go.

He hitched one hip onto the edge of the desk. "I'll get to that," he said evenly, then continued with soft violence: "But first I want to know what in *hell* y'all have done to Roanna."

Lucinda sat in silence for a long time, Webb's accusation hovering in the air between them. She stared out the window, looking out over the sweep of sundrenched land, dotted here and there with the shadows of the fat, fluffy clouds drifting overhead. Davenport land, as far as she could see. She had always taken comfort in this vista, and she still loved to see it, but now that her life was nearing an end she was finding other things of far more importance.

"I didn't notice at first," she finally said, her gaze still far away. "Jessie's death was—well, we'll talk about that later. I was so preoccupied with my own grief that I didn't notice Roanna until she'd almost drifted away."

"Drifted away, how?" His tone was hard, sharp.

"She nearly died," Lucinda said baldly. Her chin trembled, and she sternly controlled it. "I'd always thought Jessie was the one who so desperately needed to be loved, to

184

make up for her circumstances . . . I didn't see that Roanna needed love even more, but she didn't demand it the way Jessie did. Strange, isn't it? I loved Jessie from the cradle, but she would never have helped me the way Roanna has, or become as important to me. Roanna's more than my right hand; these past few years, I couldn't have managed without her."

Webb waved all of that away, focusing on the one statement that had his attention. "How did she nearly die?" The thought of Roanna dying shocked him to the bone, and he felt a cold sense of dread when he remembered her guilty, miserable expression the day of Jessie's funeral. She hadn't tried to kill herself, had she?

"She stopped eating. She never ate much anyway, so I didn't notice for a long time, almost too long. Everything was so disrupted, there were seldom any routine meals, and I suppose I thought she was snacking at odd hours the way we all were. She stayed in her room a lot, too. She didn't do it deliberately," Lucinda explained softly. "She just . . . lost interest. When you left, she totally withdrew. She blames herself for everything, you know."

"Why?" Webb asked. Roanna had told him she hadn't deliberately caused trouble, but maybe she really had, and confessed to Lucinda.

"It was a long time before she could talk about it, but several years ago she told me what happened in the kitchen, that she caught you by surprise when she impulsively kissed you. She didn't know Jessie was coming down, and of course, it was just like Jessie to make a huge scene, but to Roanna's way of thinking she caused all the trouble with that kiss. If she hadn't kissed you, you and Jessie wouldn't have argued, you wouldn't have been blamed for Jessie's death, and you wouldn't have left town. With you gone . . ." Lucinda shook her head. "She's always loved you so much. We laughed about it when she was little, thought it was hero worship and puppy love, but it wasn't, was it?"

"I don't know." But he did, he thought. Roanna had never had any self-protection where he was concerned. Hell, she'd never been good at any kind of subterfuge. Her feelings had been right out in the open, her pride as totally vulnerable as her heart. Her adoration had always been there, like a piece of sunshine in his life, and he'd depended on its being there though he seldom paid much attention to it. Like the sunshine, it was something he'd taken for granted. That was why he'd been so damn mad when he thought she had betrayed him just to get back at Jessie.

Lucinda gave him a shrewd look that told him she wasn't taken in by his denial. "After David and Karen died, you and I became the centerposts of Roanna's life. She needed our love and support, but for the most part we didn't give it to her. No, let me rephrase that, because most of the blame is mine: *I* didn't give her my love and support. As long as you were here to love her, though, she got by. When you left, there was no one here for her, and she gave up. She was almost gone before I noticed," Lucinda said sadly. A tear rolled down her wrinkled cheek, and she wiped it away. "She was down to eighty pounds. Eighty pounds! She's five-seven; she should weigh at least a hundred and thirty. I can't describe to you how pitiful she looked. But one day I saw her, really *saw* her, and realized that I had to do something or I'd lose her, too."

Webb couldn't say anything. He stood up and walked over to the window, his fists jammed deep into his pockets. His shoulders were rigid as he stood with his back to Lucinda, and it was hard for him to breathe. Waves of panic washed over him. My God, she'd almost died, and he hadn't known anything about it.

"Just saying 'You need to eat' wouldn't have done the trick," Lucinda continued, the words spilling out of her as if she'd held them in for too long, and she had to share the pain. "She needed a reason for living, something to hold on to. So I told her I needed her help."

She stopped and swallowed hard before resuming. "No one had ever said they needed her. I hadn't realized . . . Anyway, I told her I couldn't manage without her, that everything was too much for me to handle by myself. I didn't realize how true that was," Lucinda said wryly. "She pulled herself back. It was a long fight, and for a while I was terrified that I'd left it too late, but she did it. It was a year before her health recovered enough that she could go to college, a year before she stopped waking us up at night with her screams."

"Screams?" Webb asked. "Nightmares?"

"About Jessie." Lucinda's voice was soft, shredded with pain. "She found her, you know. And that was the way she screamed, the same sound, as if she'd just walked in and—and stepped in Jessie's blood." The words trembled, then firmed as if Lucinda wouldn't allow that weakness in herself. "The nightmares developed into insomnia, as if staying awake was the only way she could escape them. She still suffers from it, and some nights she doesn't sleep at all. She catnaps, for the most part. If you see her dozing during the day, whatever you do, don't wake her up because that's probably the only sleep she's had. I've made it a rule that no one wakes her, for any reason. Corliss is the only one who does. She'll drop something or let a door slam, and she always pretends it's an accident."

Webb turned from the window. His eyes were like green frost. "She might do it once more, but that'll be the last time," he said flatly.

Lucinda gave a faint smile. "Good. I hate to say it of my own family, but Corliss has a mean, trashy streak in her. It'll be good for Roanna, having you here again."

But he hadn't been here when she'd needed him most, Webb thought. He'd walked out, leaving her to face the horror, and the nightmares, alone. What was it Lucinda had said? Roanna had stepped in Jessie's blood. He hadn't known, hadn't thought about the strain she must have been under. His wife had been murdered and he'd been accused of the crime; he'd been undergoing his own crisis, and he'd assigned her stress to guilt. He should have known better, because he'd been closer to Roanna than anyone else.

He remembered the way she had ignored the united condemnation of the town and slipped her little hand into his at Jessie's funeral, to give him comfort and support. Considering the wild tales that had been going around about Jessie catching him screwing Roanna, it had taken a great deal of courage for her to approach him. But she'd done it, not counting the cost to her reputation, because she'd thought he needed her. Instead of squeezing her hand, doing any little thing at all to show his trust in her, he'd rebuffed her.

She'd been there for him, but he hadn't be there for her. She had survived, but at what cost?

"I didn't recognize her at first," he mused almost absently. His gaze never left Lucinda's. "It isn't just that she's older. She's all shut down inside."

"That was how she coped. She's stronger; I think it frightened her when she realized how weak and ill she had become. She's never let herself get in that condition again. But she coped by shutting everything out, and holding herself in. It's as if she's afraid to feel too much, so she doesn't let herself feel anything. I can't reach her, and God knows I've tried, but that's my fault, too."

Lucinda squared her shoulders as if settling an old burden, one she had become so used to that she seldom noticed it now. "When she found Jessie and screamed, we all went running into the bedroom and found her standing over the body. Gloria jumped to the conclusion that Roanna had killed Jessie, and that's what she and Harlan told the sheriff. Booley had a deputy guarding her while he checked it out. We were all on one side of the room, and Roanna was on the other, all by herself except for the deputy. I'll never forget the way she looked at us, as if we had walked up and stabbed her. I should have gone to her, the way I should have gone to you, but I didn't. She hasn't called me Grandmother since," Lucinda said softly. "I can't reach her. She goes through the motions, but she doesn't even care about Davencourt. When I told her I was going to change my will to benefit you, if she could get you to come home, she didn't even blink. I wanted her to argue, to get angry, to *care,* but she doesn't." The incomprehensibility of it rang in Lucinda's voice, for how could anyone not care about her beloved Davencourt?

Then she sighed. "Do you remember how she was always like a windup toy that never wound down? Running up and down the stairs, banging doors, yelling . . . I swear, she had no sense of decorum at all. Well, now I'd give anything to see her skip, just once. She was always saying the wrong thing at the wrong time, and now she hardly talks at all. It's impossible to tell what she's thinking."

"Does she laugh?" he asked in a rough tone. He missed her laughter, the infectious giggle when she was up to some mischief, the belly laughs when he told her jokes, the joyous chuckle as she watched foals romping in the pastures.

Lucinda's eyes were sad. "No. She almost never smiles, and she doesn't laugh at all. She hasn't laughed in ten years."

189

CHAPTER

13

*R*oanna glanced at her watch. The county commissioner's meeting was taking longer than usual, and she would have to leave soon or be late for her lunch in Florence. The Davenports had no official authority in county matters, but it was almost traditional that a family representative attend the meetings. Davenport support, or lack of it, often meant life or death to county projects.

When Roanna had first begun attending the meetings in Lucinda's stead, she had been largely ignored, or at best treated to a figurative pat on the head. She had merely listened, and reported to Lucinda; to a large degree, that was still what she did. But Lucinda, when she had taken action on the matters that interested her, had made a point of saying, "Roanna thinks" or "Roanna's impression was," and soon the commissioners had realized that they had better pay attention to the solemn young woman who seldom spoke. Lucinda hadn't lied; Roanna did relay her thoughts and impressions. She had always been observant but so active that she had often missed details, much as a speeder can see a highway sign but pass it too fast to read the message. Now Roanna was still and silent, and her brown eyes roamed from face to face, absorbing nuances of expression, tones, reactions. All of this went straight back to Lucinda, who then made her decisions based on Roanna's impressions.

Now that Webb had returned, he would be attending the meetings just as he had used to do. This was likely the last time she would be sitting here, listening and assessing, another place where her usefulness was at an end. In some distant part of her psyche she was aware of hurt, and fear, but she refused to allow them to surface.

The meeting was finally dawdling to an end. She checked her watch once again and saw that she had perhaps five minutes before she *had* to leave or be late. Normally she took the time to chat with everyone, but today she had time only for a quick word with the commissioner.

He was coming toward her, a short, stocky, balding man with a deeply lined face. The creases rearranged themselves into a smile as he approached her in her usual position close to the back of the room. "How are you today, Roanna?"

"Fine, thank you, Chet," Roanna replied, thinking that she might as well tell him about Webb's return. "And you?"

"Can't complain. Well, I could, but my wife tells me no one's interested in listening." He laughed at his own joke, his eyes twinkling. "And how's Miss Lucinda feeling?"

"Much better, now that Webb's home," she said calmly.

He gaped at her in astonishment, and for a second, dismay was written plainly on his face. He blurted, "My God, what are ya'll going to do?" before the rest of her statement sank in and he realized that commiseration wasn't appropriate. He turned beet red and started to sputter in his attempt to retrench. "I—ah, that is—"

Roanna lifted her hand to stop his verbal stumbling. "He'll be taking up the reins again, of course," she said as if Webb's return was the most natural thing in the world. "It will take him a few weeks to review everything, but I'm certain he'll be contacting you soon."

The commissioner sucked in a deep breath. He looked faintly ill, but he had recovered his composure. "Roanna, I don't think that's such a good idea. You've been handling things just fine for Miss Lucinda, and folks around here will be more comfortable with you—"

Roanna's eyes were very clear and direct. "Webb is taking over again," she said softly. "It would distress Lucinda if anyone chose not to do business with us, but of course that's their choice."

His windpipe bobbed as he swallowed. Roanna had just made it very plain that anyone who didn't accept Webb would find themselves without Davenport support or patronization. She never got angry, never yelled, never insisted on a point, and seldom even voiced an opinion, but folks in the county had learned not to discount the influence this somber-eyed woman had with Lucinda Davenport. Moreover, most people liked Roanna; it was as simple as that. No one would want an open rift with the Davenports.

"This will probably be the last monthly meeting that I'll attend," she continued.

"Don't be too sure of that," a deep, lazy voice said from the doorway just behind her.

Startled, Roanna turned to face Webb as he stepped into the room. "What?" she said. What was he doing here? He hadn't even changed clothes. Had he been so afraid she would mess up something that he'd rushed down to the commissioner's meeting without even taking the time to unpack?

"Hello, Chet," Webb was saying easily, holding out his hand to the commissioner.

The commissioner's face turned red. He hesitated, then his politician's instincts took over and he shook Webb's hand. "Webb! Speak of the devil! Roanna was just telling me you were back at Davencourt. You're looking good, real good."

"Thanks. You're looking prosperous yourself."

Chet patted his belly and gave a hearty laugh. "Too prosperous! Willadean says I'm on a seafood diet—I eat everything I see!"

People milling about in the room had noticed Webb, and

an agitated buzz was growing in volume. Roanna glanced at Webb, and the glint in his green eyes told her that he was well aware of the stir his presence was causing and wasn't the least concerned about it.

"Don't think you're off the hook," he said to Roanna, turning a smile on her. "Just because I'm home doesn't mean you get to goof off from now on. We'll probably come to the meetings together."

Despite her shock, Roanna nodded gravely.

Webb looked at his watch. "Don't you have a lunch engagement in Florence? You're going to be late if you don't hurry."

"I'm on my way. 'Bye, Chet."

"See you at the next meeting," the commissioner said, still in that falsely jovial tone as she maneuvered past him and into the hallway.

"I'll walk you to your car." Webb nodded at the commissioner and turned to fall into step with Roanna.

She was acutely aware of him just at her elbow as they walked down the hall. His tall form easily dominated her even though she was wearing high heels. She didn't know what to think about what had just happened, so she didn't let herself jump to any conclusions. Maybe he truly intended they should work together, maybe he'd just been saying that to smooth the way. Only time would tell, and she wouldn't let herself hope. If she didn't hope, then she couldn't be disappointed.

A wave of double takes followed them down the hall as people recognized Webb and turned to stare. Roanna walked faster, wanting to get out of the building before a confrontation could develop. She reached the end of the hall, and Webb's arm extended in front of her to open the door. She felt the brush of his body against her back.

They exited into the glare and sticky humidity of the hot summer morning. Roanna fished her keys out of purse and slipped her sunglasses on her nose. "What made you come to town?" she asked. "I wasn't expecting you."

"I figured now was as good a time to break the ice as any."

His long legs easily kept up with her hurried pace. "Slow down, it's too hot for a race."

Obediently she slacked her pace. Her car was parked close to the end of a row, and if she hurried all that distance, she would be drenched in sweat by the time she got to it. "Were you serious about the meetings?" she asked.

"Dead serious." He had put on his own sunglasses, and the dark lenses kept her from reading his expression. "Lucinda has been singing your praises. You already know what's going on, so I'd be a fool if I didn't use you."

One thing Webb wasn't, particularly where business was concerned, was a fool. Roanna felt a wave of dizziness at the thought of actually working with him. She had been prepared for anything, she'd thought, from being ignored to being evicted, but she hadn't considered that he would want her help.

They reached her car, and Webb plucked the keys from her hand. He unlocked the door and opened it, then handed the keys back. She waited a moment for the wave of pent-up heat in the car to dissipate, then slipped behind the wheel. "Be careful," he said, and closed the door.

Roanna glanced in the rearview mirror as she pulled out of the parking lot. He was striding back toward the building; perhaps he was parked up that way, or he was going back inside. She let her gaze move hungrily over that wide, muscled back and long legs, just for a second's delight, then she forced her attention back to her driving and merged into traffic.

Webb unlocked his own car and got inside. The impulse that had sent him into town had been a simple one, but strong. He had wanted to see Roanna. That was all, just see her. After the disturbing things Lucinda had told him, the old protective instincts had taken over and he'd wanted to see for himself that she was all right.

She was, of course, more than all right. He had seen for himself how deftly she had handled Chet Forrister, her composure unruffled by the commissioner's opposition—

and on Webb's own behalf. Now he understood exactly what Lucinda had been telling him when she'd said Roanna was stronger, that she'd changed. Roanna no longer needed him to fight her battles.

The realization left him feeling oddly bereft.

He should have been glad, for her sake. The young Roanna had been so painfully vulnerable, an easy target for anyone who wanted to take a verbal potshot at her tender emotions. He had constantly been stepping in to shield her, and his reward had been her unflagging adoration.

Now she had forged her own armor. She was cool and self-contained, almost emotionless, keeping people at a distance so their slings and arrows couldn't reach her. She had paid for that armor with pain and despair, almost with her own life, but the steel was strong. She still suffered, in the form of insomnia and nightmares when she did manage to sleep, but she handled her own problems now.

When he had walked into Davencourt today and seen her standing there on the stairs, wearing that elegantly understated silk dress and creamy pearls, with her dark chestnut hair in a sleek, sophisticated style, he had been rendered almost speechless at the contrast between the rowdy, untidy girl she had been and the classy, classic woman she was now.

She was still Roanna, but she was different. When he looked at her now, he didn't see the urchin with the unruly tongue, the awkward teenager. He looked at her and thought of the slender body beneath the silk dress, the texture of her skin that rivaled the dress in luxurious silkiness, the way her nipples had peaked at his slightest touch during those long hours in the motel in Nogales.

He had covered her naked body with his own, pulled her legs wide open, and taken her virginity. Even now, sitting in the contained, roasting heat of the car, he shivered with the power of the memory. God, he remembered every little detail—how it had felt pushing into her, the hot, soft tightness of her body as he sheathed himself inside her. He remembered how delicate she had felt beneath him, her smaller body dominated by his size, his weight, his strength. He had wanted to cradle her in his arms, protect her, soothe her, pleasure her—everything but stop. There was no way he could have stopped.

Those memories had been driving him crazy for the past ten days, depriving him of sleep, interrupting his work. When he'd seen her again today, he had been shaken by a wave of pure possessiveness. She was his. She was his, and he wanted her. He wanted her so much that his hands had started shaking. It had taken all of his self-control not to climb the stairs to where she stood, take her arm, and march her the rest of the way upstairs to one of the bedrooms, any bedroom, where he could lift her skirt and bury himself inside her once more.

He had restrained himself for one reason, and one reason only. Roanna had carefully built her inner fortress, but every fortress had a weakness, and he knew exactly what her weakness was.

Him.

She could protect herself against everyone but him.

She hadn't tried to hide it, or deny it. She had told him with devastating honesty that all he had to do was snap his fingers and she would come running. She would have gone up those stairs with him and let him do anything he wanted to her.

Webb drummed his fingers on the hot steering wheel. It seemed there was one more dragon Roanna needed him to fight, and that was his own sexual desire for her.

He had told her that he would come home if she would let him use her sexually, and she hadn't hesitated. If that was what he wanted, then she would do it. If he needed a sexual outlet, she would be available. She would do it for Lucinda, for Davencourt, for him—but what about herself?

He knew he could walk into Roanna's bedroom at any time and have her, and the temptation was already eating at him. But he didn't want Roanna to give herself to him out of guilt, or duty, or even because of her misguided hero worship. He was no hero, damn it, he was a man. He wanted her to want him as a man, male to her female. If she slipped into his bed merely because she was horny and wanted the relief he could give her, he would be delighted even by that, because it was simple and uncomplicated by other people's motives, or even her own.

God, what about his own motives?

Sweat dripped into his eye, stinging, and with a muffled curse he turned the ignition switch, starting the motor so the air conditioner would blast into life. He was going to give himself a heat stroke, sitting in a closed car in the middle of summer while he tried to sort through a tangle of emotions.

He loved Roanna; he'd loved her all her life, but as a sister, with an amused, protective indulgence.

He hadn't been prepared for the force and heat of the physical desire that had flared when she had thrown her arms around his neck and kissed him, ten long years ago. It had come from nowhere, like swirling gases that had been compressed until they reached critical mass, then exploded into a white hot star. It had shaken him, made him feel guilty. Everything about it had felt wrong. She'd been too young; he'd always thought of her as a sister; he'd been married, for God's sake. The guilt in that situation had been all his. Even though his marriage had been collapsing, he *had* still been married. He'd been the experienced one; he should have gently turned the kiss into a gesture of impulsive affection, something that wouldn't have embarrassed her. Instead, he'd pulled her tighter and turned the kiss into something quite different, a deeper, adult kiss, laden with sexuality. What had happened had been his fault, not Roanna's, but she was still trying to pay the price.

Most of the original barriers to a sexual relationship between them were gone. Roanna was a woman now, he wasn't married, and he didn't feel at all brotherly toward her. But other barriers remained: the pressures of family, Roanna's own sense of duty, his pride.

He snorted at himself as he put the car in gear. God, yes, let's not forget his male pride. He didn't want her to give herself to him for Davencourt, family, any of those unimportant reasons. He wanted her to lie hot and panting beneath him for no other reason than she wanted *him*. Nothing else would do.

The bastard was back. The news was all over the county and reached the bars that night. Harper Neeley shook with rage every time Webb Tallant's name was mentioned. Tallant had gotten away with killing Jessie, and now he was back to start lording it over everyone again as if nothing had ever happened. Oh, that stupid fat-ass sheriff hadn't arrested him, said there wasn't enough evidence for a conviction, but everyone knew he'd been bought off. The Davenports and the Tallants of this world never had to pay for the shit they committed. It was the ordinary people who did time, not the la-di-dah rich folks who lived in their big, fancy house and thought the rules didn't apply to them.

Webb Tallant had bashed Jessie's head in with an andiron. He still wept when he thought about it, his beautiful Jessie with her hair all matted with blood and brains, one side of her head flattened. Somehow the bastard had found out about him and Jessie, and killed her for it. Or maybe Tallant found out that the little bun in the oven hadn't been his. Jessie had said she'd handle it, and she was a slick one if he'd ever seen one, but this time she hadn't been slick enough.

No one had ever belonged to him the way Jessie had. She'd been wild, that girl, wild and wicked, and it had excited him so much he'd nearly creamed his pants the first time she'd come on to him. She'd been excited, too, her eyes bright and hot. She'd loved the danger of it, the thrill of doing the forbidden. That first time she had been like an animal, clawing and bucking, but she hadn't come. It had taken him a while to figure it out. Jessie had liked to screw for a lot of reasons, but pleasure hadn't been one of them. She'd used her body to mess with men's heads, to gain power over them. She'd fucked him to get back at her son-of-a-bitch husband, to get back at everyone and show them she didn't give a damn. She'd never meant for anyone else to know, but *she* knew, and that was how she got her rocks off.

But once he'd figured it out, he hadn't let her get away with it. Nobody used him, not even Jessie. Especially not Jessie. He knew her the way no one else ever had or ever would, because inside she was like him.

He started her out with kinky little games, never pushing her too far at once. She'd taken to it like a cat to cream, something even a little more forbidden for her to gloat over when she was sitting up at the big house, acting like a perfect lady and laughing at how easily she fooled everybody because she'd just spent the afternoon screwing her brains out with the one man guaranteed to make them all piss in their lace drawers.

They'd had to be careful; they couldn't go to any local motel, and it wasn't always possible for her to come up with an excuse for being absent and unreachable for several hours at a time. Usually they'd just meet in the woods somewhere. They'd been in the woods when he'd decided he'd had enough of her game playing and finally showed her who was boss.

By the time he'd let her go, she'd been covered with bruises and bites, but she'd come so many times she'd barely been able to sit her horse. She'd complained bitterly about having to be careful and not let anyone see the marks on her body, but her eyes had been shining. He'd fucked her so long and so hard that he'd been pumped dry and she'd been raw, and she had loved it. Always before women had whined and blubbered when he got rough with them, but not Jessie. She came back for more, and dished out her own medicine. He'd gone home with his back clawed bloody more times than once, and every burning weal had reminded him of her and fed his hunger for more.

There'd never been another woman like his girl. She'd come back for more, too, and pushed for rougher and more kinky games, the dirtier the better. They'd gone on to butt fucking, and that had given her a real thrill, the most forbidden thing she could do with the most forbidden man. Wicked, wicked Jessie. He'd loved her so much.

There wasn't a day that had gone by that he hadn't thought about her, missed her. No other woman could turn him on the way she had.

That goddamn Webb Tallant had killed her, killed both her and the kid. Then he'd waltzed away, free as a jaybird, and left town before he could be made to pay.

But he was back.

And this time, he was going to pay.

He'd have to be careful not to be seen, but he'd sneaked around out at Davencourt enough, back when he was meeting Jessie, that he knew his way around on the property. It was big enough, hundreds of acres, that he could approach the house from any angle he chose. It had been a while since he'd been there; ten years, as a matter of fact. He'd have to make sure the old lady hadn't gotten a guard dog and that no alarm system had been installed. He knew there hadn't been one before, because Jessie had tried more than once to talk him into sneaking into her bedroom while her husband was away on a trip. She'd liked the idea of screwing him under her grandmother's roof and in her husband's bed. He'd had sense enough to refuse, but damn, it had been tempting.

Assuming there was no alarm system, there were a hundred ways to get into that old house. All those doors and windows . . . It would be child's play. He'd gotten into houses a lot better guarded than Davencourt. The fools probably felt safe, as far out of town as they were. Country folks just never got in the habit of taking the precautions that townspeople did automatically.

Oh, yes. Webb Tallant was going to pay.

CHAPTER

14

I think we'll have a welcome-home party for Webb," Lucinda mused the next day, tapping her teeth with one fingernail. "No one would dare not accept, because then I'd know exactly who they were. That way they'd be forced to be polite to him, and it would get all those uncomfortable first meetings over with at the same time."

There were moments when Roanna was forcibly reminded that, though Lucinda had married into the Davenport family over sixty years before and had, in her own mind, thoroughly become a Davenport, if you scratched the surface you found a Tallant. The Tallants were nothing if not strong-willed and audacious. They might not always be right, but it didn't always matter, either. Put them on a path and point them at a target, and they rolled over every obstacle you put in their way. Lucinda's goal was to reinstate Webb's standing in the county, and she didn't mind twisting arms to achieve that goal.

Belonging to the best circles in the Quad Cities didn't necessarily depend on how much money you had, though it helped. Some families of very modest means were acknowledged as belonging to that select social strata, by dint of having an ancestor who had actually fought in The War, and it wasn't either of the World Wars that was meant. Some of the younger set actually referred to it as the Civil War, but the more genteel called it the War of Northern Aggression, and the most genteel of all would delicately refer to the Late Unpleasantness.

Business associates would immediately see how things stood with the Davenports and would treat Webb as if nothing had ever happened. After all, he'd never been arrested, so why should his wife's death be allowed to cut into the bottom line?

Those who ruled the social calendar, however, adhered to a stricter standard. Webb would find himself uninvited to the dinners and parties where so much business was discussed, which would be a disadvantage for the Davenport interests. Lucinda cared about the money, but she cared about Webb even more, and she was determined that he wouldn't be shunned. She would invite everyone to her home, and they would come because they were her friends. She was ill, and it might be the last party she ever gave. Leave it to Lucinda to use her own approaching death as a means of getting her way. Her friends might not like it, but they would come. They would also be polite to Webb under his own roof; though it was technically still Lucinda's roof, everyone would assume that Webb had returned home to claim his inheritance, which he had, so it would soon be his. And having accepted *his* hospitality, they would then be obliged to extend their own to him.

Once that had happened, they would pretend they'd never had any doubts about him at all, and he would be welcome everywhere. After all, you could hardly vilify someone you had invited into your home. That just wasn't done.

"Are you out of your mind?" Gloria demanded. "No one will come. We'll be humiliated."

"Don't be silly. Of course people will come, they wouldn't dare not to. It went well yesterday with Mr. Whitten, didn't it, Roanna?"

"Mr. Whitten lives in *Huntsville,*" Gloria replied, saving Roanna the necessity of a reply. "What would he know?"

"He knew what happened, that much was obvious from his face. But being an intelligent man, he decided that if *we* have faith in Webb, then those horrible accusations couldn't be true. Which they weren't," Lucinda said firmly.

"I agree with Mother," Lanette said. "Think of the embarrassment."

"You always agree with her," Lucinda replied, her eyes glittering with the light of battle. She had set her course and wasn't about to be swayed from it. "If you ever disagreed, then your opinion would carry more weight, my dear. Now, if Roanna told me my party was a bad idea, I'd be a lot more likely to listen."

Gloria snorted. "As if Roanna ever disagrees with *you.*"

"Well, she does, on a regular basis. We seldom see eye to eye on every detail of a business decision. It pains me to admit that she's right more often than not."

That wasn't perhaps a blatant lie, Roanna thought, but it wasn't exactly the truth either. She never argued with Lucinda; she occasionally saw things differently, but she would simply present her case and Lucinda would make the final decision. That was a far cry from open disagreement.

The three of them turned to her, Lucinda with open triumph, Gloria and Lanette disgruntled at having her opinion valued over theirs.

"I think it should be Webb's decision," she said quietly. "He's the one who'll have to be on display."

Lucinda scowled. "True. If he isn't willing, there's no point in even talking about it. Why don't you ask him, dear. Maybe you can get his attention off that computer screen for five minutes."

They had taken a break for lunch and had finished eating but were now lingering over their iced tea. Webb had requested a couple of sandwiches and coffee while he continued to work. He'd been in the study until eleven the night before and had gotten up at six to resume his reading. Roanna knew because she had been awake at both times, silently curled in her big chair and counting down the hours. It had been a particularly bad night; she hadn't slept at all, and she was so tired now she was afraid she would fall into a deep sleep when she did go to bed. Those were the times when she was most likely to wake up somewhere else in the house and not remember how she'd gotten there.

It was Webb's presence that had unsettled her to the point she couldn't even doze. Both she and Lucinda had worked with him last night, going over reports, until Lucinda had become tired and gone to bed. After that, alone with him in the study, Roanna had become increasingly uneasy. Did he prefer not being alone with her, after what had happened? Did he think she was pushing herself at him, by staying there without Lucinda's buffering presence?

After less than an hour she had excused herself and gone to her room. She'd taken a bath to calm her frazzled nerves, then settled in her chair to read. The words on the page hadn't made sense, though; she couldn't concentrate on them. Webb was in the house. He'd moved his clothes into the room next to hers. Why had he done that? He'd made it plain, back in Nogales, that he wasn't interested in having an affair with her. There were three other bedrooms he could have used, but he'd chosen that one. The only explanation she could think of was that it simply didn't matter to him if she was next door; her proximity was of no interest, one way or the other.

She would try to stay out of his way as much as possible, she'd thought. Show him all the current files, answer any questions he had, but otherwise she wouldn't bother him.

At eleven she heard him in the room next door, saw the spill of light onto the veranda. She had reached up and turned off her lamp so he wouldn't see her own light and know she was still awake after pleading fatigue an hour and a half before. In the darkness she had leaned her head back, closed her eyes, and listened to him moving around, picturing in her mind what he was doing.

She heard the shower, and knew he was naked. Her heart thumped at the thought of his tall, steely muscled body, and her breasts tightened. She could scarcely believe that she'd actually made love with him, that she'd lost her virginity in a cheap motel room on the Mexican border, and that it was the closest to heaven she was ever likely to get. She thought of the crisp hair on his chest and the tightness of his buttocks. She remembered how his hard, hair-roughened thighs had held her own thighs spread wide, how she had dug her fingers into the deep valley of muscle down the middle of his back. For one wonderful night she'd lain in his arms and known both desire and fulfillment.

The shower cut off, and about ten minutes later the splash of light on the veranda was extinguished. Through her own open veranda doors she had heard the click as he opened his doors to let in the fresh night air. Was he still naked? Did he sleep raw, or in his underwear? Maybe he wore pajama bottoms. It struck her as odd that she had lived in the same house with him from age seven to seventeen, and didn't know if he wore anything to bed.

Then there was silence. Was he in bed, or was he standing there looking out at the peaceful night? Had he stepped out onto the veranda? He would be barefoot; she wouldn't be able to hear him. Was he standing there even now? Had he glanced to the right and noticed that her doors were open?

Finally, her nerves raw, Roanna had crept to the window and peeked out. No one, naked or otherwise, stood on the veranda enjoying the night. As quietly as possible she had closed her doors and gone back to her chair. Sleep had escaped her, though, and once again she had endured the slow passage of time.

"Roanna?" Lucinda prodded, and Roanna realized she'd been sitting there daydreaming.

Murmuring a vague apology, Roanna pushed back her chair. She had a meeting at two with the organizers of this year's W. C. Handy Festival in August, so she would just stick her head in the study door, ask Webb his opinion of Lucinda's plan, then escape upstairs to change clothes. Perhaps, by the time she returned, he would have tired of paperwork and she wouldn't have to endure another evening of exquisite torture, sitting at his elbow, listening to his deep voice, marveling at the speed with which he assimilated information—in short, reveling in his presence—while at the same time wondering if he thought she was sitting too close, or making too much of every opportunity to bend over him. Even worse, had he wished she would simply go away and get out of his hair?

When she opened the door, he looked up inquiringly from the papers in his hand. He was leaned back in his chair, the master of his space, his booted feet propped comfortably on the desk.

"I'm sorry," she blurted. "I should have knocked."

He stared at her in silence for a long moment, his dark brows drawing together over his nose. "Why?" he finally asked.

"This is yours now." Her reply was simply made, without inflection.

He took his feet off the desk. "Come in and close the door."

She did but remained standing there by the door. Webb stood and came around the desk, then leaned against the edge of it with his arms crossed over his chest and his legs stretched out. It was a negligent position, but if his body was relaxed, his gaze was sharp as it raked over her.

"You don't ever have to knock on that door," he finally said. "And let's get one thing straight right now: I'm not taking your place, I'm taking Lucinda's. You've done a good job, Ro. I told you yesterday that I'd be a fool if I shut you out of the decision-making process. Maybe you thought you'd get to spend your days with the horses now that I'm back, and you will have more time for yourself, I promise, but you're still needed here, too."

Roanna blinked, dazed by this turn of events. Despite what he'd said to her after the commissioner's meeting, she hadn't thought he had really meant it. A part of her had automatically dismissed it as the type of thing Webb had done when she was little, reassuring her to keep her from being upset, pretending that she was important to anything or anyone. She had stopped letting herself believe in fairy tales on the night she had stumbled into a pool of blood. Very likely, she had thought, she would bring Webb up to speed, and then her usefulness would be at an end. He'd handled everything by himself before—

Her mind stopped, startled. No, that wasn't true. He had taken *most* of the work on his shoulders, but Lucinda had still been involved. And that was before he'd had his property in Arizona to oversee as well. Silent joy spread through her, warming the corners of her heart that had already begun to chill as she prepared herself for being replaced. He really *did* need her.

He'd said she had done a good job. And he'd called her Ro.

He was watching her with a sharply intent gaze. "If you don't smile," he said softly, "then I can't tell if you're pleased or not."

She stared at him, perplexed, searching his face for a clue to what he really meant. Smile? Why would he want her to smile?

"Smile," he prompted. "You remember what a smile is, don't you? The corners of your mouth turn up, like this." He pushed the corners of his mouth up with his fingers, demonstrating. "It's what people do when they're happy. Do you hate paperwork, is that it? Don't you want to help me?"

Tentatively she stretched the corners of her mouth, curling them upward. It was a hesitant, fleeting little smile, barely forming before it was gone and she was regarding him solemnly once more.

But evidently that was what he'd wanted. "Good," he said, straightening from his relaxed perch on the desk. "Are you ready to get back to work?"

"I have a meeting at two. I'm sorry."

"What kind of meeting?"

"With the organizers of the Handy Festival."

He shrugged, losing interest. Webb wasn't a jazz fan.

Roanna remembered why she was there. "Lucinda sent me to ask what you think of having a welcome-home party."

He gave a short laugh, immediately realizing the implications. "She's going on the attack, huh? Are Gloria and Lanette trying to talk her out of it?"

He didn't seem to need an answer, either that or her silence was answer enough. He thought it over for all of five seconds. "Sure, why the hell not? I don't give a damn if it makes everyone uncomfortable. I stopped caring ten years ago what people think of me. If anyone thinks I'm not good enough to deal with them, then I'll take Davencourt's business elsewhere; it's up to them."

She nodded and reached for the door handle, slipping out before he could make any more strange demands that she smile.

Webb returned to his chair, but he didn't immediately pick up the file he'd been studying before Roanna's entrance. He stared at where she'd been standing, poised like a doe on the verge of fleeing. His chest still hurt as he remembered that pathetic excuse for a smile, and the look almost of fright that had been in her eyes. It was difficult to read her now, she kept so much hidden and gave so little response to the world around her. It grated at him, because the Roanna he remembered had been as open as anyone he'd ever known. If he wanted to know how she felt about anything now, he had to pay intensely close attention to every nuance of her expression and body language, before she managed to stifle them.

She had been stunned when he'd told her that he still needed her help. He silently thanked Lucinda for giving him the key to handling Roanna. The idea of anyone needing her got to her faster than anything else, and she couldn't help responding to it. For a split second he'd seen the wonder, the pure joy, that had lit the depths of her eyes, and then it had been so quickly hidden that if he hadn't been deliberately watching her he wouldn't have seen it at all.

He'd lied. He could handle everything without her help,

even with the added burden of his properties in Arizona. He thrived on pressure, his energy level seeming to increase with the demands made on his time. But she needed to feel needed, and he needed her to be close by.

He wanted her.

The phrase beat like a refrain through his mind, his veins, every cell of his body. Want. He hadn't taken her in Nogales out of revenge or because of that damned bargain he'd made with her, or even to keep from hurting her feelings by pulling back after going that far. The simple fact was he'd taken her because he wanted her and was ruthless enough to use whatever means necessary to get her. The tequila was no excuse, though it had relaxed his control over his more uncivilized instincts.

He'd lain awake in his bed last night, thinking of her in the next room, wondering if she was awake, his damned imagination driving him crazy.

Knowing that he could have Roanna any time he wanted was more powerful than any chemical aphrodisiac ever discovered or invented. All he had to do was get out of bed and walk out onto the veranda, then slip through the French doors into her room. She had insomnia; she would be awake, watching him come toward her. He could simply get into bed with her and she would take him into her arms, her body, without question or hesitation.

Erotic dreams of that one kiss they'd shared so long ago had haunted his sleep for years. That had been bad enough, but the dreams had been only imagination. Now that he *knew* exactly how it felt to make love to her, now that reality had taken the place of imagination, the temptation was a constant, gnawing hunger that threatened to shred his self-control.

God, she'd been so sweet, so shy, and so damn tight he broke out in a sweat remembering how it had felt when he'd entered her. He had looked down at her as he made love to her and watched the expression on her face, watched the delicate pink of her nipples darken with arousal. Even though he'd hurt her, she had clung to him, arching her hips up to take him even deeper. It had been so easy to bring her to climax that he'd been enchanted, wanting to do it time and again so he could watch her face as she convulsed, feel her body flexing and throbbing around him.

The night had been exquisite torture, and he knew he would be fighting the same battle every night, with his frustration growing by the minute. He didn't know how long he could endure it before his self-control broke, but for Roanna's sake he had to try.

He'd been back at Davencourt a little over twenty-four hours, and he'd had a hard-on for what seemed like most of that time, certainly for the hours he'd spent in her company. If she'd seemed even the least inclined to flirt with him, in any way signal that she wanted him, too, he probably couldn't have withstood the temptation. But Roanna seemed totally unaware of him as a man, despite the hours they had spent in bed together. The idea was infuriating, but it seemed likely that she had indeed slept with him just to get him to come back to Davencourt.

Even that thought, instead of dampening his ardor, only intensified it. He wanted to toss her over his shoulder and carry her away for some hot, lazy sex on a sun-drenched bed, *prove* to her that she wanted him, that Davencourt and Lucinda had nothing to do with it. The fact was, where Roanna was concerned, his sexual instincts were so damn primitive he expected to start grunting and swinging clubs any minute now.

And that was after only one day.

The grudge he'd held against her all those years was gone. Maybe it had been destroyed during the night they'd spent together, and he just hadn't noticed it at the time. Habit was a powerful thing; you got so used to something that you expected it to be there even when it wasn't. If any vestige had been left, she had demolished it the next morning with her quiet dignity and the utter defenselessness with which she had said, "All you had to do was snap your fingers, and I'd have come running." Not many women would have laid themselves on the line like that; none that he knew, in fact, except for Roanna. He'd been staggered by the courage it had taken for her to say that, knowing what a weapon she had put in his hands if he'd been inclined to use it.

He wasn't. He lifted his hand and snapped his fingers, watching the motion. Like that. He could have her just like that. He wanted her, God knows he wanted her so much he ached. But what he wanted more than anything, even more than he wanted to make love to her, was to see her smile again.

By the time she drove home late that afternoon, Roanna was aching with fatigue. She usually found organizational meetings deadly dull anyway, and this one had dragged on with hours of debate on insignificant details. As usual, she had sat quietly, though this time she had been concentrating more on holding her head upright and her eyes open than she had been on what people were saying.

By the time she turned south onto Highway 43, the sun and heat were almost more than she could fight. She blinked drowsily, glad that she was so close to home. It was almost time for supper, but she planned to lie down for a nap instead. She could eat whenever she chose, but sleep was a lot harder to achieve and far more precious.

She made a right turn off the highway onto a secondary road, and a mile or so after that she turned left onto Davencourt's private road. If she hadn't been so sleepy, she would have been driving faster, and she might have missed the blur of motion in her peripheral vision. She slowed even more, turning her head to see what had caught her attention.

At first she saw only the horse, plunging and rearing, and her first thought was that it had lost its rider and bolted, and now the trailing reins were caught on some underbrush. She forgot her tiredness as urgency flooded her muscles. She slammed on the brakes, shoved the gear shift into park, and jumped out of the car, leaving the motor running and the door open. She could hear the horse's squeals of fear and pain as it reared again.

Roanna didn't think about her expensive shoes or her silk dress. She didn't think of anything except reaching the horse before it hurt itself. She leaped the shallow ditch on the opposite side of the road, then ran awkwardly across the small field toward the trees, her high heels sinking into the earth with each step. She plunged through knee-high weeds that stung her legs, snagged her hosiery on some green briers, turned her ankle when she stepped in a hole. She ignored all of that as she ran as fast as she could, intent only on getting to the horse.

Then the horse sidled sideways, and she saw the man.

She hadn't noticed him before because he'd been on the other side of the horse, and the undergrowth had partially blocked her view.

The horse's reins weren't caught on anything. The man was holding them in one fist, and in the other fist he held a small tree limb that he was using to beat the horse.

Fury roared through her, pumping strength into her muscles. She heard herself yell, saw the man look in her direction with a startled expression on his face, then she surged through the undergrowth and threw her weight against him, knocking him to the side. She couldn't have done it if he'd been expecting it and braced himself, but she caught him by surprise. "Stop it!" she stormed, placing herself between him and the frightened horse. "Don't you dare hit this animal again!"

He regained his balance and swung toward her, gripping the limb as if he would use it on her. Roanna registered the danger in his face, the venomous anger in his eyes, but she stood her ground. Her detachment didn't include standing by and watching any animal in general, but horses in particular, being abused. She braced herself, waiting for him to swing at her. If she charged him, she could get inside the blow and maybe knock him off balance again. If she could, she wouldn't waste any more time but get on the horse and get away from him as fast as she could.

His eyes were a hot electric blue as he advanced a step toward her, his arm drawn back ready to strike. His face was dark red, his lips drawn back over his teeth in a snarl. "You damn little bitch—"

"Who are you?" Roanna demanded, taking a half step toward him herself to show that she wasn't afraid. It was a bluff—she was suddenly very much afraid—but the anger inside her was still so strong she stood her ground. "What are you doing on our land?"

Maybe he thought better of hitting her. For whatever reason, he halted, though he was slow to let his arm drop. He stood a few feet away, breathing hard and glaring at her.

"Who are you?" she demanded again. Something about him was eerily familiar, as if she'd seen that expression before. But she knew she'd never seen *him* before, and she thought she would remember if she had, because those vivid blue eyes and thick shock of gray hair were very distinctive. He was a thickly built man, probably in his fifties, whose wide shoulders and barrel chest gave the impression of an almost brutish strength. What disturbed her the most, though, was the sense almost of evil that emanated from him. No, not evil. It was more impersonal than that, a simple and total lack of conscience or morals. That was it. His eyes, for all their hot color, were cold and flat.

"Who I am ain't none of your business," he sneered. "And neither is what I'm doing."

"When you do it on Davenport land, it is. Don't you dare hit this horse again, do you hear?"

"It's my horse, and I'll do whatever I damn well please to it. The bastard threw me."

"Then maybe you should learn how to ride better," she retorted hotly. She turned to catch the dangling reins and murmur soothingly to the horse, then patted its neck. It snorted nervously but calmed down as she continued to gently stroke it. The horse wasn't a valuable purebred like Lucinda's babied darlings; it was of an indeterminate breed with indifferent formation, but Roanna couldn't see any reason why it should be mistreated.

"Why don't you just go about your own business, missy, and I'll forget about teaching you some manners."

The menacing voice made her whirl. He was closer, and there was a feral look in his expression now. Swiftly Roanna stepped back, maneuvering so that the horse was between her and the man.

"Get off our land," she said coldly. "Or I'll have you arrested."

His heavily sensual mouth twisted in another sneer. "I guess you would. The sheriff's an ass-licker, especially when it comes to a Davenport ass. It wouldn't make any difference to you that I didn't know I was on your precious property, would it?"

"Not when you're beating your horse," Roanna replied, her tone still cold. "Now leave."

He smirked. "I can't. You're holding my horse."

Roanna dropped the reins and took another cautious step back. "There. Now get off our property, and if I ever see you mistreating an animal again, I'll have you brought up on charges of cruelty. Maybe I don't know your name, but I can describe you, and probably not too many people look the way you do." None that she knew of; his eyes were very distinctive.

He turned dark with temper again, and violence moved in those eyes, but he evidently thought better once more of what he had been about to do and merely reached for the reins. He swung himself into the saddle with the minimum of effort that revealed him to be an experienced rider. "I'll see you again some day," he mocked, and dug his heels into the horse's sides. The startled animal leaped forward, brushing by her so closely that its massive shoulder would have knocked her down if she hadn't jumped aside.

He rode in the direction of the highway, leaning down to avoid low-hanging branches. He was out of sight in only a moment, though it took longer than that for the thud of the horse's hooves to fade from her hearing.

Roanna made her way over to a sturdy oak and leaned against it, closing her eyes and shaking.

That had been one of the most foolish, foolhardy things she'd ever done. She had been extremely lucky and she knew it. That man could have seriously hurt her, raped her, maybe even killed her—anything. She had charged head-long into a dangerous situation without stopping to think. Such impulsiveness had been the main cause of trouble in her childhood and had been the trigger for the tragedy of Jessie's death and Webb's leaving.

She had thought that the reckless streak had been destroyed forever, but now she found, to her distress, that it still lurked deep inside, ready to leap to the fore. She probably would have found it before, if anything had made her angry. But horses weren't abused at Davencourt, and it had been a long time since she had allowed herself to care about much of anything at all. Webb had been gone, and the endless procession of days had all been flat and dreary.

She was still shaking in the aftermath of fear and rage, and her legs wobbled beneath her. She drew in deep breaths, trying to will herself to calmness. She couldn't go home like this, with her self-control so paper-thin. Anyone who saw her would know that something had happened, and she didn't want to rehash the whole thing and listen to the recriminations. She *knew* she'd been stupid, and lucky.

But more than that, she didn't want anyone to see the break in her composure. She was embarrassed and terrified by this unexpected vulnerability. She had to protect herself better than that. She couldn't do anything about her permanent weakness where Webb was concerned, but neither could her internal wall withstand any additional weaknesses.

When her legs felt steady enough, she left the woods and waded back across the field of weeds, this time taking care to avoid the briers. Her right ankle twinged with pain, reminding her that she had twisted it.

When she reached her car, she sat down sideways in the driver's seat, with her legs outside. Bending down, she took off her shoes and shook the dirt out of them. After a quick look around assured her that there were no cars on the road, she swiftly reached under her skirt and peeled off her shredded panty hose. She used the ruined garment to wipe off her shoes as best she could, then slipped them back on her bare feet.

There were tissues in her purse. She got one, wet it with her tongue, and rubbed at the scratches on her legs until the tiny beads of blood were gone. That, and a passage of a brush through her hair, was the best she could do. To be on the safe side, however, she would use her old childhood trick of going up the outside stairs to the second floor and circling around to her room.

She didn't know who that man was, but she hoped she never saw him again.

216

CHAPTER
15

*I*t was just like old times, trying to slip into her room without anyone seeing her. Back then, though, she had usually been trying to hide after committing some mischief or social *faux pas*. The confrontation with that unknown brute was far more serious. There was also the difference that now she was mature enough to admit her foolishness rather than tell whoppers to try to hide it. She wouldn't lie if asked, but still she had no intention of blurting out what had happened.

Roanna made it into her room without incident. Quickly she stripped and stepped into the shower, wincing as the water stung the scratches on her legs. After thoroughly washing, the best protection against any possible encounter with poison ivy that might have been lurking in the weeds and among the trees, she dabbed the scratches with an antiseptic, then followed that with a soothing application of pure aloe gel. The stinging stopped almost immediately, and without that constant reminder of the unsettling encounter, her nerves began to calm.

A few flips of the brush restored her hair to order, and three minutes spent applying an array of cosmetics hid any lingering sign of upset. Roanna stared in the mirror at the

217

sophisticated reflection; sometimes she was surprised by the image that looked back, as if it wasn't really her. Thank God for her sorority sisters, she thought. Most of the passages of her life had been marked by loss: the death of her parents, Jessie's murder, Webb's departure. College had been one passage, however, that had been good, and the credit for that belonged solely to those drawling, sharp-eyed, and saber-tongued young women who had taken the misfit under their protection and used their expertise in things social and cosmetic to turn her into an acceptable debutante. Funny how the competent application of mascara had translated itself into a smidgen of self-confidence, how the mastering of a graceful dance step had somehow untied her tongue and allowed her to carry on a social conversation.

She slipped the wires of plain gold hoops into her pierced ears, turning her head to check her appearance. She liked the way they looked, the way the ends of her slightly, purposely tousled hair curled through the hoops, as if her hair had been specifically cut to do so. That was another thing the sorority sisters had taught her, how to appreciate certain things about her own appearance. The greatest gift they had given her was constructed out of the small accomplishments of learning to dance, to apply makeup, to dress well, to function socially. The foundation had taken shape so slowly that she hadn't noticed it, a brick going into place every so often, but now it was suddenly large enough for her to *see* it, and she was puzzled by it.

Self-confidence.

How she had always envied people who had it! Webb and Lucinda both had dynamic, aggressive self-confidence, the type that founded nations and built empires. Gloria was frequently blind to anything but herself, but certain in any case that she knew better than anyone else. Jessie's self-confidence had been monumental. Loyal was confident in his dealings with the animals in his care, and Tansy ruled the kitchen. Even the mechanics at the dealership where she'd bought her car were certain of their ability to fix any mechanical problem.

That slow-forming structure was her own self-confidence. The realization made her eyes widen with mild surprise. She was sure of herself when it came to horses; that had always been true. She'd had the self-confidence, or pure foolhardiness, to confront that awful man in the woods today and force him to stop mistreating that horse.

The sheer force of shock and anger had propelled her into action, a spirit she hadn't realized still lived inside her. The horse had been the catalyst, of course; she loved the animals so much, and it had always sent her into pure rage to see any one of them mistreated. Even so, her own actions shocked her, bringing her face-to-face with a part of herself she had thought long dead, or at least safely dormant. She no longer threw temper tantrums or insisted on having her way about things, but she *did* make her opinions known when it suited her. She kept a great deal of herself private, but that was her own decision, her own way of dealing with heartbreak and keeping pain at bay. She protected herself by not letting herself care, or at least not letting anyone *know* that she cared, and most of the time the appearance of indifference was enough.

She continued staring into the mirror at the face she knew so well, and yet the things she saw beyond it were new, as if she had just opened a door to a different outlook.

People in town treated her with respect, listening when she spoke, however seldom that was. There was even a group of young businesswomen in the Shoals area who regularly invited her for Saturday lunches at Callahan's, not to talk business, but to laugh and joke and . . . be friends. Friends. They didn't ask her to go with them because she was Lucinda's stand-in, or because they wanted to pitch ideas or ask favors of her. They asked her simply because they liked her.

She hadn't realized. Roanna's lips parted in surprise. She was so accustomed to thinking of herself as Lucinda's proxy that she hadn't considered she could be invited somewhere on her own account.

When had this happened? She thought, but couldn't

pinpoint a time. The process had been so gradual that there was no single outstanding incident to mark the occasion.

A sense of peace began to glow deep inside. Webb was going to have Davencourt, just as Lucinda had always planned, but the deep-seated fear Roanna had felt at having to leave its sheltering confines began to fade. She would still leave; she loved him so much that she wasn't sure of her own control where he was concerned. If she stayed, she would likely end up creeping into his bed some night and begging him to take her again.

She didn't want that. She didn't want to embarrass him, or herself. This newfound sense of worth was too new, too fragile, to survive another devastating rejection.

She began to think of where she would go, what she would do. She wanted to stay in the Shoals area, of course; her roots were generations deep, centuries strong. She had money of her own, inherited from her parents, and she would still inherit part of Lucinda's estate even though the bulk of it would go to Webb. She could do anything she wanted. The thought was liberating.

She wanted to raise and train horses.

When Lucinda died, the debt of gratitude that had been incurred when a terrified, grief-stricken seven-year-old had heard her grandmother say that she could come live with her would be paid. It was a debt of love, too, as strong as that of gratitude. It had kept her at her grandmother's side, gradually becoming Lucinda's legs and ears and eyes as her health grew fragile with age. But when Lucinda was gone, and Davencourt safely in Webb's capable hands, Roanna would be free.

Free. The word whispered through her, as gossamer as a butterfly's wing when it is newly emerged from the cocoon.

She could have her own home, something that was solely hers, and she would never again be dependent on anyone else for the roof over her head. Thanks to Lucinda's training, she now understood investments and finances; she felt confident that she was capable of managing her own money, so that she would always be secure. She would raise her own horses, but that would only be a sideline. She would go into business for herself as a trainer; people would bring their horses to her for schooling. Even Loyal said that he'd never seen anyone better able to gentle a frightened or misused animal, or even one that was just plain cussed.

She could do it. She could make a go of it. And for the first time in her life, she would be living for herself.

The grandfather clock in the foyer gonged softly, the sound barely audible here at the back of the huge house. Startled, she glanced at her own clock and saw that it was supper time, and she still wasn't dressed. The nap she had planned to take was impossible now with adrenaline still humming through her veins, so she might as well eat.

Hurriedly she went to her closet and took out the first outfit that came to hand, silk slacks and a matching sleeveless tunic. The pants would hide the scratches on her legs, and that was all she cared about. She knew how to choose flattering and appropriate clothes now, but had never learned to take pleasure in clothing.

"I'm sorry I'm late," she said as she entered the dining room. Everyone was already seated; Brock and Corliss were the only ones absent, but then they seldom ate supper at home. Brock spent what time he could with his fiancée, and God only knew where Corliss spent her time.

"What time did you get home?" Webb asked. "I didn't hear you come in." His eyes were narrowed on her just the way he'd looked at her when she was a kid and he'd caught her trying to slip in unnoticed.

"About five-thirty, I think." She hadn't noted the exact time, because she had still been so upset. "I went straight upstairs to take a shower before supper."

"The heat is so sticky, I have to shower twice a day," Lanette agreed. "Greg's company wanted to transfer him to Tampa. Can you imagine how much worse the humidity is down there? I simply couldn't face it."

Greg glanced briefly at his wife, then returned his attention to his plate. He was a tall, spare man who seldom spoke, wore his graying hair in a crew cut, and to Roanna's knowledge did nothing for fun or relaxation. Greg went to work, came home with more work in his bulging briefcase, and spent the hours between supper and bedtime hunched over paperwork. So far as she knew, he was one of a horde of pencil pushers in middle management, but suddenly she realized that she didn't really know what he did at work. Greg never talked about his job, never related funny stories about his co-workers. He was simply there, a dinghy dragged along in Lanette's wake.

"A lateral transfer?" Webb asked, his cool green gaze flicking from Greg to Lanette and back again. "Or a promotion?"

"Promotion," Greg said briefly.

"But it meant moving," Lanette explained. "And the living expenses would be so much higher that we'd have been *losing* money on that so-called promotion. He turned it down, of course."

Meaning she had flatly refused to move, Roanna thought as she methodically applied herself to the chore of eating. Living here at Davencourt, they had no housing expenses, and Lanette used the extra money to swan around in the best social circles. If they moved, they would then have to provide their own roof, and Lanette's standard of living would suffer.

Greg should have gone and left Lanette to follow or not, Roanna thought. Like herself, he needed to break away from Davencourt and have a place of his own. Maybe Davencourt was *too* beautiful; it was more than just a house to the people who lived here, it was almost a being in and of itself. They wanted to possess it, and instead it possessed them, holding them captive with the knowledge that, after Davencourt, no other home could be as grand.

But she would break away, she promised herself. She had never thought she could possess Davencourt, so she wasn't bound here by envy's chains. Fear had held her here, and duty, and love. The first reason was already gone, and the remaining two would soon follow, and she would be free.

After supper, Webb said to Lucinda, "If you aren't too

tired, I want to talk to you about an investment I've been considering."

"Of course," she said, and they walked together to the dining room door.

Roanna remained at the table, her expression blank. She forked up one last bite of the strawberry shortcake Tansy had served for dessert, forcing herself to eat that one even though she wanted it no more than she had the ones preceding it.

Webb paused at the door and looked around, a slight frown pulling his dark brows together as if he'd just realized she wasn't with them. "Aren't you coming?"

Silently she got up and followed them, wondering if he'd really expected her to automatically assume she was included, or if she was an afterthought. Probably the latter; Webb had always been accustomed to discussing his business decisions with Lucinda, but for all the things he'd said about wanting Roanna to continue with her present responsibilities, he didn't think of her as having any authority.

He was right, she thought, ruthlessly facing the truth. She had no authority beyond what either he or Lucinda granted her, which wasn't true authority. Either of them could pull her up short at any time, divest her of even the semblance of power.

They entered the study and took their accustomed seats: Webb at the desk that had so recently been hers, Roanna in one of the wing chairs, Lucinda on the sofa. Roanna felt jittery inside, as if everything had been jostled, switched around. The past couple of hours had been filled with a series of insights into her own character, nothing great and dramatic but nevertheless small explosions that left her feeling as if nothing was the same, and hadn't even been as she had always perceived it.

Webb was talking, but for the first time in her life Roanna wasn't hanging on his every word as if it came from the lips of God Almighty himself. She barely even heard him. Today she had faced down a brute, and realized that people liked her for herself. She had made a decision concerning the rest of her life. As a child she had been helpless to control her life, and for the past ten long years she had let life pass her by, withdrawing to a safe place where she couldn't be hurt. But now she *could* control her life; she didn't have to let things happen as other people dictated, she could set her own course, make her own rules. The feeling of power was both heady and frightening, but the excitement of it was undeniable.

"—a sizable investment on our part," Webb was saying, "but Mayfield has always been reliable."

Roanna's interest suddenly focused, caught by the name Webb had just mentioned, and she remembered the gossip she had heard just that afternoon.

Lucinda nodded. "It sounds interesting, though of course—"

"No," Roanna said.

Silence settled over the room, complete except for the muted ticking of the old mantel clock.

It was difficult to tell who was the most startled, Lucinda, Webb, or Roanna herself. She had sometimes thought Lucinda should rethink a decision, and quietly given her reasoning, but she had never openly, flatly disagreed. The no had just popped out. She hadn't even couched it in let's-think-it-over terms, but stated it definitely, firmly.

Lucinda sat back on the sofa, blinking a little in surprise. Webb swiveled his chair a little so he was looking directly at Roanna and merely stared at her for a long moment that strained every nerve in her body. There was a strange glitter in his eyes, bright and hot. "Why?" he finally asked, his tone soft.

Roanna desperately wished that she'd kept her mouth shut. That impulsive no had been based on gossip she'd heard that afternoon at the music festival organizational meeting. What if Webb listened to her, then gave her the condescending smile of an adult listening to a child's improbable but amusing scenario, and turned back to his discussion with Lucinda? The precious new sense of confidence would wither inside her.

Lucinda had grown accustomed to listening to Roanna's observations, but Roanna had always offered them as simply that, and left the final decision to her grandmother. Never before had she flatly said, "No."

"Come on, Ro," Webb coaxed. "You watch people, you notice things we don't. What do you know about Mayfield?"

She took a deep breath and squared her shoulders. "It's just what I heard today. Mayfield desperately needs money. Naomi left him yesterday, and the word is she's asking for a huge settlement, because she caught him in the laundry room with one of Amelia's college friends who's been visiting for a couple of weeks. Moreover, according to gossip, the hanky-panky has been going on since Christmas, and it appears that the college friend, who is all of nineteen, is four months pregnant."

There was an oasis of silence, then Lucinda said, "As I remember, Amelia did have her friend over for the Easter holidays."

Webb snorted, a grin widening his mouth. "Sounds as if Mayfield had his own personal arising, doesn't it?"

"Webb! Don't be blasphemous!" But for all her genuine shock at the comment, Lucinda's sense of humor had a bawdy streak, and she fought a smile as she cast a quick, concerned glance at Roanna.

"Sorry," Webb promptly apologized, though his eyes continued to sparkle. He had caught the look Lucinda gave Roanna, as if she were alarmed that Roanna should hear something off-color. It was an old-fashioned attitude, that a virgin, no matter what her age, should be shielded from sexual innuendo. That Lucinda still considered Roanna a virgin meant that there hadn't been any romantic interests at all in Roanna's life, even in college.

Lucinda had been absolutely correct, Webb thought, his heart beating fast as an image of that night in Nogales flashed through his mind. Roanna *had* been a virgin, until roughly one hour after she had walked up to him in that bar. It had taken him about that long to have her stripped, spread, and penetrated.

The memory shimmered through him like soft lightning, heating every nerve ending, making him ache. The feel of her soft, slender body beneath him had been . . . perfect. Her breasts, round and delicious and so delicately formed . . . perfect. The hot, tight sheathing of his cock . . . perfect. And the way her arms had wound so trustingly around his neck, the way her back had arched, the blind, exalted expression on her face as she came . . . God, it had been so perfect it left him breathless.

His dick was hard as a spike. He shifted uncomfortably in the chair, glad that he was sitting behind the desk. That's what he got for letting himself think of that night, of the utter ecstasy of coming inside her. Which he had, he realized. Several times, in fact. And not once had he used a rubber.

He'd never before in his life been so careless, no matter how much he'd had to drink. The fine hairs stood up on his body as an almost electrical thrill ran through him. The thought of birth control hadn't once entered his mind that night; with primal male instinct he had taken her time and again, imprinting himself on her flesh, and in the most primitive claiming he had spurted his semen into her. During those long hours, his body had taken control from his mind, not that his mind had been in top form anyway. The flesh had no conscience; with instincts formed over thousands of years, he had claimed her as his own and sought to forge an unbreakable bond by making her pregnant, so that their two selves would mingle into one.

It was an effort to keep his face impassive, not to leap up and grab her, demand to know if she carried his child. Hell, it hadn't even been two weeks yet; how could she know?

"Webb?"

Lucinda's voice intruded on his consciousness, and he wrested his thoughts from the shattering direction they had taken. Both Lucinda and Roanna were watching him. Roanna's expression was as calm and remote as usual, but at that moment he was so acutely attuned to her that he thought he could see a hint of anxiety in her eyes. Did she expect him to dismiss what she'd said as mere gossip? Was she waiting so impassively for one more blow to her self-esteem?

He rubbed his chin as he regarded her. "What you're saying is that Mayfield's personal life is a mess, and you think he's so desperate for money that he isn't using good judgment."

She held his gaze. "That's right."

"And you heard all this at your meeting today?"

Solemnly she nodded.

He grinned. "Then thank God for gossip. You've probably saved us from a big loss—Mayfield, too, come to that, because he needs our backing to swing the deal."

Lucinda sniffed. "I doubt Burt Mayfield will feel very grateful, but his personal mess is his own fault."

Roanna sat back, a little dizzy at the ease with which they had both accepted her analysis. Her emotions were so unsteady that she didn't know how to act, what to do, so she sat quietly and did nothing. Occasionally she could feel Webb look at her, but she didn't let herself meet his gaze. Her feelings were too close to the surface right now, her control too tenuous; she didn't want to harass him and embarrass herself by staring at him with doglike devotion. The stress of the past few hours was taking its toll on her anyway; the adrenaline high had faded, and she was dreadfully tired. She didn't know if she could sleep; in fact she was so tired that she was afraid she *would* sleep, because it was when she was most exhausted and finally fell into a deep sleep that the sleepwalking episodes occurred. But sleep or not, she very much wanted to lie down, just for a while.

Then suddenly Webb was beside her, his hand on her arm as he lifted her to her feet. "You're so tired you're wobbling in your chair," he said in an abrupt tone. "Go on up to bed. Mayfield's proposal was all we needed to discuss."

Just that small touch was enough to make Roanna want to lean into him, rest against his strength, feel the heat and hardness of his body against her one more time. To keep

227

from giving in to the impulse, she made herself move away from him. "I am tired," she admitted quietly. "If you're sure that's all, I'll go upstairs now."

"That's all," Webb said, a frown pulling his eyebrows together.

Roanna murmured a good-night to Lucinda and left the room. Webb watched her go with narrowed eyes. She had pulled away from him. For the first time in his memory, Roanna had avoided his touch.

"Will she sleep?" he asked aloud, not looking at Lucinda.

"Probably not." She sighed. "Not much, anyway. She seems . . . oh, I don't know, a bit edgy. That's the most she's put herself forward in years. I'm glad you listened to her instead of just shrugging it off. I had to teach myself to pay attention to what she says. It's just that she notices so much about people, because they do all the talking and she just listens. Roanna picks up on the little things."

They chatted for a few minutes longer, then Lucinda carefully rose from the couch, proudly refusing to reveal the difficulty of the movement. "I'm a bit tired, too," she said. "My days of dancing 'til dawn are over."

"I never had any," Webb replied wryly. "There was always work to be done."

She paused, watching him with a troubled look. "Was it too much?" she asked suddenly. "You were so young when I gave Davencourt to you. You didn't have time to just be a boy."

"It was hard work," he said, shrugging. "But it was what I wanted. I don't regret it." He had never regretted the work. He'd regretted a lot of other things but never the sheer exhilaration of pushing himself, learning, accomplishing. He hadn't done it just for Davencourt, he'd done it for himself, because he'd gotten off on the power and excitement of it. He'd been the golden boy, the crown prince, and he'd reveled in the role. He'd even married the princess, and what a disaster that had turned out to be. He couldn't blame Lucinda for that even though she had happily promoted his and Jessie's marriage. It was his own blind ambition that had led him willingly to the altar.

Lucinda patted his arm as she passed, and he watched her, too, as she left the room, noting the care with which she took each step. She was either in pain or far weaker than she wanted anyone to guess. Because she wouldn't want anyone to fuss over her, he let her go without comment.

He sighed, the sound soft in the quiet of the room. Once this room had been his own domain, and bore the uncompromising signs of purely masculine use. Not much had been changed other than the addition of the computers and fax, because Davencourt wasn't a house given to swift or dramatic changes. It aged subtly, with small and gradual differences. This room, however, now seemed softer, more feminine. The curtains were different, lighter in color, but it was more than that. The very scent of the room had changed, as if it had absorbed the inherent sweetness of female flesh, the perfumes and lotions Lucinda and Roanna had used. He could detect very plainly Lucinda's Chanel; it was all she had worn in his entire memory. Roanna's scent was lighter, sweeter, and was strongest when he was sitting at the desk.

The faint perfume lured him. He resumed his seat at the desk and shuffled through some papers but after a few minutes gave up the pretense and instead leaned back, frowning as his thoughts settled on Roanna.

She had never pulled away from him before. He couldn't get that out of his mind. It disturbed him deep inside, as if he'd lost something precious. He'd sworn he wouldn't take advantage of her; hell, he'd even felt a bit noble about it, because he'd been denying himself something he really wanted: her. But she was so damn *remote,* as if that night in Nogales had never happened, as if she hadn't spent her childhood years tagging along at his heels and beaming worshipfully up at him.

She was so self-contained, so closed in on herself. He kept looking at her with a grin, expecting her to grin back in one of those moments of humor they had always shared, but her smooth, still face remained as solemn as always, as if she had no more laughter in her.

His thoughts moved back to their lovemaking. He wanted to see Roanna smile again, but even more than that, he wanted to know if his baby was inside her. As soon as he could manage it, he was going to have a private conversation with her—something that might prove to be more difficult than he'd ever imagined, given the way she'd begun avoiding him.

The next afternoon, Roanna sighed as she leaned back in the big leather chair, massaging her neck to relieve the stiffness. A neat stack of addressed invitations was on one corner of the desk, but a glance at the guest list told her that there was at least a third of the envelopes still to be addressed.

Once Lucinda had gotten Webb's okay for the party, she had begun making her battle plans. Everyone who was anyone had to be invited, which put the guest list at a staggering five hundred people. A crowd that size simply wouldn't fit into the house, not even a house as large as Davencourt, unless they wanted to open up the bedrooms. Lucinda had been unfazed; they would simply throw open the French doors onto the patio, string lights in the trees and shrubbery, and let people wander in and out as they chose. The patio was better for dancing anyway.

Roanna had begun work immediately. There was no way Tansy could handle preparing food for that many people, so she had set herself to locating a caterer who could handle that size party on such short notice, because the date Lucinda had selected was less than two weeks away. She had chosen that date intentionally, not wanting to give people time to deliberate too much, but time enough to buy new dresses and schedule appointments with hairdressers. The few caterers in the Shoals area were already booked for that date, so Roanna had been forced to hire a firm from

Huntsville that she'd never dealt with before. She only hoped everything worked out okay.

There was a ton of decorations stored in the attic and hundreds of strands of lights, but Lucinda had decided that only peach-colored lights would do because it would be such a mellow, flattering color for everyone. There were no peach lights in the attic. After a dozen phone calls, Roanna had tracked some down at a specialty store in Birmingham, and they were shipping the lights overnight.

There weren't enough chairs, even allowing for the people who would be dancing or milling around rather than sitting. More chairs had to be brought in, a band had to be hired, flowers had to be ordered, and a printer had to be found who could print the invitations *immediately*. That last accomplished, Roanna was now occupied with addressing the envelopes. She had been doing it for the past three hours, and she was exhausted.

She could remember Lucinda doing this chore years ago. Once she had asked why Lucinda didn't hire someone to do it, because it had seemed so horribly boring, having to sit for hours and address hundreds of envelopes. Lucinda had replied haughtily that a lady took the trouble to personally invite her guests, which Roanna had taken to mean it was one of those old southern customs that would continue no matter how illogical. She had promised herself at the time that *she* would never do something so boring.

Now she patiently worked through the guest list. The job was still boring, but she understood now why customs continued; it gave one a sense of continuity, of kinship with those who had gone before. Her grandmother had done this, as had her great-grandmother, her great-great-grandmother, going back an unknown number of generations. Those women were a part of her, their genes still living in her, though it looked as if she would be the end of the line. There had only ever been one man for her, and he wasn't interested. End of story, end of family.

Roanna resolutely pushed all thoughts of Webb out of her

mind so she could concentrate on the job at hand. She was accustomed to doing any paperwork at the desk, but Webb had been working there that morning. She still felt a tiny shock whenever she saw him sitting in the chair she had come to regard as *hers,* a shock that had nothing to do with the surge of joy she always felt at the very sight of him.

She had retreated to the small, sunny sitting room at the back of the house, because it was the most private, and began writing at the escritoire there. The chair had proven to be an instrument of torture to one sitting in it for longer than fifteen minutes, so she had gotten a lap desk and moved to the sofa. Her legs had gone to sleep. When Webb had left after lunch to visit Yvonne, with relief Roanna had taken advantage of his absence to work in the study. She settled into the chair, and everything felt just right. The desk was the right height, the chair was comfortable and familiar.

She had *belonged* in this chair, she thought. She refused to let herself feel resentment, however. She had felt needed here for the first time in her life, but soon she would have something that belonged solely to her. Lucinda's death would be the end of one part of her life and the beginning of another. Why fret over this symbol of power when she would soon be moving on anyway? Only to Webb could she have given it up without heartbreak, she thought, because all of this had been promised to him long before she assumed, by default, the stewardship of Davencourt.

There was a great deal of difference between handling financial paperwork and addressing envelopes, at least in the significance of it, but the physical requirements were the same. Working at last in relative comfort, she let her mind slip into neutral as she worked through the invitations.

At first she was scarcely aware of the fatigue creeping through her body, she was so accustomed to it. She forced herself to ignore it and carefully wrote out a few more addresses, but suddenly her eyelids were so heavy she could barely hold them open. Her fears for the past two nights that she would fall deeply asleep and sleepwalk had been groundless; despite the fatigue that dragged at her, she had merely dozed in fits and starts, managing to get perhaps a total of two hours' sleep each night. Last night, again, she had been almost painfully aware of Webb's presence next door, and she had awakened herself several times listening for his movements.

Now she became aware of how quiet the house was. Webb was gone, and Lucinda was napping. Greg and Brock were both at work. Gloria and Lanette might be against having the party, but they had both gone shopping for new dresses, and Harlan had gone with them. Corliss had left right after breakfast, with a careless "I'll be back later," and no indication where she was going.

Despite the efforts of the air-conditioning, the study was warm from the fierce summer sunlight pouring through the windows. Roanna's eyelids drooped even more and closed completely. She always tried not to nap during the day because that only made it more difficult for her to sleep at night, but sometimes the fatigue was overpowering. Sitting there in the warm, quiet room, she lost the battle to stay awake.

Webb noticed when he pulled into the garage that Roanna's car was in its bay, and Corliss had returned as well, but Gloria and Lanette were still out shopping. It was the presence of Roanna's car, however, that caused a hot little thrill of anticipation to shoot through him. She'd had afternoon meetings both days since he'd come home, and he had half-expected her to be gone this afternoon, too, even though she hadn't said anything about an appointment. In the tightly knit structure of small towns, business and social obligations often overlapped, with the former being conducted at the latter. Until he was fully integrated into county society again, Roanna would have to fulfill those obligations by herself.

Somehow he hadn't expected that he would see so little of her. In the past, Roanna had always been right on his heels no matter what he was doing. When she'd been seven or eight, he'd actually had to keep her from following him into the bathroom, and even then she had huddled in the hallway waiting for him. Back then, of course, she had just lost her parents and he had been her only security; the frantic clinging had gradually ceased as she adjusted. But even when she'd been a teenager, she'd always been right there, her homely little face turned up to him like a sunflower to the sun.

But she wasn't homely now; she had grown into a striking woman with the sort of strong, chiseled bone structure that wouldn't yield much to age. He'd braced himself to resist constant temptation; he couldn't take advantage of her heartbreaking vulnerability just to satisfy his lust. Damn it all to hell, though, instead of being vulnerable she was downright remote with him, and most of the time she wasn't even around. It was as if she actively avoided him, and the realization jolted him deep inside. Was she embarrassed because she'd slept with him? He remembered how closed her expression had been the next morning. Or did she resent it because he was going to inherit Davencourt instead of her?

Lucinda said Roanna had no interest in running Davencourt, but what if she was wrong? Roanna hid so much behind that calm, remote face. Once he'd been able to read her like a book, and now he found himself watching her whenever he could, trying to decipher any flicker of expression that might hint at her feelings. For the most part, though, all he saw was the fatigue that drained her, and the mute patience with which she endured it.

If he'd realized how much trouble this damn party would be for her, he never would have agreed to it. If she was still working on it when he got inside, he was going to put his foot down. Her face had been drawn and wan, and dark circles lay under her eyes, evidence that she hadn't been sleeping. Insomnia was one thing; staying awake at night and working incessantly during the day was something else. She needed to do something she enjoyed, and he thought a long, leisurely ride was just the ticket. Not only did she love riding, but the physical exercise might force her body into sleep that night. He was getting antsy himself; he'd gotten accustomed to spending long hours in the saddle almost every day, and he missed the exercise as well as the soothing company of the horses.

He entered the kitchen and smiled at Tansy, who was humming happily as she meandered around the kitchen, never getting in a hurry or seeming to have any design in her movements, but nevertheless putting together huge, scrumptious meals. Tansy hadn't changed much in all the years he'd known her, he thought. She had to be in her sixties, but her hair was still the same salt and pepper it had been since he'd come to live at Davencourt. She was short and plump, and her kindhearted nature shone out of her blue eyes.

"Lemon icebox pie for dessert tonight," she said, grinning, knowing that it was his favorite. "Be sure you save enough room for it."

"I'll make a point of it." Tansy's icebox pie was so good he could make a meal of it by itself. "Do you know where Roanna is?"

"Sure do. Bessie was just here, and she said Miss Roanna's asleep in the study. I'm not surprised, I'll say that. You could tell just by looking at the poor child that the last few nights have been bad, even worse than usual."

She was asleep. Relief warred with disappointment, because he'd been looking forward to that ride with her. "I won't disturb her," he promised. "Is Lucinda awake from *her* nap yet?"

"I imagine so, but she hasn't come downstairs." Tansy sadly shook her head. "Time's weighing heavy on Miss Lucinda. You can always tell when old folks start going, 'cause they stop eating food they used to love. It's nature's way of winding down, I guess. My mama, rest her soul, loved kraut and wienies better'n anything, but a few months before she passed on she said they just didn't taste good no more, and she wouldn't eat 'em."

Lucinda's all-time favorite food was okra. She loved it

235

fried, boiled, pickled, any way it could be prepared. "Is Lucinda still eating her okra?" he asked quietly.

Tansy shook her head, her eyes sad. "Said it don't have much taste this year."

Webb left the kitchen and walked silently down the hall. He turned the corner and stopped when he saw Corliss with her back to him, opening the study door and peeking inside. He knew immediately what she was about to do; the little bitch was going to slam the door and awaken Roanna. Fury shot through him, and he was already moving as she stepped back and opened the door wide, as wide as her arm would allow. He saw the muscles in her forearm tighten as she prepared to slam the door with all her strength, and then he was on her, his steely fingers biting into the nape of her neck. She gave a stifled little squeak and froze.

Webb eased the door shut, then dragged her away from the study, still holding her neck in a tight grip. He hauled her head around so that she was looking at him. He'd seldom in his life been more angry, and he wanted to shake her as if she were a rag. On the scale of things, waking Roanna from a nap was nothing more than petty and spiteful, no matter how desperately she needed the sleep. But he didn't give a damn about the scale of things, because Roanna *did* need that nap, and the spitefulness angered him all the more because it was so senseless. Corliss wouldn't accomplish or gain a damn thing by disturbing Roanna; she was simply a bitch, and he wasn't going to put up with it.

Her face was a picture of alarm as she stared up at him, still with her neck arched back in an uncomfortable position. Her blue eyes were rounded with startlement at being caught when she had thought herself alone, but already a sly look was creeping into them as she began trying to figure out a way to slither out of this predicament.

"Don't bother with the excuses," he said bluntly, keeping his voice low so Roanna wouldn't be disturbed. "Maybe I'd better spell things out, so you'll know exactly where you stand. You'd better pray that the wind never catches a door and slams it while Roanna's asleep, or that a stray cat never knocks anything over, and God forbid you should actually forget to be quiet. Because no matter what happens, if you're anywhere on the property, I'm going to blame it on you. And do you know what will happen then?"

Her face twisted as she realized he wasn't going to listen to any of her excuses. "What?" she taunted. "You'll get out your trusty andiron?"

His hand tightened on her neck, making her wince. "Worse than that," he said in a silky tone. "At least from your point of view. I'll throw you out of this house so fast your ass will leave skid marks on the stairs. Is that clear? I have a real low tolerance for parasites, and you're so close to the limit that I'm already reaching for the flea powder."

She flushed a dark, ugly color and tried to jerk away from him. Webb held her, lifting his eyebrows at her as he waited for a response.

"You bastard," she spat. "Aunt Lucinda thinks she can force people to accept you, but they won't ever. They'll be nice to you for her sake, but as soon as she's dead, you'll find out what they think of you. You only came back because you know she's dying, and you want Davencourt and all the money."

"I'll have it, too," he said, and smiled. It wasn't a nice smile, but he didn't feel nice. Contemptuously he released her. "Lucinda said she would change her will if I'd come back. Davencourt will belong to me, and you'll be out on your ass. But you're not only a bitch, you're a stupid one. As it stood before, Roanna was going to inherit instead of me, but you've acted like a malicious spoiled brat to her. Do you think she'd have let you go on living here, either?"

Corliss tossed her head. "Roanna's a wimp. I can handle her."

"Like I said: stupid. She doesn't say anything now because Lucinda's important to her, and she doesn't want her upset. But one way or the other, you'd better be looking for somewhere else to live."

"Grandmother won't *let* you throw me out."

Webb snorted. "Davencourt doesn't belong to Gloria. It isn't her decision."

"It doesn't belong to you yet, either! There's a lot that can happen between now and when Aunt Lucinda dies." She made the words sound like a threat, and he wondered what mischief she was considering.

He was tired of dealing with the little bitch. "Then maybe I'd better add another condition: If you start shooting off your mouth and causing trouble, you're outta here. Now get out of my sight before I decide you're already more trouble than you're worth."

She flounced away from him, sashaying her ass to show him she wasn't scared. Maybe she wasn't, but she should damn sure take him at his word.

He quietly opened the study door to make certain they hadn't awakened Roanna with their argument. He'd tried to keep his voice low, but Corliss hadn't had any such concern, and grimly he promised himself that she'd be out on the street tonight if Roanna's eyes were open.

But she still slept, curled in the big office chair with her head tucked into the wing. He stood in the doorway, watching her. Her dark chestnut hair was tousled around her face, and sleep had brought a delicate flush to her cheeks. Her breasts moved up and down in a slow, deep rhythm.

She had slept like that the night they'd spent together— what time he'd let her sleep. If he'd know then how rare real, restful sleep was for her, he wouldn't have awakened her all those times. But afterward, each time, she had curled in his arms just that way, with her head pillowed on his shoulder.

A sharp pang of longing went through him. He'd like to hold her that way again, he thought. She could sleep in his arms for as long as she wanted.

CHAPTER
16

Corliss was shaking as she climbed the stairs, but the trembling was as much inside as out. She needed something, fast. She hurried into her suite and locked the door, then began to frenziedly search all of her favorite hiding places: inside the tiny rip in the lining on the bottom of the sofa, the empty cold cream jar, the bottom of the lamp, the toe-shapers for her shoes. She found exactly what she'd known she would find, nothing, but she needed a fix bad enough that she looked anyway.

How dare he talk to her like that? She'd always hated him, hated Jessie, hated Roanna. It simply wasn't fair! Why should they get to live at Davencourt while she had to live in that stupid little house? All of her life she'd been looked down on at school as the Davenports' poor relation. But sometimes good things did happen, like when Jessie was killed and Webb blamed for it. Corliss had silently celebrated; God, it had been so hard to keep from laughing at that turn of events! But she had made all the proper noises, looked properly sad, and when Webb had left, pretty soon things had fallen into place and her family had moved into Davencourt, where they should have been all those years anyway.

239

She'd had a lot of friends then, people who knew how to really party, not the snooty my-great-great-granddaddy-fought-in-the-War crowd, the ones who wore pearls and the men didn't cuss in the ladies' presence. What bullshit. Her friends knew how to have *fun.*

She'd been smart, she'd stayed away from the hard drugs. No mainlining for her, no sirree. That shit would kill you. She liked booze, but she *loooved* that sweet white powder. One snort, and no worries; she felt on top of the world, the best, the prettiest, the sexiest. Once she'd been so damn sexy that she'd taken on three guys, one after the other, then all three together, and worn them all out. It'd been great, she'd been fantastic, she'd never had sex like that since. She'd like to do it again, but it took more to fly now, and really she'd rather enjoy that than concentrate on screwing. Besides, a couple of times she'd had a little problem a month or so later, and she'd had to go to Memphis where no one knew her to have it taken care of. Wouldn't do to have a bun in the oven ruining her fun.

But all of her little hiding places were empty. She didn't have any coke, and she didn't have any money. Desperately she roamed the suite, trying to think. Aunt Lucinda always kept a good bit of money in her purse, but the purse was in her bedroom and the old lady was still in her suite, so she couldn't get at it. Grandmother and Mama had gone shopping, so they would have taken all their cash with them. But Roanna was asleep in the study . . . Corliss laughed to herself as she slipped from her rooms and hurried down the hallway to Roanna's room. Guess it was a good thing Webb had kept her from slamming that door after all. Let dear little Roanna sleep, the stupid bitch.

Silently she entered Roanna's bedroom. Roanna always put her purses away in the closet like a good little girl. It took Corliss only a moment to filch Roanna's wallet and count the money. Only eighty-three bucks, damn it. Even someone as dense as Roanna would notice if a couple of twenties went missing. She seldom bothered searching

Roanna's purse for that reason, because Roanna didn't normally carry much cash.

She eyed the credit cards but resisted the temptation. She would have to sign for a cash advance on them, and anyway the bank teller might know she wasn't Roanna. That was the trouble with hick towns, too many people knew your business.

The automatic teller bank card was something else, though. If she could just find Roanna's PIN . . . Swiftly she began pulling scraps of paper out of the little pockets of the wallet. No one was supposed to write down their PIN, but everyone did. She found a slip of paper, neatly folded, with four numbers on it. She snickered to herself as she took an ink pen from the bottom of Roanna's purse and scribbled the numbers on her palm. Maybe it wasn't the PIN, but so what? All the machine would do was not give her the money, it wasn't as if it would call Roanna and tell on her.

Smiling, she slipped the bank card into her pocket. This was better than sneaking a twenty here and a twenty there. She'd get a couple of hundred, put the card back before Roanna missed it, and have some fun tonight. Hell, she'd even put the transaction slip in the folder where Roanna kept things like that; that way, there wouldn't be a discrepancy when the bank statement came out. This was a good plan; she'd have to use it again, though it would be smart to use Aunt Lucinda's card occasionally, if she could get it, and alternate rather than using the same one all the time. Variety was the spice of life. It also cut down on her chances of getting caught, which was the most important thing; that, and getting money.

By eight o'clock that night, Corliss felt much better. After hitting the automatic bank machine, it had taken her some time to find her regular supplier, but at last she had located him. The white powder beckoned, and she wanted to sniff it all up at once, but she knew it would be smarter if she rationed it, because there was no telling how often she

241

would be able to sneak a bank card. She allowed herself just a single line, enough to take the edge off.

Then she was in the mood for fun. She hit her favorite bar, but none of her friends were there, and she sat by herself, humming a little. She ordered her favorite drink, a strawberry daiquiri, which she liked because it packed quite a punch the way the bartender made them for her but still looked like one of those cute drinks it was okay for a nice girl to drink.

The longer she sat there, though, the more her mood darkened. She tried to hang on to the drug-induced euphoria, but it faded as it always did, and she wanted to cry. The daiquiri was good, but the alcohol didn't work the same way coke did. Maybe if she got a real buzz on, it would help.

The hour dragged past, and still none of her friends came in. Had they gone somewhere else tonight and not told her? She felt a sense of panic at being abandoned. Surely no one had heard that Webb had threatened to throw her out of Davencourt, not yet.

Desperately she sipped the daiquiri, trying not to stick herself in the eye with the stupid little turquoise paper parasol. Either the straw was shorter than usual, or that damn parasol had grown. She hadn't had this kind of trouble with the first two drinks. She glared at the bartender, wondering if he was playing a practical joke on her, but he wasn't even looking at her, so she decided he wasn't.

The carcasses of the other two little paper parasols lay in front of her. One was yellow, the other was pink. Put them all together and she'd have a pretty little parasol bouquet. Whoopee. Maybe she'd save them to put on Aunt Lucinda's grave. That was a thought; by the time the old bat kicked off, she should have enough little parasols collected to make a real pretty wreath.

Or maybe she could stuff them down Webb Tallant's throat. Death by parasol; that had a nice ring to it.

The bastard had scared her half to death this afternoon when he'd grabbed her like that. And the look in his eyes— God! That was the coldest, meanest look she'd ever seen, and for nothing! Little Miss Mealy-Mouth's beauty sleep hadn't been disturbed, and God knows she needed all she could get. Corliss snickered, but her mirth died when she remembered the threats Webb had made.

She *hated* him. Why did he have everything? He didn't deserve it. It had always galled her that he was the chosen favorite when he wasn't any closer kin to Aunt Lucinda than she was. He was mean and selfish, the old bitch was going to give Davencourt to him, and he wasn't going to let her live there after Aunt Lucinda died. It just wasn't fair!

As much as she disliked Roanna, at least Roanna was a real Davenport, and she wouldn't feel as bad if Davencourt went to her. Like hell, she wouldn't. Roanna was a stupid wimp, and she didn't deserve Davencourt either. The only good thing about Roanna having the house was that Corliss knew she could handle Roanna with one hand tied behind her back. She'd have that little mouse so buffaloed Roanna would be handing over money instead of forcing Corliss to sneak it.

But if Aunt Lucinda wasn't going to leave Davencourt to Roanna, then it just wasn't fair that Webb should get it! Aunt Lucinda might not think that Webb had killed Jessie, but Corliss had her own opinion, and it was even stronger after the look she'd seen on his face that afternoon. She had no doubts that he could kill. Why, for a minute she'd thought he was going to kill *her,* and over a little joke she'd been about to play. She'd only been thinking about slamming the door, she hadn't actually done it. But he'd grabbed her and hurt her neck, the bastard.

Someone slid onto the stool beside her. "You look like you need another drink," a smooth masculine voice purred in her ear.

Corliss cast a dismissive glance at the man beside her. He was good-looking enough, she supposed, but way too old. "Get lost, Pops."

He chuckled. "Don't let the gray hair fool you. Just because there's snow on the roof doesn't mean there's no fire in the furnace."

"Yeah, yeah, I've heard it all before," she said, bored. She took another draw on the daiquiri. "You may be too old to cut the mustard, but you can still spread the mayonnaise. Big deal. Beat it—and you can take that any way you like."

"I'm not interested in fucking you," he said, sounding as bored as she had.

She was so shocked by the bluntness that she looked at him then, really looked at him. She saw the thick hair that had gone mostly gray, and a body that was still powerful and in shape even though he had to be in his fifties. It was his eyes that riveted her, though; they were the bluest eyes she'd ever seen, and looking into them was like looking into a snake's eyes: flat, totally devoid of feeling. Corliss shivered, but couldn't help feeling fascinated.

He nodded at the parasols littering the bar. "You've been pouring the booze down pretty fast. Have a bad day?"

"You don't know the half of it," she said, but then laughed. "Things are looking up, though."

"So why don't you tell me about it," he invited. "You're Corliss Spence, aren't you? Don't you live out at Davencourt?"

That was often one of the first questions people asked when meeting her for the first time. Corliss loved the distinction it gave her, the sense of being someone special. Webb was going to take that away from her, and she hated him for it. "Yeah, I live there," she said. "For a while longer, anyway."

The man lifted his glass to his mouth. From the color of the liquid, it looked like straight bourbon. He sipped it as he stared at her with those cold blue eyes. "Looks to me like you'd already be hauling ass out of there. It must be pretty uncomfortable living with a killer."

Corliss thought of Webb's hand biting into the back of her neck, and she shivered. "He's a bastard," she said. "I'll be moving out soon. He attacked me today for no reason!"

"Tell me about it," he urged again, and held out his hand. "By the way, my name's Harper Neeley."

Corliss shook hands with him and felt a little thrill of

fascination. He might be an old guy, but there was something about him that gave her the shivers. For now, though, she was more than willing to tell her new friend anything he wanted to know about how hateful Webb Tallant was.

Roanna wished she hadn't succumbed to the nap that afternoon. It had helped immeasurably at the time, but now she faced another long night. She had come upstairs at ten and gone through the ritual of showering, putting on her nightgown, brushing her teeth, getting in bed, all for nothing. She had known immediately that sleep would be a long time coming, if at all, so she had gotten out of bed and curled up in her chair. She picked up the book she'd been trying to read for the past two nights and finally managed to get interested in it.

Webb came up at eleven, and she snapped off her reading light while she listened to him showering. She watched the splash of light from his room, wondering if he would back between it and the windows so she could see his shadow on the veranda. He didn't; his light went out, and there was silence from the other room.

The light from her lamp attracted mosquitoes, so Roanna always kept her veranda doors closed while she was reading, and she wasn't able to hear if he opened his own doors that night. She sat quietly in the dark, waiting until he'd had time to fall asleep, hoping she might become sleepy herself. She watched the fluorescent hands of her clock move past midnight; only then did she turn her lamp back on and resume reading.

An hour later she yawned and let the book drop into her lap. Even if she couldn't actually sleep, she was so tired that she wanted to lie down. She glanced outside and saw that an evening storm was building; she could see the red arc of lightning, but it was so far away she couldn't hear any thunder. Perhaps if she opened her doors and got into bed, the storm would sweep nearer, bringing the sweet rain with it. Rain was the best sedative, soothing her into what was usually her most restful sleep.

She was so tired that it was a long moment before she realized that lightning wasn't red. There was no storm.

Someone was on the balcony, his darker form barely discernible in the shadows.

He was watching her.

Webb.

She recognized him immediately, so swiftly that she didn't have time to panic at the thought of a stranger on the veranda. He was smoking, and the cigarette glowed in a red arc as he lifted it to his lips. The fiery end burned even brighter when he inhaled, and in the brief flare she could make out the hard outline of his face, the slash of his high cheekbones.

He was leaning against the veranda railing, just outside the frame of light from her windows. A faint, silver light gleamed on his naked shoulders, cast from the stars dotting the night sky. He was wearing dark pants, perhaps jeans, but nothing else.

She had no idea how long he'd been out there, smoking and silently watching her through the glass French doors. She inhaled deeply, her physical awareness of him suddenly so intense that she ached with the force of it. Slowly she nestled her head against the back of the chair and stared back at him. She was acutely aware of her bare flesh beneath the fabric of the modest nightgown: the breasts he had kissed, the thighs he had parted. Was he remembering that night, too?

Why wasn't he asleep? It was almost one-thirty.

He turned and flicked the cigarette over the railing, into the dew-wet grass below. Roanna's gaze automatically followed the movement, the arc of fire, and when she looked back, he was gone.

She didn't hear his doors close. Had he gone back inside, or was he strolling around on the veranda? With her own doors closed, she wouldn't have heard his open or close. She reached up and turned off the lamp, plunging her room into darkness again. Without the light on she could clearly see the balcony, bathed in that faint, silvery starlight. He wasn't there.

She was shaking a little as she crawled into bed. Why had he been watching her? Had there been any intent to it, or had he simply been outside smoking and looked through her windows because her light was on?

Her body ached, and she hugged her arms over her throbbing breasts. It had been two weeks since that night in Nogales, and she yearned to feel his hot, naked flesh against her again, his weight pressing her down into the mattress, moving over her, into her. The soreness left by the loss of her virginity had long since faded, and she wanted to feel him there again. She wanted to go to him in the silence of the night, slip into bed beside him, give him the gift of her own flesh.

Sleep had never been further away.

He gave her a sharp glance when she entered the study the next morning. She had used makeup to mask the dark circles beneath her eyes, but he immediately noted the effort. "It was a bad night for you, wasn't it?" he asked brusquely. "Did you get any sleep at all?"

She shook her head but kept her expression blank so he wouldn't guess at her physical torment. "No, but eventually I'll get tired enough to sleep. I'm used to it."

He closed the file that had been open on the desk, punched the exit key on the keyboard, and turned off the computer. He got to his feet with an air of decision.

"Go change clothes," he ordered. "Jeans and boots. We're going for a ride."

At the word *ride* her whole body was consumed with eagerness and renewed energy. Even as tired as she was, a ride sounded like heaven. A horse moving smoothly beneath her, the breeze flowing over her face, the fresh, heated air soothing her lungs. No meetings, no schedule, no pressure. But then she remembered that there *was* a schedule, and a meeting, and she sighed. "I can't. There's a—"

"I don't care what kind of meeting you have," he interrupted. "Call and tell them you won't be there. Today, you're going to do nothing but relax, and that's an order."

Still she hesitated. For ten years her entire existence had been focused on duty, on taking care of business, on helping fill the gap left by his departure. It was difficult to abruptly turn her back on the foundation of those ten years.

He put his hands on her shoulders and turned her toward the door. "That's an order," he repeated firmly, and gave her a light swat on the rump to send her on her way. It was supposed to be a swat, but instead his touch gentled the motion to a pat. He drew his hand back before it could linger, before his fingers could cup the firm buttock he had just touched.

She stopped at the door and looked back at him. He noted that she was blushing a little. Because he'd patted her ass? "I didn't know you smoked," she said.

"I usually don't. A pack lasts me a month or longer. I end up throwing most of them away because they've gone stale."

She started to ask him why he'd been smoking last night if he didn't normally smoke any more than that but held the words back. She didn't want to pester him with personal questions the way she had when she was a kid. He'd had a lot of patience with her, but now she knew that she'd been a bother to him.

Instead she quietly went upstairs to change clothes, and her heart lifted as she did. An entire day to herself with nothing to do but ride! Pure heaven.

Webb must have called down to the stable, because Loyal was waiting with two horses already saddled. Roanna gave him a shocked look. She'd always taken care of her own horse from the time she'd been big enough to lift a saddle. "I would have saddled him myself," she protested.

Loyal grinned at her. "I know you would, but I thought I'd save you some time. You don't get to ride nearly enough, so I wanted you to have a few extra minutes."

Buckley, her old favorite, was fifteen years old now, and she rode him only on more leisurely trails, over easy terrain.

The horse Loyal had chosen for her today was a sturdy bay, not a streak of lightning, but with legs like iron and a lot of stamina. Webb's horse, she noticed, had much the same characteristics. Loyal evidently figured they were going out for more than a Sunday trot.

Webb came out of one of the stalls where he'd been patting the inhabitant, a frisky yearling who had gotten into rough play with some other yearlings and a kick had opened up a cut on his leg. "Your salve still works magic," he said to Loyal. "That cut looks like it's a week old instead of just two days."

He took the reins from Loyal, and they swung into their saddles. Roanna felt her body change, the old magic sweeping over her muscles the way it always had. Instinctively she aligned herself with the horse's rhythm from the first step he took, his strength flowing upward into her lithe, graceful limbs.

Webb held his horse a pace back from hers, mainly for the pleasure of watching her. She was the best rider he'd ever seen, period. His own horsemanship was of the quality that, had he had the desire, he could have competed successfully in either of the opposing equestrian poles, show jumping or rodeo, but Roanna was better. Sometimes, every decade or so, there would be an athlete on the scene whose grace of movement transcended the sport, turning every meet, game, or competition into a work of art, and that was what it was like to watch Roanna ride. Even when the pace was easy, as it was now, and they were riding simply for the pleasure of it, her body was fluid as she adjusted to and controlled every nuance of the animal's motion beneath her.

Would she look like that if she were riding him? Webb's breath caught. Would her sleek thighs tighten and relax, lifting her, then letting her slide down onto his erection, so that she enveloped him with one smooth motion while her torso moved in that graceful sway—

He cut the thought off as blood rushed to his loins, and he shifted uncomfortably. Getting a hard-on while horseback

249

riding wasn't a good idea, but it was difficult to dispel the image. Every time he looked at her he saw the curve of her buttocks, and he remembered touching them, caressing her, driving deep and hard, and coming inside her with a force that made him feel as if he were exploding.

He was going to do himself a serious injury if he didn't stop thinking about it. He wiped the beads of sweat from his brow and deliberately wrenched his gaze away from her bottom. He looked instead at the trees, the horse's ears, anything except her, until his erection had subsided and he was comfortable again.

They didn't talk. Roanna was so often silent anyway, and now she seemed totally absorbed in the pleasure of the ride and he didn't want to disturb her. He enjoyed the freedom himself. He'd been working almost from the minute he set foot back on Davencourt land, and he hadn't taken the time to acclimate himself. His eyes were accustomed to stark, dramatic mountains and an endless sweep of sky, to cactus and scrub bushes, to clouds of dust and air so clear you could see for fifty miles. He was used to dry, searing heat, to arroyos that would abruptly flood from a rain the day before, far upstream.

He'd forgotten how damn *green* this place was, every shade of green in creation. It soaked into his eyes, into the pores of his skin. The air was thick and hazy with humidity. Hardwoods and evergreens rustled softly in a breeze so slight he couldn't feel it, wildflowers nodded their technicolor heads, birds darted and soared and sang, insects buzzed.

It hit him hard, low down in the gut. He'd developed a real love for Arizona and would never give up that part of his life, but this was *home*. This was where his roots were, sunk generations deep into the rich soil. Tallants had lived here for almost two hundred years, and hundreds of years longer than that if you counted the Cherokee and Choctaw heritage that ran in his family.

He hadn't let himself miss Alabama when he left. He had concentrated solely on the future and what he could build with his own two hands in the new home he'd chosen. But now that he was back, it was as if his soul had revived. He'd handle his family, ill-tempered and ungrateful as some of them were. He didn't like having so many Tallants living off the Davenports and not doing a damn thing to earn their keep. Lucinda was the tie between the Davenports and the Tallants, and when she died . . . He looked at the slim figure riding in front of him. The family hadn't been prolific, and untimely deaths had decimated their ranks. Roanna would be the only surviving Davenport, the last of the line.

No matter what he had to do, he would hold the Davenport legacy intact for her.

They rode for hours, even skipping lunch. He didn't like for her to miss any meals, but she looked so relaxed, with a flush on her cheeks, that he decided it was an acceptable trade-off. He would make certain from now on that she had time for a ride every day if she wanted, and it wouldn't be a bad idea if he applied the same decision to himself.

She didn't bubble over with enthusiasm the way she once would have done, talking nonstop and making him laugh with her quirky, sometimes rowdy observations. That Roanna would never return, he thought with a pang. It wasn't just trauma that had changed her into this controlled, reserved woman; she had grown up. She would have changed anyway, though not to this extent; time and responsibility had a way of transforming people. He missed the mischievous imp, but the woman got to him in a way no one else ever had. This volatile mixture of lust and protectiveness was driving him crazy, the two instincts warring with each other.

He'd stood on the balcony the night before and watched her through the windows while she read. She'd been isolated in a soft pool of light, curled in a huge chair that dwarfed her slender body. The light had picked up the red in her chestnut hair, making it gleam with rich, dark tones. A modest white nightgown had swathed her to her ankles, but he could see the faint shadow of her nipples beneath the cloth, the darkness at the junction of her thighs, and he knew that the gown was all she wore.

He'd known that he could go into her room and kneel down in front of that chair, and she wouldn't protest. He could slide his hands under the gown to cup her bottom and pull her forward. He'd been hard as rock, thinking of it, imagining the feel of her sliding down onto him.

Then she had looked up, as if she'd felt the heat of his thoughts. Her whiskey-brown eyes had been mysterious, shadowed pools as she stared back at him through the glass. Beneath the white cloth, her nipples had hardened into tiny peaks.

Just like that, her body had responded to him. A look. A memory. He could have had her then. He could have her now, he thought, watching her.

Was she pregnant?

It was too soon for her body to show any sign, but he wanted to strip her naked anyway, turn her this way and that with his big hands so he could minutely examine every inch of her in the bright sun, memorize her so that in the future he would be able to tell even the smallest change in her.

He was going to go out of his mind.

Roanna reined in. She felt exhilarated from the ride, but her muscles were telling her that it had been a while since she'd been in the saddle for such a long time. "I need to walk for a while," she said, dismounting. "I'm getting a little stiff. You can go on if you want."

She almost hoped that he would; it was a strain, being alone with him, riding with him in such perfect accord, the way they had before. Relaxed, with her guard down, several times she had almost turned to him with a teasing comment. She had caught herself each time, but the close calls made her nervous. It would be a relief to be alone.

But he dismounted as well and fell into step beside her. Roanna glanced at his expression and just as quickly looked away. His jaw was set, and he was staring straight ahead as if he couldn't bear to even look at her.

Stricken, she wondered what she had done wrong. They walked in silence, the horses clopping along behind them.

She hadn't done *anything* wrong, she realized. They had barely spoken. She had no idea what was bothering him, but she refused to automatically take the blame on herself the way she had always done before.

He put his hand on her arm and drew her to a halt.

The horses stopped, shifting behind them. She gave him a questioning look and went still. His eyes were a deep, intense green, glittering with a heat that had nothing to do with anger. He stood very close to her, so close that she could feel the damp heat of his sweaty body, and his broad chest was rising and falling with hard, deep breaths.

The impact of male lust hit her like a blow, and she swayed. Dazedly she tried to think, to pull back, but something inside her responded of its own volition. *He wanted her!* Happiness bloomed inside her, an internal golden glow that blotted out years of sadness. The reins dropped from her limp fingers, and she surged forward as if pulled by an invisible chain, rising on tiptoe as her arms went around his neck and her soft mouth lifted to his.

He stiffened in her embrace, just for a second, then he too dropped his reins, and his arms went around her, crushing her hard against him. His mouth was just as hard on hers, his tongue plunging deep. He was almost savaging her, the pressure of the kiss bruising her lips, his grip compressing her ribs. She could feel the ridge of his erection grinding against the soft juncture of her thighs.

She couldn't breathe; a giddy blackness began to creep over her consciousness. Desperately she wrenched her mouth away from him, her head falling back like a flower too heavy for its fragile stem. Her body was on fire and she didn't care, didn't care what he did to her, let him take her here, now, on the ground without even a blanket to cover the earth. She had craved his touch, ached for him—

"No!" he said hoarsely, putting his hands on her hips and forcing her away from him. "God damn it, no!"

The shock was as staggering as that blatant look of lust had been. Roanna stumbled, her knees too wobbly to hold her upright. She grabbed her horse's mane, clenching her fingers on the coarse hair and letting the big animal take her weight as she leaned against him. All color washed out of her face as she stared at Webb. "What?" she gasped.

"I told you," he said in a savage tone. "What happened in Nogales won't happen again."

An icy hollow formed in the pit of her stomach. My God, she had misunderstood. She'd misread that expression on his face. He hadn't wanted her at all, he'd been angry about something. She had wanted so desperately for him to want her that she had ignored everything he'd said and listened only to her own eternal, hopeless longing. She had just made a colossal fool of herself, and she thought she would die of shame.

"I'm sorry," she managed to choke out, backing away from him. The well-trained horse backed up, too, keeping pace with her. "I didn't mean—I know I promised—Oh, *God!*" With that despairing wail, she threw herself onto the horse's back and kicked him into a gallop.

She heard him yell something, but she didn't stop. Tears blurred her eyes as she bent over the horse's neck. She didn't think she would ever be able to face him again, and she didn't know if she would ever be able to recover from this final rejection.

Webb stared after her, his own face white, his hands knotted into fists at his side. He cursed himself, using every vicious term he'd ever heard. God, he couldn't have handled that any worse! But he'd been in an agony of desire all day, and when she had thrown herself against him like that, he'd lost it. The red tide of lust had swamped him, and he'd stopped thinking, plain and simply. He'd have pushed her to the ground and taken her right there, pounded her into the dirt, but she had pulled away from him and her head had fallen back as limply as any rag doll's, and he'd realized how roughly he was treating her.

He'd forced her into bed with him in Nogales, using blackmail as a means of slaking his lust for her. This time he'd been about to use brute force. He'd hauled himself back from the edge, but just barely. God, just barely. He had only kissed her, hadn't even touched her breasts or taken off any of her clothes, and he'd been on the verge of orgasm. He could feel the dampness of preliminary semen on his underwear.

And then he'd pushed her away—Roanna, who had already suffered so much rejection that she had withdrawn from everyone rather than give them the power to hurt her again. Only he retained that power, he was her only vulnerability, and with raw, savage frustration blinding him, he had pushed her away. He'd wanted to explain, to say that he didn't want to take advantage of her the way he had in Nogales. He wanted to talk to her about that night; he wanted to ask when her period was due, if she was already late. But the clumsy words that had come out of his mouth had been like a blow to her, and she had fled before he could say anything else.

There was no point in trying to catch her. Her horse wasn't the fastest thing on four legs, but then neither was his. She had the advantage of weighing about half what he did, and being the better rider to boot. Chasing after her would be a wasted effort, and hard on his mount in this heat.

But he had to talk to her, had to say something, anything, that would chase the haunted, empty look from her eyes.

Roanna didn't go back to the house. She wanted only to hide and never have to face Webb again. She felt shredded inside, and the pain was so new and raw that she simply couldn't face anyone.

She knew she couldn't avoid him forever. She was bound to Davencourt for as long as Lucinda lived. Somehow, tomorrow, she would find the strength to see him and pretend that nothing had ever happened, that she hadn't literally thrown herself at him again. Tomorrow she would have her protective shell rebuilt; maybe some cracks would show where she had mended it, but the walls would hold. She would apologize, pretend it hadn't been important. And she would endure.

She stayed away for the rest of the afternoon, stopping at a shady creek to water the horse and let him graze on the soft, fresh grasses nearby. She sat in the shade and blanked her mind, letting the time drip away as she did at night when she was alone and the sleepless hours stretched before her. Anything could be gotten through, one second at a time, if she refused to let herself feel.

But when the purple and lavender shades of twilight began to darken the world around her, she knew she couldn't delay any longer and reluctantly mounted the horse and turned his head toward Davencourt. An anxious Loyal came out to meet her.

"Are you all right?" he asked. Webb must have been in a black mood when he returned, but Loyal didn't ask what had happened; that was her business, and she'd tell him if she wanted. But he did want to know if she was physically okay, and Roanna managed to nod.

"I'm fine," she said, and her voice was steady, if a trifle husky sounding. Odd; she hadn't cried, but still the strain was evident in her tone.

"You go on up to the house," he said, his brow still furrowed with concern. "I'll take care of the horse."

Well, that was twice in one day. Her protective shell must not be as far along in reconstruction as she'd hoped. She was tired enough, devastated enough, that she simply said, "Thanks," and dragged herself toward the house.

She thought about sneaking up the outside stairs again, but somehow that seemed like too much effort. She had sneaked up those stairs too often in her life, she thought, instead of facing things. So she walked up the front steps, opened the front door, took the main stairs. She was halfway up them when she heard the thud of boot heels and Webb said from the foyer, "Roanna, we need to talk."

It took every ounce of strength she had, but she turned to face him. If anything, he looked as strained as she felt. He was standing at the foot of the stairs, his hand on the newel post and one foot on the first step, as if prepared to come after her if she didn't obey. His eyes were hooded, his mouth a grim line.

"Tomorrow," she said, her voice soft, and turned away . . . and he let her go. With every step she expected to hear him coming after her, but she reached the top of the stairs and then her room, unhindered.

She took a shower, dressed, went down for supper. Her instinct was to hide away in her room, just as it had been to take the back stairs, but the time for that was past. No more hiding, she thought. She would face what she had to face, handle what she had to handle, and soon she would be free.

Webb watched her broodingly during supper, but afterward he didn't try to maneuver her into a private conversation. She was tired, more exhausted than she thought she'd ever been before, and though with what had happened weighing on her mind she doubted she would even doze that night, still she wanted to lie down, had to lie down. She said good-night to everyone and returned to her room.

As soon as she stretched out in her comfortable bed, she felt the odd, limp weightiness of drowsiness come over her. Whether it was the ride, the accumulated lack of sleep, the stress, or a combination of all of it, she fell deeply asleep.

She didn't know when Webb silently entered the room through the balcony doors and checked on her, listening to her deep, even breathing to make certain she was asleep, watching her for a while, then leaving as quietly as he had entered. On this night, she wasn't awake to watch the hands on the clock sweep inexorably around.

She didn't remember dreaming; she never did.

In the deepest hour of the night she left her bed. Her eyes were open but strangely unseeing. She walked without haste, without hesitation, to her door and opened it. Her bare feet were sure and silent on the carpet as she drifted down the hall, ghostly in her white nightgown.

She wasn't aware of anything until a sudden bursting pain shot through her head. She heard a strangely distant cry, and then there was only darkness.

CHAPTER
17

Webb bolted out of bed, instantly awake and horribly certain that he'd heard Roanna crying out, but the sound hadn't come from her room. He grabbed up his pants and jerked them on, fastening them as he ran out the door. The cry had sounded as if it came from the direction of the stairs. God, what if she'd fallen down them—

The rest of the family had been awakened, too. He heard a babble of voices, saw lights coming on, doors opening. Gloria poked her head out just as he ran past. "What's going on?" she asked fretfully.

He didn't bother to answer, all his attention focused on getting to the stairs. Then he saw her, lying crumpled like a broken doll in the front hall that ran at a right angle to the stairs. He turned on the overhead light, the chandelier almost blinding in its brilliance, and his heart almost stopped. Blood, wet and dark, matted her hair and stained the carpet beneath her head.

He heard a clatter downstairs, as if someone had stumbled into something.

Webb looked up and saw Brock standing there blinking sleep from his eyes, not quite understanding what was going on. "Brock," he snapped. "There's someone downstairs."

258

His cousin blinked again, then comprehension cleared his gaze. Without a word he ran down the stairs. Greg didn't hesitate as he followed his son.

Webb knelt beside Roanna and gently pressed his fingers to her neck, hardly daring to breathe. Panic swelled in him like a balloon, suffocating him. Then he felt her pulse throbbing under his fingertips, reassuringly strong, and he went weak with relief. He ignored the rising crescendo of voices around him and gently turned her over. Harlan was blustering, Gloria and Lanette were clinging to each other and making moaning sounds. Corliss stood frozen just outside her bedroom door, her eyes wide with terror as she stared down at Roanna's limp form.

Lucinda struggled through the press of bodies and sank heavily to her knees beside him. Her color was pasty, and her trembling hand dug into his arm. "Roanna," she whispered, her voice catching. "Webb, is she—?"

"No, she's alive." He wanted to say she'd just been knocked out, but her injury could be more serious than that. She hadn't regained consciousness, and the fear was growing in him again. Impatiently he looked at Gloria and Lanette, driving each other into higher levels of hysteria, and dismissed them as useless. His gaze snapped over to Corliss.

"Corliss! Call 911. Get the paramedics out here, and the sheriff." She just stared at him, not moving, and he barked, *"Now!"* She swallowed convulsively and darted back into her suite. Webb heard her voice, high and trembling, as she talked to the 911 operator.

"What happened?" Lucinda moaned, stroking Roanna's face with shaking fingers. "Did she fall?"

"I think she surprised a burglar," Webb said, his voice tight with anger and anxiety, and the fear he was barely holding at bay. He wanted to pick Roanna up in his arms, cradle her against his chest, but common sense told him to let her lie still.

She was still bleeding, her blood soaking into the carpet. A dark red stain was spreading out from where her head lay.

"Corliss!" he yelled. "Bring a blanket and a clean towel!"

She was there in just a moment, stumbling over the blanket she was dragging, and simultaneously struggling to pull on a robe over her rather skimpy silk sleepshirt. Webb took the blanket and carefully tucked it around Roanna, then folded the towel and as gently as possible slipped it under her head, cushioning it from the floor and positioning the pad so that it pressed against the bleeding wound.

"W-will she be all right?" Corliss asked, her teeth chattering from shock.

"I hope so," he said grimly. There was a savage pain in his chest. What if she *wasn't* all right? What would he do?

Lucinda collapsed backward, her legs folding under her. She buried her face in her hands and began sobbing brokenly.

Gloria stopped wailing, the sound ceasing as if it had been cut with a knife. She dropped to her knees beside her sister and put her arms around her. "She'll be all right, she'll be fine," she crooned in reassurance, smoothing Lucinda's white hair.

Roanna stirred, moaning a little as she tried to lift her hand to her head. She didn't have the strength or the coordination, and her arm fell limply back to the carpet. Webb's heart leaped wildly. He picked up her hand and cradled it in his. "Roanna?"

At his tone, Lucinda pulled away from Gloria, frantically scrambling closer. Her expression was both terrified and hopeful.

Roanna took two deep breaths, and her eyelids fluttered open. Her gaze was unfocused, confused, but she was regaining consciousness, and that was what mattered.

Webb had to swallow a lump in his throat. "Roanna," he said again, leaning over her, and with an obvious effort she looked at him, blinking as she tried to clear her vision.

"You're fuzzy," she mumbled.

He could hardly breathe, his heart was pounding so violently. He placed her fingers against his rough cheek. "Yeah, I need to shave."

"Not that," she said, her words slurred. She took another deep breath, as if exhausted. "Four eyes."

Lucinda gulped back her sobs, choked laughter mingling with the tears as she reached for Roanna's other hand.

A tiny frown pulled at Roanna's brow. "My head hurts," she announced in confusion, and closed her eyes again. Her speech was clearer. She tried again to touch her head, but Webb and Lucinda were each holding a hand, and neither of them was inclined to let go.

"I imagine it does," Webb said, forcing himself to speak calmly. "You've got a hell of a bump back there."

"Did I fall?" she murmured.

"I guess so," he replied, not wanting to alarm her until he knew something for certain.

Brock and Greg came panting back up the stairs. Brock was wearing only a pair of jeans, zipped but not snapped, and his sturdy chest gleamed with sweat. He had picked up a poker from somewhere, and Greg had taken the time to get the .22 squirrel rifle from its rack over the fireplace in the den. Webb looked inquiringly at them, and they shook their heads. "He got away," Greg mouthed silently.

Sirens were wailing in the distance. Greg said, "I'd better put this up before the sheriff gets here. I'll let them in." He went back downstairs to return the rifle to its rack, lest he alarm a deputy already on edge with adrenaline.

Roanna tried to sit up. Webb put his hand on her shoulder and pressed her back down, alarmed at how little effort it took to do so. "No you don't. You're going to stay right here until a medic says it's all right for you to move."

"My head hurts," she said again, a bit truculently.

It had been so long since he'd heard that tone in her voice that he couldn't help grinning, despite the terror that had been clawing at his insides and was only now beginning to truly subside. "I know it does, honey. Sitting up will only make it worse. Just lie still."

"I want to get up."

"In a minute. Let the paramedics take a look at you first." She gave an impatient sigh. "All right." But before the sirens had wound to a stop outside, she was trying again to sit up, and he knew she was disoriented. He'd seen it before in injured people; the instinct was a primitive one, to get up, keep moving, put distance between yourself and whatever had caused the injury.

He could hear Greg explaining as he led a veritable parade of people up the stairs. There were six paramedics and at least that many deputies, with more arriving, from the sound of the sirens as additional vehicles speeded up the road.

Webb and Lucinda were shouldered to the side as the paramedics, four men and two women, gathered around Roanna. Webb backed against the wall. Lucinda clung weakly to him, trembling, and he put a supporting arm around her. She leaned heavily against him, using his strength, and with dismay he felt how fragile her once strong body felt in his grip.

More deputies arrived, and the sheriff. Booley Watts was retired now, but the new sheriff, Carl Beshears, had been Booley's chief deputy for nine years before being elected sheriff, and he had worked on Jessie's case. He was a compactly muscular man with iron gray hair and cold, suspicious eyes. Booley had operated with a sort of good-old-boy Andy Taylor kind of manner; Beshears was more brusque, straight to the point, though he had learned to temper the bulldog, straight-ahead tactics he'd learned in the marines. He began gathering the family together, ushering them to the side. "Folks, let's get out of the medics' way now, and let them take care of Miss Roanna." His steely gaze lit on Webb. "Now, what happened here?"

Until then, Webb hadn't realized the similarities between what had happened to Roanna tonight and Jessie's death ten years earlier. He had been concentrating on Roanna, terrified for her, taking care of her. The old, cold fury began to build in him as he realized Beshears suspected him of attacking Roanna, perhaps trying to kill her.

He ruthlessly suppressed his anger, though, because now wasn't the time for it. "I heard Roanna scream," he said in as even a tone as he could manage. "The sound came from the front of the house, and I was afraid she'd gotten up without turning on any lights and fallen down the stairs. But when I got here, I saw her lying just where she is now."

"How did you know it was Roanna screaming?"

"I just did," he said flatly.

"You didn't think it could be anyone else in the house who'd gotten up?"

Lucinda gathered herself, galvanized by the obvious suspicion in Beshears's voice. "Not usually," she said in a firm tone. "Roanna suffers from insomnia. If anyone is wandering around the house at night, it's likely to be her."

"But you were awake," Beshears said to Webb.

"No. I woke up when I heard her scream."

"We all did," Gloria put in. "Roanna used to have nightmares, you know, and that's what *I* thought was happening. Webb ran past my door just as I opened it."

"You're sure it was Webb."

"I know it was," Brock put in, squarely facing the sheriff. "I was right behind him."

Beshears looked frustrated, then shrugged, evidently deciding he didn't have a tie between the two events after all. "So, did she fall or what? The dispatcher said it was a call for the paramedics *and* the sheriff's department."

"Just as I got to her," Webb said, "I heard something downstairs."

"Like what?" Beshears's eyes sharpened again.

"I don't know. A crash." Webb looked at Brock and Greg.

"Brock and I went downstairs to take a look," Greg said. "A lamp had been knocked over in the den. I went outside while Brock checked the rest of the house." He hesitated. "I *think* I saw someone running, but I couldn't swear to it. My eyes hadn't adjusted to the dark."

"What direction?" Beshears asked briefly, already beckoning to one of his deputies.

"To the right, toward the highway."

The deputy approached, and Beshears turned to him. "Y'all get some lights and check the yard on the other side of the driveway. There's a heavy dew tonight, so if anybody's been through there, it'll show on the grass. There may have been an intruder in the house." The deputy nodded and departed, taking several of his fellows with him.

One of the paramedics came over. He had obviously leaped out of bed to answer the call; a ball cap covered his uncombed hair, and his eyes were puffy from sleep. But he was alert, his gaze sharp. "I'm pretty sure she's going to be all right, but I want to transport her to the hospital to be checked out and to have that cut in her head stitched up. Looks like she's got a mild concussion, too. They'll probably want to keep her for twenty-four hours, just to make certain she's okay."

"I'll go with her," Lucinda said, but suddenly staggered. Webb grabbed her.

"Lay her down on the floor," the paramedic said, reaching for her, too.

But Lucinda batted their hands away and pulled herself erect once more. Her color still wasn't good, but she glared fiercely at them. "Young man, I will not lie down on the floor. I'm old and upset, that's all. You tend to Roanna and don't pay any attention to me."

He couldn't treat her without her permission, and she knew it. Webb looked down at her and thought about picking her up and carrying her to the hospital himself, bullying her into letting a doctor check her. She must have known what he was thinking, because she looked up and managed a smile. "It's nothing to fret about," she said. "Roanna's the one who needs seeing to."

"I'll go with her to the hospital, Aunt Lucinda," Lanette said, surprising everyone. "You need to rest. You and Mama stay here. I'll go put on some clothes if y'all will gather up the things she'll need."

"I'll drive," Webb said. Lucinda started to protest again, but Webb put his arm around her. "Lanette's right, you need to rest. You heard what the paramedic said, Roanna will be all right. It would be different if she were in danger, but she isn't. Lanette and I will be there with her."

Lucinda clutched his hand. "You'll call me from the hospital, let me talk to her?"

"Just as soon as she's settled," he promised. "They'll have to do X-rays first, I imagine, so it could take a while. And she might not feel like talking," he warned. "She'll have a hell of a headache."

"Just let me know she's all right."

With that, Lucinda and Gloria went down the long hall to the back bedrooms, to gather the personal items Roanna would need for even a short stay in the hospital. Webb and Lanette went to their own rooms to dress. It took him less than two minutes, and he reached Roanna's side just as they were transferring her to a stretcher to carry her downstairs.

She was fully conscious now, and her eyes were wide with alarm as she looked up at him. He took her hand again, folding her cold, slender fingers against his rough, warm palm. "I don't like this," she said fretfully. "If I need stitches, why can't I just drive to the emergency room? I don't want to be *carried.*"

"You have a concussion," he replied. "It's not safe for you to drive."

She sighed and gave in. He squeezed her hand. "Lanette and I are going to be with you. We'll be right behind the ambulance."

She didn't protest again, and he almost wished she had. Every time he looked at her, he was hit by another wave of panic. She was paper white, what part of her face that wasn't covered by blood. The dark, rusty stain was spread over her face and neck, where it had run down from the laceration on her scalp.

Lanette came hurrying down, carrying a small overnight case, just as they were sliding the stretcher into the ambulance. "I'm ready," she said to Webb, already moving past him toward the garage.

Sheriff Beshears fell into step beside Webb. "The boys

found marks in the dew," he said. "Looks like someone took out running across the yard. Somebody's been messing with the lock on the kitchen door, too, there's some scratches on the metal. Miss Roanna's lucky, if she came face-to-face with a burglar and a bump on the head's all she got."

Remembering how she had looked like a crumpled little doll lying in the hall, with blood spreading around her, Webb thought Beshears's definition of *lucky* was different from his own.

"I'll be at the hospital later on to ask her some questions," the sheriff continued. "We'll do some more checking around here."

The ambulance was pulling out. Webb turned away and strode to the garage, where Lanette was waiting for him.

It took several hours and a shift change at Helen Keller Hospital before Roanna had been scanned, stitched, and settled into a private room. Webb impatiently waited in the hallway while Lanette helped her to clean up and get dressed in a fresh nightgown.

The bright morning sun was shining through the windows when he was finally allowed to reenter the room. She was lying in bed, looking almost normal now that most of the blood had been washed away. Her hair was still matted with it, but that would have to be taken care of later. A white pad covered the stitches in the back of her head, and stretchy gauze had been wrapped around her head to hold the bandage in place. She was very pale, but all in all she looked much better.

He eased down on the side of the bed, careful not to jar her. "The doctor told us to wake you up every hour. That's a helluva thing to do to an insomniac, isn't it?" he teased.

She didn't smile as he'd hoped. "I think I'll save you the trouble and just stay awake."

"Do you feel like talking on the phone? Lucinda was frantic."

Carefully she pushed herself higher in the bed. "I'm okay, it's just a headache. Will you dial the number for me?"

Just a headache from a bruised brain, he thought grimly as he picked up the receiver and punched the number for an outside line, then the number at Davencourt. She still thought she'd fallen, and no one had told her any differently. Sheriff Beshears wasn't going to get a lot of information from her.

Roanna talked briefly to Lucinda, just long enough to reassure her that she felt all right, a blatant lie, then gave the phone back to Webb. He was going to give Lucinda his own reassurances, but to his surprise it was Gloria who came on the line.

"Lucinda had another spell after y'all left," she said. "She's too stubborn to go to the hospital, but I've called her doctor and he's going to stop by this morning."

He glanced at Roanna; the last thing she needed to hear right now was that Lucinda was ill. "Keep her in line," he said briefly, and lowered his voice as he turned away so Roanna wouldn't be able to hear him. "I'm not going to say anything to the others now, so don't mention it to them just yet. I'll call in a couple of hours and check on her."

He got off the phone just as Sheriff Beshears came in and tiredly settled himself into one of the two chairs in the room. Lanette was in the other, but Webb wasn't inclined to sit anyway. He wanted to be closer to Roanna's side.

"Well, you're looking better than the last time I saw you," Beshears said to Roanna. "How do you feel?"

"I don't believe I'll go dancing tonight," she said in that solemn way of hers, and he laughed.

"Don't guess you will. I want to ask you a few questions if you feel up to it."

A puzzled look crossed her face. "Of course."

"What do you remember about last night?"

"When I fell? Nothing. I don't know how it happened."

Beshears shot a quick look at Webb, who gave a tiny shake of his head. The sheriff cleared his throat. "The thing is, you didn't fall. It looks like someone broke into Davencourt last night, and we figure you walked right up on him."

If Roanna had been pale before, now she was absolutely

267

white. Her face took on a pinched, frightened expression. "Someone hit me," she murmured. She didn't say anything else, didn't move. Webb, watching her closely, had the distinct impression she was drawing in on herself, holding everything inside, and he didn't like it. Deliberately he reached out and took her hand, squeezing it to let her know she wasn't alone, and he didn't give a damn what conclusions Beshears drew about his action.

"You don't remember *anything?*" the sheriff persisted, though his gaze flickered briefly to their clasped hands. "I know everything's confused now, but maybe you caught a glimpse of him and you just haven't realized it yet. Let's take it step by step. Do you remember leaving your room?"

"No," she said tonelessly. Her hand was motionless in Webb's grip. Once she would have been clinging to him, but now she didn't hold on to him at all. It wasn't just that she didn't seem to need him anymore, but that she didn't want to even be around him. For a while, when she had been so confused, all the barriers had been down and she had seemed to be comforted by his presence, to need him. But now she was pulling away from him again, putting emotional distance between them even though she made no effort to physically pull away. Because of what had happened between them yesterday, or was it something else, a detail about her injury? Did she remember something after all? Why didn't she want to tell the sheriff?

"What's the last thing you remember?" Beshears asked.

"Going to bed."

"Your folks say you have insomnia. Maybe you were awake, and you heard something and went to see what it was."

"I don't remember," she said. The pinched look was more pronounced.

He sighed and got to his feet. "Well, don't fret about it. A lot of folks don't remember at first what happened right before they took a bump on the noggin, but sometimes it comes back to them after a while. I'll be checking back with you, Miss Roanna. Webb, come on out in the hall with me, and I'll tell you what we've done so far."

Webb went with him, and Beshears strolled down the hall toward the elevators. "We followed the trail through the weeds all the way to that pasture road that cuts off from the highway, just past the turnoff going up to Davencourt," he said. "I figure he left his car parked there, but it's been a couple of weeks since we've had any rain and the ground was too hard for us to get any tread marks. Just to be sure, we brought in a couple of dogs, and they followed the trail as far as the pasture road, too, but nothing after that. It's a good place to hide a car; the brush is so thick anything parked even twenty yards up the road would be damn hard to see even in the daylight, much less at night."

"He got in through the kitchen door?"

"That's what it looks like. We couldn't find any other sign of entry." Beshears snorted. "I thought he was a fool at first, for not going in through some of those fancy glass doors y'all got all over the house, but maybe he was pretty smart. You think about it, the kitchen is the best place. Everyone should be upstairs in bed at that time of night, so he don't want to risk waking anyone by going through any of the upper veranda doors. The doors on the patio are on the side of the house, visible from the stables. But the kitchen door is on the back, and you can't see it from the driveway, the stables, or anywhere else."

They had reached the elevators, but Beshears didn't stop to punch the button to call it. He and Webb strolled on to the end of the hall, out of earshot of anyone getting off the elevator on that floor.

"Was anything taken?" Webb asked.

"Not that anyone can tell. That lamp's knocked over in the den, but except for that and the lock on the kitchen door nothing looks like it was touched. Don't know what he was doing in the den, unless he got rattled when Miss Roanna screamed. I suppose he ran back downstairs, looking for a quick way out, but the front door has a double lock on it and he couldn't figure it out in the dark. He ran into the den, saw it doesn't have an outside door, and accidentally blundered into the lamp. Looks like he finally went out the kitchen door, same as he got in."

Webb roughly ran his hand through his hair. "This won't happen again," he said. "I'll have a security system installed this week."

"Y'all should already have had one." Beshears gave him a look of disapproval. "Booley used to go on and on about how easy it would be to break into that house, but he never could talk Miss Lucinda into doing anything about it. You know how old folks are. With the house so far out of town, she felt safe."

"She didn't want to feel like she was in a fortress," Webb said, remembering the comments Lucinda had made over the years.

"This will probably change her mind. Don't bother with one of the systems that automatically call for help, because y'all are so far out of town it would be a waste of money. Put in a loud alarm that'll wake everyone up, if you want, but remember that wires can be cut. Your best bet is to put good locks on the doors and windows, and get a dog. Everybody should have a dog."

"Lucinda's allergic to dogs," Webb said wryly. He wasn't about to get one now and make her miserable for the few remaining months of her life.

Beshears sighed. "Guess that's why you never had one. Well, forget that idea." They turned and walked back toward the elevators. "Miss Lucinda had another spell after y'all left."

"I know. Gloria told me."

"Stubborn old woman," Beshears commented. They reached the elevators, and this time he punched the button. "Call me if Roanna remembers anything, 'cause otherwise we don't have jack shit."

Roanna rested quietly the remainder of the day, though she was troubled by nausea. The doctor ordered a mild medication to remedy that, and she ate most of her lunch, a light meal of soup and fruit. Lanette was surprisingly good in a sickroom, making sure Roanna had plenty of ice water in the bedside pitcher where she could reach it, and helping her to the bathroom when she needed to go. Otherwise she sat patiently, reading a magazine she'd bought in the gift shop, or watching television with the sound turned low.

Webb was restless. He wandered in and out of the room, moodily watching Roanna's face whenever he was there. Something about her manner bothered him more and more. She was *too* quiet. She had reason to be upset and alarmed, but instead she was showing very little response to anything. She avoided meeting his gaze and pleaded a headache when he tried to talk to her. The nurses checked on her regularly and said she was doing okay, her pupil responses were normal, but still he was uneasy.

He called back twice to check on Lucinda, but both times Lucinda answered the phone herself and wouldn't let him talk to Gloria. "I'm fine," she said crossly. "Don't you think the doctor would have put me in the hospital if anything serious was wrong? I'm old, I have cancer, and my heart isn't what it used to be. What else do you think could be wrong? Frankly, I can't think why I'd bother even taking medicine for a cold."

Both times she asked to talk to Roanna, and both times Roanna insisted that she felt well enough to talk. Webb listened to her side of the conversation and realized how guarded she sounded, as if she were trying to hide something.

Had she seen her assailant after all?

If so, why hadn't she told Beshears? There was no reason he could think of for her to keep something like that secret, no one she would be protecting. She was definitely hiding something, though, and he was determined to find out what. Not right now, not while she was still rocky, but as soon as she was home, he was going to sit her down in a private place for a little talk.

Lanette said she would stay overnight, and Webb finally

left at nine that night. He was back at six-thirty the next morning, though, ready to take Roanna home as soon as she was released. She was ready, already dressed in street clothes and looking much better than she had the day before. Twenty-four hours of enforced rest had done her a lot of good, even under the circumstances.

"Did you sleep any?" he asked.

She shrugged. "As much as anyone does in a hospital, I suppose."

Behind her, Lanette met his eyes and shook her head.

It was after eight when the doctor came in and checked her pupil responses, then smiled and told her to go home. "Take it easy for about a week," he said, "then see your family doctor for a checkup."

Webb drove them home then, easing over every bump and railroad track in an effort not to jar her head. Everyone at home at the time came out to meet her, and his plan to have a private talk with her was soon demolished. He didn't have a chance to be alone with her all day long. She was promptly put to bed, though she complained a bit irritably that she would rather be in her chair, but nothing would satisfy Lucinda except bed rest. Lucinda and Gloria fussed over her, Bessie was in and out at least ten times asking if she was comfortable, and Tansy left her kitchen domain to personally bring up the meal trays she had prepared with Roanna's favorites. Even Corliss stirred herself to visit and uncomfortably ask if she was all right.

Webb kept watch, knowing he'd get his chance.

It didn't come until late that night, when everyone else had gone to bed. He waited in the darkness, watching the veranda, and as he had expected, it wasn't long before a light came on in the next room.

He knew her veranda doors were locked, because he'd locked them himself before leaving her room the last time. He went out into the hallway, where the lights had been left burning at night since Roanna had been hurt, and quietly entered her room.

She had gotten out of bed and was once again ensconced

in that huge, soft-looking chair, though she wasn't reading. He supposed her head still hurt too much for her to do any reading. Instead she'd turned on her television, with the sound so low he could barely hear it.

She looked around with a guilty expression when the door opened. "Caught you," he said softly, shutting the door behind him.

Immediately he caught a hint of uneasiness in her face, before she smoothed her expression to blankness. "I'm tired of being in bed," she explained. "I've rested so much I'm not in the least bit sleepy."

"I understand," he said. She'd been in bed for two days, no wonder she was sick of it. "That isn't what I wanted to talk about."

"I know." She looked down at her hands. "I made a fool of myself day before yesterday. It won't happen again."

So much had happened since then that for a moment he stared blankly at her, then realized she was talking about what had happened when they were riding. He'd been a clumsy idiot, and typically, Roanna was taking the blame for it.

"You didn't make a fool of yourself," he said harshly, walking over to the veranda doors to check them again, just to make certain they were locked. "I didn't want to take advantage of you, and I handled it all wrong." He stood there, watching her reflection in the glass. "But that's something we'll talk about later. Right now, I want to know what it is you aren't telling the sheriff."

She kept her gaze on her hands, but he saw how still she went. "Nothing." He could see the guilt, the discomfort, even in the reflection.

"Roanna." He turned around and went over to her, squatting down in front of the chair and taking her hands in his. She was sitting in what was evidently her favorite position, with her feet pulled up onto the seat and tucked her under nightgown. He looked at the bandage on her head rather than the shadowy peaks of her nipples poking against the white cloth, because he didn't want anything to distract

273

him from what he wanted to find out, and just being close to her was bad enough. "You can fool the others, but they don't know you the way I do. I can tell when you're hiding something. Did you see who hit you? Do you remember more than you're telling?"

"No," she said miserably.

"Then what is it?"

"Nothing—"

"Ro," he said warningly. "Don't lie to me. I know you too well. What are you hiding?"

She bit her lip, worrying it between her teeth, and her golden brown eyes lifted to him, filled with a distress so intense he almost reached out for her in comfort. "I walk in my sleep," she said.

He stared at her, astounded. Whatever he'd been expecting, that wasn't it. "What?"

"I'm a sleepwalker. I guess that's part of the reason I have insomnia," she explained in a soft tone, looking down again. "I *hate* waking up in strange places, not knowing how I got there, what I've done, if anyone has seen me. I only do it when I'm in a deep sleep, so—"

"So you don't sleep," he finished. He felt himself shattering inside as he realized the sheer enormity of the burden she carried, the pressure under which she lived. God, how did she stand it? How did she function? For the first time, he sensed the slender core of pure steel in her. She wasn't little, needy, insecure Roanna any longer. She was a woman, a Davenport, Lucinda's granddaughter, with her share of the Davenport strength. "You were sleepwalking night before last."

She inhaled deeply. "I must have been. I was so tired, I went to sleep as soon as I got in bed. I don't remember anything until I woke up in the hall with a splitting headache and you and Lucinda leaning over me. I thought I *had* fallen, though I've never had any accidents before when I was sleepwalking."

"Jesus." He stared at her, shaken by the image that came to mind. She had walked up to the burglar like a lamb to slaughter, not seeing him even though her eyes had been open. Sleepwalkers *looked* awake, but they weren't. Possibly the burglar even thought she could identify him. Attempted burglary and assault weren't crimes that warranted murder to avoid arrest, but she could be in danger anyway. Not only were new locks going on everywhere, as well as an alarm system that would wake the dead if there was an unauthorized intrusion, but he would make damn certain everyone in the county knew she had a concussion and didn't remember anything about the incident. An article about the attempted burglary had been in the paper, and as a follow-up, he would have that information printed as well.

"Why didn't you tell the sheriff that you walk in your sleep?"

"Lanette was there," she said, as if that were reason enough.

It was, but it took him a moment to think it through. "No one knows, do they?"

She gave a slight shake of her head, then winced and stopped the motion. "It's embarrassing, knowing that I wander around in my nightgown, but it's more than that. If anyone knew . . ."

Again, it didn't take a genius to follow her thoughts. "Corliss," he said grimly. "You're afraid the little bitch would play nasty tricks on you." He rubbed his thumbs over the backs of her hands, feeling the slender, elegant bones just under the skin.

She didn't respond to that, just said, "It's better if no one knows."

"She won't be here much longer." He was glad he could make that promise.

Roanna looked startled. "She won't? Why?"

"Because I told her she'd have to move out. She can stay until Lucinda . . . She can stay for a few more months if she behaves herself. If she doesn't, she'll have to leave before then. Lanette and Greg will have to find another place to live, too. Greg makes good money, there's no excuse for them to be sponging off Lucinda the way they have."

"I think living here was Lanette's decision, hers and Gloria's."

"Probably, but Greg could have said no. I don't know about Brock. I've always liked him, but I didn't expect him to be a moocher."

"Brock has a plan," Roanna explained, and unexpectedly a faint smile touched her pale lips. "He's living here so he can save as much money as possible before he gets married. He's going to build his own house. He and his fiancée have already had an architect draw up the blueprints."

Webb stared at her mouth, enchanted by that tiny, spontaneous smile. He hadn't had to coax that one out of her. "Well, at least that's a plan," he grumbled to hide his reaction. "Gloria and Harlan are in their seventies; I'm not going to make them move. They can live here the rest of their lives if they want."

"I know you don't want the house crammed with relatives," she said. "I'll be moving out, too—"

"You aren't going anywhere," he interrupted harshly, rising to his feet.

She looked at him in bewilderment.

"This is your home, damn it. Did you think I was trying to tell *you* to get out?" He couldn't keep the anger out of his voice, not just at the thought of her leaving, but that she had thought he would want her to.

"I'm just a distant cousin, too," she reminded him. "How would it look for us to be living here together, even with Gloria and Harlan here? It's different now, because the house is so full, but when the others move out people will gossip if I don't, too. You'll want to get married again someday, and—"

"This is your home," he repeated, grinding his teeth together in an effort to keep his voice down. "If one of us has to move out, I will."

"You can't do that," she said, shocked. "Davencourt will be yours. It wouldn't be right for you to leave just so I'll have a place to stay."

"Haven't you ever thought that it should be yours?" he

snapped, goaded beyond endurance. "You're the Davenport. Don't you resent the hell out of me for being here?"

"No. Yes." She watched him for a moment, her eyes shadowed and unreadable as the words lay between them. "I don't resent you, but I envy you, because Davencourt is going to be yours. You were raised with that promise. You shaped your life around taking care of this family, this house. Because of that, you've earned it, and it should be yours. I knew when I went to find you in Arizona that Lucinda would change her will, giving everything to you again; we discussed it beforehand. But even though I envy you, I've never thought of Davencourt as mine. It's been home since I was seven years old, but it wasn't *mine*. It was Lucinda's, and soon it'll be yours."

She sighed, and gingerly rested her head back against the chair. "I have a degree in business administration, but I got it only because Lucinda needed help. I've never been interested in business and finance, while you thrive on it. The only kind of work I've ever wanted to do is train horses. I don't want to spend the rest of my life in business meetings; *you* take that part of it, and welcome to it. I won't be left destitute, and you know it. I have my own inheritance."

He opened his mouth and she held up her hand to stop him. "I'm not finished. When I'm no longer needed here —" She paused, and he knew she was thinking of Lucinda's death, as he did. It was always there, looming in their future whether they could bring themselves to speak openly of it or not. "When it's over, I'm going to set up my own stables, my own house. For the first time something will belong to *me*, and no one else will ever be able to take it away."

Webb's fists clenched. Her gaze was very clear, yet somehow distant, as if she looked back at all the things and people that *had* been taken from her when she'd been too young and helpless to have any control over her life: her parents, her home, the very center of her existence. Her self-esteem had been systematically stripped from her by Jessie, with Lucinda's unknowing assistance. But she had had him

277

as her bulwark until he, too, had turned from her, and since then Roanna had allowed herself to have no one, to care for nothing. She had in effect put herself in dormancy. While her life was on hold she had devoted herself to Lucinda, but that time was coming to an end.

When Lucinda died, Roanna planned to leave.

He glared down at her. Everyone else wanted Davencourt, and they weren't entitled to it. Roanna was legitimately entitled to it, and she didn't want it. *She wanted to leave.*

He was so pissed off that he decided he'd better go back to his room before he really lost his temper, something she wasn't in any shape to endure and that he didn't want to do anyway. He stalked to the door, but paused there for the last word. "We'll work all that out later," he said. "But you are *not* moving out of this house."

CHAPTER
18

It was the day of Lucinda's welcome-home party for him, and as Webb drove home he wondered how big of a disaster it would be. He didn't care, but it would disturb Lucinda a great deal if things didn't go exactly as she had planned. From what he'd experienced that afternoon, things weren't looking good.

It hadn't been much, not even a confrontation, but as a barometer of public sentiment it had been fairly accurate. He'd had lunch at the Painted Lady with the chairman of the agricultural commission, and the comments of the two women behind him had been easily overheard.

"He certainly has a lot of brass on his face," one of the women had said. She hadn't raised her voice, but neither had she lowered it enough to ensure she couldn't be heard. "If he thinks ten years is long enough for us to forget what happened . . . Well, he has another think coming."

"Lucinda Davenport never could see any fault in her favorites," the other woman commented.

Webb had looked across at the commissioner's face, which was turning dark red as the man studiously applied himself to his lunch and pretended he couldn't hear a thing.

279

"You'd think even the Davenports would balk at trying to force a murderer down our throats," the first woman said.

Webb's eyes had narrowed, but he hadn't turned around and confronted the women. Suspected murderer or not, he'd been raised to be a southern gentleman, and that meant he wouldn't deliberately embarrass the ladies in public. If men had been saying the same things he would have reacted differently, but not only were the two verbal snipers female, they were rather elderly, from the sound of their voices. Let them talk; his hide was tough enough to take it.

But the social matriarchs wielded a lot of power, and if they all felt the same way, Lucinda's party would be ruined. He didn't care for himself; if people didn't want to do business with him, fine, he'd find someone who did. But Lucinda would be both hurt and disappointed, and blame herself for not defending him ten years ago. For her sake, he hoped—

The windshield shattered, spraying Webb with tiny bits of glass. Something hot hummed by his ear, but he didn't have time to worry about it. His reflexive dodge had jerked the steering wheel in his hand, and the right wheels of the car bumped violently as the car veered onto the shoulder of the road. Grimly he fought for control, trying to ease the car back onto the pavement before he hit a hole or a culvert that would send him careening into the ditch. He was effectively blinded by the shattered windshield, which had held together but turned white with a thick webbing of fractures. A rock, he thought, though the truck in front of him had been far enough away that he wouldn't have expected the tires to throw a rock that far. Maybe a bird, but he would have seen something that big.

He got all four wheels back onto the pavement, and the car's handling smoothed. Automatically he braked, looking out the relatively undamaged right side of the windshield in an effort to judge his distance to the shoulder of the road and whether or not he would have enough room to pull off. He was almost to the side road that led to Davencourt's private road. If he could reach the turn off, there wouldn't be as much traffic—

The windshield shattered again, this time farther to the right. Part of the broken glass sagged from the frame, little diamond bits held together by the safety film that prevented the glass from splintering. *Rock, hell,* he thought violently.

Someone was shooting at him.

Quickly he leaned forward and punched the safety film with his fist, tearing it down so he could see in front of him, then he pushed the gas pedal to the floor. The car rocketed forward, the force jerking him back in the seat. If he stopped and gave the shooter a stationary target, he'd be dead, but it was damn hard to make an accurate shot at someone going eighty-five miles an hour.

Remembering that hot humming he'd heard just beside his right ear after the first shot, he made a rough estimate of the trajectory of the first bullet and mentally placed the gunman on a high bank just past the cutoff for the side road. He was almost to the road now, and if he turned onto it, the gunman would have a broadside shot at him. Webb kept the gas pedal down and roared past the cutoff, then past the thickly wooded pasture road where Beshears thought the burglar had hidden his car—

Webb narrowed his eyes against the whistling wind and stood on the brakes, spinning the steering wheel as he threw the car into a state-trooper-turnaround, a maneuver he'd mastered when he'd been a wild-ass teenager running this same road, with its long, flat straightaway. Smoke boiled from his tires as they left rubber on the pavement. Another car blew past him, horn blaring. His car rocked and skidded, then straightened out with its hood pointing back in the direction from which he'd come. This was a four-lane divided highway, so that meant he was going the wrong way, against traffic. Two cars were headed straight toward him. He hit the gas again.

He reached the pasture road just before he would have collided head-on with one of those cars, and took the turn on two wheels. He braked immediately and threw the transmission into park. He jumped out of the car before it stopped rocking, dodging into the thick cover to the side and leaving the car to block the exit from the pasture road, just in case this was where the shooter had left his car. Was it the same man who had broken into the house, or coincidence? Anyone who used this highway on a regular basis, which was thousands of people, could have noticed the pasture road. It looked like it was a hunting road leading up into the woods, but the trees and bushes cleared out after about a quarter of a mile and opened up onto a wide field that butted up against Davencourt land.

"Fuck coincidence," he whispered to himself as he weaved his way silently through the trees, taking advantage of the natural cover to keep anyone from getting a clear shot at him.

He didn't know what he'd do if he came face-to-face with someone carrying a hunting rifle while he himself was barehanded, but he didn't intend for that to happen. His had been a fairly typical rural upbringing in spite of, or perhaps because of, the advantage of living at Davencourt. Lucinda and Yvonne had made certain he fit in with his classmates, and the people he'd be dealing with the rest of his life. He'd hunted squirrel and deer and possum, learning early how to slip through thick woods without making a sound, how to stalk game that had eyes and ears a lot better than his. The rustlers who had taken his cattle and high-tailed it into Mexico had found out how good he was at tracking and at not being seen if he didn't want to be. If the gunman was in here, he'd find him, and the man wouldn't know he was anywhere around until it was too late.

There was no other vehicle parked on the pasture road. Once he'd established that, Webb hunkered down and listened to the sounds around him. Five minutes later, he knew that he was stalking the wind. No one was there. If he'd figured the trajectory correctly, then the shooter had taken another route off that high bank.

He stood up and walked back to his car. He looked at the demolished windshield, with those two small holes punched in it, and got seriously pissed off. Those had been good shots; either one or both of them could have killed him if the angle of fire had been corrected just a hair. He opened the door and leaned in, examining the seats. There was a ragged hole in the back of the driver's headrest, just about an inch from where his right ear had been. The bullet had had enough power, even after going through the windshield, to completely pierce the seat and make an exit hole in the back windshield. The second bullet had torn a hole in the back seat where it entered.

He picked up the cellular phone, flipped it open, and called Carl Beshears.

Carl drove out without lights or sirens, at Webb's request. He didn't even bring a deputy with him. "Keep it quiet," Webb had said. "The fewer people who know about this, the better."

Now Carl walked around the car, looking at every detail. "Damn, Webb," he finally said. "Someone's got a real hard-on for you."

"Tough. I'm not in the mood to get fucked."

Carl cast a quick look at Webb. There was a cold, dangerous look on his face, an expression that boded ill for anyone who crossed him. Everyone knew Webb Tallant had a temper, but this wasn't temper: this was something else, something deliberate and ruthless.

"Got any ideas?" he asked. "You've been back in town—what, a week and a half? You're making enemies real fast, serious ones."

"I think it's the same man who broke into the house," Webb said.

"Interesting theory." Carl thought about it, stroking his jaw. "So you don't think it was just a burglar?"

"Not now, I don't. Nothing has happened at Davencourt for the past ten years, until I came home."

Carl grunted, and stroked his jaw some more as he studied Webb. "Are you saying what I think you're saying?"

"I didn't kill Jessie," Webb growled. "That means someone else did, someone who was in our rooms. Normally, I would have been there. I never did go in for the late-night bar scene, and I didn't fool around with other women. Maybe Jessie surprised him, the way Roanna did. Roanna met up with him in the front hall; mine and Jessie's rooms were on the front left side, remember? Corliss has the rooms now, I sleep in a bedroom on the back. But the so-called burglar wouldn't have known that, would he?"

Carl whistled softly between his teeth. "That would make you the intended victim all along, which means this is the third attempt to kill you. I tend to believe you, son, mainly because there wasn't a reason for you to kill Miss Jessie. That's what had us so buffaloed ten years ago. Whoever did it must have thought it was real funny, you being blamed for killing her. That would be better than killing you himself. Now, who hated you enough to try to kill you ten years ago, and stay mad this long?"

"Damn if I know," Webb said softly. For years he'd thought Jessie's secret lover must have killed her, but with these new developments that didn't make sense. It would have made sense for the murderer to try to kill him, but not for him to kill Jessie. It would even have been reasonable, if he wanted to think of murder as reasonable, for the two of them to plot to kill him. That would get him out of the way, and Jessie would have inherited more of the Davenport fortune. If she had simply divorced him, her inheritance wouldn't have been as much, because despite Jessie's threats she had to have known that Lucinda wouldn't have disinherited him just because they'd divorced. To her credit, he didn't think Jessie had been involved in a plot to murder him. Like Roanna, she had simply been in the wrong place at the wrong time, but for Jessie the bad timing had been fatal.

Carl took a length of string from his pocket and tied one end of it around a pen. "Come hold this windshield up as straight as you can," he said, and Webb complied. Carl passed the free end of the string through the first bullet hole, threading it through until the pen caught on the outside and held. Then he tied the other end around another pen, this time securing the string under the pen's clip, and passed that pen through the holes in the back of the headrest.

He looked at the trajectory and whistled softly again. "At the distance he was shooting from, if he'd adjusted his sights just a teeny bit to the right, that bullet would have caught you smack between the eyes."

"I noticed it was a fine shot," Webb said sarcastically.

Carl grinned. "Thought you might be a man who appreciated good marksmanship. How about the second bullet?"

"It went on through the trunk."

"Well, any good deer rifle would shoot a bullet with that much power over that distance. No way of tracing it, even if we could have found one of the slugs." He eyed Webb. "You took a chance, stopping here like this."

"I was mad."

"Yeah, well, if there's a next time, cool off before you decide to go after someone who's armed. I'll have the car towed in, and my boys will go over it, but I don't think we'll find anything that will help us."

"In that case, I'd just as soon no one else knows about this. I'll take care of the car."

"Mind telling me why you want to keep it quiet?"

"Number one, I don't want him on guard. If he's relaxed, maybe he'll make a mistake. Number two, you can't do a whole hell of a lot anyway. You can't give me an escort everywhere I go, and you can't keep a twenty-four-hour watch on Davencourt. Number three, if Lucinda finds out, it just might kill her."

Carl grunted. "Webb, your folks need to know to be careful."

"They do. The so-called burglar spooked them. We have new deadbolt locks now, more secure windows, and we're wired to an alarm that, if it goes off, will set every dog inside a thirty-mile radius to howling. It's not any secret in Tuscumbia that we've done this, either."

"So you think he knows, and isn't likely to try getting into the house again?"

"He's gotten in twice before without any trouble. Instead of trying it again, this time he tried to shoot me off the road. Sounds as if he heard the news."

Carl crossed his arms and stared at him. "Miss Lucinda's big party is tonight."

"You think he could be among the guests," Webb said. He'd already thought of that himself.

"I'd say there's a good chance. You might want to take a look at the guest list and see if you recognize the name of someone you didn't get along with, somebody who came out on the short end of some business deal. Hell, he wouldn't even have to be invited; from what I hear, so many people will be there that he could waltz right in and no one would notice."

"You were invited, Carl. Are you coming?"

"Couldn't keep me away. Booley will be there, too. Is it okay if I run all of this by him? That old dog is still pretty sly, and if he knows to be watching, he might see something."

"Sure, tell Booley. But no one else, you hear?"

"All right, all right," Carl grumbled. He looked at Webb's car again. "You want me to give you a ride up to the house?"

"No, everyone would ask questions. Take me back to town. I have to get something else to drive anyway, and I'll arrange to have this one taken care of. As far as anyone is concerned, I had car trouble." He looked at his watch. "I'll be pushing it to get home in time for the party."

The guests were due to arrive in only half an hour, and Webb was nowhere around. All of the family was already there, including his mother and Aunt Sandra. Yvonne was beginning to pace, because it wasn't like Webb to be late to anything, and Lucinda was growing increasingly fretful.

Roanna sat very still, holding her own worry inside. She didn't let herself think about car accidents, because she couldn't bear it. Her own parents had died that way, and since then she shrank from the very idea of an automobile accident. If she passed one on the highway, she never rubbernecked but carefully kept her gaze averted and got past the accident site as soon as she could. Webb couldn't have been in an accident, he simply couldn't

Then they heard the front door open, and Yvonne rushed to the door. "Where have you *been?*" Roanna heard her demand with a mother's asperity.

"I had car trouble," Webb replied as he took the stairs two at a time. He was back downstairs in fifteen minutes, freshly shaved and wearing the black-tie apparel on which Lucinda had insisted.

"Sorry I'm late," he said to everyone as he crossed to the liquor cabinet and opened the doors. He poured himself a shot of tequila and tossed it back, then set the glass down and gave them a reckless grin. "Let the games begin."

Roanna couldn't take her eyes off him. He looked like a buccaneer despite the fineness of his clothes. His thick dark hair was still black with dampness and brushed into a severe style. He moved with the lithe grace of a man accustomed to formal clothes, without a trace of self-consciousness. The jacket sat perfectly on his broad shoulders, and the trousers were just snug enough to look trim without being binding. Webb had always worn his clothes well, no matter what they were. She had thought no one could look better than he did in jeans and boots and chambray work shirt, and now she thought no one looked better in black tie. Jet studs marched down the front of his snow white shirt, which had rows of tiny tucks, and matching jet cuff links gleamed darkly at his thick wrists.

She hadn't talked privately with him since the night he'd come to her room, and she had told him why she hadn't seen the burglar. Webb had forbidden her to work at all until the family doctor had checked her and given her the all clear, which he'd done just the day before. Truth to tell, for the first several days after she'd gotten home from the hospital, she hadn't felt like working or doing anything except sitting very still. The headache had been persistent, and if she had moved around much, she suffered a recurrence of that nausea that went with concussion. It was only

287

in the past two days that the headache had gone away, and the nausea with it. She didn't think she would risk dancing tonight, though.

Webb had been busy, and not just with work. He had overseen the installation of steel-reinforced doors on the main entrances, dead-bolt locks on even the French doors, and an alarm system that had made her pull a pillow over her head to buffer the sound when it was tested. If she couldn't sleep and wanted the veranda doors open so she could enjoy the fresh air, first she had to punch in a code on a small box installed by the window of every room. If she opened the doors without entering the code, the resulting blast would jolt everyone out of their beds.

Between her headache and his work, there simply hadn't been time for a private talk. In the drama of her injury, most of her embarrassment had faded away. After his midnight visit to her room, the subject hadn't come up again, as if they both wanted to avoid it.

"My, you look handsome," Lucinda said now, eyeing Webb up and down. "Better than you did before, if you don't mind my saying so. Wrestling cows, or whatever it was you did in Arizona, certainly kept you in shape."

"Steers," he corrected, his eyes gleaming with amusement. "And, yes, I wrestled a few of them."

"You said you had car trouble," Yvonne said. "What's wrong with it?"

"The transmission went out," he said smoothly. "I had to have it towed."

"What are you driving then?"

"A pickup truck." His eyes gleamed greenly as he said it, and Roanna saw the fine tension in him, a sort of heightened state of alertness, as if he were poised for some sort of crisis that only he anticipated. At the same time there was an obvious amusement in the line of his mouth, and she saw him glance expectantly at Gloria.

"A truck," Gloria said with disdain. "I hope it doesn't take long to get your car repaired."

The amusement became even more pronounced, though Roanna wondered if she was the only one who saw it. "Doesn't matter," he said, and grinned in wicked relish. "I bought the truck."

If he'd expected a tirade, Gloria didn't disappoint him. She launched into a lecture on "how it looks for one of *our* family to drive such a *common* vehicle."

When she segued into the part about the image they had to uphold, Webb's eyes gleamed even brighter. He said, "It's four-wheel drive, too. Big tires, like the kind bootleggers use so they can get into the woods." Gloria stared at him, aghast and momentarily silenced, as her face turned red.

Lucinda was hiding her smile behind her hand. Greg coughed and turned away to look out the window.

Corliss was also looking out the window. She said, "My God, it looks like that scene in *Field of Dreams.*"

Lucinda, understanding exactly what she meant, stood up and said with evident satisfaction, "Of course it does. If I give a party, they will come."

That remark elicited laughter from everyone except Roanna, but Webb noticed that a smile briefly touched her lips. That was the third one, he thought.

Soon the house was brimming over with laughing, chattering people. Some of the men wore black tie, but most of them were in dark suits. The women were arrayed in a variety of styles ranging from above-the-knee cocktail dresses to tea length to more formal long gowns. Everyone in the Davenport and Tallant families wore long gowns, again at Lucinda's direction. She knew exactly how to make an impression and set the tone.

Lucinda looked good, better than she had in a long time. Her white hair was in a queenly twist on the back of her head, and her pale peach gown, aided by a skillful application of cosmetics, lent its delicate color to her face. She had known what she was doing by insisting on peach-colored lights.

While Lucinda held court with her friends, Roanna

quietly saw to it that everything ran smoothly. The caterer was very efficient, but disaster had been known to strike even the most rigidly organized of parties. Waiters hired for the evening moved through the crowd with trays laden with glasses of pale gold champagne or with a dazzling array of hors d'oeuvres. For those who had heartier appetites, a huge buffet had been set up. Out on the patio, the band had already begun playing old standards, luring people outside to dance under the peach fairy lights.

Roanna noticed Webb moving through the crowd, talking easily with people, stopping to tell a joke or make a few remarks about politics, then going on to another group. He seemed perfectly relaxed, as if it hadn't occurred to him that anyone might look askance at him, but still she could see his increased tension in the hard, bright glitter of his eyes. No one would say anything derogatory about him in his presence, she realized. There was a power about him that made him stand out even in this crowd of social elites, a personal assurance that not many people had. He really didn't give a damn what any of them thought. Not for his own sake, at least. He came across as both relaxed and self-assured but ready to act if necessary.

Around ten o'clock, when the party had been going strong for over two hours, he came up behind her as she was surveying the buffet table to make certain nothing needed replenishing. He stood so close that she felt the heat of his big body, and he rested his right hand on her waist. "Are you feeling all right?" he asked in a low voice.

"Yes, I'm fine," she said automatically as she turned to face him, repeating the same words she had used at least a hundred times that night in answer to the same question. Everyone had heard about the burglar, and her concussion, and wanted to know about it.

"You look fine," everyone else had said, but Webb didn't. Instead he was looking at her hair.

The stitches in her scalp had been removed just the day before when she had gone to the family doctor. Today, in preparation for the party, she had gone to her hairdresser, who had gently arranged her hair in a sophisticated twist that concealed the small shaved patch.

"Can you tell?" she asked anxiously.

He knew what she meant. "No, not at all. Is your head still sore?"

"Just a little. It's tender rather than actually sore."

He lifted his hand from her waist and flicked one of her dangling earrings, setting the gold stars to dancing. "You look good enough to eat," he said quietly.

She blushed, because she had hoped she looked attractive tonight. The creamy gold of her gown complemented her warm complexion and the dark chestnut of her hair.

She looked up at him, and her breath caught in her chest. He was looking down at her with a hard, intense, *hungry* cast on his face. Time suddenly seemed to stand still around them, people fading from her consciousness, the noise and music muted. Her blood throbbed through her veins, slowly, powerfully.

This was the way he had looked the day they'd gone riding together. She had mistaken it for lust . . . or *had* she been mistaken?

They were utterly alone there in the middle of the crowd. Her body quickened, her breath coming fast and shallow, her breasts rising as if to his touch. The ache of wanting him was so intense that she thought she would die. "Don't," she whispered. "If you don't mean it . . . don't."

He didn't reply. Instead his gaze moved slowly down to her breasts, lingered, and she knew her nipples were visibly erect. A muscle twitched in his jaw.

"I want to make a toast."

Lucinda knew how to make herself heard in a crowd without appearing to raise her voice. Slowly the chatter of hundreds of voices stilled, and everyone turned toward her as she stood slightly alone, frail but still queen.

The spell that had held Roanna and Webb in its grip was shattered, and Roanna shuddered in reaction as they both turned to face Lucinda.

"To my grand-nephew, Webb Tallant," Lucinda said

clearly, and lifted her glass of champagne to Webb. "I missed you desperately while you were away, and I'm the happiest old lady in Colbert County now that you're back."

It was another of her masterful strokes, forcing people to toast him, acknowledge him, accept him. All over the room glasses were lifted to Webb, champagne was drunk to his return, and a chorus of "Welcome home" filled the room. Roanna, whose hands were empty, gave him a fleeting, rueful smile.

Number four, he thought. That was two in one night.

Her nerves felt raw from the silently charged interval that had passed between them. She slipped away into the crowd and worked her way outside to make certain everything was okay on the patio. Couples strolled over the grounds, their way lit by the thousands of lights woven into the trees and bushes, the maze of electrical cords carefully covered with foam stripping and taped over so no one would trip over them. The band had moved out of old standards, having sufficiently warmed up the dancing crowd, and was now playing more lively tunes, specifically "Rock Around the Clock." At least fifty people were bopping their hearts out on the dance floor.

The tune ended to applause and laughter, and then there was one of those errant little pockets of silence in which the words "killed his wife" were clearly heard.

Roanna stopped, her expression freezing. The silence spread as people looked uncomfortably at her. Even the band members stood still, not knowing what was going on but aware that something had happened. The woman who had been talking turned around, her face dark red with embarrassment.

Roanna stared steadily at the woman, who was a Cofelt, a member of one of the oldest families in the county. Then she looked around at all the other faces, frozen in the lovely peach light as they watched her. These people had come to Webb's home, enjoyed his hospitality, and still talked about him behind his back. It wasn't just Cora Cofelt, who had been unlucky enough to be heard. All of these faces were guilty because they too had been saying the same thing she had. If they had possessed any good judgment to begin with, she thought with growing fury, they would have realized ten years ago that Webb couldn't possibly have killed his wife.

It was common courtesy that a hostess do nothing to embarrass one of her guests, but Roanna felt anger move through her. She trembled with the rush of emotion, the sheer energy. It flowed through her until even her fingertips tingled.

She had endured a lot on her own account. But, by God, she wasn't going to stand there and let them slander Webb.

"You people were supposed to have been Webb's friends," she said in a clear, strong voice. She had seldom in her life been angrier, except at Jessie, but this was a different kind of anger. She felt cool, perfectly in control of herself. "You should have known ten years ago that he would never have harmed Jessie, you should have supported him instead of putting your heads together and whispering about him. Not one of you—*not one*—expressed any sympathy to him at Jessie's funeral. Not one of you spoke up in his behalf. But you've come to his house tonight as guests, you've eaten his food, you've danced . . . and you're still talking about him."

She paused, looking from face to face, then continued. "Perhaps I should make my family's position clear to everyone, in case there's been any misunderstanding. We support Webb. Full stop, period. If anyone of you here feels you can't associate with him, then please leave now, and your association with the Davenports and the Tallants will be at an end."

The silence on the patio was thick, embarrassed. No one moved. Roanna turned to the band. "Play—"

"—something slow," Webb said from behind her. His hand, hard and warm, curled around her elbow. "I want to dance with my cousin, and her head is still too sore for bopping."

A spatter of self-conscious laughter ran around the patio. The band began playing "Blue Moon," and Webb turned her into his arms. Other couples moved together and began swaying to the music, and the crisis was over.

He held her with the distance of cousins, not the closeness of a man and a woman who had lain naked together amid tangled sheets. Roanna stared at his throat as they danced. "How much did you hear?" she asked, her voice quiet and level once more.

"Everything," he said carelessly. "You were wrong about one thing, though."

"What was that?"

A rumble of thunder sounded in the distance, and he looked up at the dark sky as a sudden cool breeze arrived with the promise of rain. After days of teasing, it looked as if a storm was finally coming. When he glanced back down at her, his green eyes were glittering. "There was one person who offered me sympathy at Jessie's funeral."

CHAPTER
19

*T*he party was over, the guests gone home. The band had unplugged and loaded up, and they, too, were gone. The caterer and her staff had cleaned, washed, and efficiently stored everything in two vans and driven away, tired but well paid.

Lucinda, exhausted by the superhuman effort she had made that night, had gone immediately up to bed, and everyone else had soon followed.

The storm had lived up to its promise, arriving with great sheets of lightning, window-rattling thunder, and torrents of rain. Roanna watched all the drama from the dark safety of her room, snugly curled in her chair. The veranda doors were thrown open so she could get the full effect of it, smell the freshness of the rain and watch the wind sweep it across the land in battering waves. She was cuddled under a light, baby-soft afghan, deliciously chilled by the dampness in the air. She was relaxed and a little drowsy, hypnotized by the rain, her body sinking into the chair's comforting depths in utter relaxation.

The worst of the storm had already passed, and the rain had settled down into a steady, heavy downpour accompanied by an occasional flash of lightning. She was content to sit there, remembering—not the scene on the patio, but that moment before Lucinda's toast when she and Webb had been caught in a private bubble of suspended time, desire pulsing thickly between them.

It *had* been desire, hadn't it? Sweet, hot. His gaze had drifted, as heated as a torch, down to her breasts. They had throbbed, her nipples lifting to him. She hadn't been mistaken in his intent, she couldn't have been. Webb had wanted her.

Once she would have gone to him, heedless of everything except her desire to be with him. Now she remained in her own room, watching the rain. She wouldn't chase after him again. He knew that she loved him, he'd known it all her life. The ball was now in his court, for him to hit it back or let it go by. She didn't know what he would do or if he would do anything at all, but she had meant what she'd told him at the party. If he wasn't serious in his attentions, then she didn't want them.

Her eyes drifted shut as she listened to the rain. It was so soothing, so peaceful; she felt at rest, whether or not she slept that night.

A faint scent of cigarette smoke came to her. She opened her eyes, and he was there, standing in the open doors, watching her. His gaze bored through the darkness of the room. The sporadic flashes of lightning revealed her to him, her eyes shadowed and calm, her body relaxed and waiting . . . waiting.

In the same brief moments of illumination she could see the way he lounged there with one shoulder against the door frame, a negligent posture that in no way concealed the tension in his coiled muscles, the intensity of the way he watched her, like a predator focusing on its prey.

He had partially undressed. His coat was gone and his black tie. The snowy white shirt was unbuttoned and pulled free of his pants, and it hung open across his broad chest. A half-smoked cigarette was in his hand. He turned and flicked it over the veranda railing, out into the rain, and then he was silently crossing the room to her, his tread lithe and pantherish.

Roanna didn't move, didn't say anything in either welcome or rejection. This move was his.

He knelt in front of the chair and put his hands on her legs, smoothing the afghan across her knees. The heat of his touch burned her through the covering.

"God knows, I've tried to stay away from you," he muttered.

"Why?" she asked, her voice low, the question simple.

He gave a rough laugh. "God knows," he said again.

Then he tugged gently on the afghan, pulling it away from her and dropping it to the floor beside the chair. Just as gently he slipped his hands under the hem of her nightgown and caught her ankles. He pulled her legs out of their tucked position, straightening them, and spread them so that he was between them.

Roanna caught a deep, shuddering breath.

"Are your nipples hard?" he whispered.

She could barely speak. "I don't know . . ."

"Let me see." And he slid his hands all the way up her body, under the nightgown, and closed his fingers over her breasts. Until he touched them, she hadn't realized how desperate she had been for this. She moaned aloud at the relief, the pleasure. Her nipples stabbed his palms. He rubbed his thumbs over them and laughed softly. "I do believe they are," he whispered. "I remember the way they taste, the way they feel in my mouth."

Her breasts lifted into his hands with every quick, sighing breath. Desire was coiling hotly in her loins, loosening her, turning her flesh warm and pliable to his touch.

He lifted the nightgown up and over her head, pulling it away and dropping it to the floor as he had the afghan. She sat naked before him in the huge chair, her slender body dwarfed by its bulk. Lightning flickered again, briefly revealing the details of breast and loin, tightly puckered nipples and opened thighs. His breath hissed through his teeth, his broad chest expanding. Slowly he stroked his hands up her legs, pushing her thighs wider and wider apart until she was fully exposed to him.

The damp night air washed over her, the breeze cooling the heated flesh between her legs. The feeling of exposure, of vulnerability, was too sharp to be borne, and with a soft, panicked sound she tried to close her legs.

His hands tightened on her thighs. "No," he said. Slowly he leaned forward, letting his body touch her, lightly press down on her, and his mouth closed over hers with a sweetness, a tenderness, that was devastating. The kiss was as gentle as a butterfly's wings, as leisurely as summer. With the utmost delicacy he cherished her mouth, lingered over the kiss. At the same time his wicked fingers moved boldly between her legs, opening the secret folds that protected the soft opening of her body. One big finger probed at her, making her squirm, then it pushed deep inside. Roanna arched helplessly, moaning into his mouth, overcome by the startling sense of being penetrated.

He kept on kissing her, the sweetness of his mouth gentling her for the marauding thrust of his fingers. It was almost diabolical, that contrast of intensity, arousing every aspect of her sensuality. She was both seduced and ravished, enticed and taken.

His lips left her mouth, slid hotly down her throat, then were at her breasts. He sipped delicately, sucked hard. Roanna sank into a dark, whirling storm of pure desire, trembling with need. She put her hands on his head, feeling the thick, cool silk of his hair between her fingers. She felt dizzy, drunk with arousal, with the heated musky scent of his skin. He was hot, so hot, his body heat burning through his shirt.

His mouth moved downward, over her trembling stomach muscles. His tongue probed her shallow navel, making her loins clench wildly as a bolt of pleasure shot through her. Down, down . . .

He gripped her buttocks hard, pulling them forward so that her bottom was right on the edge of the chair, then draped her legs over his shoulders. She made an incoherent sound of panic, of helpless anticipation.

"I told you," he muttered. "Good enough to eat."

Then he kissed her, his mouth hot and wet, his tongue swirling around her straining, yearning nub. Her hips lifted wildly, her heels digging into his back. She cried out, muffling the sound with her own hand. She couldn't stand it, it was too intense, it was torture and ecstasy all at once, and her hips bucked in an effort to escape the sensation. He gripped her bottom tighter, pulling her harder against his mouth, and his tongue stabbed deep into her. She climaxed violently, shuddering, biting her hand to keep from screaming from the force of it.

When the sensations finally ebbed and released her from their dark whirlpool, she lay sprawled limply in the chair with her legs still spread on his wide shoulders. She couldn't move. She had no strength, not even enough to open her eyes. Whatever he wanted to do to her now, she was open, compliant, completely vulnerable to his desire.

He lifted her thighs off his shoulders and she felt him moving, felt the brush of bare skin against her as he stripped out of his shirt. She forced her heavy eyelids open as he undid his pants and pushed them down. His urgency was a hot, wild thing. He hooked one arm around her bottom and dragged her forward even more, off the chair and onto his thighs, onto his thick, thrusting penis. It speared upward into her, so hard that she felt bruised, so hot that she felt burned. Her weight aided in her own penetration, pushing her down so that he went even deeper, and she choked on a soft scream.

Webb groaned, leaning back on his hands so that his body arched powerfully beneath her. "You know what to do," he said from between clenched teeth. "Ride."

She did. Automatically her body responded, rising and falling, her thighs clasping his hips, flexing as she lifted herself almost completely off him only to slide back down. She rode him slowly, so that she took him by increments.

Her body was magic, moving with the fluid grace that had always captivated him; she enveloped him with a downward glide, then tormented him with the threat of release as she moved upward again, almost off of him . . . *no, no* . . . then back down, and he groaned at the wet heated relief of being surrounded by her flesh, held, caressed. He was stallion-hard inside her, and finally she rode him hard, moving fast, slamming herself down onto him. Sensation built unbearably, and he thrust upward, hard. Helplessly she cried out, her sweet inner flesh pulsing and hugging him as she came again.

A harsh cry tore out of his throat and he reared up, throwing her back against the chair. He pinned her to it with his weight as he plunged and bucked, spurting hotly into her.

He lay heavily on her, trembling and sweating. His release had been so powerful that he couldn't speak, couldn't think. Sometime later a measure of strength returned to his muscles and he withdrew from her, bringing a wordless murmur of protest from her lips. He stood and kicked his pants off, then lifted her up into his arms and carried her to the bed. He stretched out on the bed beside her, and she curled into his embrace and went to sleep. Webb buried his face against her hair and let the darkness claim him, too.

Some unknown time later she moved out of his arms and got up from the bed. Webb awoke at once, disturbed by her absence. He blinked sleepily at the pale form of her naked body. "Ro?" he murmured.

She didn't answer but walked calmly, deliberately toward the door. Her bare feet were silent. It almost looked as if she were drifting over the floor.

The hair stood up on the back of his neck and he shot out of bed. His hand slapped against the door just as she reached out for the doorknob. He peered at her face. Her eyes were open, her expression as serene as a statue's.

"Ro," he said, his voice rough. He put his arms around her and pulled her against him. "Wake up, darlin'. Come on, baby, wake up." He shook her a little.

She blinked once or twice and yawned as she cuddled closer. He held her tighter and felt tension slowly rob her body of pliancy as she realized that she was out of bed, standing at the door.

"Webb?" Her voice was choked, shaken. She shivered, her skin roughening with a chill. He picked her up and carried her back to the bed, sliding her beneath the warm covers and getting in beside her. He held her close to the warmth of his own body, held her as the shivers became shudders.

"Oh, my God," she said against his shoulder, the words almost toneless with strain. "I did it again. I don't have any clothes on. I almost walked out of here *naked.*" She began pushing against him, trying to squirm away. "I need my nightgown," she said frantically. "I can't sleep like this."

He controlled her struggles, pressing her down into the mattress. "Listen to me," he said, but she kept trying to pull away from him, and finally he rolled on top of her, ruthlessly controlling her delicate body with his much bigger, stronger one.

"Shh, shh," he murmured against her ear. "You're safe with me, baby. I woke up as soon as you moved away from me. You don't have to worry; I won't let you leave this room."

Her breath was coming in gasps, and two tears rolled out of the corners of her eyes into the hair at her temple. He rubbed the wet tracks with his beard-stubbled cheek, then kissed the last traces away. She was soft beneath him; his penis was stiff and urgent. He tugged her thighs apart. "Hush, now," he said, and stabbed deeply into her.

She gasped again, but stilled at his penetration. He lay on her and felt her slowly calm. It was a gradual process, her body changing beneath him, around him, as her distress faded and her physical awareness of him, and what he was doing, increased. "I won't let you leave," he whispered in reassurance as he began to move inside her.

At first she was simply quiescent, accepting his possession, and that was enough. Then his hunger grew and he wanted more than her compliance, and he began stroking her in ways that made her cry out, made her flesh heat and begin to press urgently against him. She began to climax and he pressed deep into her, pulsing with his own release.

Afterward she tried again to get up, to put on her nightgown, but he held her tightly. She needed to trust him, to be able to fall asleep knowing that he would wake up if she tried to leave, that he wouldn't let her roam the house in defenseless sleep. Until she had that assurance, sleep would remain difficult for her.

Roanna huddled against him, devastated by what had almost happened. She began to cry again, choked sobs that she tried to stifle. She hadn't cried in years, but she was helpless to stop, as if the very fierceness of the pleasure she received from his lovemaking had battered down the walls of her defenses, so that she couldn't hold *any* emotion at bay.

It was too much, all of it, everything that had happened since Lucinda had sent her to Arizona in search of Webb. Within an hour of finding him, she had been lying beneath him, and nothing had been the same since. How long had it been? Three weeks? Three weeks that comprised shattering ecstasy and devastating pain, three weeks of tension and sleepless nights and fear, and the more recent days when she had felt herself changing inside, facing life and in the process beginning to live again.

She loved Webb, loved him so much that she felt it in every pore of her body, every particle of her soul. Tonight he had made love to her, not with anger, but with a breath-taking possessiveness and sensuality. She hadn't gone to him, he had come to her, and he was holding her as if he never intended to let her go.

But if he did—if, when morning came, he said it had been a mistake—she would survive. It would hurt, but she would go on. She had learned that she could endure almost anything, that her future was still out there.

Oddly, realizing that she could live without him made his presence all the sweeter. She cried until she couldn't anymore, and he held her the entire time, stroking her hair, murmuring to her. Exhausted both emotionally and physically, she slept.

It was six o'clock when she woke, the morning already bright and sweet, the storm long gone and the birds singing with mad abandon. The veranda doors were still standing open, and Webb was leaning over her.

"Thank God," he muttered roughly as he saw her eyes flutter open. "I don't know how much longer I could have waited." Then he mounted her, and she forgot about the morning, about the household awakening around them. For all his impatience, he made love to her with a lingering enjoyment they hadn't been able to savor the night before.

When it was over, he gathered her trembling body close and wiped the tears, this time of ecstasy, from her eyes. "I think we've found the cure for your insomnia," he teased, his voice still hoarse and strained from his own climax.

She gave a hiccupping little laugh and buried her face against his shoulder.

Webb closed his eyes, that small, happy sound reverberating through his entire body. His throat clogged, and his eyes burned. She had laughed. Roanna had laughed.

Her small laugh died away. She kept her face pressed to him, and her fingers moved along his ribcage. "I can handle not sleeping," she said quietly. "But knowing that I walk in my sleep . . . terrifies me."

He moved his hand down her spine, stroking each vertebrae. "I promise you," he said, "that if you're in bed with me, I won't let you leave the room."

She shivered, but it was from the delicious sensations his stroking fingers were causing as they moved along her spine, probing and caressing. She arched inward, the movement pressing her body more firmly against him. "Don't try to distract me," she said. "I really would feel more secure if I wore my nightgown."

He shifted so that he was lying to face her, gathering her in. "But I don't want a nightgown between us," he murmured, coaxing her. "I want to feel your skin, your breasts. I want you to go to sleep and know that I won't let anything happen to you—unless I'm the one doing it."

She was silent, and he knew that he hadn't convinced her, but for now she wasn't going to argue the point. Slowly he combed his fingers through her tangled curls, letting the strands drift down so that the sunlight caught them, highlighting the reds and golds and richest browns. He thought of the night he had first taken her, and damned himself for his callousness. He thought of the empty nights since then, when he could have been making love to her, and damned himself for his stupidity.

"I thought I was being noble by not taking advantage of you," he said in lazy amusement.

"Stupid," she said, rubbing her cheek against his hairy chest. She nuzzled one of his flat nipples and caught it with her teeth, lightly biting. He sucked in his breath, undone by her uncomplicated sensuality.

He tried to explain further. "I blackmailed you into that first night. I didn't want you to think you had no choice."

"Dumb." She tilted her head back and looked up at him, whiskey eyes drowsy with sensual completion. "I thought you didn't want me."

"Ye gods," he muttered. "And you called *me* dumb."

She smiled and returned her head to its resting place on his chest. Number five. They were coming more often now, he thought, but were just as precious.

He thought of the shots that someone had taken at him the day before, of the danger she had already faced because of him. He should get the hell away from Davencourt, out of her life, for her safety and that of everyone else in the house. But he couldn't, because he had already been careless of her safety even before returning to Davencourt.

He put his hand on her belly, spanning the narrow distance between her hipbones. For a moment he studied the contrast between his big, rough, sun-browned hand and the silky smoothness of her stomach. He had made it a principle all his life to protect a woman from pregnancy, and AIDS had made the practice even more sensible. All his fine principles had flown out the window when he'd had Roanna beneath him; not once had he worn a rubber when he was making love to her, not in Nogales and not last night. He flattened his palm on her belly. "Have you had a period since that night in Nogales?"

His tone was soft, even, but the words hung between them as if he had shouted. She went very still in that way of hers, motionless except for her breathing. Finally she replied with caution, "No, but I've never been regular. A lot of times I'll completely skip a month."

He'd wanted certainty but realized he wasn't going to find it yet. He rubbed his hand over her stomach, then up to lightly cup a breast. He loved her breasts, so firm and high and elegantly shaped. He watched in sensual delight as the nipple immediately began to pucker, standing up as if begging for attention. Were her nipples slightly darker than they had been that first night? God, he loved her reaction, the immediate response to him. "Have your breasts always been this sensitive?"

"Yes," she whispered, her breath catching as pleasure flooded through her. At least they were whenever *he* looked at them, or touched them. She could no more stop her reaction to him than she could halt the tides.

He wasn't immune himself. Though it hadn't been long since they'd made love, his sex stirred as he watched color flush her breasts and cheeks. "How did you manage to stay virgin for twenty-seven years?" he marveled, thrusting himself against the cleft of her bare thighs.

"You weren't here," she said simply, and the open honesty of her love humbled him.

He nuzzled her hair, feeling himself grow more urgent. "Can you take me again?" To make his meaning plain, he pushed his erection even harder against her.

For answer she lifted her thigh, sliding it along his hip, up to his waist. Webb reached down and guided himself to the soft, swollen opening and pushed inside.

He didn't feel any urgent need for orgasm, just the need for *her*. They lay together, gently rocking to keep the level of sensation. The morning was getting older, and the chances were increasing that they would be caught naked in bed together. Of course, everyone was more likely to sleep late today after the party last night, so he judged it fairly safe to indulge themselves for a while longer. He didn't want to embarrass her, but neither did he want to let her go.

He loved being inside her, loved the tight clasp of her body. They began to slip apart, and he put his hand on her bottom to anchor her to him. She might not think so, but he'd bet the ranch that she was pregnant, and the thought of her carrying his baby at once thrilled him to his bones and scared him half to death.

Maybe it wasn't the most romantic conversation to be having while they were making love, but he tilted her chin up and looked square into her eyes, so she would know he meant it. "You have to eat more. I want you to put on another fifteen pounds, minimum."

A shadow of insecurity darkened her eyes, and he cursed aloud even as he thrust deeper into her. "Don't look like that, damn it. After last night, there's no way you can doubt how much you turn me on. Hell, what about right *now?* I wanted you when you were seventeen, and I sure as hell want you now. But I also want you strong and healthy enough to carry my baby."

It took her a moment to catch her breath after that strong thrust. She moved against him, an enticing wiggle to make herself more comfortable. "I don't think I'm—" she began, then stopped, and her whiskey eyes widened. "You wanted me then?" she whispered.

"You were sitting on my lap," he said wryly. "What did you think, that I was carrying a lead pipe around in my pocket?" He thrust again, letting her feel every inch of him. "And after the way I kissed you—"

"I kissed you," she corrected. Her face was growing flushed, and she clung tighter to him.

"You started it, but I didn't push you away, did I? As I remember, it took about five seconds before I had my tongue halfway down your throat."

She made a little hum of pleasure, perhaps at the memory, more likely at what he was doing to her now. A hard surge of sensation brought him to the realization that the need for orgasm was abruptly urgent, for both of them. He stroked her bottom, trailing his fingers down the cleft until he reached the point of their union. Gently he rubbed her, feeling how stretched and tight her soft flesh was around him. She whimpered, arched, and dissolved. It took only two thrusts for him to join her, and they strained together in completion.

He was still sweating a long time later, when he maneuvered out of her arms and out of bed. "We have to stop before someone comes looking for us," he muttered. Swiftly he dressed, stepping into wrinkled black pants and picking up his equally wrinkled shirt. He leaned down to kiss her. "I'll be back tonight." He kissed her again, then straightened, winked at her, and sauntered out onto the veranda as casually as if it were perfectly natural for him to be leaving her room, half naked, at eight o'clock in the morning. She didn't know if anyone saw him or not because she jumped up, grabbed her nightgown, and darted into the bathroom.

She was still quivering with excitement and pleasure as she showered. Her skin was so sensitive from his lovemaking that even the act of bathing felt sexual. She couldn't believe the raw sexuality of the night, but her body had no such difficulty.

Her hands moved over her wet abdomen. Was she pregnant? It had been three weeks since Nogales. She didn't feel any different, she didn't think, but then it had been an eventful three weeks and her attention hadn't been on her menses. Her periods were so irregular anyway that she never paid much attention to the calendar or how she felt. He seemed oddly certain, though, and she closed her eyes as sweet weakness made her tremble.

She was glowing when she went down to breakfast. Webb was already there, halfway finished with his usual hefty meal, but he paused with his fork in midair when she entered the room. She saw his eyes linger on her face, then slip down her body. Tonight, she thought. Tonight, he'd promised. She filled her plate with more than she usually took and made an effort to eat most of it.

It was Saturday, but there was still work to be done. Webb had already gone into the study, and Roanna was lingering over her second cup of coffee when Gloria came down. "Lucinda isn't feeling well," she said fretfully as she began dipping scrambled eggs onto a plate. "Last night was too hard on her."

"She wanted to do it," Roanna said. "It was important to her."

Gloria looked up, and her eyes were sheened with tears. Her chin wobbled a bit before she controlled it. "It was silly," she grumbled. "All that trouble for a party."

But Gloria knew, as they all did: that had been Lucinda's last party, and she had wanted to make it memorable. It had been her effort to set aright the wrong she felt she had done to Webb ten years ago by not standing up for him.

Lucinda had been holding her decline at bay by sheer willpower, because there had still been things she wanted to accomplish. Those things were done now, and she had no more reason to fight. The snowball was rolling downhill now, picking up speed and hurtling toward its inevitable end. From long, quiet talks with Lucinda, Roanna knew this was what she wanted, but it wasn't easy to let go of the woman who had been the family's bulwark for so long.

Booley Watts called Webb that afternoon. "Carl told me what happened," he drawled. "Interesting as hell."

"Thanks," Webb said.

Booley chuckled, the sound ending in a wheeze. "Carl and I both watched the crowd last night, but we didn't see anything out of the way except for that little scene on the patio. Roanna was something, wasn't she?"

"She took my breath away," Webb murmured, and he wasn't thinking just of the lovemaking that had happened later. She had been standing in the middle of the crowd like a pure, golden candle, her head high, her voice loud and clear. She hadn't hesitated to wade into battle on his behalf, and the last part of him that had held on to the image of "little Roanna" had faded away. She was a woman, stronger than she knew and perhaps beginning to realize that strength. She was a Davenport and, in her own way, every bit as queenly as Lucinda.

Booley's voice intruded into his thoughts. "Have you thought of anybody who would carry a grudge against you for that long, a grudge serious enough that Jessie was killed because of it?"

Webb sighed tiredly. "No, and I've wracked my brain trying to come up with something. I've even gone over old files, hoping I'll notice a detail, remember something that would make sense out of all this."

"Well, keep thinking. That's what bothered me about Jessie's murder from the beginning: there just didn't seem to be any sense to it, no reason that I could see. Hell, even drive-by shootings have a reason behind them. So whoever killed Jessie—and I'm saying now that I don't believe you did it—killed her for a reason no one else knows. If your theory's right, then the reason didn't apply to her anyway. Someone was after you, and she got in the way."

"Come up with the motive," Webb said, "and we come up with the killer."

"That's the way it's always worked for me."

"Then let's hope we can figure it out before he takes another shot at me . . . or someone else gets in his way."

He hung up and rubbed his eyes, trying to put the pieces of the puzzle together but they simply refused to fit. He stretched and stood up. He had to go into town on an errand, so he had a decision to make: play it safe and take a roundabout route, or drive his usual route and hope he got shot at so he'd have another chance at catching the gunman—assuming the shot missed. Some choice.

Lucinda came down for supper that evening, the first time all day she'd been out of her room. Her color was waxy, and the palsy in her hands was worse than it had been before, but she was jubilant over the success of the party. Several of her friends had called her during the course of the day and told her it had been simply wonderful, which meant she had accomplished her aim.

They were all at the table except for Corliss, who had gone out earlier in the day and hadn't yet returned. After chattering excitedly for several minutes, Lucinda looked at Roanna and said, "Dear, I'm so proud of you. What you said last night really made a difference."

Everyone else, except for Webb and Roanna, looked confused. Lucinda had never missed much that was going on, though probably it was one or more of her cronies who had filled her in on what had happened on the patio.

"What?" Gloria asked, looking from Lucinda to Roanna and back.

"Oh, Cora Cofelt made a snide remark about Webb, and Roanna took up for him. She managed to make everyone feel ashamed of themselves."

"Cora Cofelt?" Lanette was aghast. "Oh, no! She'll never forgive Roanna for embarrassing her."

"On the contrary, Cora herself called me today and apologized for her own bad manners. Admitting when you're wrong is the mark of a lady."

Roanna didn't know if that was a dig at Gloria or not, for Gloria had certainly never admitted being wrong about anything. Lucinda and Gloria loved each other, and in a crisis they could each be relied on to support the other, but their relationship had its sharp edges.

Webb's eyes met hers, and he smiled. Slowly, blushing a little, she smiled in return.

Number six, he thought triumphantly.

The front door slammed, and heels clattered unsteadily across the foyer tile. "Yoo-hoo!" Corliss yelled. "Where is everybody? Yoo—"

"Damn it!" Webb said violently, shoving his chair back from the table. The alarm went off, shrieking like all the fiends in hell. Everyone jumped and covered their ears. Webb ran from the room, and after a second Brock followed him.

"Oh, no, the horses," Roanna cried, and darted for the door. When the alarm had been tested, the horses had all panicked. Webb had debated changing the alarm to one less shrill but had opted for the safety of his family over the nervousness of the horses.

The godawful racket stopped as she reached the hall, and instead she heard Corliss whooping with uncontrollable laughter and Webb cussing with every breath he drew. Brock turned on Corliss and yelled, "Shut up!"

Everyone else piled into the hall behind Roanna as Corliss straightened from where she was clinging to the huge, carved newel post at the bottom of the stairway. Corliss's face twisted with fury. She worked her mouth and spat a gob of saliva at her brother. "Don't tell me to shut up," she sneered. The spit missed Brock, but he looked down at the wet splatter on the floor with disgust etched on his face.

Lanette stared at her daughter in horror. "You're drunk!" she gasped.

"So?" Corliss demanded belligerently. "Just having a li'l fun, nothin' wrong with that."

Webb gave her a look that would have frozen antifreeze. "Then you can have your fun somewhere else. I warned you, Corliss. You have a week to find somewhere else to live, then I want you out."

"Oh, yeah?" She laughed. "You can't throw me out, big boy. Aunt Lucinda might have one foot in the grave, but until they're both there, this place isn't yours."

Lanette covered her mouth with her hand, staring at Corliss as if she didn't recognize her. Greg took a threatening step forward, but Webb stopped him with a look. Lucinda drew herself up, her expression hardening as she waited for Webb to handle the situation.

"Three days," he grimly said to Corliss. "And if you open

your mouth again, the deadline will be tomorrow morning.
He glanced at Roanna. "Come on, we'd better go help get
the horses settled down."

They went out the front door and around the house; they
could hear the horses' frightened whinnies as soon as they
stepped outside, and the thuds as the ones in the stable
kicked frantically at their stalls. Webb's long legs made one
stride for every two of hers, and Roanna was practically
running to keep up with him. Loyal and the few stable
hands who were still at work at that hour were doing their
best to soothe the terrified animals, crooning to them, trying
to hold them still. True, most of the words they were using
were lurid curse words, but they were uttered in the softest
of tones.

Roanna ran into the stable and added her own special
croon to the lullaby. The horses outside were just as
frightened as the animals in the stable, but they weren't as
likely to hurt themselves because they had room to run. The
horses in the stable were mostly animals with injuries or
illnesses, and they could damage themselves even more in
their panic to escape.

"Hush," Loyal said to the hands, and they fell silent,
letting Roanna sing. They all continued their petting, but
Roanna's voice had a unique quality to it that caught the
attention of every animal in the stable. She'd had the gift
from childhood, and Loyal had used it more than once to
settle a frightened, nervous horse.

Webb moved down the rows of stalls, stroking sleek,
sweating necks, just as they all were doing. Roanna sang
softly, going from stall to stall, her voice pitched at just the
right tone so that the horses' ears pricked forward as if
trying to catch every note. Within five minutes, all the
occupants of the stalls were calm, if still sweating.

"Get some cloths, boys," Loyal murmured. "Let's get my
babies dried off."

Roanna and Webb helped with that, too, while Loyal
checked each animal for any new injury. They all seemed to
be all right, except for their original ailments, but Loyal

shook his head at Webb. "I don't like that damn squeal," he said flatly. "And the horses ain't going to get used to it, it's too high pitched. Hurts their ears. Hurts mine too, come to that. What the hell happened?"

"Corliss," Webb said disgustedly. "She's shit faced and didn't enter the code when she came in."

Loyal scowled. "What Miss Lucinda was thinking to let that little bitch, pardon my French, move into Davencourt, I don't know."

"Neither do I, but she's moving out within three days."

"Not soon enough if you ask me."

Webb looked around and located Roanna at the far end of the stable. "There's some trouble going on, Loyal. Until it's settled, I'm keeping the alarm because it's loud enough to wake you even down here, and we may need your help."

"What kind of trouble, boss?"

"Someone shot at me yesterday. I think it's the same person who broke into the house last week and maybe even the same person who killed Jessie. After Corliss leaves, if that alarm goes off, then it's a real emergency. In a worse-case scenario, you may be the only one who can help us."

Loyal eyed him consideringly, then gave one abbreviated nod. "Reckon I'll make sure my rifle's cleaned and loaded," he said.

"I'd appreciate it."

"Miss Roanna doesn't know, does she?"

"No one does except for me, Sheriff Beshears, and Booley Watts. And now you. It's hard to catch someone if they're looking for the trap."

"Well, I hope this varmint gets caught real soon, because I'm not going to rest easy as long as I know that damn siren can go off at any time and make every horse here go wild."

313

CHAPTER
20

*T*he house was still in an uproar when Webb and Roanna returned to it, with Corliss now sitting on the stairs weeping hysterically and begging Lucinda not to let Webb throw her out. Not even her own mother was taking her side this time; drunkenness was bad enough, but to *spit* at her brother was totally unacceptable.

Brock was nowhere in sight, probably having removed himself from the temptation to do physical damage to his sister.

To Corliss's sobbing entreaties, Lucinda merely gave her a cold look. "You're right, Corliss. Despite my own foot in the grave, I *am* still the owner of this house. And as the owner, I give Webb full authority to act on my behalf, no questions asked."

"No, no," Corliss moaned. "I can't leave, you don't understand—"

"I understand that you're leaving," Lucinda replied, not bending an inch. "You're disgusting. I suggest you go to your room now, before Webb's threat to make you leave in the morning begins to sound even more delightful than it already does."

314

"Mama!" Corliss turned to Lanette, a pleading expression on her tear-blotched face. "Tell her to let me stay!"

"I'm very disappointed in you," Lanette said softly and stepped past her daughter on her way upstairs.

Greg leaned down and hauled Corliss to her feet. "Upstairs," he said sternly, turning her around and bodily forcing her upward. They all watched until the pair reached the top of the stairs and turned toward Corliss's suite. They could hear her sobbing until a door closed firmly behind her.

Lucinda sagged. "The ungrateful little wretch," she muttered. Her skin tone was even more waxy than before. "Are the horses all right?" she asked Roanna.

"None of them were injured, and they're quiet now."

"Good." Lucinda put a trembling hand to her eyes, then took a deep breath and straightened her shoulders once more. "Webb, could I talk to you, please? We need to go over some details."

"Of course." He put a supporting hand under her arm to steady her as they walked to the study. He glanced over his shoulder at Roanna, and their eyes met. His were steady and warm with promise. "Go finish your supper," he said.

When he and Lucinda were alone in the study, she dropped heavily onto the couch. She was breathing hard and perspiring. "The doctor said that my heart's giving out, too, damn it," she muttered. "There, I've used a cuss word." She peeped up at Webb to see his reaction.

He couldn't help grinning at her. "You've used them before, Lucinda. I've heard you cuss that roan mare you used to ride until it was a wonder her ears didn't singe and drop off."

"She was a bitch, wasn't she?" The words were fondly uttered. As hardheaded as the mare had been, Lucinda had always gotten the best of her. Until just a few years before, Lucinda had been strong enough to handle almost any horse she straddled.

"Now, what details do you want to discuss?"

"My will," she said baldly. "I'm having the lawyer in tomorrow. I'd better get that chore taken care of, because it's beginning to look like my time's a bit shorter than I expected."

Webb sat down beside her and took her frail, palsied hand in his. She was too shrewd and mentally tough for him to even consider trying to comfort her with platitudes, but damn it, he hated to let her go. "I love you," he said. "I was damn mad at you for not defending me after Jessie was killed. It hurt like hell that you thought I could have done it. I still hold a grudge about that, but I love you anyway."

Tears swam briefly in her eyes, then she blinked them away. "Of course you hold a grudge. I never thought you'd totally forgive me, God knows I don't deserve that consideration. But I love you, too, Webb. I always knew you were the best choice for Davencourt."

"Leave it to Roanna," he said. His own words took him by surprise. He'd always thought of Davencourt as his, always expected to have it. He'd worked hard for it. But as soon as the words were out of his mouth he knew they were right. Davencourt should be Roanna's. Despite what Lucinda thought, despite even what Roanna thought, she was more than capable of handling it.

Roanna was tougher and smarter than any of them knew, even including herself. Webb was only now beginning to understand the strength of her character. For years everyone had thought of her as fragile, irreparably damaged emotionally by the trauma of Jessie's death, but instead Roanna had been protecting herself, and enduring. It took a special kind of strength to endure, to accept what couldn't be changed and simply hunker down and wait it out. More and more lately Roanna was coming out of her shell, showing her strength, standing up for herself with a quiet maturity that didn't attract much attention, but was there.

Startled, Lucinda blinked several times. "Roanna? Don't you think I've talked this over with her? She doesn't want it."

"She doesn't want to spend her life reading financial

statements and watching stock reports," he corrected. "But she loves Davencourt. Give it to her."

"You mean split the inheritance?" Lucinda asked in bewilderment. "Give the house to her and the financial holdings to you?" She sounded shocked; that had never been done. Davencourt and all it entailed had always been kept intact.

"No, I mean leave it all to her. It should be hers anyway." Roanna needed a home. She had told him so herself; she needed something that was *hers,* that could never be taken away from her. "She's never really felt as if she belonged anywhere, and if you leave everything to me, she'll feel as if she wasn't good enough to have Davencourt, even if she did agree to the terms of the will. She needs her home, Lucinda. Davencourt should have Davenports living here, and she's the last one."

"But . . . of course she would live here." Lucinda looked at him uncertainly. "I never thought that you would make her leave. Oh, dear. That would look funny, wouldn't it? People would talk."

"She told me that she plans to buy her own place."

"Leave Davencourt?" The very idea shocked Lucinda. "But this is her home."

"Exactly," Webb said softly.

"Well." Lucinda sat back, mulling over this change in her plans. Except it wasn't a change, she realized. It was simply leaving everything as it already stood, with Roanna as her heir. "But . . . what will you do?"

He smiled, a slow smile that lit his entire face. "She can hire me to handle the financial dealings for her," he said lightly. Suddenly he knew exactly what he wanted, and it was like a light being turned on inside him. "Better yet, I'm going to marry her."

Lucinda was truly speechless now. It was an entire minute before she could manage a squeaky "What?"

"I'm going to marry her," Webb repeated with growing determination. "I haven't asked her yet, so keep it quiet." Yes, he was going to marry her, one way or the other. It felt

317

as if a piece of the puzzle had suddenly been placed in its correct position. It felt right. Nothing else would ever be as right. Roanna had always been his—and he had always been Roanna's.

"Webb, are you sure?" Lucinda asked anxiously. "Roanna loves you, but she deserves to be loved in return—"

He gave her a level look, his eyes very green, and she fell silent in astonishment. "Well," she said again.

He tried to explain. "Jessie—I was obsessed with her, I suppose, and in a way I loved her because we grew up together, but it was mostly ego on my part. I never should have married her, but I was so locked into the idea of inheriting Davencourt and marrying the crown princess that I didn't realize what a disaster our marriage would be. Roanna, now . . . I've loved her for as long as she's been alive, I reckon. When she was little I loved her like a brother, but now she's all grown up, and I'm damn sure not her brother." He sighed, looking back over the years at how relationships had gotten tangled up with inheritances. "If Jessie hadn't been killed, we'd have gotten divorced. I meant what I said that night. I was fed up, through with her. And if we'd been divorced, instead of things happening the way they did, I'd have been married to Roanna for a long time now. The way Jessie died split us all apart, and I've wasted ten years because of a grudge."

Lucinda searched his face, looking for the truth, and what she found made her sigh with relief. "You really do love her."

"So much it hurts." Gently he squeezed Lucinda's fingers, taking care not to hurt her. "She's smiled at me six times," he confided. "And laughed once."

"Laughed!" Tears welled again in Lucinda's eyes, and this time she let them fall. Her lips trembled. "I'd like to hear her laugh again, just once more."

"I'm going to try real hard to make her happy," Webb said.

"When do you plan to get married?"

"As soon as possible, if I can talk her into it." He knew Roanna loved him, but convincing her that he loved her in return might take some doing. Once she would have married him under any circumstances, but now she would quietly turn stubborn if she thought something wasn't right. On the other hand, he wanted Lucinda to be at their wedding, so that meant it had to happen quickly, while she was still able to attend. And there might be another, more private reason for a quick wedding.

"Oh, posh!" Lucinda scoffed. "You know she would walk through fire to marry you!"

"I know she loves me, but I've learned not to think she'll automatically do anything I ask. Those days are long gone. I wouldn't like having a doormat for a wife anyway. I want her to have the confidence to stand up for what *she* wants."

"The way she stood up for you."

"The way she's always stood up for me." When no one else had been there, Roanna had been at his side, slipping her little hand into his and offering what comfort she could. She had been far stronger than he, strong enough to make the first move, to reach out. "She deserves the inheritance," he said. "But besides that, I don't want her to ever feel that she had to please me in order to stay in her home."

"She might feel the same way about you," Lucinda pointed out. "Whenever you're nice to her, she might think it's only because she holds the purse strings. I've been in that situation," she added dryly, no doubt thinking of Corliss.

Webb shrugged. "I'm not a pauper, Lucinda, as you know damned well, since you had me investigated. I have my Arizona holdings, and they're going to be worth a good-sized fortune before I get through with them. I assume Roanna read the same report you did, so she knows my financial situation. We'll be equals, and she'll know that I'm with her because I love her. I'll take care of the financial dealings if she really isn't interested; I don't know if she'll want to stay involved with that part of it or not. She says she doesn't like it, but she has the Davenport knack, doesn't she?"

"In a different way." Lucinda smiled. "She pays more attention to people than she does to numbers on a sheet of paper."

"You know what she really wants to do, don't you?"

"No, what?"

"Train horses."

She laughed softly. "I might have known! Loyal has been using some of her training ideas for years now, and I have to say we have some of the best-behaved horses I've ever been around."

"She's magic with a horse. They're where her heart is, so that's what I want her to do. You've always had horses just for the pleasure of it, because you love them, but Roanna wants to get into it as a business."

"You have it all planned out, don't you?" She smiled fondly at him, because even as a boy Webb had mapped out his strategy, then followed through on it. "No one else around here knows about your properties out west. People will talk, you know."

"That I married Roanna for her money? That I was determined to get Davencourt any way I could? That I'd married Jessie for it and then, when she died, moved on to Roanna?"

"I see you've thought of all the angles."

He shrugged. "I don't give a damn about the angles as long as Roanna doesn't believe any of them."

"She won't. She's loved you for twenty years, and she'll love you for another twenty."

"Longer than that, I hope."

"Do you know how lucky you are?"

"Oh, I've got an idea," he said softly. He was surprised it had taken him so long to get that idea, though. Even though he'd *known* that he loved Roanna, he hadn't thought of it as a romantic, erotic love; he'd been stuck in the big-brother mode even after they had kissed the first time and he'd almost lost control. He hadn't been jolted out of it until she had walked up to him in the bar in Nogales, a woman, with a gap of ten years between their meetings so he hadn't *seen* her grow up. That night was burned in his memory, and still he'd struggled with the misapprehension that he had to protect Roanna from his own lust. God, what a dope. She positively reveled in his lust, which made him about the luckiest man alive.

Now, all he had to do was convince her to marry him, and clear up the small matter of attempted murder—his own.

Roanna was standing out on the veranda watching the sunset when he entered her room. She turned and glanced over her shoulder when she heard the door open. She was gilded by the last rays of the sun, turning her skin golden, her hair glinting red and gold. He came on through and out onto the veranda with her, turning to lean against the railing so that he faced the house, and her. Looking at her was so damn easy. He kept rediscovering the angles of those chiseled cheekbones, seeing anew the golden lights in her whiskey-colored eyes. The open collar of her shirt let him see enough of her silken skin to remind him how silky she was all over.

He felt the beginning twinges of lust in his groin but nevertheless asked an utterly prosaic question. "Did you finish your supper?"

She wrinkled her nose. "No, it was cold, so I ate a slice of lemon icebox pie instead."

He scowled. "Tansy made another pie? She didn't tell me."

"I'm sure there's some left," she said comfortingly. She looked up at the vermillion streaks in the sky. "Are you really going to make Corliss leave?"

"Oh, yes." He let both his satisfaction and determination come through in those two words.

She started to speak, then hesitated.

"Go on," he urged. "Tell me, even if you think I'm wrong."

321

"I don't think you're wrong. Lucinda needs peace now, not constant turmoil." Her expression was distant, somber. "It's just that I remember what it's like to be terrified of having nowhere to live."

He reached out and caught a tendril of her hair, winding it around his finger. "When your parents died?"

"Then, and later, until—until I was seventeen." Until Jessie died, she meant, but she didn't say it. "I was always afraid that if I didn't measure up, I'd be sent away."

"That would never have happened," he said firmly. "This is your home. Lucinda wouldn't have made you leave."

She shrugged. "They were talking about it. Lucinda and Jessie, that is. They were going to send me away to college. Not just to Tuscaloosa; they wanted me to go to some women's college, in Virginia, I think. It was someplace far enough away that I couldn't come home regularly."

"That wasn't why." He sounded shocked. He remembered the arguments. Lucinda had thought it would be good for Roanna to be away from them, force her to mature, and Jessie, of course, had egged her on. He saw now that, to Roanna, it must have seemed that they didn't want her around.

"That's what it sounded like to me," she said.

"Why did it change when you were seventeen? Was it because Jessie was dead and wasn't there to keep bringing up the subject?"

"No." That remote look was still in her eyes. "It was because I didn't care anymore. Going away seemed like the best thing to do. I wanted to get away from Davencourt, from people who knew me and felt sorry for me because I wasn't pretty, because I was clumsy, because I was so socially graceless." Her tone was matter-of-fact, as if she were discussing a menu.

"Hell," he said wearily. "Jessie made a career out of making you miserable, didn't she? Damn her. It should be against the law for people under the age of twenty-five to get married. I thought I was king of the mountain when I was in my early twenties, so damn sure I could tame Jessie and turn her into a suitable wife—my idea of suitable, of course. But there was something missing in Jessie, maybe the ability to love, because she didn't love anyone. Not me, not Lucinda, not even herself. I was too young to see it, though." He rubbed his forehead, remembering those last horrible days after her murder. "Maybe she did love *someone,* though. Maybe she loved the man whose baby she carried. I'll never know."

Roanna gasped, shock running through her. She turned to face him. "You knew about him?" she asked incredulously.

Webb straightened away from the railing, his gaze sharpening. "I found out after she was killed." He caught her shoulders, his grip urgent. "How did you know?"

"I—I saw them together in the woods." She wished she had controlled her reaction to finding out he knew about Jessie's lover, but it had been such a shock. She had protected that secret all these years, and he'd known anyway. But she hadn't known that Jessie was pregnant when she was killed, and that made her feel sick.

"Who was it?" His tone was hard.

"I don't know, I'd never seen him before."

"Can you describe him?"

"Not really." She bit her lip, remembering that day. "I only saw him once, the afternoon of the day Jessie was killed, and I didn't get a good look at him. I didn't tell you then because I was afraid . . ." She paused, a look of unutterable sadness crossing her face. "I was afraid you'd fly off the handle and do something dumb and get in trouble. So I kept quiet."

"And after Jessie was killed, you didn't say anything because you thought I would be arrested, that they'd say I killed her because I'd found out she was cheating on me." He'd kept his silence on the same subject and nearly choked on his bitterness. It made him ache inside to know that Roanna had kept the same secret and for the same reason. She had been so young, already traumatized by finding Jessie's body and briefly being suspected of murder herself, hurt by his own rejection of her, and still she'd kept quiet.

Roanna nodded, searching his face. The sunlight was fading fast, and the shades of twilight were veiling them in mysteriously shadowed blues and purples, wrapping them in that brief moment when the earth hovered between day and night, when time seems to stop and everything seems richer, sweeter. His expression was guarded, and she couldn't tell what he was thinking or feeling.

"So you kept it to yourself," he said softly. "To protect me. I'll bet you nearly choked on it, with Jessie accusing us of sleeping together when you'd just seen her with another man."

"Yes," she said, her voice strained as she remembered that horrible day and night.

"Did she know you'd seen her."

"No, I was quiet. In those days I was good at sneaking around." The glance she gave him was full of wry acknowledgment of what an undisciplined handful she had been.

"I know," he said, his tone as wry as her look. "Do you remember where they met?"

"It was just a clearing in the woods. I could take you to the area but not to the exact spot. It's been ten years; it's probably grown over by now."

"If it was a clearing, why couldn't you see the man?"

"I didn't say I couldn't see him." Feeling uncomfortable, Roanna moved restlessly under his hands. "I said I couldn't describe him."

Webb frowned. "But if you saw him, why can't you describe him?"

"Because they were having sex!" she said in stifled exasperation. "He was naked. I'd never seen a naked man before. Frankly, I didn't look at his face!"

Webb dropped his hands in astonishment, peering at her through the fading twilight. Then he began to laugh. He didn't just chuckle, he roared with mirth, his entire frame shaking. He tried to stop, took one look at her, and started again.

She punched him on the shoulder. "Hush," she muttered.

"I can just hear you telling Booley about it," he chortled,

almost choking with laughter. "S-sorry, Sheriff, I didn't notice his f-face because I was looking at his—Woof!" This time she punched him in the belly. The breath rushed out of him and he bent over, clutching his stomach and still laughing.

Roanna lifted her chin. "I was not," she said with dignity, "looking at his woof." She strode into her room and started to close the veranda doors in his face. He barely slipped through the rapidly shrinking opening. Roanna set the alarm for the doors, then pulled the curtains closed over them.

He slipped his arms around her before she could move away, pulling her snugly back against him. "I'm sorry," he apologized. "I know you were upset."

"It made me *sick,"* she said fiercely. "I hated her for cheating on you."

He bent to rub his cheek against her hair. "I think she must have been planning to have the baby and pretend it was mine. But first she had to get me to have sex with her, and I hadn't touched her in four months. There was no way in hell she could pass it off as mine as things stood. When she caught us kissing, she probably thought all her plans had gone up in smoke. She knew damn well I wouldn't pretend the baby was mine just to prevent a scandal. I'd have divorced her so fast her head would spin. She was crazy jealous of you anyway. She wouldn't have been nearly as furious if she had caught me with anyone else."

"Me?" Roanna asked incredulously, turning her head to stare at him. "She was jealous of *me?* Why? She had everything."

"But you were the one I protected—from her, most of the time. I took your side, and she couldn't stand that. She had to be first in everything and with everybody."

"No wonder she was always trying to talk Lucinda into sending me away to college!"

"She wanted you out of the way." He brushed her hair to one side and lightly kissed her neck. "Are you certain you can't describe the man you saw her with?"

"I'd never seen him before. And since they were lying down, I couldn't really see his face. I got the impression that he was older, but I was only seventeen. Thirty seemed old to me then." His teeth nipped at her neck, and she shivered. She could feel him losing interest in his questions; quite literally, in fact. His growing erection pushed at her bottom, and she leaned back against him, closing her eyes as warm pleasure began to fill her.

Slowly he slid his hands up her body and put his palms over her breasts. "Just what I thought," he murmured, moving his love bites to her earlobe.

"What?" she gasped, reaching back to brace her hands on his thighs.

"Your nipples are already hard."

"Are you fixated on my breasts?"

"I must be," he murmured. "And assorted other body parts, too."

He was very hard now. Roanna turned into his arms, and he walked her backward to the bed. They fell down upon it, Webb bracing his weight on his arms to keep from crushing her, and in the cool darkness their bodies came together with a fire and intensity that left her weak and shaking in his arms.

He held her close to his side, her head cradled on his shoulder. Left weak and boneless, utterly relaxed, Roanna felt drowsiness begin to ease over her. Evidently he was right about her insomnia: tension had kept her sleepless for ten years, but after his lovemaking she was too relaxed to resist. But sleep was one thing; the sleepwalking was something else entirely and disturbed her on a much deeper level. She said, "I need to put on my nightgown."

"No." His refusal was instant and emphatic. His arms tightened around her as if he would prevent her from moving.

"But if I walk in my sleep—"

"You won't. I'm going to hold you all night long. You won't be able to get out of bed without waking me up." He kissed her long and slow. "Go to sleep, sweetheart. I'll watch over you."

But she couldn't. She could feel the tension coming back, invading her muscles. A habit of ten years' duration couldn't be broken in a single night, or even two. Webb might understand the dread she felt at the thought of walking through the night so defenselessly, but he couldn't *feel* the panic and helplessness of not waking up in the same place where she'd gone to sleep, not knowing how she'd gotten there or anything that had happened.

He felt the tension that kept her from relaxing. He held her closer, tried to soothe her with reassurances, but finally he evidently came to the conclusion that nothing would help except complete exhaustion.

She had thought she was accustomed to his lovemaking, that she already knew the extent of his sensuality. She found that she was wrong.

He brought her to climax with his hands, with his mouth. He put her astride his hard, muscled thigh and rocked her to completion, though she clutched at him and begged him to fill her. Finally he did, pulling her off the bed and turning her so that she was on her knees, bent over with her face buried in the covers. He drove into her from behind, slamming into her buttocks with the force of his thrusts, reaching around to the front of her sex to caress her at the same time. She cried out hoarsely and stifled the sound against the mattress as she climaxed a fourth time, and still he wasn't finished. She was dissolving, going beyond peaks to a state where the pleasure simply went on and on, like the waves of the tide. It happened again, fast, and she reached back to grab his hips and pull him hard into her as she pulsed around him. Her action caught him by surprise and with a low, savage cry he joined her, shuddering and jerking as he came.

They were both shaking violently, so weak they could barely crawl back onto the bed. Sweat dripped from their bodies, and they clung together like shipwreck survivors.

This time there was no way to fight off the sleep that claimed her as surely as he had.

She woke once, only enough to be aware that he was still holding her, just as he had promised, and she drifted back to sleep.

The next time she awoke she was sitting up in bed, and Webb's fingers were hard around her wrist. "No," he said softly, implacably. "You aren't going anywhere."

She went back into his arms, and began to believe.

She woke for the last time at dawn, when he got out of bed. "Where are you going?" she asked, yawning and sitting up.

"To my room," he replied, pulling on his pants. He smiled at her, and she felt herself melting inside all over again. He looked tough and sexy, with his dark hair tousled and his jaw darkened with beard stubble. His voice was still rough with sleep, and his eyelids were a little puffy, giving him a heavy-lidded, just-had-sex look. "I have to get something," he said. "Stay right there, and I mean *right there*. Don't get out of bed."

"All right, I won't." He left by the hallway door, and she lay back down and cuddled under the sheet. She wasn't certain she *could* get out of bed. She remembered the night that had just passed, the things that had happened between them. She ached deep inside, and her thighs felt weak, sore. That hadn't been mere lovemaking, that had been a melding that went beyond the mere physical. There were deeper levels of intimacy than she had ever imagined, and yet she knew there were still delights as yet untasted.

He was back in only a moment, carrying a plastic bag with a pharmacist's name on it. He placed the bag on the bedside table.

"What's that?" she asked.

He shucked off his pants again and got into bed beside her, tucking her close to his side. "An early pregnancy test."

She stiffened. "Webb, I really don't think—"

"It's possible," he interrupted. "Why don't you want to know for certain?"

"Because I—" She stopped herself that time, and her eyes were somber when she looked up at him. "Because I don't want you to feel obligated."

He went still. "Obligated?" he asked carefully.

"If I'm pregnant, you'll feel responsible."

He snorted. "Damn right. I'd *be* responsible."

"I know, but I don't want . . . I want you to want me for myself," she said softly, trying to hide the longing but knowing that she hadn't quite succeeded. "Not because we were careless and made a baby."

"Want you for yourself," he repeated just as softly. "Haven't the last two nights given you an idea about that?"

"I know you want me physically."

"I want *you*, period." He cupped her face in his hand, stroking his thumb over the soft curve of her mouth. His eyes were very serious. "I love you, Roanna Frances. Will you marry me?"

Her lips trembled under his touch. When she'd been seventeen, she had loved him so desperately that she would have jumped at any chance to marry him, under any conditions. She was twenty-seven now, and she still loved him desperately—loved him enough that she didn't want to trap him into another marriage in which he would be miserable. She knew Webb, knew the depths of his sense of responsibility. If she were pregnant, he would do anything to take care of his child, and that included lying to the mother about his feelings for her.

"No," she said, her voice almost soundless as she refused what she wanted most on this earth. A tear slipped from the corner of her eye.

He didn't insist, didn't lose his temper, though she had halfway expected that. His expression remained serious, intent, as he caught the tear with a gentle thumb. "Why not?"

"Because you're asking in case I'm pregnant."

"Wrong. I'm asking because I love you."

"You're just saying that." And she wished he would stop saying it. In how many dreams had she heard him whisper those words? It wasn't fair that now he should say it, now when she didn't dare let herself believe him. Oh, God, she loved him, but she deserved to be loved for herself. At last she knew the truth of that, and she couldn't cheat herself of that final dream.

"I'm not 'just' saying anything. I love you, Ro, and you have to marry me."

Under the serious expression was a certain smugness. She studied him, looking beneath the surface with her somber brown gaze that saw so much. There was a self-satisfied glint deep in his green eyes, a fierce triumph, the way he had always looked when he'd pulled off a difficult deal.

"What have you done?" she asked, her eyes widening with alarm.

Amusement curled the edges of his mouth. "When Lucinda and I talked last night, we agreed that it would be better to leave the terms of her will as they stand. Davencourt will be better off in your hands."

She went white. "What?" she whispered, something almost like panic edging into her tone. She tried to pull away from him but he forestalled the movement, cuddling her even closer so that her next protest was muffled against his neck.

"But it's been promised to you since you were fourteen! You worked for it, you even—"

"I even married Jessie for it," he finished calmly. "I know."

"That was the bargain. You'd come back if Lucinda changed her will in your favor again." She felt a great hollow fear growing in the pit of her stomach. Davencourt was the lure that had brought him back, but she and Lucinda had both been aware that he had built his own life in Arizona. Maybe he preferred Arizona to Alabama. Without Davencourt to keep him here, after Lucinda died he would leave again, and after these past two nights she didn't know if she could stand it.

"That's not quite true. I didn't come back because of the bargain. I came back because I needed to tie up old loose

330

ends. I needed to make my peace with Lucinda; she was a big part of my life, and I owe her a lot. I didn't want her to die before we cleared the air between us. Davencourt is special, but I've done all right in Arizona," he said in calm understatement. "I don't need Davencourt, and Lucinda thought you didn't want it—"

"I don't," she said firmly. "I told you, I don't want to spend my life in business meetings and studying stock reports."

He gave her a lazy smile. "Pity, when you're so good at it. I guess you'll have to marry me, and I'll do it for you. Unlike you, I get my kicks making money. If you marry me, you can very happily spend your time raising kids and training horses, which is what you would have been doing even if Lucinda had left Davencourt to me. The only difference now is that it will all belong to you, lock, stock, and barrel, and you'll be the boss."

Her head was whirling. She wasn't quite certain that she'd heard what she thought she'd heard. Davencourt was going to be hers, and he was staying anyway? Davencourt was going to be hers . . .

"I can hear those wheels turning," he murmured. He tilted her head up so that she was looking at him. "I came back for one final reason, the most important one. I came back because of you."

She swallowed. "Me?"

"You." Very gently he stroked one finger down her spine to the cleft of her buttocks, then retraced the caress up her back. She shivered delicately, melting against him. He knew what he was doing with that small, delicate touch. His purpose wasn't to arouse her but to soothe her, reassure her, reestablish the trust with which she gave her body over to him during lovemaking. The very fact that he *wasn't* making love to her now was proof of how intent he was on accomplishing his aim.

"Let me see if I can make this any clearer," he mused softly, brushing his lips against her forehead. "I loved you when you were a snot-nosed kid, into so much mischief it's a wonder my hair didn't turn prematurely gray. I loved you when you were a teenager with long, skinny legs and eyes that broke my heart every time I looked at you. I love you now that you're a woman who makes my brain go soft, my legs go weak, and my dick get hard. When you walk into a room, my heart damn near jumps out of my chest. When you smile, I feel as if I've won a Nobel Prize. And your eyes still break my heart."

The soft litany washed over like the sweetest of songs, soaking into her flesh, her soul, her very being. She wanted so much to believe him, and that was why she was afraid to, afraid she would let her own desires convince her.

When she didn't speak, he began those gentling caresses again. "Jessie really did a number on you, didn't she? She made you feel so unloved and unwanted that you still haven't gotten over it. Haven't you figured out yet that *Jessie lied?* Her whole life was a lie. Don't you know that Lucinda dotes on you? With Jessie dead, she was finally able to get to know you without Jessie's poison ruining everything, and she adores you." He picked up her hand and carried it to his lips, where he kissed each fingertip, then began nibbling on the sensitive pads. "Jessie's been dead ten years. How long are you going to continue letting her ruin things for you?"

Roanna tilted her head back, searching his expression with solemn, wondering eyes. With a sense of amazement, she realized she had never seen him look more determined, or more intent. That hard face looking back at her was the face of a man who had made up his mind and was damn sure going to get what he wanted. He meant it. He didn't want to marry her because she would have Davencourt, because *he* could have had it without any strings. Lucinda would have honored her bargain. He didn't want to marry her because she might be pregnant—

As if he were reading her mind, and perhaps he was, he said, "I love you. I can't tell you how much, because the words don't exist. I've tried to count the ways, but I'm no

Browning. It doesn't matter if you're pregnant or not, I want to marry you *because I love you.* Period."

"All right," she whispered, and trembled at the enormity of the step she was taking, and from the joy that was blooming inside her.

Her breath whooshed out of her as he crushed her to his chest. "You know how to make a man sweat," he said fiercely. "I was getting desperate. What do you think about getting married next week?"

"Next week?" She all but shouted the words, at least as much as she was able to, crushed against his chest the way she was.

"You didn't think I was going to give you time to change your mind, did you?" She could hear the smile in his voice. "If you have your heart set on a big church wedding, I suppose I can wait if it doesn't take too long to arrange. Lucinda . . . Well, I think we should be married within a month, at the most."

Tears sprang to her eyes. "That soon? I hoped she . . . I hoped she would last through the winter, maybe see another spring."

"I don't think so. The doctor told her that her heart is failing, too." He rubbed his face against her hair, seeking comfort. "She's a tough old bird," he said roughly. "But she's ready to go. You can see it in her eyes."

They held each other quietly for a moment, already grieving for the woman around whom the entire family revolved. But Webb wasn't a man to be deterred for long from his set course, and he leaned back from her, giving her an inquiring look. "About that wedding—"

"I don't want a big church wedding," she said forcefully, shuddering at the idea. "You did that with Jessie, and I don't want to repeat it. I was miserable that day."

"Then what kind of wedding do you want? We could have it here, in the garden, or at the country club. Do you want just family present, or invite our friends, too? I know *you* have some, and maybe I can scare up a couple."

She pinched him for that remark. "You know darn well you have friends, if you can bring yourself to forgive them and *let* them be friends again. I want to get married in the garden. I want our friends to be here. And I want Lucinda to walk with me down the aisle, if she's able. A big wedding would be too much for her, too."

One corner of his lip quirked at all of those decisive "I wants." He suspected that before long, even though she professed not to be interested in Davencourt's business concerns, she would be poking her nose into it, butting heads with him over some of his decisions. He couldn't wait. The thought of Roanna arguing with him made him weak with delight. Roanna had always been stubborn, and she still was, even though her methods had changed. "We'll work out the details," he said. "We'll get married next week if we can, two weeks max, all right?"

She nodded, smiling a little mistily.

Number seven, he thought triumphantly. And this one had been open, natural, as if she were no longer wary about showing joy.

Twisting, he reached for the plastic bag on the bedside table and withdrew the contents. He opened the box, read the instructions, then gave her the small plastic wand with a wide slot on the side. "Now," he said, with a determined glint in his green eyes, "go pee-pee on the stick."

Ten minutes later he knocked on the bathroom door. "What are you doing?" he asked impatiently. "Are you all right?"

"Yes," she said in a muffled voice.

He opened the door. She was standing nude in front of the sink, her face blank with shock. The plastic stick lay on the rim of the bowl.

Webb looked at the stick. The slot had been white; now it was blue. It was a simple test: if the color of the slot changed, the test was positive. He eased his arms around her, pulling her into the comforting warmth of his body. She was pregnant. She was going to have his baby. "You really didn't think you were, did you?" he asked curiously.

She shook her head, her expression still stunned. "I don't—I don't feel any different."

"I imagine that will start changing soon." His big hands slid down to her flat belly, gently massaging. She could feel his heart thumping hard and fast against her back. His penis rose to jut insistently against her hip.

He was excited. He was aroused. She was stunned at the realization. She had been thinking he would feel only responsibility for the baby; she hadn't considered that he would be excited at the prospect of being a father. "You want the baby," she said, her amazement plain in both face and voice. "You *wanted* me to be pregnant."

"I sure as hell did." His voice was rough, and he tightened his arms around her. "Don't *you* want it?"

Her hand drifted downward, lightly settling over the place where her child, his child, was forming inside her. Radiant wonder lit her face, and her gaze met Webb's in the mirror. "Oh, yes," she said softly.

335

CHAPTER
21

Corliss slipped into Roanna's bedroom. She was alone upstairs, because all the others had either gone to work or were downstairs at breakfast. She had been trying to eat, but with her pounding headache and upset stomach, it had been more of a pretense than anything else. She needed some coke, just a little of it to make her feel better, but all the money she'd gotten before was already gone.

When Webb and Roanna had entered the breakfast room, she had made a point of getting up and leaving in dignified, offended silence, but they hadn't cared, the bastards. She had stopped just outside the door and listened, waiting to hear what they said about her. They hadn't mentioned her at all, as if she weren't important enough for discussion. Webb had told her to leave Davencourt and *poof!* just like that she didn't matter any more. Instead, Webb had announced that he and Roanna were getting married.

Married! Corliss couldn't believe it. The thought made her mind fog with rage. Why would anyone, especially someone like Webb, want to marry a mealymouth like Roanna? Corliss hated the bastard, but she didn't underestimate him. Despite what he'd said, she could have handled Roanna, she was sure of it. She couldn't handle Webb,

336

though. He was too hard, too mean. He was going to throw her out of Davencourt. And that's why she had to get rid of him.

She couldn't leave Davencourt. She felt sick with panic at the prospect. Nobody seemed to care that she *needed* to live here. She couldn't go back to that dinky little house in Sheffield, back to being just a poor relation to the rich Davenports. She was somebody now, Miss Corliss Spence, of Davencourt. If Webb threw her out, she'd become a nobody again. She wouldn't have any means of getting money for her expensive little habit. The thought was unbearable. She had to get rid of Webb.

She prowled through Roanna's room. She'd get to the money, but first she wanted to poke around a little. She'd gone first into Webb's room, hoping to find something of *his* she could use, but—surprise, surprise! It didn't look as if he'd slept there. His bed was perfectly made, not a wrinkle in it. Somehow she couldn't see him making his own bed, not the arrogant Webb Tallant.

Well, wasn't he the sly one? No wonder he hadn't wanted his old suite. He'd chosen this room beside Roanna's so they would have a cozy little arrangement, alone here at the back of the house.

She'd gone then into Roanna's room, and sure enough, the bed was a wreck, and both pillows bore the imprint of a head. Who ever would have thought it of prissy Roanna, who didn't even date? But she sure didn't mind screwing, from the looks of that bed. Smart of her, too. Corliss hated to admit it, but this was one time Roanna had been the smart one. She'd made certain Webb wouldn't tell *her* to leave, by setting herself up as a convenient source of sex, and somehow she'd convinced him to marry her. Maybe she was better in bed than she looked. Corliss would have slept with him herself if she'd thought of it. It pissed her off that she hadn't.

She wandered into the bathroom and opened the mirrored door to the medicine cabinet. Roanna never kept

337

anything interesting in there, no birth control pills or condoms, no diaphragm, just toothpaste and boring shit like that. She didn't even have any good cosmetics Corliss could borrow.

She glanced down at the small trash can and went still. "Well, well," she said softly, bending down to pick up the box. A do-it-yourself pregnancy test.

So that was how Roanna had done it.

She was a fast worker, Corliss had to give her that. She must have made her plans and gotten in bed with him first thing, when she'd gone to Arizona. She probably hadn't expected to get pregnant so fast, but what the hell, sometimes you took a chance and hit the jackpot.

Wouldn't Harper Neeley be interested in hearing about this?

She didn't bother with the money after all. This was too good to wait. Quickly she slipped out of Roanna's room and went back to her own. Harper was her only hope. He was one strange dude; he scared her, but he excited her, too. He looked like there was nothing too low or raunchy for him to do, nothing he would balk at. It was weird the way he hated Webb, almost to the point he couldn't think about anything else, but that was to her advantage. Harper had messed up twice, but he would keep trying. He was like a gun; all she had to do was point him and fire.

She called him to set up a meeting.

Harper's eyes gleamed with a cold, feral light that made Corliss shiver inside with both fear and satisfaction. His reaction had been more than she'd expected.

"Are you sure she's pregnant?" he asked softly, leaning back in his chair so that the front legs came off the floor. He was poised on the back legs of the chair like an animal preparing to spring.

"I saw the damn test," Corliss replied. "It was on top in the trash can, so she must have done it just this morning. Then they came downstairs all smiley-faced and Webb said they're getting married. What about my money?"

Harper smiled at her, his eyes so very blue and empty. "Money?"

Panic nibbled at her nerves. She needed some money; she'd been in too much of a hurry to get out of Roanna's room, and now she really needed a line or two to hold her steady. She was really on edge; she only had two days left before Webb made her move. Harper had to do something, but the waiting was killing her. She wouldn't be able to hold it together unless she could get just a little coke to tide her over.

"You never said anything about money," he drawled, and his smile made cold shivers go over her again. Nervously she looked around. She didn't like this place. She met Harper at a different place every time, but always before, the locations had been public: a truck stop, a bar, places like that. After the first time, they'd always met out of town, too.

This time he'd given her directions to a ratty little trailer out in the middle of nowhere. There were junk cars in the yard and discarded carcasses of old chairs and box springs piled haphazardly against the trailer, as if they'd just been tossed outside and never thought of again. The trailer was tiny, consisting of a cramped little kitchen with a cramped little table and two chairs as the dining area, a cracked Naugahyde couch and a nineteen-inch television sitting on a rickety end table, and beyond that she could see a closet-sized bathroom and a bedroom in which the double bed took up most of the floor space. Dirty dishes, beer bottles, crumpled cigarette packs, overflowing ashtrays, and dirty clothes littered every surface.

This wasn't where Harper lived. There had been a different name, crudely lettered, on the mailbox, but she couldn't remember what it was. He'd said the trailer belonged to a friend. Now she wondered if the "friend" had ever heard of Harper Neeley.

"I've got to have money," she blurted. "That was the deal."

"Nope. The deal was you'd pass along information about Tallant, and I'd take care of your problem for you."

"Well, you've done a piss-poor job of it!" she snapped.

He blinked slowly, his cold blue gaze growing even colder, and belatedly she wished she'd kept her mouth shut.

"It's taking longer than I expected," she said, moderating her tone to a plea. "I'm broke, and I need things. You know how girls are—"

"I know how cokeheads are," he said indifferently.

"I'm not a cokehead!" she flared. "I just use a little every now and then to settle my nerves."

"Sure, and your shit don't stink either."

She flushed, but something in the way he was looking at her made her afraid to push him any further. Nervously she got up from the couch, peeling her thighs from the Naugahyde where sweat had made her stick to the damn thing. She saw his gaze drop down to her legs, and she wished she hadn't worn shorts. It was just so damn hot, and she hadn't expected to be sitting on Naugahyde, for God's sake. She wished she hadn't worn these shorts especially, but they were her favorites because they were so short and tight, and they were white besides, which really showed off her tan.

"I got to go," she said, trying to hide her agitation. Harper had never tried anything with her, but then they'd never been in a place where he could. It wasn't that he was ugly, far from it, for an old dude, but he scared the living shit out of her. Maybe if they'd been someplace where she wasn't so alone, like a motel, where someone would hear if she screamed, because Harper looked like a man who made women scream.

"You ain't wearing any panties," he observed, never moving from his balanced position on the back legs of the chair. "I can see your pussy hair through your shorts."

She knew that; that was one reason she liked the shorts so much. She loved the way men glanced at her, then did a double take and looked again, with their eyes all bugged out and their tongues all but flapping like a dog's. It made her feel sexy, hot. But when Harper looked at her, she didn't feel hot, she felt scared.

He tilted even further back in the chair and reached into

340

the right pocket of his jeans. He pulled out a Baggie filled with about an ounce of white powder, twisted into a little pouch and secured with red yarn tied around the neck of the pouch. The yarn drew her gaze, held it. She'd never seen a cocaine bag tied up with red yarn before. It looked exotic, unreal.

He swung the little bag back and forth. "Would you rather have this, or money?"

Money, she tried to say, but her lips wouldn't form the words. Back and forth the little bag went, back and forth. She stared at it, hypnotized, fascinated. There was snow in that little bag, a Christmas present all tied up with red yarn.

"M-maybe just a taste," she whispered. Just a taste. That was all she needed. A little snort to chase away the edginess.

Carelessly he turned and swiped everything off the surface of the dirty little table, knocking newspapers and ashtrays and dirty dishes to the floor where it joined the rest of the litter and looked right at home. The owner of the trailer might not even notice. Then he untied the red yarn and carefully poured a portion of the white powder onto the table. Eagerly Corliss started forward, but he gave her a cold look that stopped her in her tracks. "Just wait," he said. "It's not ready for you yet."

A magazine insert, one of the stupid little cards that magazines stuck all through the pages, giving the reader an opportunity to become a subscriber, was lying on the floor. Harper picked it up and began to divide the tiny white mound into uniform lines on the table. Corliss watched his quick, sure movements. He'd done this before, many times. That puzzled her, because she thought she knew how to spot the cokers, and Harper didn't have any of the signs.

The little lines were perfect now, four of them. They weren't very long, but they would do. She quivered, staring at them, waiting for the word that would release her from her position.

Harper took a piece of straw from his pocket. It was a regular soda straw, cut down to not much longer than an inch. It was shorter than she liked, so short she'd have to bend down right over the table and take care that her hand didn't brush the lines and disturb them. But it was a straw, and when he held it out to her, she eagerly took it.

He pointed to a place on the floor. "You can stand there."

The trailer was so tiny that it was only one step forward. She took it, then looked at the table and back at him. She would have to bend all the way forward and stretch to reach the lines. "That's too far," she said.

He shrugged. "You'll manage."

She reached out and braced her left hand on the table and carefully held the little straw in her right. She bent forward, inching, hoping she wouldn't fall and turn the table over. The lines came closer and she lifted the straw to her nose, already anticipating the rush, the sizzle of ecstasy as her head expanded, the glow—

"You're not doing it right," he said.

She froze, her gaze still on those sweet little lines. She had to have them. She couldn't wait much longer. But she was afraid to move, afraid of what would happen if she moved before Harper said she could.

"You have to drop your drawers first."

His voice was expressionless, as if they were playing May I? But now she knew what he wanted, and relief almost made her knees sag. It was just screwing, nothing important. So what if he was older than anyone else she'd ever screwed? The little lines beckoned, and how old he was didn't matter.

Hastily she straightened and unbuttoned her shorts, let them drop to her ankles. She started to step out of them, but he stopped her again. "Leave them there. I don't want your legs spread, it's tighter when they're together."

She shrugged. "Whatever cranks your tractor."

She didn't pay any more attention to him as he moved behind her. She bent forward, eagerly focused on the cocaine, left hand braced on the table, right hand holding the straw. The tip of the straw touched the white powder, and she inhaled sharply just as he shoved into her, driving deep, the force of his thrust making the straw skid across the table and knock the cocaine out of its neat lines. She was dry, and he hurt her. She chased after the coke with the straw and he shoved again, making her miss. She whimpered, frantically adjusting her position and inhaling as hard as she could to suck up any particle the tip of the straw might touch.

The coke was scattered all over the table. There was no point in trying to aim, only to time her inhalations as his thrusts rhythmically pushed her forward. Corliss held the short straw to her nose, avidly sweeping the tip across the table, sucking hard through her nose as she went back and forth, back and forth, and it didn't matter any more that he was hurting her, damn him, because she was managing to inhale enough, and the glow, the rush, was spreading through her. She didn't care what he did as long as he could get the coke for her, and as long as he took care of Webb Tallant before the bastard kicked her out of Davencourt.

That afternoon when Roanna returned from a meeting of the Historical Society, she opened the garage door and saw that Corliss had returned before her and taken advantage of her absence to take her parking slot again. Sighing, she pressed the button on the remote control to lower the garage door again, and parked her car to the side. Corliss would be gone in two days; she could be patient that long. If she said anything about the parking space, there would be another big scene that would upset Lucinda, something she wanted to avoid.

She was walking across the yard to the back door when something moved softly in her heart, and she stopped and looked around. It was one of the most beautiful days she'd ever seen. The sky was a deep, pure blue and the air was unusually clear, without the usual haze of humidity. The heat was so intense it was like a touch, releasing the rich, heavy fragrance from the rose bushes, which had been carefully cultivated over decades and were laden with blooms. Down at the stables, the horses were prancing around and tossing their glossy heads, full of energy. That morning, Webb had asked her to marry him. And above all that, she was carrying his child.

Pregnant. She was actually pregnant. She was still a little stunned, as if it couldn't possibly be happening to her, and she had been so distracted she had no idea what had been discussed at the Historical Society meeting. She was accustomed to being the only person inhabiting her body. How did she get used to the concept of someone else living inside her? It was alien, and it was frightening. How could something so strange be so precious? She was so happy she wanted to weep.

That, too, felt alien. She was happy. She examined the emotion cautiously. She was going to marry Webb. She was going to raise kids and horses. She looked up at the huge old house and felt a wave of pure elation and possessiveness sweep over her. Davencourt was *hers*. It was her home now, truly and for real. Yes, she was happy. Even with Lucinda's inevitable passing coming closer and closer, she was filled with a rich contentment.

Webb was right; Jessie had poisoned enough of her life, convinced her that she was too ugly and clumsy for anyone to love her. Well, Jessie had been a spiteful bitch, and she'd been lying. Roanna felt the knowledge seep into her pores. She was a capable, likable human being, and she had a special talent with horses. She *was* loved; Lucinda loved her, Loyal loved her, Bessie and Tansy loved her. Gloria and Lanette had been concerned when she'd been injured, and Lanette had been surprisingly helpful. Brock and Greg liked her. Harlan—well, who knew about Harlan? But most of all, Webb loved her. Sometime during the day, the certainty of that had penetrated the layers of her soul. Webb loved her. He'd loved her all her life, just as he'd said. He was certainly aroused by her, which meant that her looks weren't all that odd either.

She smiled a private little smile as she remembered how he'd made love to her the night before, and again that morning, after the pregnancy test had shown positive. There was no doubting his physical reaction to her, any more than he could doubt her desire for him.

"I saw that," he said from where he lounged in the kitchen doorway. She hadn't heard him open the door. "You've been standing there daydreaming for five minutes, and you just got a mysterious little smile on your face. What are you thinking about?"

Still smiling, Roanna walked toward him, her brown eyes heavy lidded and filled with an expression that made him catch his breath. "Riding," she murmured as she walked past, deliberately brushing her body against his. "And woofs."

His own eyes grew heavy, and color stained his cheekbones. It was the first seductive move Roanna had made toward him, and it had brought him to a full, immediate erection. Tansy was behind him in the kitchen, cheerfully going about her daily baking and concocting. He didn't care if she noticed his aroused state. He turned around and silently, purposefully followed Roanna.

She glanced over her shoulder at him as they went up the stairs, her face glowing with promise. She walked faster.

The bedroom door was barely closed behind them before Webb had her in his arms.

Getting married involved running a lot of errands, Roanna thought the next morning as she drove down the long, winding private road. The guest list for the wedding was much smaller than the one for Lucinda's party had been, with a total of forty people, including family, but there were still details to be taken care of.

She and Webb were to have their blood tests later that afternoon. This morning, she had arranged for the flowers and the caterer and the wedding cake. Normally wedding cakes took weeks to prepare, but Mrs. Turner, who specialized in wedding cakes, had said she could do an "elegantly simple" one in the eleven days left until the chosen wedding date. Roanna understood that "elegantly simple" was a tactful way of saying less elaborate, but that was what she preferred anyway. She had to stop by Mrs. Turner's house and pick out the design she liked best.

She also had to shop for a wedding gown. If she couldn't find anything she liked in the Quad Cities on such short notice, she would have to go to Huntsville or Birmingham.

Fortunately, Yvonne had been ecstatic about the prospect of Webb's second marriage. She had tolerated Jessie but never really liked her. Roanna suited her to a T, and she had even said that she'd always wished Webb had waited for Roanna to grow up rather than marrying Jessie. Yvonne had thrown herself into the preparations, taking over the onerous chore of invitations and volunteering to handle the logistics of everything else once Roanna had made her choices.

Roanna reached the side road and stopped, waiting for an oncoming car to pass. Her brakes felt mushy when she applied them, and she frowned, experimentally pumping the pedal again. This time it felt fine. Perhaps the level of brake fluid was low, though she kept the car well maintained. She made a mental note to stop at a service station and have it checked.

She turned right onto the side road, traveling toward the highway. The car that had just passed was at least a hundred yards ahead of her. Roanna gradually accelerated, her thoughts drifting to the style of gown she wanted: something simple, in ivory rather than pure white. She had some gold-hued pearls that would look gorgeous with an ivory gown. And a fairly slim skirt in the Empire style would suit her far better than a full-skirted, fairy princess gown.

There was a curve in the road, then a stop sign where the road intersected with Highway 43, a busy four-lane highway, with traffic continually zooming past. Roanna rounded the curve and saw the car ahead of her halted at the stop sign, left turn signal blinking, waiting for an opening in the traffic to enter the highway.

A car turned onto the side road, coming toward her, but

the traffic was too heavy for the car stopped at the intersection to make it across to the other side. Roanna put her foot on the brake pedal to slow down, and the pedal went to the floorboard without any resistance at all.

Alarm shot through her. She pumped the pedal again, but there was no response the way there had been the first time. If anything, the car seemed to pick up speed. She had no brakes, and both lanes of the road were occupied.

Time warped, stretching like elastic. The road elongated in front of her, while the oncoming car loomed twice its normal size. Thoughts flashed through her mind, lightning fast: Webb, the baby. A deep ditch was to the right, and the shoulder was narrow; there was no room for her to swing past the car stopped at the intersection, even if there hadn't been the danger of shooting across four lanes of traffic.

Webb! Dear God, Webb. She gripped the steering wheel, anguish almost choking her as the seconds churned past and she ran out of time. She couldn't die now, not now when she had Webb, when his child was just beginning its life inside her. She had to do something . . .

But she already knew what to do, she realized, memory gleaming like a bright thread through the terror that threatened to engulf her. She'd been a terrible driver, so she had taken a driving course when she was in college. She knew how to handle skids and lousy road conditions; she knew what to do in case of brake failure.

She knew what to do!

The car was shooting forward, as if it were on a downhill course and the roadway was greased.

The driving instructor's voice sounded in her head, calm and prosaic: *Don't take a solid hit if you can help it. Don't let yourself hit anything head on, that's when the worst damage occurs. Turn the car, slide into a collision, dissipate the force.*

She reached for the gear shift. Don't try to put it into park, she thought, remembering those long-ago lessons. The instructor had said it likely wouldn't go into park anyway. She could hear his voice as clearly as if he was sitting beside her: *Put the gear into low range and pull the emergency brakes. The emergency brakes work on a cable, not on pneumatic pressure. A loss of brake fluid won't affect them.*

The stopped car was just fifty yards ahead now. The oncoming car was less than that.

She pulled the gear shift into low and reached for the emergency brake lever, pulling it with all her strength. Metal shrieked as the transmission ground down, and black smoke boiled up from her tires. The stench of burning rubber filled the car.

The rear end of the car will likely come around. Steer out of the skid if you can. If you don't have room, and you see you're going to hit someone or be hit, try to maneuver so it's an indirect collision. Both of you will be more likely to walk away.

The rear end swung into the other lane, in front of the oncoming car. A horn blared, and Roanna caught a glimpse of a furious, terrified face, just a blur in the windshield. She turned into the skid, felt the car began to slide in the other direction, and quickly spun the steering wheel to correct that skid, too.

The oncoming car swept past with inches to spare, horn still blaring. That left only the car in her lane, still sitting patiently at the stop sign, turn signal blinking.

Twenty yards. No more room, no more time. With the left lane clear now, Roanna sent the car into a spinning slide across it. A cornfield stretched out on the other side of the road, nice and flat. She left the road and plunged across the shoulder, the car still skidding sideways. She crashed into the fencing, wood splintering, and a whole section came down. The car plowed down head-high stalks of corn as it bumped and thudded across the furrows, clods of dirt flying in all directions. She was thrown forward, and the seat belt bit hard into her hips and torso, jerking her back as the car shuddered to a stop.

She sat there with her head resting on the steering wheel, too weak and dazed to get out of the car. Numbly she took stock of herself. Everything seemed to be all right.

She became aware that she was trembling uncontrollably. She'd done it!

She heard someone yelling, then there was a tapping on the window beside her. "Ma'am? Ma'am? Are you all right?"

Roanna lifted her head and stared into the scared face of a teenage girl. Willing her shaking limbs to obey, she unclipped the seat belt and tried to get out. The door didn't want to open. She shoved, and the girl pulled from the outside, and together they forced it open enough for Roanna to climb out. "I'm okay," she managed to say.

"I saw you run off the road. Are you sure you're okay? You hit that fence pretty hard."

"The fence got the worst of it." Roanna's teeth began chattering, and she had to lean against the car or sink to the ground. "My brakes failed."

The girl's eyes widened. "Oh, gosh! You ran off the road to keep from hitting me, didn't you?"

"It seemed like a better idea," she said, and her knees sagged.

The girl sprang forward, sliding an arm around her. "You *are* hurt!"

Roanna shook her head, forcing her knees to stiffen as the girl showed signs of bursting into tears. "No, I'm just scared, that's all. My legs feel like limp noodles." She took a few deep, steadying breaths. "I have a cell phone in the car, I'll just call someone to come—"

"I'll get it for you," the girl said, wrenching the door open wider and scrambling inside to find the cellular phone. After a brief search she located it under the right front seat.

Roanna took some more calming breaths before she called home. The last thing she wanted to do was unduly alarm Webb or Lucinda, so that meant she had to steady her voice.

Bessie answered the phone, and Roanna asked for Webb. He came on the line a moment later. "You haven't been gone five minutes," he teased. "What else have you thought of?"

349

"Nothing," she said, and was proud of how calm she sounded. "Come down to the intersection and get me. I had trouble with the brakes on my car and ran off the road."

He didn't reply. She heard a violent, muffled curse, then there was a clatter and the phone went dead. "He's on his way," she said to the girl, and pressed the END button on the phone.

Webb bundled Roanna into his truck, thanked the teenager for checking on her, and drove back to Davencourt so fast that Roanna clung to the overhead strap to steady herself. When they reached the house, he insisted on carrying her inside.

"Put me down!" she hissed as he swung her up into his arms. "You'll have everyone worried to death."

"Hush," he said, and kissed her, hard. "I love you and you're pregnant. Carrying you makes *me* feel better."

She looped her arm around his neck and hushed. She had to admit, the warmth and strength of his big body was very soothing, as if she were absorbing some of it through her skin. But as she had predicted, the fact that she wasn't walking on her own brought everyone scurrying, frightened questions on their lips.

Webb carried her into the living room and placed her on one of the couches as carefully as if she were made of fine crystal. "I'm all right, I'm all right," she kept saying to the chorus of questions. "I'm not even bruised."

"Get her something hot and sweet to drink," Webb said to Tansy, who rushed to obey.

"Decaffeinated!" Roanna called after her, thinking of the baby.

After assuring himself for the tenth time that she was unhurt, Webb stood up and told her he was going out to have a look at her car. "I'll go with you," she said in relief at the prospect of escaping from all the cosseting, getting up, but she was immediately drowned out by a chorus of protests from the women in the household.

"You most certainly will not, young lady," Lucinda said, at her most autocratic. "You've had a shock to your system, and you need to rest."

"I'm not hurt," Roanna said again, wondering if anyone was actually listening to what she said.

"Then *I* need for you to rest. It would fret me no end if you went off gallivanting, when common sense says you should give yourself time to get over the shock."

Roanna gave Webb a speaking glance. He lifted one eyebrow and shrugged, not at all sympathetically. "Can't have you gallivanting," he murmured, and dropped his gaze lower, to her belly.

Roanna sat back down, warmed by the silent communication, the shared thought about their child. And while Lucinda was blatantly using emotional blackmail to get her way, it was done out of genuine concern, and Roanna decided there wouldn't be any harm in letting herself be fussed over for the rest of the day.

Webb went outside to get into his truck, and stared thoughtfully at the spot where Roanna's car had been parked. There was a dark, wet stain on the ground, visible even from where he was. He walked over and hunkered down, examining the stain for a moment before touching it with his finger, then sniffing the oily residue. Definitely brake fluid, a lot of it. She must have had only a little fluid left in the lines, and it would have been pumped out the first time she used her brakes.

She could have been killed. If she had gone across the highway instead of into a cornfield, she very likely would have been seriously injured, at the least, if not killed outright.

A cold sense of dread touched him. The shadowy, unknown assailant could have struck again, but this time at Roanna. Why not? Hadn't he done it before with Jessie? And with more success, too.

He didn't use the cellular phone, with its insecure channels, or go back inside to face the inevitable questions

351

Instead he walked down to the stables and used Loyal's phone. The trainer listened to the conversation, his thick, graying brows pulling together as his eyes began to snap with anger.

"You think somebody tried to hurt Miss Roanna?" he demanded as soon as Webb hung up.

"I don't know. It's possible."

"The same person who broke into the house?"

"If her brakes have been sabotaged, then I'd have to say yes."

"That would mean he was here last night, messing around with her car."

Webb nodded, his expression stony. He tried not to let his imagination run away with him until he knew for certain if Roanna's car had been tampered with, but he couldn't stop the stomach-tightening panic and anger at the thought of the man being so close.

He drove out to the intersection, all the while carefully scanning around him. He didn't think this would be a trap designed to get him out in the open, because there was no way to predict exactly where Roanna's accident would happen. Though he was acutely aware that this was roughly the same location where he had been shot at from ambush, he was more afraid that this hadn't been aimed at him, but specifically at Roanna. Maybe she hadn't simply been in the wrong place at the wrong time the night she'd been hit on the head. Maybe she'd been lucky instead, that she'd managed to scream and alert the household before the bastard had been able to finish the job.

Jessie had been killed, but by God, he wouldn't let anything happen to Roanna. No matter what he had to do, he'd keep her safe.

He parked the truck on the shoulder next to the downed section of fencing and waited for the sheriff. It wasn't long before Beshears drove up, and Booley was riding in the front seat with him. The two men got out and joined Webb, and together they waded through the flattened cornstalks to where the car sat. They were all grim and silent. After the other two incidents, it was asking a bit much to believe that Roanna's brakes had failed on their own, and they all knew it.

Webb lay down on his back and wormed his way under the car. Broken corn stalks scraped his back, and tiny insects buzzed around his ears. The smell of grease and brake fluid filled his nostrils. "Carl, hand me your flashlight," he said, and the big flashlight was passed under the car to him.

He turned it on and directed the beam to the brake line. He spotted the cut almost immediately. "Y'all want to take a look at this?" he invited.

Carl lay down and grunted as he squirmed under the car to join Webb, cussing as the cornstalks gouged his skin. "I'm too old for this," he muttered. "Ouch!" Booley declined to join them, as the weight he'd added since retirement would have made it a tight fit for him.

Carl hauled himself into position next to Webb and scowled when he saw the line. "The son of a bitch," he growled, lifting his head to examine the line as close as he could without touching it. "Cut almost through. A nice fresh, clean cut. Even if she'd managed to make it onto the highway okay, she'd have wrecked when she got to the stop light on 157. Guess it was pure luck she ran into this field the way she did."

"Skill, not luck," Webb said. "She took some driving courses in college."

"No fooling. Wish more folks would take something like that, then we wouldn't have to pick pieces of them up off the highway." He glanced at Webb, saw the tightening of his mouth, and said, "Sorry."

Carefully they wormed their way out from under the car, though Carl cussed again when a stalk caught his shirt and tore a small hole in it.

"Did you check the other cars at the house?" Booley asked.

"I took a quick look under all of them. Roanna's was the only one touched. She usually parks in the garage, but she left her car outside last night."

"Now, that's a bit coincidental." Carl scratched his chin, a sign that he was thinking. "Why didn't she park in the garage?"

"Corliss was parked in her slot. We've had some trouble with Corliss lately, and I told her she had to move out. I started to make her move her car, but Ro told me to leave it alone and not cause a fuss that would upset Lucinda."

"Maybe you should've made that fuss anyway. You reckon Corliss would do something like this?"

"I'd be surprised if she knew a brake line from a fishing line."

"She got any friends who would do it for her?"

"I've been away for ten years," Webb replied. "I don't know who she hangs out with. But if she had anyone tamper with a brake line, it would be mine, not Roanna's."

"But yours was in the garage."

"Corliss has a control for the doors. We all do. If she was behind it, it wouldn't matter if the car was inside the garage or not."

Carl scratched his chin again. "None of this ties together, does it? It's like we've got pieces from ten different puzzles, and nothing goes together. It just don't make a lick of sense."

"Oh, it all fits," Booley said grimly. "We just don't know how."

354

CHAPTER

22

The house was quiet that night when Webb finally entered Roanna's room. As usual, she was curled up in her chair with a book in her lap, but she looked around with a warm welcome in her eyes. "What took you so long?"

"I had some last-minute paperwork I needed to do. With all the excitement today, I'd forgotten about it." He knelt in front of her, searching her eyes with his. "Are you honestly okay? You aren't hiding anything from me?"

"I'm *fine*. Not a single bruise. Do you want me to pull off my clothes and show you?"

His eyes turned smoky, and his gaze dropped to her breasts. "Yes."

She felt herself begin to warm and soften inside, and her nipples beaded the way they always did when he looked at her. He laughed softly, but got to his feet and caught her hands, pulling her up. "Come on."

She thought they were going to the bed, but instead he directed her to the door. She gave him a confused look. "Where are we going?"

"To another bedroom."

"Why?" she asked, bewildered. "What's wrong with this one?"

355

"Because I want to try another bed."

"Yours?"

"No," he said briefly.

Roanna resisted the pressure on her back as he urged her toward the door. She turned and gave him a long, steady regard. "Something's wrong." She said it as a statement, not a question. She knew Webb too well; she'd seen him angry and she'd seen him amused. She knew when he was tired, when he was worried, when he was aggravated as all hell. She thought she'd seen him in all his moods, but this one was new. His eyes were hard and cool, with an alertness that made her think of a hungry cat stalking prey.

"Let's just say I'd feel better if you were in a different room tonight."

"If I go, will you tell me why?"

That bladelike gaze sharpened even more. "Oh, you'll go," he said softly.

She drew herself up and faced him, not backing down an inch. "You can reason with me, Webb Tallant, but you can't order me around. I'm not a fool or a child. Tell me what's going on." Just because she loved him to distraction didn't mean she couldn't think for herself.

He looked briefly frustrated, because once she wouldn't have balked at doing anything he told her. But she'd been a child then, and now she was a woman; he needed to be reminded of that every so often. He made a rapid decision. "All right, but come on. And be as quiet as you can; I don't want to wake anyone. When we get to the other room, don't turn on any lights either."

"The bed won't have any sheets on it," she warned.

"Then bring something to put around you in case you get cold."

She picked up her afghan and went quietly with him down the hall to one of the unoccupied bedrooms, the last one on the left side. The curtains were open, letting in enough light from the quarter moon that they could see how to maneuver. Webb went over to the windows and looked out, while Roanna sat down on the bed.

"Tell me," she said.

He didn't turn away from the windows. "I suspect we might have a visitor tonight."

She thought about it for a few seconds, and her stomach knotted at the obvious answer. "You think the burglar will come back?"

He gave her a brief glance. "You're quick, you know that? I don't think he was a burglar. But, yes, I think he'll come."

He could see the side lawn from this room, she realized, while from either of their rooms he could have seen only the back. "If he isn't a burglar, why would he come back?"

Webb was silent a moment, then said, "Jessie's killer was never caught."

She was suddenly chilled, and pulled the afghan around her shoulders. "You think . . . you think whoever killed Jessie was in the house again that night, and hit me?"

"I think it's possible. Your accident today wasn't an accident, Ro. Your brake line had been cut. And someone took a couple of shots at me the other day when I was late getting here for the party. I didn't have car trouble; my windshield was shot out."

Roanna sucked in a deep, shocked breath, her mind reeling. She wanted to jump up and yell at him for not having said something before, she wanted to throw something, she wanted to get her hands on whoever had tried to shoot him. She couldn't do any of that, however. If she wanted him to finish telling her what was going on, she had to sit there and not make a lot of noise. She pulled herself together and tried to reason it out. "But . . . why would whoever killed Jessie want to kill you? And me?"

"I don't know," he said in frustration. "I've gone over and over everything that happened before Jessie died, and I can't think of anything. I didn't know she had a lover until Booley told me she was pregnant when she died, but why would he have killed Jessie? It would have made sense if he'd tried to kill me, but not Jessie. And if Jessie was killed because of something else she was doing, there wouldn't be a reason for the killer to come after you and me. We don't know who he is, and after ten years he should feel safe from discovery, so why take the risk of starting it all again?"

"So you don't think her lover is the one?"

"I don't know. There's no reason for it. On the other hand, if *I'm* the real target and have been all along, that means Jessie died because she was my wife. I thought she might have surprised the killer, the same way you did, and he killed her so she couldn't identify him. I made sure it's common knowledge that you can't remember anything about the night you were attacked, so he wouldn't have that as a reason for coming back. But when your brake line was cut, I knew it had to be more than that. Tampering with your car was directed specifically at you."

"Because we're getting married," she said, feeling sick inside. "But how could he have found out so fast? We just decided yesterday morning!"

"You started making arrangements yesterday," Webb said, shrugging. "Think of the people you called, all the people they must have told. News travels. Whoever it is must hate me a lot, to go after first Jessie, then you."

"But Jessie's death had to be unplanned," Roanna argued. "No one could have known that y'all would argue that night or that you would have gone to a bar. Normally you would have been at home."

"I know," he said, exhaling hard in frustration. "I can't think of a reason for any of it. No matter how I look at it, some of the details don't fit."

She got up from the bed and went over to him, needing his closeness. He put his arms around her and hugged her to him, tucking the afghan more securely around her shoulders. She laid her head on his chest, softly breathing in the warm, musky scent of his skin. It was unthinkable that anything should happen to him.

"Why do you think he'll come back tonight?"

"Because he's made several attempts in a short period of time. He keeps coming back, trying something different. Loyal is watching from the stables. If he sees anything, he'll call me on the cellular phone, then notify the sheriff."

"Are you armed?"

He tilted his head toward the dresser. "There."

She turned her head and in the dimness could see a darker shape lying on top of the dresser. Abruptly she knew what was different about his mood. This was how he must have been when he'd tracked the rustlers into Mexico: the hunter, the predator. Webb was a man not normally inclined to violence, but he would kill to protect his own. He wasn't excited or on edge; the thud of his heart beneath her head was steady. He was coolly, ruthlessly determined.

"What if nothing happens tonight?" she asked.

"Then we'll watch again tomorrow night. Eventually, we'll get him."

She stood with him for a long time, staring out at the moonlit night until her eyes ached. Nothing moved, and the crickets chirped undisturbed.

"You're sure the alarm is on?"

He pointed to the code box beside the veranda doors. A tiny green light was steadily shining. A red light flashed if a door was opened, and if the code wasn't entered within fifteen seconds, the alarm sounded.

Webb appeared to have the patience of Job and the stamina of a marathoner. He stood unmoving, keeping watch, but Roanna couldn't manage to stand still for that length of time. She paced slowly around the dark bedroom, hugging the afghan around her, until Webb said softly, "Why don't you lie down and get some sleep?"

"I have insomnia, remember?" she shot back. "I only sleep after—"

She stopped, and he chuckled. "I could say something crude, but I won't. I kind of like this strange type of insomnia," he teased. "It gives me incentive."

"I haven't noticed that you needed any."

"After we've been married thirty years or so, I might—" He broke off, every line of his big body tensing.

Roanna didn't hurry to the window, though that was her first urge. She was wearing a white nightgown; her appearance at the window might be spotted. Instead she whispered, "Do you see someone?"

"The son of a bitch is slipping up the outside stairs," he murmured. "I didn't see him until just now. Probably Loyal didn't either." He took the cellular phone from his pocket and punched the numbers for Loyal's private line. A few seconds later he said quietly, "He's here, coming up to the veranda by the outside stairs." That was all. He closed the phone and returned it to his pocket.

"What do we do?" she whispered.

"Wait and see what he does. Loyal is calling the sheriff, then he's coming over as backup." He shifted his position a little, so he had a better angle to watch the silent intruder. The moonlight slanted across his face. " He's going around to the front . . . He's out of sight now."

A red light blinked, catching Roanna's attention. She stared at the code box. "Webb, he's in the house! The light's blinking."

He swore softly and moved across the room to get the pistol from the top of the dresser.

Still watching the light, Roanna said, startled, "It's stopped blinking. It's green again."

He swung around and stared at the code box. "Someone let him in." His voice was almost soundless, but laden with a quiet menace that didn't bode well for someone. *"Corliss."*

He kicked off his shoes and silently went to the door.

"What are you going to do?" Roanna asked fiercely, trying to keep her voice down. It was difficult, with anger and fear rushing through her veins with every beat of her heart. She trembled with the need to go with him, but she forced herself to stand still. She had no means of protecting herself, and the last thing he needed was to have to worry about her.

"Try to get behind him." He opened the door the tiniest crack, looking down the hallway for the intruder. He couldn't see anything. He decided to wait, hoping the man would give away his position. He thought he heard a faint whisper of sound but couldn't be certain.

Seconds ticked past, and Webb took the risk of opening the door a bit more. He could see all the way to the front of the house now, on this side of the house, and the hallway was empty. He slipped out of the room and down the back hallway, his bare feet soundless on the carpet, keeping close to the wall. When he approached the corner he slowed, lifting the pistol and pulling the hammer back. With his back flattened against the wall, he took a quick look around the corner. A dark figure loomed at the other end of the hallway. Webb jerked back, but not in time—he'd been seen. A thunderous shot reverberated through the house, and plaster flew from the wall.

Webb swore viciously even as he threw himself into the open, rolling, bringing his own weapon around. He squeezed off a shot, the heavy pistol bucking in his hand, but the dark figure at the other end darted toward Lucinda's door. Smoke filled the hallway, and the stench of cordite burned in his nostrils as Webb scrambled to his feet and threw himself forward.

As he'd expected, the shots had the entire family opening their doors, poking their heads out. "God damn it, get back in your rooms," he yelled furiously.

Gloria ignored him and stepped completely out into the hallway. "Don't swear at me!" she snapped. "What on earth is going on?"

Behind her, the assailant stepped out into the hallway, but Gloria was between them and Webb couldn't get off a shot. Roughly he shoved her, and with a cry she sprawled to the floor.

And he froze, suddenly helpless. The man had one arm hooked around Lucinda's neck, holding the frail old woman in front of him as a shield. The gun was steady in his other hand, the barrel laid against Lucinda's temple, and a savage grin was on his face.

"Unload the gun real slow," he ordered, backing toward the front hallway. Webb didn't hesitate. There was an expression on the man's face that told him Lucinda would be dead if he didn't obey. With deliberate movements he flipped open the cylinder and removed all the bullets.

"Throw them behind you," the man said, and Webb obeyed, tossing the bullets down the hallway. "Now kick the gun toward me."

Carefully he bent and placed the empty weapon on the carpet, then took his foot and shoved it toward the man, who made no move to pick it up. He didn't have to; he had separated the bullets from the weapon, so there was no way anyone could pick up a bullet, get to the pistol and reload it, then fire, before he could shoot them.

Lucinda was standing very still in his grip, as colorless as her nightgown. Her white hair was rumpled as if he had dragged her from her bed, and perhaps he had, though more likely she had jumped up at the first shot and was coming to see what had happened when he grabbed her.

The man looked around, his savage grin growing even bigger as he saw all the people standing frozen in their bedroom doors, except for Gloria, who was still lying on the carpet and whimpering softly.

"Everybody!" he suddenly bellowed. "I want to see everybody! I know who you all are, so if anybody tries to hide, I'll put a bullet in the old biddy's head. You got five seconds! One—two—three—"

Harlan stepped out of the bedroom and bent to help Gloria to her feet. She clung to him, still whimpering. Greg and Lanette came out of their rooms, ashen faced.

"—four—"

Webb saw Corliss and Brock appear from the other hallway.

The man looked around. "There's one more," he said, sneering. "We're missing your little brood mare, Tallant. Where is she? You think I'm fooling around about killing this old bitch?"

No, Webb thought. No. As much as he loved Lucinda, he couldn't bear the thought of risking Roanna. Run, he silently pleaded with her. Run, darling. Get help. *Run!*

The man looked to the left and gave a pleased laugh. "There she is. Come on out, darlin'. Join the happy crowd."

Roanna slipped forward, moving to stand between Corliss and the front double doors of the veranda. She was as pale as Lucinda, her slender figure almost insubstantial. She stared at the man and gasped, going even whiter.

"Well, ain't this nice?" the man crowed, grinning at Roanna. "I see you remember me."

"Yes," she said faintly.

"That's good, because I remember you real well. Me and you got some unfinished business. You gave me a scare when you walked up on me here in the hall that night, but I heard tell that little bump on the head gave you a concussion, and you don't remember nothing about it. That right?"

"Yes," she said again, her eyes huge and dark in her white face.

He laughed, evidently pleased by the irony. His cold eyes swept over them all. "A real family reunion. All of you get together, over here in the front hall, under the light so I can see all of you real good." He moved back, out of reach, holding Lucinda's head arched back as Webb silently shepherded the others forward, grouping them together with Corliss, Brock, and Roanna.

Webb spared a single murderous look at Corliss. She was watching the man as if fascinated, but there wasn't a single flicker of fear on her face. She had let him in, and she was too stupid to realize he would kill her, too. All of them were dead, unless he did something.

He tried to move closer to Roanna, hoping that perhaps he could shield her with his body, that somehow she might survive. "Uh-uh," the man said, shaking his head. "You stand still, you bastard."

"Who *are* you?" Gloria shrilled. "Turn loose of my sister!"

"Shut up, bitch, or I'll feed the first bullet to you."

"It's a good question," Webb said. He stared at the man with a cool, hard gaze. "Who the hell are you?"

Lucinda spoke, her bloodless lips moving. "His name," she said clearly, "is Harper Neeley."

The man gave a rough, feral laugh. "I see you've heard of me."

"I know who you are. I made it a point to find out."

"Did you, now? That's real interesting. Wonder why you never visited. We're family, after all." He laughed again.

Webb didn't want his attention on Lucinda, didn't want him watching any of them except himself. "Why, God damn it?" he snarled. "What do you want? I don't know you, I've never even heard of you." If he could stall long enough, Loyal might be able to work himself into position and do something, or the sheriff would arrive. All he had to do was stall.

"Because you killed her," Neeley said viciously. "You killed my girl, you fucking bastard."

"Jessie?" Webb stared at him, astonished. "I didn't kill Jessie."

"God damn you, don't lie!" Neeley roared, jerking the pistol from Lucinda's temple to point it at Webb. "You found out about us, and you killed her!"

"No," Webb said sharply. "I didn't. I didn't have any idea she was cheating on me. I didn't know until after the autopsy when the sheriff told me she was pregnant. I knew it couldn't be mine."

"You knew! You knew and you killed her! You killed my girl and you killed my baby, and I'm going to make you watch while I kill *your* baby. I'm going to shoot this little bitch right in the stomach and you're going to stand there and watch her die, and then I'm going to do you—"

"He didn't kill Jessie!" Lucinda's voice rang out over Neeley's. She lifted her white head high. "I did."

The pistol wavered slightly. "Don't try to mess with me, old woman," Neeley panted.

Webb kept his attention glued to Neeley; the man's eyes were gleaming hotly, sweat beading on his face as he worked himself into a frenzy. He was planning to kill nine people. He'd already wasted one shot. The pistol was an automatic;

how many bullets did it have in the clip? Some carried as many as seventeen, but still, after the first shot he could hardly expect them all to stand there like sheep waiting for the slaughter. He had to realize that he was in an almost impossible situation, but that made him all the more unstable. He had nothing to lose.

"I killed her," Lucinda repeated.

"You're lying. It was him, everybody knows it was him."

"I didn't mean to kill her," Lucinda said calmly. "It was an accident. I was scared, I didn't know what to do. If Webb had actually been arrested, I would have confessed, but Booley couldn't find any evidence because there wasn't any. Webb didn't do it." She gave Webb a look of sorrow, of love, of regret. "I'm sorry," she whispered.

"You're lying!" Neeley howled, jerking her hard against him and tightening his arm around her throat. "I'll break your goddamn neck if you don't shut up!"

Greg jumped for him. Quiet, unassuming Greg, who had let Lanette run their lives without even opening his mouth to give an opinion. Lanette screamed, and Neeley jerked back, firing once. Greg stumbled and fell forward, all of his coordination suddenly gone, his legs and arms moving spasmodically. He sprawled on the floor, his chest heaving and his eyes wide with surprise. Then he gave a funny little cough that turned into a moan, as blood slowly spread beneath him.

Lanette stuffed her fingers into her mouth, staring in horror at her husband. She started forward, instinctively going to him.

"Don't move!" Neeley screamed, waving the pistol erratically. "I'll kill the next one who moves!"

Corliss was staring down at her father, her mouth open, her expression stunned. "You shot my daddy," she said in amazement.

"Shut up, you fucking bitch. Stupid," he sneered. "You're so fucking stupid."

Webb caught the faintest movement out of the corner of his eyes. He didn't dare move, didn't dare turn his head, as terror seized him. Roanna shifted again, just the slightest of movements, taking her a fraction of an inch closer to the doors.

On the code box to the left of the doors, Webb saw the green light change to red.

Roanna had opened the door.

Fifteen seconds. The deafening blare would be all the diversion he would get. He began counting, hoping he could time it right.

Tears streamed down Corliss's face as she stared down at Greg, feebly writhing on the floor. "Daddy," she said. She looked back at Neeley and her face twisted with rage, and something else. *"You shot my daddy!"* she screamed, lunging at Neeley, her hands extended like claws.

He pulled the trigger again.

Corliss skidded, her torso jerked backward even as her feet tried to keep moving. Lanette screamed hoarsely, and the pistol swung unevenly toward her.

The alarm went off, the shrill, deafening sound painful in its intensity. Neeley's finger tightened on the trigger even as Webb was moving, and the bullet plowed into the wall right over Lanette's head. Neeley shoved Lucinda to the side, his free hand coming up to cover one ear as he tried to bring the pistol around. Webb hit him, driving one shoulder hard into the man's stomach, slamming him back against the wall. With his left hand he grabbed Neeley's right wrist, holding it up so he couldn't shoot anyone else even if he pulled the trigger.

Neeley shoved back, gathering himself. He was enraged, and as strong as an ox. Brock threw himself into the fray, adding his strength to Webb's as they both forced Neeley's arm back, pinning it to the wall, but still the man pushed back against them. Webb drove his knee upward, slamming it into Neeley's groin. A choked, guttural sound exploded from him, then he gasped soundlessly, his mouth working. He began sliding down the wall, taking them with him, and the movement wrenched his arm free of their grasp.

Webb grabbed for the gun as the three of them sprawled on the floor in a tangle. Neeley got his breath back with a high-pitched shriek of laughter, and only then did Webb realize that the shriek of the alarm had stopped, that Roanna had silenced it as quickly as she had set it off.

Neeley was scrabbling around, turning his body, still laughing in that shrill, maniacal tone that made the hair stand up on Webb's neck. He was staring at something, and laughing as he struggled, squirming on the floor, trying to bring the pistol around one more time—

Roanna.

She was kneeling beside Lucinda, tears running down her face as she looked from her grandmother to where Webb was struggling with Neeley, obviously torn between the two of them.

Roanna.

She was a perfect target, a little isolated from everyone else because Lanette, Gloria, and Harlan had rushed to Greg and Corliss. Her nightgown was a pristine white, perfect, impossible to miss at this range.

The gray metal of the barrel inched around, despite his and Brock's best efforts to hold Neeley's arm still, to wrestle the gun away from him.

Webb roared with fury, a great rush of it that surged through his muscles, his brain, obscuring everything in a red tide. He lunged forward that extra inch, his hand clamping down on Neeley's, slowly forcing the gun back, back, until he literally broke it free as the bones in Neeley's thick fingers popped under the pressure.

He screamed, writhing on the floor, his eyes going blank with pain.

Webb staggered to his feet, still holding the gun. "Brock," he said in a low, harsh voice. "Move."

Brock scrambled away from Neeley.

Webb's face was cold, and Neeley must have read his death there. He tried to surge upward, reaching for the gun, and Webb pulled the trigger.

At almost point blank range, one shot was all he needed. The reverberation faded away, and in the distance he could hear the faint wail of sirens.

Lucinda was trying feebly to sit up. Roanna helped her, bracing the old woman with her own body. Lucinda was gasping for breath, her color absolutely gray as she pressed her hand to her chest. "He—he was her father," she gasped desperately, reaching out to Webb, trying to make him understand. "I couldn't—I couldn't let her h-have that baby." She choked and grimaced, pressing harder on her chest with her other hand. She collapsed back against Roanna, her body going limp and sagging to the floor.

Webb looked around at his family, at the blood and destruction and grief. Over the groans of pain, the sobs, he said in a steely voice, "This stays in the family, do you understand? I'll do the talking. Neeley was Jessie's father. He thought I killed her, and he was out for revenge. That's it, do you understand? All of you, *do you understand?* No one knows who really killed Jessie."

They looked back at him, the survivors, and they understood. Lucinda's terrible secret remained just that, a secret.

Three days later, Roanna sat by Lucinda's bed in the cardiac intensive care unit, holding the old lady's hand and gently stroking it as she talked to her. Her grandmother had suffered a massive heart attack, and her body was already so frail that the doctors hadn't expected her to live through the night.

Roanna had been by her bedside all that night, whispering to her, telling her of the great-grandchild that was on its way, and despite all logic and medical knowledge, Lucinda had rallied. Roanna stayed until Webb had forced her to go home and rest, but was back as soon as he would allow it.

They all marched to Webb's orders, the family closing ranks behind him. There was so much to get through that they were all numb. They had buried Corliss the day before. Greg was in intensive care in Birmingham. The bullet had clipped his spine and the doctors expected him to have some paralysis, but they thought he would be able to walk with the aid of a cane. Only time would tell.

Lanette was like a zombie, moving silently between her daughter's funeral and her husband's hospital bed. Gloria and Harlan were in almost the same state, shocked and bewildered. Brock handled the funeral arrangements and took care of the others, his good-looking face lined with grief and fatigue, but his fiancée was at his side the entire time, and he took comfort from her.

Roanna looked up when Webb came into the small cubicle. Lucinda's eyes brightened when she saw him, then filmed with tears. It was the first time she had been awake when he'd been to visit. She groped for his hand, and he reached out to gently take her fingers in his.

"So sorry," she whispered, gasping for breath. "I should have . . . said something. I never meant for you . . . to take the blame."

"I know," he murmured.

"I was so scared," she continued, determined to get it said now after all the years of silence. "I went to your rooms . . . after you left . . . try to talk some sense into her. She was . . . wild. Wouldn't listen. Said she was . . . going to teach you . . . a lesson." The confession came hard. She had to gasp for breath between every few words, and the effort was making perspiration shine on her face, but she focused her gaze on Webb's face and refused to rest. "She said she would . . . have Harper Neeley's baby . . . and pass it off . . . as yours. I couldn't . . . let her do it. Knew who he was . . . her own father . . . abomination."

She drew a deep breath, shuddering with the effort. On her other side, Roanna held tightly to her hand.

"I told her . . . no. Told her she had to . . . get rid of it. Abortion. She laughed . . . and I slapped her. She went wild . . . knocked me down . . . kicked me. I think . . . trying to kill me. I got away . . . picked up the andiron . . . She came at me again. I hit her," she said, tears rolling down her face.

"I . . . loved her," she said weakly, closing her eyes. "But I couldn't . . . let her have that baby."

369

There was a soft scraping sound at the sliding glass doors. Webb turned his head to see Booley standing there, his expression weary. He gave Booley a hard stare and turned back to Lucinda.

"I know," he murmured as he bent over her. "I understand. You just get well now. You have to be at our wedding, or I'll be mighty disappointed, and I won't forgive you for *that.*"

He glanced at Roanna. She too was staring at Booley, a cool look in those brown eyes that dared him to do or say anything that would upset Lucinda.

Booley jerked his head at Webb, indicating that he wanted to talk to him outside. Webb patted Lucinda's hand, carefully placed it on the bed, and joined the former sheriff.

Silently they walked out of the CICU and down the long hall, past the waiting room where relatives kept endless vigils. Booley glanced into the crowded room and continued strolling.

"Guess it all makes sense now," he finally said.

Webb remained silent.

"No point in it going any further," Booley mused. "Neeley's dead, and there wouldn't be any use in pressing any sort of charges against Lucinda. No evidence anyway, just the ramblings of a dying old woman. No point in stirring up a lot of talk, all for nothing."

"I appreciate it, Booley," said Webb.

The old man clapped him on the back and gave him a level, knowing look. "It's over, son," he said. "Get on with your life." Then he turned and walked slowly to the elevator, and Webb retraced his steps to the CICU. He knew what Booley had been telling him. Beshears hadn't asked too many questions about Neeley's death, had in fact skirted around some things that were fairly obvious.

Beshears had been around. He knew an execution when he saw one.

Webb quietly reentered the cubicle, where Roanna was once again talking softly to Lucinda, who seemed to be dozing. She looked up, and he felt his breath catch in his chest as he stared at her. He wanted to grab her in his arms and never let her go, because he had come so close to losing her. When she had explained about her confrontation with Neeley over his treatment of his horse, Webb's blood had run cold. It had been just after that when Neeley had broken into the house for the first time, and when Roanna walked up on him, he had to have thought she would recognize him. He would have killed her then, Webb was certain, if Roanna hadn't awakened enough to scream when Neeley hit her. His idea of putting it about that the concussion had caused her to lose her memory about that night, just as a precaution, had undoubtedly saved her life, because otherwise Neeley would have tried to get to her sooner, before Webb managed to have the alarm installed.

As it was, Neeley had been within a hair's breadth of settling that pistol sight on her, and that had signed his death warrant.

Webb went to her, gently touching her chestnut hair, stroking one finger down her cheek. She rested her head on him, sighing as she rubbed her cheek against his shirt. She knew. She had been watching. And as she had knelt beside Lucinda, when he had turned back to her after pulling the trigger, she had given him a tiny nod.

"She's asleep," Roanna said now, keeping her voice to a whisper. "But she's going to come home again. I know it." She paused. "I told her about the baby."

Webb knelt on the floor and put his arms around her, and she bent her head down to him, and he knew that he held his entire world there in his arms.

Their wedding was very quiet, very small, and took place over a month later than they had originally planned.

It was held in the garden, just after sunset. The gentle shades of twilight lay softly over the land. Peach lights glowed in the arbor where Webb waited beside the minister.

A few rows of white chairs had been set up on each side of

371

the aisle, and every face was turned toward Roanna as she walked down the carpet laid out on the grass. Every face was beaming.

Greg and Lanette sat in the first row; Greg was in a wheelchair, but his prognosis was good. With physical therapy, the doctors said, he would likely regain most of the use of his left leg, though he would always limp. Lanette had cared for her husband with a fierce devotion that refused to let him give up, even when his grief over Corliss had almost defeated him.

Gloria and Harlan were also in the first row, both of them looking much older as they held hands, but they too were smiling.

Brock pushed Lucinda's wheelchair to keep pace with Roanna's stately stride. Lucinda was dressed in her favorite peach, and she wore her pearls and makeup. She smiled at everyone as they passed. Her frail, gnarled fingers were linked with the slender ones of her granddaughter, and they went together up the aisle, just as Roanna had wanted.

They reached the arbor and Webb reached out for Roanna's hand, drawing her to his side. Brock positioned Lucinda's wheelchair so that she was in the traditional place as matron of honor, then took up his own position as best man.

Webb's gaze briefly met Lucinda's. There was a serene, almost translucent quality to her. The doctors had said she wouldn't have long, but she had confounded them once again, and it was beginning to look as if she might make it through the winter after all. She was saying now that she wanted to wait until she knew if her great-grandchild was a boy or a girl. Roanna had immediately stated that she had no intention of letting the doctor or ultrasound technician tell her the baby's sex before its birth, and Lucinda had laughed.

Forgive me, she had said, and he had. He couldn't hold on to anger, to hurt, when he had so much to look forward to.

Roanna turned her radiant face up to him, and he almost kissed her right then, before the ceremony even started.

"Woof," he whispered, so low that only she could hear him, and he felt her stifle a giggle at what had turned into their private code for "I want you."

She smiled more readily these days. He'd lost count, at least in his mind. His heart still noted each and every curve of her lips.

Their fingers twined together, and he lost himself in her whiskey-colored eyes as the words began, washing over them in the soft purple twilight: "Dearly beloved, we are gathered here together . . ."

POCKET BOOKS
PROUDLY PRESENTS

SON OF THE MORNING

Linda Howard

**Available
from
Pocket Books**

The following is a preview of
Son of the Morning. . . .

THE STONE WALL OF THE DUNGEON WAS COLD AND damp against her back as Grace eased down the narrow, uneven steps. There was no railing, and she had to feel her way in the dark, for a candle would have alerted the guard to her presence.

The weight of the heavy iron candlestick pulled at her arm. Below she could see the single guard, sitting on a crude bench with his back resting against the wall, a rough skin of wine at his elbow. Good—if she was lucky, he had drunk himself into a stupor. Even if he had a hard Scottish head for spirits, at least the liquor would have slowed his reflexes. She hoped he was asleep, because given where he was sitting, she would have to approach him practically head-on. The light was poor and she could hide the candlestick against her leg, but if he stood up it would be much more difficult to hit him hard enough to knock him out. She was so sore and battered from the trip through time that she didn't trust her strength; better if she could simply lift the candlestick and swing downward, letting gravity aid her.

Ahead was the flicker of torchlight, but it didn't penetrate up the inky, curving stairs. Grace cautiously moved her foot forward, searching for the edge of each step while trying not to scrape her shoe against the stone. The air was cold, and fetid; the smell assaulted her nose, making it crinkle in disgust. The odor of human waste was unmistakable, but beneath that lay the sharper, more unpleasant odors of blood, and fear, and the sweat of pain. Men had been tortured, and died, in these foul depths that never saw the sun.

It was up to her to make certain Black Niall didn't join their ranks.

Huwe of Hay would sleep until morning, under the influence of whiskey and Seconal. Given how much he had drunk, she only hoped she hadn't overdosed him; as crude and disgusting as he was, she didn't want to kill him. The risks she'd run, back in Real Time, in getting the variety of drugs she carried had certainly been justified. Without the Seconal, she could never have escaped from Huwe at all, much less avoided being raped.

Her searching foot found no more steps. The floor was hard-packed dirt, uneven and treacherous. She stood still for a moment, taking deep, silent breaths as she tried to steady her nerves. The guard still sat slumped on the bench, his head nodded forward onto his chest. Was he truly asleep, drunk, or merely playing possum? As careful as she'd been, had he still heard some betraying rustle, and was he now trying to lure her closer?

It didn't matter; she had no choice. She couldn't leave Black Niall here, to be tortured and killed. He was the Guardian, the only person alive who knew both the secrets and the location of the hidden treasures of the Templars. She needed him, for only with his knowledge, his cooperation, could she keep Parrish from getting his hands on that treasure in Real Time. She wanted Parrish stopped, and she wanted Parrish dead; for that, she needed Black Niall.

If the guard was awake and merely being crafty, she would arouse less suspicion by approaching him directly, as if she had nothing to hide. Moreover, if he saw her, he wouldn't expect any threat from a woman. Her heart thumped wildly, and for a moment black spots swam before her eyes. Panic made her stomach lurch, and she thought she might throw up. Desperately she sucked in deep breaths, fighting back both nausea and weakness. She refused to let herself falter now, after all she'd been through.

Cold sweat broke out on her body, trickled down her spine. Grace forced her feet to move, to take easy, measured strides that carried her across the rough floor as if she had nothing at all to hide. The torchlight danced and swayed under the spell of some unheard music, casting huge, wavering shadows on the damp stone walls. The guard still didn't move.

Ten feet. Five. Then she stood directly in front of the guard, so close that she could smell the stench of his unwashed body, sharp and sour. Grace swallowed, and steeled herself for the blow she had to deliver. Sending up a quick prayer that she wouldn't cause him any lasting damage, she used both aching arms to raise the candlestick high.

Her clothing rustled with her movements. He stirred, opening bleary eyes and peering up at her. His mouth gaped open, revealing rotted teeth. Grace swung downward, and the massive iron candlestick crashed against the side of his head with a solid thunk that made her cringe. Anything he might have said, any alarm he might have yelled, dissolved into a grunt as he slid sideways, his eyes closing once more.

Blood trickled down the side of his head, matting in his filthy hair. Tears stung her eyes, but she turned sharply away, need shouldering aside regret.

There were two cells, and only one of them was barred. "Niall!" she whispered urgently as she grasped the massive bar. How was she best to communicate with him? Despite her study and preparation, she understood barely one word in thirty of the burred, rolling Gaelic the Highlanders spoke; reading it was one thing, pronouncing it something else. She felt more certain of herself in

Old English or Old French, both of which Niall also spoke, but Latin hadn't changed at all since his time, so that was the language she chose.

"I have come to free you," she said softly as she struggled with the bar. My God, it was heavy! It was like wrestling with a tree trunk, six feet long and a good ten inches thick. Her hands slipped on the wood, and a splinter dug deep into her little finger. Grace bit off a cry of pain as she jerked her hand back.

"Are you hurt?"

The question was in a deep, calm tone, and came very clear to her ears as if he was standing against the other side of the door. Hearing it, Grace froze, her eyes closing as she struggled once more with tears and an electrifying surge of emotion that threatened to overwhelm her. It was really Black Niall, and oh, *God,* he sounded just as he had in her dreams. The voice was like thunder and velvet, capable of a roar that would freeze his enemies, or a warm purr that would melt a woman into his arms.

"Only . . . only a little," she managed, struggling to remember the correct words. "A splinter . . . The bar is very heavy, and it slipped."

"Are you alone? The bar is too big for a mere woman."

Mere? *Mere?* "I can do it!" she said fiercely. What did he know? She had survived on the run for months, she had managed to get here, against all odds, and moreover, she was the one on the *free* side of the door. Anger mixed with exhilaration, surging through her veins, making her feel as if she would burst through her skin. Abandoning any attempt to lift the bar with her hands, she bent her knees and lodged her shoulder under it, driving upward with all the strength in her back and legs.

The weight of the bar bit into her shoulder. Gritting her teeth, Grace braced her legs and strained. She could feel the blood rush to her face, feel her heart and lungs labor. Her knees wobbled. Damn it, she *wouldn't* let this stupid piece of wood defeat her! A growl of refusal burst past her lips and she summoned every ounce of strength in her aching body, gathering it for one final effort. Her thigh muscles screamed, her back burned. Desperately she shoved upward, forcing her legs to straighten, and one end of the bar rose. It teetered for a moment, then began sliding down through the other bracket. The rough wood scraped her cheek, snagged her clothes. Using both hands, ignoring the need for quiet, she shoved the bar forward until it was free of one bracket.

Instead of continuing its slide through the other bracket, the bar slowed, then began tipping back toward her. Grace scrambled out of the way as one end hit the floor with a reverberating thud. The bar stood braced there, one end on the floor and the other balanced against the second bracket.

She stood back, breathing hard, trembling in

every muscle, but the triumph that roared through her was fierce and sweet. Heat radiated from her, banishing the cold as if she stood close to a fire, and she couldn't even feel the pain of her injured hand. She felt invigorated, invincible, and her breasts rose tight and aroused beneath her clothing.

"Open the door," she invited, the words coming out breathlessly despite her efforts to steady her voice, and she couldn't resist a taunt: "If you can."

A low laugh came to her ears, and slowly the massive door began to open, pushing the huge bar before it. Grace took another step back, peering hungrily into the black space yawning open between the door and the frame, waiting for her first glimpse of Black Niall in the flesh.

He came through the door as casually as if he were on vacation, but there was nothing casual in the black gaze that swept over the unconscious guard and then leapt to her, raking her from head to foot in a single suspicious, encompassing look. His vitality seared her like a blast, and almost palpable force, and she felt the blood drain from her face.

He could have stepped straight from her dreams.

He was there, just as he had been in the images that had plagued her for endless nights, as she had been when his essence had pulled her across seven centuries. Slowly, like a lover's hand drifting over the face of a beloved, barely touching as if too strong a contact would destroy the spell, her gaze traced his features. The broad, clear forehead; the eyes, as black as night, as old as sin; the thin, high-bridged Celtic nose; the chiseled cheekbones; the firm and unsmiling lips, the uncompromising chin and jaw. He was big. Mercy, she hadn't realized how big he was, but he was over a foot taller than she, at least six-four. His long black hair swung past his shoulders, shoulders that were two feet wide, and the hair at his temples was secured in a thin braid on each side of his face.

His shirt and kilt were dark with dried blood. He didn't have his plaid, but he didn't seem to feel the cold. He was wilder than she could have imagined, and yet he was exactly as she had dreamed. The reality of him was like a blow, and she swayed.

He looked around, his face hard and set, every muscle poised for action. "You are alone?" he asked again, evidently doubting that she had managed the bar by herself.

"Yes," she whispered.

No enemies rushed from the inky shadows, no alarm was raised. Slowly he returned his gaze to her, and even in the poor, unsteady light from the torch she knew he could see how violently she was trembling.

"Frail but valiant," he murmured, coming closer. Despite herself, she would have shrunk back, but he moved with the deceptive speed of an attacking tiger. One hard arm passed around her waist, both supporting and capturing her, drawing her against him. "Who are you? No relation of Huwe's, I'll wager, with such a pretty face—and a command of Latin."

"N-no," she stammered. The contact with him was going to her head, making her feel giddy. She lifted her right hand to brace against his chest; it was her injured hand, and she flinched.

Instantly he caught her hand, turning it toward the light. The long, jagged splinter had entered her finger lengthwise, and the end protruded just above the bend of the first knuckle. He made a softly sympathetic sound, almost a croon, and lifted her hand to his mouth. With delicate precision he caught the end of the splinter in his animal-white teeth, and steadily drew it out. Grace flinched again at the pain, rising on tiptoe against him, but he held her hand steady in his powerful grip. He spat the splinter out, then sucked hard at the sullenly bleeding wound. She could feel his tongue flicking against her skin, laving her hurt, and a moan that had nothing to do with pain slipped from her lips.

He lifted his mouth from her hand then, and the look he gave her was sharp and hot, startlingly aware. "I've no time for more, but I'll have the taste of ye," he murmured, this time in Scots English, and somehow she understood him.

He lifted her, turning to pin her against the wall. His big, iron-muscled body ground against her, from shoulder to knee, and her breath caught at the fullness of his arousal. Instantly he took advantage of her parted lips and set his mouth to hers. Her blood surged at the ravaging kiss; his taste was hot, tart, and uncivilized. He used his tongue with soul-searing skill, demanding her response, then deepening his advantage when she helplessly gave it. His hands moved over her body, cupping her breasts, her bottom, moving her against him.

He was panting when he lifted his head, his lips swollen and shiny, his eyes narrow with lust. "A pity I must go," he whispered, letting her slide to her feet. "Perhaps we'll meet again."

Shaking, Grace leaned against the wall, her mind a blank. He crossed swiftly to the unconscious guard and relieved him of his sword and dagger. He moved so fast that he had already reached the stairs before realization sank into Grace's mind. She struggled upright, her eyes wide. "No, wait!" she cried. "Take me with you!"

He didn't even pause, his powerful legs taking the stairs two at a time. "Another time, lass," he said, and disappeared upward into the darkness.

Oh, damn! She didn't dare call out again. She launched herself after him, but her legs were still shaking from the effort of lifting the bar, and from the effects of that kiss. She barely had the strength to climb the stairs, and there was no sign of him when she emerged from the dungeon.

She didn't dare sound an alarm, for after all, she didn't want him recaptured. But she didn't dare remain, either. Somehow she had to escape from this grimy hold and find Black Niall again. He wasn't a hero, damn him, no knight in shining armor. He was an arrogant brute, and he was her only hope.

Look for
Son of the Morning
Wherever Paperback Books Are Sold